'A strength of Tea Cooper's novels is the [...] which comes from thorough research, but w[...] the protagonists are women with intelligence, agency and courage. *The Butterfly Collector* will be enjoyed by those who like well-researched historical fiction with a mystery to solve.' —*Denise Newton Writes*

'Fans of Natasha Lester and Kate Morton will absolutely devour *The Fossil Hunter*. It is the kind of story you can easily get swept up in. Readers interested in Australian history, museums, and the fascinating world of fossils will be especially delighted with Cooper's stunning new historical novel.' —*Better Reading*

'Cooper fills the page with strong and intriguing female characters. There is a soupçon of romance but the real focus is on these trail-blazing women. Highly recommended.' —*Booklist*

'Elegant ... Cooper's confident prose and deep empathy for her characters will keep readers hooked as she unspools her intrigue-filled mystery. Historical fans will want to dig this one up.' —*Publishers Weekly* on *The Fossil Hunter*

'Cooper again indulges her love of museums and historical relics to produce a fascinating tale.' —*The Australian* on *The Fossil Hunter*

'Tea Cooper's meticulous prose and deft phrasing delight the reader.' —Historical Novel Society (US) on *The Cartographer's Secret*

'Cooper gets to the heart of a family's old wounds, puzzles, and obsessions, while providing a luscious historical rendering of the landscape. This layered family saga will keep readers turning the pages.' —*Publishers Weekly* on *The Cartographer's Secret*

'Weaving together historical facts with fabulous fiction, Tea delivers a richly imagined world. Her research is impeccable and the era vividly drawn ... [she] excels at writing complex, strong female characters. Evie and Lettie, and their dual timelines and tales, are completely mesmerising. I devoured this novel over the weekend and haven't stopped thinking about it since. *The Cartographer's Secret* is an excellent Australian historical.' —*Better Reading*

'A new Australian historical fiction book by Tea Cooper always gives reason to celebrate. So many of her previous works are both engaging and masterfully crafted tales of mystery and intrigue that allow her readers to journey alongside strong heroines and enticing tales. In her latest, Tea once again provides the perfect blend of fact and fiction in this riveting historical mystery.' —*Great Reads and Tea Leaves* on *The Cartographer's Secret*

'... a delicate union between historical fact and compelling fiction. *The Cartographer's Secret* presents a remarkable voyage of adventure, exploration, mystery and family secrets ... a delightful tale that historical fiction fans will not want to miss. ... Take a trek back into Australia's stimulating past, thanks to the masterful writing of Tea Cooper.' —*Mrs B's Book Reviews*

'... a mesmerising historical mystery.' —*Herald Sun* on *The Cartographer's Secret*

'Take a journey into the heart of Australia's past, in the company of the strong and inspirational characters in Tea Cooper's latest triumph, *The Girl in the Painting*. A stunning historical timepiece ... one of Australia's leading historical fiction specialists.' —*Mrs B's Book Reviews*

'Refreshing and unique, *The Woman in the Green Dress* sweeps you across the wild lands of Australia in a thrilling whirl of mystery, romance, and danger. This magical tale weaves together two storylines with a heart-pounding finish that is drop-dead gorgeous.' —J'nell Ciesielski, author of *The Socialite*

'Readers of Kate Morton and Beatriz Williams will be dazzled. *The Woman in the Green Dress* spins readers into an evocative world of mystery and romance in this deeply researched book ... One of the most intelligent, visceral and vibrant historical reads I have had the privilege of visiting in an age.' —Rachel McMillan, author of *The London Restoration*

'... boasts strong female protagonists, an infectious fascination with the past, and the narrative skill to weave multiple timelines into a satisfying whole ... easy to devour.' —*Sydney Morning Herald* on *The Woman in the Green Dress*

'... weaves a seductive narrative of secrets, memories, lost love and mystery ... a freshly drawn bittersweet saga that draws nuggets of "truth" with timeless magic and might-have-beens.' —*North & South Magazine* (NZ) on *The Woman in the Green Dress*

'Cooper weaves historical fact and creative fiction through the two periods with success. The plot ... contains Cooper's signature mix of colonial and indigenous social history, scientific discovery, mystery and a hint of romance.' —Historical Novel Society on *The Woman in the Green Dress*

'Cooper is a welcome inclusion to the rising ranks of female-centred historical Australian novels.' —*Herald Sun* on *The Naturalist's Daughter*

Tea Cooper is an established Australian author of historical fiction. In a past life she was a teacher, a journalist and a farmer. These days she haunts museums and indulges her passion for storytelling. She is the internationally bestselling author of several novels, including *The Butterfly Collector*; *The Naturalist's Daughter*; the *USA Today*–bestselling *The Woman in the Green Dress*; *The Girl in the Painting*; *The Cartographer's Secret*, winner of the prestigious Daphne du Maurier Award; and *The Fossil Hunter*.

www.teacooperauthor.com

Also by Tea Cooper

The Horse Thief
The Cedar Cutter
The Currency Lass
The Naturalist's Daughter
The Woman in the Green Dress
The Girl in the Painting
The Cartographer's Secret
The Fossil Hunter
The Butterfly Collector

(Available in ebook)
Matilda's Freedom
Lily's Leap
Forgotten Fragrance
The House on Boundary Street

The TALENTED *Mrs Greenway*

TEA COOPER

First Published 2023
First Australian Paperback Edition 2023
ISBN 9781867239192

THE TALENTED MRS GREENWAY
© 2023 by Tea Cooper
Australian Copyright 2023
New Zealand Copyright 2023

Published by
HQ Fiction
An imprint of Harlequin Enterprises (Australia) Pty Limited (ABN 47 001 180 918), a subsidiary of HarperCollins Publishers Australia Pty Limited (ABN 36 009 913 517)
Level 19, 201 Elizabeth St
SYDNEY NSW 2000
AUSTRALIA

® and TM (apart from those relating to FSC®) are trademarks of Harlequin Enterprises (Australia) Pty Limited or its corporate affiliates. Trademarks indicated with ® are registered in Australia, New Zealand and in other countries.

A catalogue record for this book is available from the National Library of Australia
www.librariesaustralia.nla.gov.au

Map by Giacomo Pantalone

Printed and bound in Australia by McPherson's Printing Group

MIX
Paper | Supporting responsible forestry
FSC
www.fsc.org
FSC® C001695

To all women whose stories remain hidden,
we hear you, and we acknowledge you.

a map of
SYDNEY TOWN
1824

1/8 mile   1/4 mile   3/8 mile   1/2 mile

Fort Philip

Argyle Street

Greenway's House

Quarry

Commissariat Store

St Philip's Church

Orphan School

Mrs Reibey's Warehouse

Bridge St.

Obelisk

Fountain

Military Barracks

Tank Stream

Bent St.

Government House

George Street

Pitt Street

Castlereagh St.

Hunter Street

Elizabeth St.

Macquarie St.

Court House

Convicts' Barracks

St James Church

To Turnpike Gate

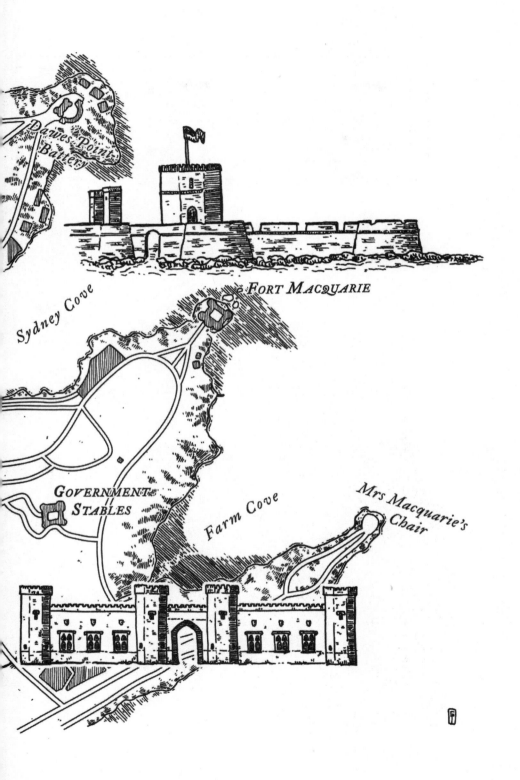

Dawes Point Battery

FORT MACQUARIE

Sydney Cove

GOVERNMENT STABLES

Farm Cove

Mrs Macquarie's Chair

One

1806
Manali House, six miles east of Bath, England

'Miss Fripp, I was hoping I might find you here.'

The pencil fell to Mary's lap, and she lifted her gaze to the silhouette, blocking the sun. Miss Fripp? Her husband, James, was her senior by more years than she cared to count. She didn't correct the gentleman standing before her in the garden—many had made the mistake of believing her to be James's daughter, not his wife.

Shading her eyes with the flat of her hand, she admired the man's neatly fitted moss-coloured velvet tailcoat, his brilliant white cravat and, in the sudden change from shadow to light, the planes of his face came into focus—high cheekbones, a long, somewhat sharp nose and startling hazel-green eyes that glinted in the sunlight. His skin wore a healthy glow yet there was a weathered look about him of a man who spent a lot of time out of doors. She detected a musky, very masculine scent.

'Francis Howard Greenway.' For some unknown reason he emphasised the name *Howard* before making a sweeping bow, a heavy lock of his reddish hair falling over his high forehead. 'At your service, Miss. I've been requested by Captain Fripp to quote on repairs and renovations to the house and stables.'

She leapt to her feet. He had? She'd rather hoped James would discuss the proposal with her before he made a move. He was aware of her interest in architecture and her feelings for her home, the house Papa had built. In a surprising mood of bonhomie, spurred no doubt by the quantity of brandy he had consumed, James had told her of his intention to have the house and stables 'brought up to scratch'. He'd discovered a local architect who had studied under the famous architect John Nash in London and believed he could negotiate a reduced price. He'd failed to mention he'd already made a start. 'You've spoken with my husband?'

A hint of colour stole across Mr Greenway's cheeks. 'I beg your pardon, Mrs Fripp. Unfortunately, Captain Fripp appears to have forgotten our appointment and I took it upon myself to appraise the house and its surrounds.'

How unusual. Mudd, stable master and general factotum, rarely approved any unescorted visitor, and since Papa's death he'd extended his role as groom to that of guardian. He must have taken James into town because Mudd wouldn't allow anyone to roam the grounds alone.

Mr Greenway lifted his chin and surveyed the vista. 'I thought perhaps I'd find a vantage spot to survey the house.'

She'd sat and listened to James's grandiose ideas but when he'd spoken of tacking a new wing on the side of Papa's simple Palladian country house to accommodate additional reception and gaming rooms, she'd made the foolish mistake of lamenting the resulting loss of symmetry. She'd decided the addition of a portico might balance James's proposed additions. Her gaze darted to her sketchpad, still lying beneath the tree where it had fallen when she'd jumped up, and she bent to retrieve her drawing but Mr Greenway moved faster. 'May I?'

She nodded and with damp palms waited while he studied her sketch. 'It would seem we are of like mind. The house is a delightful example of Palladian architecture, influenced by Inigo Jones, no doubt. It would be a great shame to detract from the classic features, such harmony, clarity and order—and, as you have so rightly shown, perfect symmetry. The addition of the portico is a touch of genius ...' With her sketchpad dangling from his fingers he strolled off, examining the building from various angles.

Mind afire, she scampered after him, skipping steps to match his determined stride.

Finally she caught up when he settled on the grassy knoll overlooking the house, her sketchpad still in hand. He'd pulled out a measuring compass and stubby pencil and with a few deft strokes adjusted the height of the portico.

A feather-light breeze tickled her skin, and she bit back a curl of annoyance. She should be pleased at his interest, but a sense of violation overtook her. Stepping closer, she studied his handiwork.

'Do you think perhaps ...?' She bit back her words. Who was she to question a man who had studied under John Nash?

'There!' He gave a satisfied grunt and held up her sketchpad. 'I believe that has corrected your errors.'

'Errors?' No, simply a different vision. Her skin prickled again—definitely not caused by the breeze.

'Indeed. There are certain principles which should be adhered to as laid down by Sir William Chambers, architect to their Royal Highnesses the Prince of Wales and Princess Dowager of Wales. Anyone who purports to have an interest in architecture should study his treatise.'

Her shoulders dropped and her foolish pride slipped. Papa's library contained a great many books on architecture, some of which he'd brought back from India. It was an interest he'd developed over the years, and one they'd shared, but she'd never heard of Chambers. 'There is a manual?'

'Not so much a manual, a treatise laying down the basic principles of architecture. I have found it invaluable.' He pocketed his measuring compass, patting to ensure it was securely lodged.

'How I wish I could pursue my own interests.' The words popped out of her mouth before she had time to think. She must have taken him by surprise because he flinched, tipped up his face, and deep in his eyes she caught a momentary flicker of something unexpected—quite what she couldn't be sure.

'You have talent, a talent that should be fostered. You should travel, expand your view of the world.'

'I am a married woman, Mr Greenway. My husband requires that I remain at home.' Ready to dance to his pipe and drum. Perhaps matters might be different if she had fulfilled her obligations and provided the necessary heir and spare, but in the three years since their marriage she'd failed. She hadn't managed to conceive, and James was rapidly losing patience.

'Why should marriage prevent you from furthering your interest in architecture?' He held her gaze, and her reply flew away with the birds.

He wouldn't understand. Papa had determined her life: her home, her education and the arrangement of her marriage, and she'd blindly accepted first his authority and, after his passing, that of the husband he had chosen for her.

Mr Greenway's gaze narrowed, his intense scrutiny making her cheeks burn. 'There is nothing to prevent a woman displaying an interest in architecture. Besides, this is your home, is it not? And isn't it a woman's role to manage the household?'

'The internal functioning perhaps.' Truth be told, not even that. Mrs Rudge, the housekeeper and cook James had employed, ruled the house with her wooden spoon and barely tolerated any interference. 'Not the building or repairs to the house. That's why Captain Fripp has engaged you.'

'Tosh and nonsense. There are plenty of women who have an interest in architecture.' Her cheeks grew warm as his face broke into the most engaging smile. 'Lady Elizabeth Wilbraham is but one example—the first to pave the way. She was responsible for the design and fit-out of her own home, Wotton House, in Buckinghamshire.'

Mary's heart leapt. How could she have forgotten? Papa had attributed the beautiful sash windows he'd installed in the library to Lady Wilbraham's designs. 'I wish I could have met her.'

She shook her head at her stupidity. A peeress wouldn't have entertained a woman of her standing, the country daughter of a retired sea captain. And it was beside the point.

'She passed away almost one hundred years ago,' she added.

'But her genius remains—Wotton House is a perpetual reminder of the lasting value of classical architecture. Have you not visited London and seen the work of Sir Christopher Wren? Lady Wilbraham was his sponsor.'

'I have never travelled beyond Gloucestershire.'

'A matter that should be remedied. Your husband may have mentioned that I spent several years in London studying under Nash—my designs have been exhibited at the Royal Academy. I, too, prefer the neoclassical style.'

'Neoclassical ...'

'Grand scale and simple geometric forms, the use of Greco-Roman motifs and proportions, a dramatic use of columns, rather as you have here.' He tapped the page in her sketchbook then handed it back. 'I must take my leave. I will submit my designs to Captain Fripp. My brothers, John and Olive, will undertake the necessary repairs and structural improvements required before work can progress. In the meantime, work on your drawings and we can compare our thoughts. Good afternoon, ma'am.' He replaced his hat, straightened his moss-green coat and with a long, loping gait disappeared down the carriageway.

The days passed in a haze as Mary scoured the shelves holding Papa's architectural books and found references to Christopher Wren, another west countryman as it turned out, but no mention of Lady Wilbraham. She found plenty of tomes revealing the splendours of Ancient Rome, Athens and the Mughal Empire, but nothing like the book by Chambers that Mr Greenway had mentioned. She thought of little else in the intervening days, while she worked on her plan for the house, filled with a longing for Mr Greenway's opinion. James remained absent, in London according to Mudd, and the Greenway brothers did not appear to begin the repairs.

Summer had come early to the hills and the cerulean sky played host to scudding clouds that sent shadows skittering across the grassy slopes. Knowing James was away, Mary made no effort and simply pulled on a faded Indian muslin day dress and tucked her heavy hair into a sloppily wound chignon then snatched up her sketchpad and headed for the knoll above the house, the scent of the grass sweet beneath her slippered feet.

She threw herself down, her back against the gnarled oak tree, and opened her sketchpad. Mr Greenway's corrections had thrown her design into a completely different light, changed not only the perspective of her drawing but also her vision. With the addition of four columns the symmetry was restored. She squinted into the distance, holding her pencil up to the gauge the proportions. A bubble of happiness swelled in her breast as she imagined the reality of her design. How she wished she could share it with Mr Greenway.

'It seems my suggestions appealed.'

As if conjured from her imagination, Mr Greenway stood before her once again. Cheeks burning, she shot to her feet. 'Good morning, Mr Greenway.' She made a fumbled attempt at a curtsy and managed to tangle her foot in her hem and lurched away, leaning heavily against the tree to restore her balance.

'I had no intention of taking you by surprise. I called out but you were engrossed in your drawing.' He bent and picked up her sketchpad, and his long finger traced her redrawn lines of the columns. 'A masterful move. The contract I have agreed with Captain Fripp is for a new reception room but the repairs to the structural damage and undermining of the foundations could well be combined with some new features. A portico such as this would give the building a greater presence.'

Dragging her gaze from his hand, she looked up at the flecks of gold dancing in his eyes. The creases at the corners deepened as a slow smile lifted his lips. He really was a most attractive man.

'I was on my way to the house in search of you.'

She brought her hands together in anticipation. She couldn't wait to see what he had in mind for Manali.

He lifted his satchel from his shoulder and knelt to unbuckle the straps. 'I wanted to show you this.' He sank down, legs stretched in front of him, and patted the grass. 'I thought you might be interested.' He unrolled a large piece of paper and laid it down on the grass, his workworn hand splayed across one corner, holding it flat.

Not a plan for Manali but something even more interesting.

A great baronial castle. Its castellated battlements, carved brick chimneys and casement windows spoke of safety, security, power and luxury—she'd never seen anything so beautiful. The legends and myths Papa had read to her as a child filled her mind—a high-born medieval knight carrying his lady's favour into battle, the great Mughal empire, bejewelled maharajahs astride painted elephants ruling unchallenged, their every wish a command. She let out a long breath and sneaked a look at Mr Greenway from under her lashes.

He'd put a blade of grass between his teeth and turned his eyes to the sky. 'The plans for Manali are not yet prepared. These are for the restoration of Thornbury Castle. They were displayed at the Royal Academy and were well received.' He threw back his shoulders and smiled, pride lighting his handsome face.

'What a great honour.'

'I must admit to a familial connection on my mother's side. Charles Howard, the eleventh Duke of Norfolk, is the present incumbent. He is most interested in my ideas.' He smoothed his hand over the paper then turned his head, his chin tilted and a smile curling his full lips.

Charles Howard, the Duke of Norfolk ... so that was perhaps why he had placed such emphasis on his middle name when they'd first met—a familial connection. All so very complicated and not dreadfully important unless it perhaps oiled the wheels of commerce.

'It may be a little presumptuous, but would you like to visit?'

His question drew her attention from her musing.

'I am certain it could be arranged. The castle nestles on the northern edge of Thornbury village not twelve miles north. It was originally built during the reign of Henry VIII in the Tudor style and was one of the most magnificent buildings of its time.' He let out an audible breath. 'The home of kings, queens and dukes over the centuries, one of the last medieval castles to be built in England. Let me make some enquiries.' A strange challenge flickered in the depths of his flecked eyes. 'And in the meantime, I shall arrange a loan of a copy of Chambers's work. Would that be to your liking?'

Two

Mary waited in vain for Mr Greenway to fulfil his promise of an invitation to Thornbury Castle or the loan of Chambers's book. When James reappeared after his latest visit to London, she regaled him with her plans for the house and told him of Mr Greenway's visits. The whole idea of the portico and the addition to the stables filled her with excitement. 'We have decided that a portico would …'

'*We* have decided …' James spluttered, his already florid face turning an alarming damson colour, suggesting that by expressing her opinion she'd reached beyond his understanding. 'I think you have forgotten your role, madam—your one and only role— which you should concentrate on fulfilling.'

She batted away a rising flush of heat and inhaled, determined not to rise to the bait. She could hardly fulfil her *role* if James wasn't at home. Better to ignore his comment. 'Mr Greenway was acting on your instructions and, in your absence, spoke with me. He believes the house requires certain structural improvements before any additions can be made. He has been commissioned to undertake the restoration of Thornbury Castle.' James would have to be impressed. 'His plans were exhibited at the Royal Academy in London.'

James's fist slammed down on the table, making the plates jump. His glass jumped too, spilling a red stain across Mrs Rudge's pristine white tablecloth. 'You, madam, have surpassed your position. I have already communicated my intentions to Mr Greenway but after this outrageous liberty he has taken I am tempted to terminate our agreement.'

Mary swallowed her reply, knowing from experience James was well past rational discussion. The man Papa had entrusted her to, the man she had willingly married, had hoodwinked them both. He was interested in nothing more than the bounty Papa had handed him on a plate.

'Go and prepare yourself.'

A stone lodged in her stomach. She knew full well the way the evening would progress. Another painful, unfruitful grope beneath her nightgown—she'd shut her eyes and wait for him to finish, consoling herself with the thought that it was her role, as his wife, a role women had fulfilled since time immemorial.

One morning when the leaves had begun to turn and the garden became a riot of glorious autumn colour, James left, citing a business appointment and his intention to spend an extended period in Bath.

Mary dutifully waited at the front door until James heaved himself into the saddle, dug in his heels and disappeared in a cloud of dust. The prospect of the peace and quiet that always descended on the house when he left calmed her soul. She had no idea when he would return but she planned to make the most of every moment.

She fastened her bonnet and set off for a morning walk with a bounce in her step, intending to follow the carriageway and take the path into the woods where the oak trees would be turning. Maybe there'd be mushrooms. Mrs Rudge made a beautiful creamy mushroom fricassee which went particularly well with a roasted chicken.

When she rounded the bend a stocky, tousle-headed young man with a ruddy complexion came into view, wrangling a large package wrapped in oilskin. Hand-delivered packages were a rarity, as James insisted Mudd should pick up the mail when he went to town to collect the supplies Mrs Rudge required for the house. It was just one other matter that Mary apparently hadn't the wit to manage despite the fact that she'd handled the task quite successfully prior to Papa's passing. 'Can I help you?'

The youth's face split into a wide grin. 'You Miss Fripp?' He eased the package down and doffed his cloth cap. 'This is for you; the gaffer asked me to drop it by.'

'Gaffer?'

'Greenway. He said I was to make sure I handed it directly to you but it's a bit heavy so maybe I should carry it up to the house.'

'That would be perfect, but how do you know I am Mrs Fripp?'

'Beggin' your pardon, ma'am, Mr Greenway said Miss Fripp. Said I'd know you straight off because of your shiny chestnut hair and lovely smile.' A hint of colour stained the top of his ears.

'Did he indeed? That's very kind of him. Come this way.' Masking a smile, she led the way to the front door. 'Follow me.' She hovered for a moment in the hallway, unsure where to ask him to leave the package. If James returned unexpectedly and came across something from Mr Greenway, he would no doubt be more than unimpressed. Only a few days before he left for Bath, he'd complained that he had received a letter demanding payment for the plans Mr Greenway had drawn up. In a fit of rage James had threatened to cancel their arrangement. Unless she was very much mistaken, the package contained the book Mr Greenway had promised to lend her.

'In here.' She threw open the door to the library, a place she loved, her favourite place and one of the few rooms in the house James rarely entered, preferring the isolation of his study. A room smelling of leather and antiquity, the walls lined with shelves sagging under the weight of Papa's vast collection. Religious tracts, atlases, and books on natural history, archaeology and architecture filled every space, and between the two sash windows sat the magnificent inlaid table Papa had brought home from India.

Papa's books, his most treasured possessions, were now hers. They were a link, an almost living, breathing connection, to happier times when he had been the centre of her universe and she his—his precious gift, he'd liked to call her. Pushing aside her sketches and pencils, she made space for the package. 'Would you put it here, please.'

The boy thumped it down, dusted off his hands then reached for the leather thong securing the oilcloth.

'I can manage, thank you.' She didn't want to share the pleasure of this unusual occurrence. She clasped her damp hands to her chest then gestured to the door. He didn't move, but just raised his eyebrows, a look of expectation on his face.

He wanted a token of thanks. She pulled open the central table drawer and ran her hand around the inside hoping to find a farthing or even a halfpenny. She usually had no need of money because she rarely left the estate. If she took the young man down to the kitchen Mrs Rudge's insatiable curiosity would be aroused and before she knew it James would be questioning her about the book and ranting about outrageous liberties.

'Stay here a moment.' She slipped through the door, down the hallway and into the cloying darkness of James's study. The reek of brandy and cigars hung, turning her stomach, and she swallowed, resisting the temptation to throw back the heavy curtains and clear the air. This was no longer her domain, no longer the room where she and Papa had spent so many happy hours.

As luck would have it, a pile of coins sat on top of the desk. She snatched up a shilling and slipped out, closing the door firmly behind her, then took several deep breaths to settle her roiling stomach.

When she returned to the library she found the young man, cap in hand and saucer-eyed, studying the ceiling-high shelves. 'You read all those?'

'No, not even half of them. They belonged to my father. He was a great collector.'

She held out the shilling. 'Thank you for your trouble.'

His eyes bulged. 'That's a bit much, ma'am.'

'Not at all, the package was heavy.' Besides, she hadn't anything smaller and she doubted James would miss it. He had a cavalier approach to money, and with Papa's wealth in his control, no need to wonder where the next shilling would come from. He spent far more betting at the racetrack. She wanted the boy to leave, and could hardly resist ripping the package open. 'Take it and off you go. You can find your own way out, can't you?'

The cheeky devil winked, pocketed the shilling, rammed his cloth cap back on his head and took off without closing the door, no doubt worried she'd change her mind.

A series of firmly tied knots held the oilcloth in place. She pulled at the thong, working until it came free, releasing a slight odour of linseed, reminiscent of oil paint. The cloth fell open, revealing a large, reddish-brown leather-bound volume with gold embossing.

She opened the cover, glanced at the marbled end pages then, with damp fingers, turned to the frontispiece.

To The
Right Honourable
John Earl Of Bute
Groom Of The Stole
to
The Prince
This Book is humbly Dedicated
by
His Lordship's
Most Obedient Servant
William Chambers

Good heavens! Her heart began to thump beneath her rib cage. It seemed Mr Greenway's connections with the nobility were as he described. How else would he have acquired such a tome?

The second page contained illustrations ranging from two primitive buildings—a tent, resembling those used by the native people in the Americas, and what appeared to be a shepherd's hut—to a more complex dwelling with a pitched roof and elaborately detailed columns. The first chapter, on the facing page, was titled *Of the Origins of Buildings*. As her gaze raced across the print, she lifted the corner of the page to turn it and a small square of folded paper fell out. Inscribed across the front, in a script as bold as the writer himself, was her name: just Mary, nothing else. A personal letter from a man to a married woman such as herself was beyond scandalous. With shaking hands, she broke open the seal holding the piece of thick cartridge paper, torn undoubtedly from a sketchpad, and sank down in the chair.

7 Limekiln Street,
Mangotsfield
Dear Mary (May I call you by your own name, which I have
to admit I learnt from another, rather than that of your husband
with whom I am somewhat aggrieved?)

I had hoped to deliver this personally but unfortunately, I
have been denied permission to enter the estate. As I expect you
know your husband has reneged on our contract and no longer
wishes to engage my services. Since I relied on a handshake and
have nothing in writing I am unable to hold him to his promise.

Mary pursed her lips and inhaled. How could James do such a
thing? He couldn't back out of a gentleman's agreement. She
ought to try and bring up the subject, though she doubted he'd
pay any heed. Her gaze danced back to the letter.

However, the two occasions on which we met have remained
uppermost in my mind and I wanted to honour my commitment
to you.

I trust you will enjoy your perusal of Chambers's treatise and
when you have had your fill, I would appreciate it if you would
arrange its return to my business premises in Limekiln Street.

Your servant,
Francis Howard Greenway
(Who hopes to be known henceforth as your friend).

Through her palm the pitter-patter of her heart vibrated, and a
wave of euphoria stirred her blood. Thank heavens the package
had arrived in James's absence. The thought of James's dismissive
comments and his tirade when she'd mentioned Mr Greenway's
name still made her shudder. She tucked the letter in her sleeve,
against her skin, and then folded the oilskin and wound the

leather thong into a small ball. With a glance over her shoulder to ensure Mrs Rudge was otherwise engaged she hefted the book and darted up the stairs to her bedchamber.

Time passed in a blur. Mary spent every available hour propped up in bed, claiming a headache but in fact absorbed in Chambers's theories, and in dreams of the conversations she might have with Mr Greenway—Francis. The mere thought of his name made her chest tighten as though an invisible thread connected them.

Mrs Rudge fussed around, bringing interminable pots of tea or chicken broth and slices of buttered, toasted bread, and insisted on keeping the fire alight, convinced Mary had caught a chill on one of her morning walks in the woods.

Every time Mrs Rudge's steps sounded on the landing Mary pulled the counterpane over the book and lay back with a pained expression on her face. James returned from Bath but stayed well away, no doubt fearing he might contract her unaccustomed sickness.

On the fifth morning Mrs Rudge puffed up her pillows and placed the breakfast tray on the nightstand then hovered, arms folded and a quizzical expression on her face.

'Thank you, Mrs Rudge. I am feeling a little better this morning.' She so badly wanted to return to the book, or better still discuss with Francis the decorative aspects of Corinthian columns.

'Hmm! The captain will be disappointed.'

He knew nothing of her interest in Corinthian columns, or the book. 'Disappointed?'

'He's hopeful ...' Colour stained Mrs Rudge's plump cheeks, and she wiped her face on the corner of her pinny and heaved a sigh. 'We thought perhaps your delicate condition might signal a happy event.'

'Oh!' The air whistled out between Mary's lips. It was the furthest thing from her mind. She couldn't possibly be with child; James had been away for weeks. She tried for a rapid calculation, resorted to her fingers, gave up and tossed her hands in the air.

Mrs Rudge smiled, revealing the familiar array of crooked teeth and yawning gaps. 'A month and two weeks over, and counting.'

And how would she know? 'I'm sure you must be mistaken.'

'Who do you think supervises your bed linen and laundry?'

Mary's mouth opened and closed like a trout on the end of a line. She ought to be happy, having finally achieved the one action expected of her. She snapped her mouth closed and tried for a smile, but instead tears sprang to her eyes.

'Enough of that.' Mrs Rudge peered down at her through narrowed eyes. 'The captain's at home. Shall I send him up? You'll be wanting to tell him yourself.'

Mary slipped her hand under the bedclothes, her fingers groping for the cover of Chambers's treatise. 'Let me finish my tea and get dressed. I'll come downstairs and tell him.' She lifted the porcelain cup to her lips. Mrs Rudge didn't move, just hovered over her like some sort of avenging angel. If she got out of bed the woman would want to straighten the covers and her secret would be revealed. 'Thank you, Mrs Rudge. I can manage perfectly well. I'm sure you are busy.'

'Not too busy to help the new mother. You've been in bed for nigh on five days, you'll be light-headed the minute your feet touch the ground.'

'I assure you I am perfectly fine. Please leave.' Harsh, too harsh, and truth be told she had felt a little dizzy the last time she left her bed.

'I'm only trying to help.' Mrs Rudge's mouth turned down at the corners. 'We've all been waiting far too long for this. The captain will want the doctor to call.'

'I assure you, I am perfectly well.'

With a disgruntled harrumph Mrs Rudge turned on her heel, then paused, her hand on the doorknob. 'You leave the tray and your bed. I'll come and tidy up while you're talking to the captain.'

Once the door closed, Mary drew in a deep breath, pulled the book from under the covers and swung her legs out of bed. Her heart thundered and dark spots clouded her vision. The room wavered. Refusing to succumb to Mrs Rudge's predictions, she bent double and drew in a deep breath, sank onto her knees, and slipped the book under her bed, pushing it into the shadows against the wall.

Mary paused at the top of the stairs, hair brushed and her favourite Indian shawl draped around her shoulders to cover her nightgown. The prospect of making any further effort was more than she could manage—and for the first time in her life she had the perfect excuse.

She tiptoed down the stairs. A stillness filled the house, a heavy, suffocating closeness, as though at any moment a clap of thunder would rent the air. James's study door was firmly closed. She clenched her fist and rapped: to enter uninvited always incurred his wrath. It was the last thing she wanted to do. As she raised her hand again the door swung open, bringing with it the inevitable waft of cigars and brandy, and James's florid, beaming face. She took a step back, her breath caught and her stomach churned. Hand clasped to her mouth, she spun around and raced outside just in time to deposit the tea and toasted bread in the urn on the front steps. Wiping her mouth, she sank down and inhaled the sharp air, hoping it might clear her head.

When a hand came down on her shoulder she flinched and buried her head in her hands, the thought of facing anyone, most especially James, more than she could bear.

'I've called for Mrs Rudge. Stay still.' James remained behind her so she couldn't see his face, but his words sounded almost solicitous. He gave her back a clumsy pat. Had she the energy she would have shot to her feet in surprise. She had no recollection of him ever touching her unless it was to pin her to the mattress.

'I'm sorry,' she murmured.

'No apologies necessary. In fact, something to celebrate. A glass of brandy perhaps?'

The mere mention made her stomach heave again and she shook her head, forcing down the surge of bile.

'Ah! Mrs Rudge. Could you help Mary upstairs? She's feeling unwell. It seems our celebration will have to be put on hold for a day or two.'

Mary! What had happened to his usual 'madam'?

Mrs Rudge tucked an arm around her waist and eased her upright. 'I hate to say I told you so but perhaps you might take notice next time. I dare say I've had a lot more experience than you.'

The comment didn't merit an answer. Feeling addle-headed and pathetic, Mary meekly allowed Mrs Rudge to lead her back into the house as she tutted and harrumphed about chills, cold air and delicate conditions. James stood at the bottom of the stairs, one hand resting on the carved newel post, his chest puffed like a crowing cockerel and a satisfied smile emblazoned on his face. Which under the circumstances was understand-able—he'd blamed her for her inability to provide him with an heir, but surely he must have wondered if the responsibility lay with him.

Once Mrs Rudge had deposited her in the chair in front of the fire, she bustled around straightening the bedding and foraging in the cupboard for a clean nightgown. Mary closed her eyes and prayed to whatever god might be listening that her secret wouldn't be revealed. She hadn't the strength, nor the inclination, to explain the book hidden under the bed. The thought of James's cynical expression if she tried to justify her interest in architecture, and his displeasure if he discovered Mr Greenway's letter, was enough to unsettle her fragile stomach.

'I'll put this on your desk, shall I?'

She flashed her eyes open. Mrs Rudge stood in the middle of the room, Francis's letter clasped in her pudgy fingers. Mary's stomach churned again, and she clapped her hand over her mouth. The letter must have fallen out of the book when she'd slipped it under the bed, or had she left it on the counterpane? 'Yes, please.' Her voice wavered. 'I think I'm going to be sick again.'

Mrs Rudge tossed the letter onto the nightstand and grabbed the thankfully empty chamber-pot. The cold porcelain lip butted against her chin, her stomach griped, and she dredged up some very impressive vomiting sounds that failed to produce anything.

'False alarm.' Mrs Rudge wiped the perspiration from her forehead and replaced the chamber-pot beneath the bed. 'Let's get you back under the covers. This won't last forever. I'll bring you a nice cup of tea and some dry biscuits to settle your stomach, then you can have a rest.'

The moment Mrs Rudge left the room Mary shot out of bed, her shift drenched with sweat and the sour taste of bile coating her mouth. She retrieved Chambers's treatise then tucked the letter into her sleeve; it would do until she thought of a safer hiding place. She couldn't believe she'd got away with it. It would be safest to return the book but the thought of sending it back before she'd finished left a hollowness in her gut which had nothing to do with her condition. She slipped the book under her pillow and waited patiently for Mrs Rudge's return.

An assertive knock on the door took her by surprise. 'Come in.' The door opened to reveal James, a tray in his hands, looking for all the world like the attentive husband.

'Are you feeling somewhat recovered? I've brought your tea.'

Her mouth fell open when he placed the tray on the nightstand beside the bed and proceeded to fill the cup. What a difference a bout of sickness could make!

'Mrs Rudge suggested you drink it without milk but that you should have sugar to keep your spirits up.' He ladled a disgusting amount of sugar into the cup and held it out.

The sooner she drank it, the sooner he would leave. She lifted the cup to her lips and sipped and then, to her horror, James sat down on the edge of the bed and offered the plate of dry biscuits. 'I cannot tell you how happy I am. An heir! Mrs Rudge tells me he'll be with us in the middle of summer—late June, early July.'

Mary bit her lips. She still couldn't believe, after all this time, that she was with child. Her courses were often erratic. What if this was all a mistake? The closed, cloying atmosphere of James's study always turned her stomach, and her weakness could well have been due to the fact that she'd spent five days abed, her nose buried in Chambers's treatise. On the other occasions when she'd thought she might be carrying she'd never suffered a moment's sickness, just the painful indignity of another failure.

James reached out and patted the counterpane. 'We'll have to think of a name. I favour George, after my late father, George James Fripp. It has a certain ring to it, don't you think?'

'And if it's a girl?' She couldn't help herself.

James drew back his hand as though stung, and his face clouded. 'An heir and a spare. That was the arrangement.' He pulled his waistcoat down over his ample stomach. 'I shall leave you to rest.

I'll contact Dr Lewis and ask him to call next time he is in the area. We can't take any chances.'

Dr Lewis appeared a few days later. After much prodding and poking he pronounced her healthy and informed her the sickness would pass in a matter of weeks. He appeared to have received all the necessary intimate information from Mrs Rudge and echoed her sentiments about George's summertime arrival. Mary hadn't the strength to discuss her previous failures: time would tell and there was nothing she could do about it.

As the weeks passed and the debilitating sickness waned, she finally admitted that she was indeed carrying James's heir, although she found it difficult to summon any maternal feelings.

'Don't you fuss yourself.' Mrs Rudge straightened the bed coverings and fluffed up her pillows. 'It always takes a while for the truth to sink in. Why don't I bring you up a book or two to pass the time—one of those novels you favour?'

She was about to decline, but then Mary nodded. 'Thank you. There are some books of Papa's on the table in the library, about the Mughal palaces. I don't think I can concentrate sufficiently to read. I'll look at the pictures.' And then if Mrs Rudge came across Chambers's book, she might not pay any attention to it.

'I don't want you getting maudlin. Just because your mother …'

'Nothing like that, Mrs Rudge, I promise.' She gave a frail smile. It hadn't even crossed her mind to wonder if she might be in any danger. Mother's demise had occurred aboard ship, in the middle of the Indian Ocean with no one to help but her maid and the ship's surgeon, whose expertise revolved around broken limbs and seasickness and hadn't extended to childbirth.

'You stay abed for another few weeks and gather your strength. We don't want any slip-ups like before. I'll bring those books up with your lunch.'

As a diversion Mary busied herself imbibing every snippet of information from Chambers's treatise, making notes, and then trying her hand at reproducing some of the illustrations. She began with a Roman Doric portico, similar to her original idea for Manali, dredging up her long-forgotten mathematic skills. Although she'd never been one for arithmetic and measurements, the more drawings she reproduced the more the plans and elevations made sense.

After James's initial flurry of concern, he reverted to his old habits and spent more and more time away, maybe in London, maybe in Bath, courting Lady Luck more than like, but she relished the solitude, and at the same time, also enjoyed the company of the lady's maid he'd insisted she needed.

Leah was a gentle young woman, the daughter of one of the local families, with plump cheeks, irrepressible curly hair and honey-brown eyes. She saw to it that Mary had everything she needed, and was also a dab hand with a needle and thread; although Mary's condition was barely visible some strategic adjustments to her wardrobe had become necessary. Leah also delighted in braiding her long, and more recently abundant, hair.

By the time the new year arrived Mrs Rudge had declared Mary no longer needed to be confined to the house. Suitably rugged up, she and Leah would tramp the garden and, as Mary's stamina returned, they ventured further afield.

Three

1807

The first hint of spring came early and with it a great longing to meet Mr Greenway again. Mary had hundreds of questions she wanted answered and a sketchpad full of drawings. She couldn't imagine how it might feel to see the buildings created with pen and paper spring to life, perpetual and permanent reminders of a personal vision. Leah was the only person who'd seen her drawings and she hadn't been terribly impressed. She yearned for pastoral scenes, trees and flowers and fluffy white clouds. Try as she might Mary couldn't convince her of the intention of her drawings even when she'd sworn her to secrecy and shown her Chambers's book.

When James announced he would be spending another month away, citing business meetings and the need to secure a new mount, which demanded a trip to Ascot, Mary took matters into her own hands.

'Leah, I am going to Bath today. I have some errands to run, and it is time I called in to the seamstress. I am sorely in need of some new gowns.' The bump in her stomach was hardly visible beneath her high-waisted dresses, and certainly did not prevent her from fitting into any of the gowns Leah had adjusted. 'I'll wear my blue pelisse.'

'Oh, Bath, ma'am.' At the note of longing in her voice Mary glanced up.

'Would you like to accompany me?'

'More than anything in the world. I'd love to let my sister know I'm alive. I haven't seen her since before Christmas.'

A wave of shame washed over Mary. She'd never given a moment's thought to Leah's life before she came to Manali. 'Is it on the way?'

'Oh yes, ma'am. The Bath road runs through Mangotsfield.'

Mangotsfield. Mary couldn't control her smile. Fate had played into her hands. 'That's perfect. I have a package to deliver to Mangotsfield and then I can travel on to Bath, take some refreshments at the Pump Room, visit the seamstress in Milsom Street before I pick you up and we'll be home before dark.'

Leah gave a little skip and held out her pelisse and then her face dropped. 'Will Mrs Rudge let me go? She said this morning she had a list as long as her arm.'

'I'll speak to her, I'm sure it's nothing that can't wait until tomorrow. You go and ask Mudd to prepare the carriage, then change your clothes. We'll leave in half an hour.'

The moment Leah left the room Mary burrowed under the bed and retrieved the book and wrapped it in the oilcloth. As she was about to secure the leather thong, she remembered Francis's letter. She took it from the drawer of the nightstand and stopped. It would only be polite to write a quick thank-you note in case he was unavailable. A cold shiver crossed her shoulders at the thought. She wanted to see him—she had so much to discuss, and the mere idea was such a salve to her loneliness. But better to be prepared.

Sitting down, she tore a sheet of thick cream paper from her sketchbook, dipped the pen in the inkpot, and began to write before her courage failed her.

> *Dear Mr Greenway,*
> *I cannot thank you enough for the loan of this wonderful book.*
> *It has inspired me, and it has helped me to pass a difficult winter.*
> *I very much hope to ask your advice on my paltry designs …*

She chewed the end of the pen. There was so much more she wanted to say but she couldn't impose on his time and since he hadn't arranged to have the book collected, he must be very busy.

> *Yours, most sincerely, your friend*
> *Mary Fripp*

Before she could change her mind, she sanded the page, folded and sealed it, then tucked it into her reticule. She lifted the package and stopped. Mrs Rudge would, without a doubt, enquire as to the contents. Far better to speak to her first.

Mary found her in the kitchen, where feathers were flying, and a headless chicken was spreadeagled on the table.

'I'm going into Bath. Leah is coming with me.'

Mrs Rudge wiped the back of her hand across her forehead and groaned. 'And who's going to help me with today's chores? I haven't got fifteen hands, you know.'

Much as she'd never thought about Leah's life outside the estate, it had never crossed her mind to wonder how Mrs Rudge dealt with all the work that needed doing. Due to James's household parsimony, she'd juggled the position of both housekeeper and cook since Papa's passing. She had Janey, the maid-of-all-work, and now, thankfully, Leah to assist her, but was still constantly run off her feet.

'We'll be back before teatime. I need to call in to the seamstress—despite Leah's best attention nothing fits me anymore.' She pouted and patted her stomach, hoping to forestall any more complaints.

Mrs Rudge ran her gaze over her body. 'You ain't showing much but it's a sensible idea. You'll pop before long and then you won't want to be seen out and about. Go on, off you go, make the most of it and don't stand no nonsense from that girl; she's got a mind of her own.'

Mary stalked out of the kitchen before the thought of being confined to the house yet again dampened her high spirits. She'd rather hoped it was a thing of the past now the sickness had left her. She felt more energetic than she had for months.

Leah skidded to a halt in front of her in the hallway, her irrepressible curls captured under a very pretty straw hat, with a large velvet bag clutched in her hands. The perfect size for the book. 'Good heavens, Leah. What have you got in there?' She gestured to the bag.

'Nowt. Susan will want to load me up with supplies, so I'm prepared. She reckons I don't get fed and I haven't got the heart to tell her Mrs Rudge's cooking's better than hers.'

'Could you do something for me? I've forgotten the package I need to deliver. It's in my bedchamber, on the desk; would you go and fetch it for me? And my sketchpad,' she added as an afterthought. 'I'll tell Mudd we're ready to leave.' Without giving Leah a moment to comment she flew out of the door, heart pumping as she revelled in her good fortune.

An hour later when the carriage descended into the valley, Leah leant forward and peered out of the window, her excitement palpable. 'We just go down this hill and then you'll see the church spire and we're there. The house is next door to the vicarage, across from the common.'

Mudd drew to a halt outside what had once been a fine church in the medieval style with a tall steeple, sorely in need of repair.

'Just over there.' Leah jumped down and started across the common then came to a shuddering halt and turned back. 'Oh! I'm sorry, ma'am. Would you care to come and meet me sister? She'd love to offer you some refreshment.'

Mary didn't want to appear churlish, but it was the ideal opportunity to go and find Mr Greenway without Leah in tow. 'Thank you. I won't. I'll go and deliver my package.'

'Lucky I remembered me manners then, otherwise you might have forgotten it.' Leah delved into her bag and brought out the wrapped package and sketchpad and handed them up.

'We'll come back and collect you after I've run my errands. I expect I'll be an hour or two.'

With a wave, Leah took off again.

Mudd turned around and grinned. 'Where to?'

'We're looking for 7 Limekiln Street. It can't be too difficult to find. I believe it is a stonemason's yard, close to a quarry.'

'Greenway Brothers? Opposite the riding school. I thought that might be where you were headed.'

To her horror her cheeks pinked. The man missed nothing; he must have heard about Mr Greenway's visit all those months ago. She swallowed. 'Quite right, Mudd.' She schooled her face, trying for all the world to look as though a trip to a stonemason's yard was a most natural event. Mudd clicked his tongue and flicked the reins, and the horses took up the slack.

An incongruous Doric portico framed the small building. Above it was a relief of what looked remarkably like the goddess of wisdom and arts, Minerva, her helmet held in one hand and in the other a set of plans.

A sign confirmed their arrival:

F. GREENWAY

ARCHITECT, STATUARY and LANDSCAPE GARDENER

'Good work, Mudd.' Her mumbled words did little to cover her confusion. What in God's name had made her embark on this ridiculous errand? And then the words of Mr Greenway's letter echoed in her mind: *who hopes to be known henceforth as your friend*. What was wrong with visiting a friend? She had Mudd as a chaperone. No one could complain, and there was no reason why James would ever find out. Pushing the thought of her husband aside, she took Mudd's hand and clambered from the carriage.

'I'll wait here for you, shall I?' Mudd raised his wiry eyebrows, and a grin twitched his lips.

'Yes, please.' She held her head high and walked up the path, picking her way through an array of marble chimney pieces, busts and bronzed figures and ornamental chimney funnels.

'You'll be wanting to take Mr Greenway's book, then,' Mudd called, reaching into the carriage.

She halted in her steps and spun around. Was there anything the man didn't know? 'Thank you, Mudd.' With the package safely cradled in her arms she straightened her spine and headed towards the open door.

Before she could raise her hand to knock a man appeared in the shadows. Her heart picked up a beat but as he stepped forward a wave of disappointment washed over her. With sleeves rolled above the elbow and a layer of dust coating every inch of him, he bore little resemblance to the man who'd visited Manali. 'I'm here to see Mr Greenway.'

He nodded his head. 'Aye.'

It couldn't be, although he had the look of him. 'Mr Francis Greenway?'

'No, John. Francis isn't here.'

'Oh!' Her shoulders drooped. One of the Greenway brothers.

John brushed off his hands, spreading a cloud of dust that made her nose twitch, his gaze fixed on the package in her arms. 'Come in. Perhaps I can help. I'm his brother.' He moved back to allow her to enter. 'First door on the right.'

A beam of sunlight illuminated the small room, which obviously served as an office of sorts. Papers, plans and elevations lay strewn across a battered table, held in place by random offcuts of stone and dust. 'I have a package for Mr Greenway.'

'Leave it here and I'll see he gets it.'

No! That wouldn't do, letter or no letter. 'I need to speak to him. It's about the designs he is preparing for my home—Manali.'

John crossed his arms and peered down his long nose at her. 'And you are?'

'Mrs Fripp. Mrs James Fripp.'

'Heard tell your husband had second thoughts.'

She fanned her face with her gloves, more to give herself a moment to think than anything else, and inhaled a breath of rough-hewn sandstone. 'I would like to speak ...'

'You'll find him in Clifton, on site. Can't miss it, at the east end of the Mall. Now, if that's all, I've got work to do.'

Her dismissal. Nodding her thanks to his retreating back, she picked up the package and left.

'Mudd, do you know the road to Clifton?'

'That I do. Where exactly do you want to go?'

'The east end of the Mall.'

'Should take about an hour, maybe less. It's about seven miles.'

'Perfect.' Once there she wouldn't be more than a few minutes and Leah would be quite content with her sister, although the visit to the seamstress might have to wait for another day.

Mudd found the site with no difficulty, two miles from the centre of the town with sweeping views over the surrounding countryside.

With his auburn hair catching the sun, Mr Greenway stood out like a brightly coloured bird amongst the labyrinth of foundations, piles of cut and dressed sandstone and carefully placed pegs and lengths of string. He paced backwards and forwards, consulting a sheaf of papers and waving a hand around as he supervised a group of men scuttling about like woodlice released from beneath a log.

'Wait here, please,' Mary said. 'I won't be long.' Pulse galloping, she snatched up the book and picked her way across the disturbed earth, wishing she'd worn sturdy boots rather than the dainty slippers she'd chosen out of vanity.

Coat cast aside, shirtsleeves rolled to the elbows, dressed in well-fitting britches and boots, he bent and hefted a large piece of sandstone. Her breath hitched in her throat and her pulse thundered. It wasn't until he placed the stone and pulled the sheaf of papers from his pocket that he spotted her. She must have taken him by surprise because he stopped still, brushed his tousled hair out of his eyes and managed to lose his grip on the papers.

A puff of wind snatched the papers away and they scattered across the ground. Several blew in her direction, and she chased after them. They met in the middle of the cleared ground, and she held them out, breathless after her exertions.

'Mrs Fripp.' He stilled for a moment, his gaze roaming her face. 'To what do I owe the honour?' Taking the crumpled papers from her hands, he added them to those he held, his attention darting to the group of men settling a large block on top of a teetering stack. 'Not there, you fool, on the right,' he bellowed, waving his hand in the air to indicate the spot.

'I've brought your book back. I thought you might be in need of it. I wanted to thank you ...' She offered a self-conscious smile, her mind a complete blank. Her heart beat a ridiculous tattoo and she could hardly catch a breath. He hadn't touched her, not even her gloved hand, but her longing stretched like a ribbon between them.

The light reflected specks of gold in his hazel eyes. 'My book?'

A tight laugh exploded from her mouth, and she thrust it into his hands. 'The book you lent me. Sir William Chambers's *Treatise on Civil Architecture.*'

Greenway raised his chin a fraction, a mannerism she remembered from their previous meetings, and his eyes narrowed. She hadn't just imagined how he'd made her blood quicken when they met before.

'Ah yes. I had all but forgotten.'

Her confidence plummeted. Perhaps she had read more into his attentions than he intended. 'As I said, I would like to offer my thanks. I found it most interesting. I won't interrupt you any further.' She scuffed her toe on the dusty ground and turned, more to cover the traitorous colour in her cheeks and her disappointment than from any desire to leave.

His hand reached for her arm. 'Don't go. Just give me a moment or two. The men are due for a break.' He returned to the labourers, and after much arm waving they wandered off to the back of the site and threw themselves down, faces turned to the frail spring sun.

By the time he returned she had recovered her composure and her interest spiked as the courses of sandstone and numerous string lines formed a picture in her mind. How wonderful it would be to stand beneath a building that had once been no more than the faintest line on a pristine sheet of paper, to see the dimensions grow, the walls and roof appear, and know that she had created a place where women and men might seek shelter, and find safety and security.

'Mrs Fripp, I have a few moments to spare.' He reached for her arm again.

Mary jumped at his touch, her mind a million miles away. 'I see there will be two long wings facing the mall,' she managed.

'Yes, yes indeed. Let me show you my plans.' He shuffled through his papers and stepped closer.

Her breath caught as she viewed the glorious design and the intricate plans and elevations. As she'd guessed, there were two long wings, but set between them was a dramatic centre pavilion, temple-like in its grandeur. Six Ionic columns rising through two storeys were capped by a triangular pediment. 'It's magnificent,' she whispered. 'A temple to the gods.'

He laughed, the skin around his eyes crinkling. 'Not for the gods, more to appease society. A venue for public gatherings, concerts, gaming tables and the very popular matchmaking balls. You approve?'

'I most definitely do.' Her voice quaked, overcome by the grandeur of the proposed building. In her mind's eye she could see it complete: filled with society's finest, spacious and elegant.

'I would welcome your assistance when it comes to the interior.'

His words brought her back to earth with a bump—assistance with the interior? Why should a woman only have suggestions for the interior? She turned her face away to prevent him reading the disappointment in her eyes. What was she thinking? His design couldn't be bettered, but how she wished she could have had some part in its creation. 'I have some designs of my own inspired by Chambers. I wondered if I could impose on your time and ask for your opinion.'

'It would be my pleasure.'

'I've left my sketchpad in the carriage.' She pointed to Mudd leaning against the wheel, crowned by a wreath of pipe smoke.

'Unfortunately, now is not the moment.' He gestured to the labourers wandering out from the spot where they'd taken their rest. 'They are piece workers and time is money to them, and me. I must return.'

How foolish. Thinking she could appear from nowhere and take this man away from his work. 'Thank you for your time and the loan of the book.'

'Mary. May I call you Mary?'

She widened her eyes and inclined her head.

'I would very much like to see your drawings. Perhaps I could call on you again?'

Her heart skipped a beat. She could think of nothing she would like more. Then she remembered James and his summary dismissal of Mr Greenway—Francis. Although James had said he'd be away for a month he could return from London at any time, and in all honesty, she doubted he would be impressed if he knew of her actions today, never mind inviting Francis to the house. 'I'll let you know when it is convenient. A note to your premises in Limekiln Street will find you, will it not?'

A cloud crossed his face as though she had offended him, and then he brightened. 'I will wait until I hear from you. Let me walk you to your carriage.'

'No, I can manage quite well.' She handed him the book. 'Return to your men, and thank you once again.'

Francis nodded, half reaching towards her with his outstretched hand, then stepped back, gave a curt bow and strode away, the sun highlighting his shock of copper-coloured hair.

She found Mudd pacing up and down. 'That took longer than I expected. We're going to have to get a move on if you want to go to Milsom Street.'

'I think I'd prefer to go directly home.' She lifted a shaking hand to her forehead. 'I'm feeling a little queasy.'

'So, I won't get my pint of ale.' His florid face wore a look of disappointment.

'Never mind, I'm sure Mrs Rudge will have a tipple for you.' And she would have to come up with some excuse for their stop at Clifton. That she'd been overcome by tiredness perhaps, given her condition. 'We need to make haste because Leah will be wondering what I've been up to.'

'She won't be the only one,' Mudd muttered as he helped her into the carriage.

Four

With her husband's return from Ascot, Mary found herself once more confined to the house and, when James agreed, the immediate garden. No traipsing in the woods, so she missed the arrival of the bluebells, and as spring rolled into summer she began to rail against her confinement and long for her release.

She spent most of her time in the library, with the sash windows open to allow the warm breeze to sweeten the air, and worked her way through all the titles relating to architecture on the lower shelves. It wasn't until she stretched to ease her back that she spotted an intriguing row of small leather-bound books stacked one on top of the other on the highest shelf.

With a good deal of effort, she dragged the library steps across to the back wall, then tucked up her skirts, and climbed onto the bottom rung and gave a little wriggle. As a child she'd loved to perch on the fourth step and survey the room and the garden beyond while Papa worked away at his beloved inlaid table, but with her burgeoning stomach would her balance be compromised? The steps were stable enough and once she reached the third step, she'd be able to grab the safety rail.

Before she could change her mind she scooted up, and with one hand aiding her balance she reached out for the pile of books. Her fingers grazed the leather bindings. Leaning out, she teetered on one leg and stretched ...

'What are you doing up there?'

Almost losing her footing, she straightened up.

Hands on hips, Mrs Rudge scowled up at her. 'Come down here this instant. And do it carefully, or I'll not be held responsible.'

'I'm perfectly fine. I just need these books.'

'Come down, now.'

With a barely audible grumble, Mary reversed down and with a final act of defiance jumped off the last step.

'You simply can't be trusted, can you? Where's Leah? She's supposed to be keeping an eye on you.'

'I don't need an eye kept on me. I'm not a child.'

'No, you're not. You're a woman who should have more sense. Leah!'

'Coming.' Leah's voice wafted in on the breeze.

'What do you think you're doing out there?'

'I was just taking Mudd ...' Colour flooded Leah's downturned face.

'You're not paid to court Mudd. Mrs Fripp needs your help.' Mrs Rudge stomped out of the room.

Leah's laughter filled the room. 'Oops. Sorry, ma'am, I was just taking Mudd something to keep the wolf from the door. The captain's had him cleaning out the stables and repainting the big stall. Something to do with a new horse he's got coming, another racehorse.'

'Never mind, Leah. I just need some help with those books up on the top shelf. Do you think you can reach them?' Mary tugged at her skirt, untucking it. 'We'll need to move the steps a little to the right first.'

'Why don't I collect everything on the top shelf for you? Then I'll bring you something to eat. Much as I hate to admit it, Mrs Rudge is right. You shouldn't be up there, not in your situation.'

'Thank you, that would be perfect.' Mary cleared the surface of the table and before too long a pile of books she'd never seen sat on the table—a series of leather-bound journals.

Mostly they belonged to famous astronomers, mathematicians and explorers, but amongst them one caught her particular attention. The journal of Elizabeth Wilbraham, the very person she and Francis had discussed the first time they'd met. That Papa owned the journal didn't surprise her given he had a great interest in architecture and was an avid collector. He'd drawn the initial plans for Manali himself, and then employed an architect to oversee the building when they'd first arrived in Bath from India. Not that she could remember—she had been but a babe in arms—but she'd heard Mudd say the project had taken Papa's mind off the loss of his wife.

She sat gazing out to the gardens, listening to the birdsong while she ate the slices of ham and fresh bread Leah had brought. Papa had also played a formidable role in the landscaping of the grounds. When she was older, he had explained the choice of the name Manali for the property, his eyes filling with tears. It was the hill station in the Punjab Hills where he and Mama spent the first weeks of their marriage. The word Manali meant place of birds and beautiful hills, and suited the area outside Bath perfectly. He said India had first awakened his love of architecture: the fantastically opulent palaces of the Mughal emperors, their quirkiness and romance, their sense of presence and majesty. He had acquired a set of plans from a Frenchman that were said to be the only pictorial representation of the Mughal palaces of Delhi, Agra and Faizabad, and they'd fashioned the backdrop for hundreds of stories during Mary's childhood. Perhaps that was where her latent interest in architecture stemmed from. It had never crossed her mind to wonder before.

Many days passed as she lost herself within the pages of the journal of the formidable seventeenth-century woman, Elizabeth Wilbraham, who had managed to combine designing her own home in Buckinghamshire, and many other buildings, with raising two daughters. That a woman had pursued a profession nearly one hundred years earlier staggered her, although she had been forced to use men to supervise the construction of her buildings—something she lamented most vociferously in the pages of tightly packed script.

Mary could hardly believe her good fortune as she delved deeper. Lady Wilbraham and her husband had travelled widely in Europe and she recounted the entire trip through the pages of the journal. In the Netherlands she'd met architect Pieter Post, the creator of the Dutch baroque style, and she had studied the works of Palladio in Venetia. However, it wasn't until Mary reached the latter pages that her interest was truly piqued. Lady Wilbraham had not only become patron and sponsor to Christopher Wren, but she claimed her work was the architectural inspiration for many of his buildings.

The journal fell to her lap and she sat back, staring into the distance, imagining Francis's face alight with interest and enthusiasm and the challenge in the depths of his eyes. She couldn't wait to show him the journal, especially the passages relating to Christopher Wren.

'Madam!'

Mary leapt to her feet, the wave of dizziness making her head swirl. She reached for the back of the chair, steadied herself and inhaled deeply; the stench of tobacco, brandy and horse sweat emanating from James's person caused her stomach to convulse. 'Why have you left your bedchamber?' His anger simmered just below the surface, frightening her more than any explosion of rage. She recognised it well; the slightest thing might unleash his fury and he would wreak carnage. His irate face and belligerent stance wavered then came into focus. Shadows, dark as churned mud, underscored his eyes as his gaze raked her from head to toe and came to rest on her expanded girth.

Her hackles rose at his peremptory tone and her temper snapped. 'Am I not permitted to spend time in this room, in my father's library, in the house he built for me?'

A furious pulse pounded in the hollow of his throat. 'Remember your place, madam. Everything that you refer to is mine. The clothes you wear, the books you read, the very chair that you sit in. This house is no longer yours. You have no rights to it nor to the contents.' His hand sketched a wide arc. 'You brought the estate to our marriage—the price your father paid to secure your future. One that is in serious jeopardy.' He took two steps closer. 'How would you like to explain this?' He waved a piece of paper in the air and took several menacing steps closer. Her mind raced and a trickle of sweat made its way from her hairline down her neck. She had no idea of the relevance of the paper nor the reason for James's outburst—other than the nauseating stench of brandy and the slurring of his words.

She moistened her lips. 'What is it?' Her high-pitched, self-conscious tone made her grimace.

Her question only enraged him further. His face swelled and turned crimson; his breath came in short sharp pants. 'A letter. A letter from your paramour. That rogue, scoundrel ...' Spittle flecked the corners of his mouth and with his next exhalation peppered the air.

Whatever was he talking about? 'I beg your pardon?' She had no paramour. She'd barely set foot outside the house in the last six months. Her mouth gaped and she snatched at the paper in his hand.

With one look at the bold, sprawling handwriting an uncontrollable shudder swept her body—Francis's letter, which had accompanied Chambers's treatise. How had James come by it? Surely Mrs Rudge hadn't taken it upon herself to interfere.

The worn, curled paper spiralled in the breeze wafting through the open window and fluttered to the floor.

'Where is this book?' He swiped his hand across the tabletop, scattering the contents across the room.

'Stop! Stop!' Mary leapt to her feet, arms spread, trying to save the precious manuscripts and journals. 'It's not here. I returned it.'

A horrible silence descended. James's face seemed to swell, and his eyes, normally hidden in folds of flesh, became round and wide. 'Returned it,' he bellowed. 'Returned it?'

'To Mr Greenway's offices in Mangotsfield. Leah and Mudd chaperoned me. Mr Greenway was working on the assembly rooms in Clifton. He's responsible for overseeing the building, he is the architect.'

She didn't see the blow coming, just heard the sound, skin hitting bone, a resounding thud and then a surge of indescribable pain. Her ears rang and the air wavered.

Trying to ease the throbbing, she cradled her cheek. James loomed over her, incandescent with rage. She took a step back. Her foot skidded from under her, taking her balance with it.

An explosion of white-hot pain racked her body and her world fractured and darkened.

When Leah placed little George in Mary's arms and she stared into his soft brown eyes her heart contracted with a love so fierce she vowed to protect him forever. No matter how difficult James might make her life, he would never lay a hand on her son. A calmness descended; after years of failure, she had fulfilled her role. Not only that, but she also had someone to love, her own flesh and blood. She lifted him close, sniffed his shock of dark hair, kissed his button nose. James would never raise his hand to him; she would defend him with her life.

Once Mary was clean and tidy, Mrs Rudge ushered James into the bedchamber. He strode to her side, chest puffed out. With a look of sanctimonious satisfaction, he reached for his swaddled son. She nursed him close and turned her body to shield him.

With a frown, James reached for George again.

'Come, Mary, give the babe to his father.' Mrs Rudge leant over the bed.

Sucking in a deep breath, she relinquished her hold and Mrs Rudge placed George in his father's arms. James uttered not a word, not that there was any need. The smirk on his face said it all, and for a moment she felt for him. He'd truly believed she'd never produce an heir, that he'd never hold his son in his arms—perhaps there was something to Mrs Rudge's whispered reference that she'd overheard in the kitchens. The French Disease, common amongst sailors, regardless of their rank, often stripped a man of his ability to sire a child. She'd never raised the matter with him—she hadn't dared.

James carried his son to the window, held him up, examined his fingers and toes, and turned him this way and that. Then, with a grunt that she took to be approval, he handed him back and left the room.

Mrs Rudge found a lovely woman, a Mrs Porlock, from one of the local villages to act as wet nurse. She exuded a sense of peace and calm and quickly settled George into a routine that would have pleased an admiral of the fleet, never mind a mere captain.

But after only a couple of weeks James's enthusiasm for his son wavered and faded, and once again he took to spending more and more time in Bath, although he returned most evenings. He made no further mention of Francis's letter or her trip to Clifton, nor did he apologise for his brutish attack that had brought on George's arrival.

More than anything else Mary wanted a breath of fresh air. Summer had truly arrived in a blaze of cerulean skies and long twilights. She felt superfluous, her time with baby George restricted to a visit before Mrs Porlock settled him for the evening. Despite her protestations, James and Mrs Rudge insisted she remain in her bedchamber, fed nothing more than weak tea and watery soups. How she longed for a roasted chicken, gravy rich with cooking juices, potatoes basted in goose fat. As the days turned into a month, she began to feel she'd been dealt a life sentence.

Shunning Mrs Rudge's constant fussing, she resumed her normal habits, insisting the windows should be opened, refusing to take an invalid's meals, and returning to her beloved library, but what she truly longed for was freedom, to see the world beyond the confines of Manali, to walk in the footsteps of Lady Wilbraham.

'Leah, would you find my bonnet, the one with the blue ribbons. I want to take a drive. Ask Mudd to prepare the carriage.'

'Oh, ma'am, are you sure you're strong enough?'

'I am perfectly well.'

'I'll ask Mrs Rudge.'

Was she to be kept as a prisoner in her own house? 'Why don't you come with me, Leah? That should allay Mrs Rudge's concerns.'

Leah's face broke into a bright smile, giving Mary the sneaking suspicion she'd been manipulated, but no matter—she enjoyed Leah's company. 'Go and tell Mudd to prepare the carriage, and find your bonnet. I'll meet you outside.'

Leah bounced off and Mary collected her sketchpad from her desk, picked up a pencil and went downstairs. The door to James's study was open so she stuck her head inside. She hadn't seen him for days, maybe even a week, not that she had enquired about his movements.

The curtains were tied back, the windows were wide open and an array of brushes and buckets littered the floor in front of the fireplace, evidence that Janey, the maid-of-all-work, had once again become sidetracked and abandoned her task half-finished. It also answered her question. James was not at home and not expected back for some time.

She wandered over to the desk, as usual strewn with ledgers, receipts, bills and a half-empty decanter of brandy. Francis's letter lay to one side, crumpled as though it had been screwed up and then smoothed again, and beneath it a half-written page.

Tilting her face to one side she focussed, her hand hovering, fingers clenching and unclenching. She glanced over her shoulder. Not a sound and no one in sight.

James's spider-like handwriting slashed across the page, his anger obvious in the splotches of ink and hastily scratched-out words. From what she could decipher he was replying to a letter from Francis. It had nothing to do with the letter Francis had written to her, or her visit to Clifton; instead James denied he had agreed to any preliminary plans being drawn up for Manali. She flipped over the sheet of paper and found a reference that brought a sense of vertigo. Clutching the side of the desk, she read on:

> *Any further contact between yourself and my wife will cease and should you or your brothers set foot on the estate I will ensure your name is dragged through the mire and you never work in Bath or Bristol again.*

Her pulse raced and she snatched an irate breath. It was outrageous. What right had James to determine her pastimes? He had his friends in Bath and London, his horses—why, he spent more time and money on horses than he did on her or even his long-awaited heir. Why couldn't she have married a man who shared her interests? Someone who recognised her as a person, not a chattel. There was nothing in Lady Wilbraham's journal that even hinted at her husband's lack of support. Why, they'd even spent their honeymoon exploring the architectural wonders of Europe.

'Are you ready, ma'am?' Leah's face peeped around the corner of the door. 'Mudd's got the carriage. He wants to know where we're going and how long we'll be. Says he's still got work to do in the stables.'

'I'm quite ready.'

Mudd fussed like an old woman, handed her up and tucked a blanket over her knees. 'Where would you like to go?'

'Thornbury Castle.' The words popped out of Mary's mouth like a cherry pit.

'Thornbury? Why would you want to go there?'

Truthfully, she hadn't even thought of going until that very moment. 'It's only twelve miles away. Hurry up, Mudd, we haven't got all day if you have tasks to complete,' she snapped before she had the opportunity to think better of her decision. She pushed the blanket off her knees, leaving poor Leah scrabbling around the floor of the carriage when it lurched horribly as Mudd swung out onto the road.

'What is this place we're going to? I've never heard of it. Is it a real castle?' Leah asked once she'd crawled up on the seat.

'I've never been there but I heard all about it from Mr Greenway. He's drawn up some plans for renovations. Did you know he's related to the Duke of Norfolk?'

Leah huffed. 'How would I? Never met the man. Though I seem to be hearing a lot about him—what with you and Mudd going on and … you know the captain ain't going to be too pleased if he finds out where you've been.'

'And how's that going to happen?' Mary narrowed her eyes and pinned Leah with a stern gaze.

'Oh, my lips are sealed, ma'am. Same as Mudd's.'

Not sealed too tightly, otherwise Mudd wouldn't have been talking to Leah about Francis. Her stomach sank. Had he told James about their trip to Clifton? He wouldn't have. His loyalty rested with her. He'd been with them for years, started as a stable boy, long before she'd married James. He'd taught her to ride a horse and drive the carriage, spent hours with her exploring the countryside, as her groom, and they'd struck up quite a friendship. She'd trust him with her life.

The carriage bowled along with both Mary and Leah lost in their own thoughts, although occasionally Mary caught what might be a sideways glance from Leah.

'We should be there before long.' Mary broke the silence hoping to distract Leah from her musing. 'When the castle was built it was thought to be one of the most magnificent of the time, back in the reign of Henry VIII. Kings and queens and dukes have lived there for hundreds of years.' She dredged up everything she could remember Francis saying. How she wished she'd thought to see if there was anything in Papa's library about the place before she'd embarked on this foolhardy whim. 'It's got castellated towers,' she added lamely.

'Cast-a-what?'

'Towers and battlements to defend the castle from attack.'

Leah peered out of the window. 'I think we might be there then. Looks a bit of a wreck to me.'

Mary followed Leah's finger to the roofline appearing through the trees. 'That's why Mr Greenway is preparing plans for renovations.'

'Mr Greenway—right.' Leah's eyebrows danced and her face lit with a knowing grin.

She really must stop talking about Francis. Somehow he seemed to occupy far too many of her thoughts. No one could question the fact that he cut a fine figure in his green velvet coat but there was more that kept him in her thoughts. It was his attitude towards her. He hadn't questioned her interest in architecture, had encouraged her, shared his plans of Thornbury Castle and treated her as an equal. She let out a long sigh and snatched a glance at Leah, hoping she hadn't noticed anything untoward in her expression. 'We'll be there soon.'

When they finally drew to a halt at the intricate Gothic gatehouse Mudd opened the door. 'Doesn't look like there's anyone about. Leastways if they are they wouldn't be too comfortable. Look over there.' He pointed to the crumbling facade. 'Want me to go and see if they're ready to receive you?'

Mary cleared her throat. 'We're not expected. I just wanted to take a drive. Some fresh air, clear my head ...' Her words dried. 'Just follow the road around the perimeter. I'm simply interested in the buildings.' She gave a nonchalant wave of her hand to dismiss him.

Mudd walked the horses past the ornate, Gothic gatehouse and around the carriageway. The place might have fallen into disrepair but nevertheless there was something very appealing about it, straight out of a fairy tale, with an octagonal tower, turrets, chimneys and walled courtyards. In her mind's eye she could see how Francis's designs would bring the castle back to life. It would be an expansive project and cost a fortune—but then maybe dukes could afford to indulge their fantasies.

Once they'd made a full circuit Mary stuck her head out of the window. 'Thank you, Mudd, I think it's time we returned. I'd hate to keep you from your work.'

As was so often the case with return trips, they were back at Manali in half the time it had taken to get to Thornbury. Mudd trudged off to deal with the horses and Leah scuttled into the kitchen, leaving Mary a trifle bewildered and discombobulated. She'd missed her afternoon visit with George, and Mrs Porlock didn't appreciate interruptions to the strict routine she'd established.

Mary wandered into the library and threw herself down in the big leather armchair, inhaling the faint scent of bergamot, a subtle reminder of Papa. There was no pleasure in an interest if it wasn't shared. She pulled her sketchpad towards her and chewed the end of her pencil.

No one built castles anymore, but she did love the romance of the turrets and the arched windows and doors. Her pencil flew across the page as a smaller, more intimate creation appeared, with traceried windows, octagonal battlemented towers all around a central courtyard and a matching gatehouse. As her designs took shape her thoughts settled. She would not subdue her interest in architecture because society, and James, deemed the art the realm of men, and one day she would design—not restore, but design— a castle, maybe a fort and a great bridge. Meanwhile she would dedicate her time to creating her own architectural portfolio.

With a wry smile, she closed her sketchpad and sat staring out of the window as the twilight turned the sky to indigo and a bone-white moon rose.

Five

James barged into the library and threw himself down. Despite the early hour, he had been drinking; his bulbous nose glowed, and vivid purple spider veins traced his cheeks. Mary concentrated on her drawing, not wanting him to know she was watching him. He pushed on the table, attempted to stand, failed miserably and slumped back in the chair.

Some moments later he made a second attempt, succeeded, and staggered down the length of the table towards her. 'What's this?' The flat of his hand hit the table with a resounding thump, the inkpot jumped and an icy sense of dread shivered across her shoulders. With a shaking hand she pulled the ink closer and dipped her nib. If she could maintain a sense of calm, perhaps he would be soothed. 'Just a drawing.' She added a line to the octagonal tower.

He pushed her arm aside and snatched at her sketchpad. Her good intentions took flight, and she slammed her nib down. A blob of ink landed on the sleeve of his linen shirt. His face paled as he looked down at it, then back at her. His eyes narrowed and the sound of his laboured breathing filled the room.

She threw back the chair and lunged for the door—too late. Grabbing a fistful of her hair, he swung her around and tossed her aside. She crashed to her knees, her scalp burning, and scrambled beneath the table.

His meaty fist reached for her again and hauled her out by the hair, flipping her over onto the carpet and knocking the breath from her lungs. Turning her head, she sank her teeth into his hand and kicked out, but he slapped her away like a persistent fly, knelt on her legs and pinned her to the ground, raised his arm and backhanded her across the face.

A high-pitched roaring filled her ears and scattered starbursts filled her vision.

Before she could regain her senses, James pressed his riding jacket down over her face, blinding her. She could smell nothing but the overpowering stench of him, the brandy he drank, the pomade he used and the rank odour of his unwashed body.

She tried to suck in a breath, sensed him fumbling at his clothes, felt warm flesh, and in that moment his intention became clear. She gave an enormous lurch and almost managed to toss him aside, lashing out with her arms, scratching at his face, and squealing as loudly as she could, praying Mrs Rudge, Leah, Mudd, God, anyone, would rescue her.

His stinking jacket tightened, muffling her cries, smothering her airways, suffocating her. Blood trickled down the back of her throat and she sank back in despair, her body limp.

James lifted his weight, and she tossed aside his jacket, sucked in a breath of air and for a heartbeat believed it over until her skirt came up, covering her head. She tightened her muscles, clamped her legs, but his knee forced down and he shoved his way between her thighs, pinned her arms and crushed her beneath his heaving chest.

As he thrust into her, she let herself drift away, as she always did, thought of the books on the table, beautiful buildings, and in her mind created the perfect house she would design, where she would live, without him, free to follow her dreams.

James's vicious, thrusting climax drove her spine into the hard floor and a moment later he rolled off her and lay panting. Too wary to move, she stayed motionless, hoping he would follow his usual practice and leave her be.

After a few moments he drew down her skirt, wiped the blood and semen off himself with his handkerchief, picked up his coat—frowning at the stain where her nose had bled—and without a backwards glance, left the room.

Mary lay still. Her head and face throbbed, and blood trickled from her nose into her mouth, coppery and salty. She wiped it away with the back of her hand and rolled onto her hands and knees. Her back ached and her hips jarred as though they'd been wrenched from their sockets. A deep ache flamed in her lower belly.

She rocked back on her haunches and waited until her breathing settled, then, with the aid of the table, shakily found her feet. A gush of warmth ran down her legs. She staggered across the carpet to the door, reaching for the handle. He would never touch her again. He would never lay his hands on George. She would move into the gatehouse, raise George, and James could continue to live the life he preferred—his horses, the gambling, the drinking and socialising—the women too. She had no doubt there were others but unsurprisingly, it didn't matter to her at all.

Mary knew she was with child when the sickness arrived, but this time she had at least an understanding of the path it would take. It wouldn't last forever. Once again James's attitude softened but he made no reference to the episode in the library and, best of all, having informed her that he expected another son, he kept from her bedchamber. She too hoped for a son. She would then have fulfilled her obligations, produced an heir and a spare, and she'd move to the gatehouse, where the door would remain forever barred.

By the beginning of May the sickness abated and Mary resumed her early-morning walks, revelling in the extended time James spent away. She followed the meandering path through the woods, along the curved contours of the land, amongst the trees and gently sloping hills.

The early-morning light speared the lush green of the spring leaves, illuminating the sweet-smelling bluebells nodding their violet heads in the breeze, shaking off the dew and tilting their faces to the slanting rays of sun.

She bent and inhaled their perfume then collected a small bunch. She liked to place them on the table in the library. Mrs Rudge was never very keen and threw them away at the earliest opportunity. Steeped in the old folklore, she constantly warned of fairy enchantments. She swore that if a person heard bluebells ring, it heralded a visit from a bad fairy and imminent death. Mary always laughed away her warning tales. She preferred the story told in Mama's book on the language of flowers—that blue-bells were a symbol of constancy, gratitude and everlasting love.

As she stepped through the trees she added to the bunch then wiped the sticky sap coating her hands on the hem of her skirt and straightened up, arching her back to stretch her muscles. The pungent earthy scent of the woodland made her mouth water. How she longed for a plate of juicy mushrooms. Bending down, she scrabbled beneath the old trees. Her foolish, fruitless search made her laugh—mushrooms were an autumn treat, when the mists rolled in and the earth smelt damp. Mother Nature wouldn't be hurried, no matter what Mary's body craved.

With the bunch of bluebells clasped tightly in her hand, she returned to the path and awaited the sense of peace and tranquillity the woodlands always brought, but the day felt somehow different. Turning this way and that she searched the winding path, up the rise beneath the tunnel of leaves.

A strange vibration travelled from the soles of her feet and echoed in her chest. Something was coming, big and fast, too fast. A moment later the sound of thundering hooves filled her ears. A massive black stallion bolted at an uncontrolled gallop. It hurtled towards her, eyes rolling white, nostrils flared, legs flailing.

With a scream she lurched off the path, her cloak billowing behind her. The rider sawed on the reins, struggling to control the beast as it plunged sideways, ears flat against its head, snorting. Great wheeling hooves filled her vision. Her heartbeat roared in her ears. She scrambled towards the trees and fell to her knees, face buried in her hands, cowering into the carpet of last year's leaves, sheltered by the oak tree's massive root system.

A high-pitched, agonising squeal pierced her ears, quickly followed by a string of obscene profanities—in a voice as familiar as her own. With a final, resounding curse, James arced through the air. He landed, with a sickening thud, not six feet from where she crouched.

Freed of its burden, the stallion skittered sideways, sweating and blowing, then continued its wild race into the trees, leaving nothing but an eerie, loaded silence.

Tight, dry gasps caught in her throat and made her chest heave. She crawled from under the tree. The warm, earthy scent of the undergrowth mingled with the reek of sweat, blood and brandy.

James lay spreadeagled across the path, his head twisted askew, his sightless eyes wide and accusing.

Her mouth opened in a strangled cry. 'James!' She inched towards him, clasped his shoulders. His dead weight slipped from her hands and his body fell back to the earth, revealing a wet, sticky slick of blood staining the undergrowth.

'James!' Frantically she searched for some sign of life. There was nothing but the sound of the birds and the rustle of the foliage in the trees above and a sense of profound peace.

He couldn't be dead. Only a moment ago he'd been galloping down the track, full of life, the massive stallion beneath him, surging through the woods.

She rocked back on her heels and studied his face—calm, all signs of his perpetual anger faded—and in that moment she knew her life had changed.

Help. She had to get help. Mudd. She needed Mudd. He would know what to do. He understood horses, and men, and accidents.

Or was it an accident? If she hadn't screamed, darted from the path and petrified the horse, James would be arriving at the house, throwing the reins to Mudd and calling for Mrs Rudge, demanding a meal and more brandy to wash away the night's indulgences.

A panicked howl broke from her lips and she lifted her skirts and bolted down the path, her feet pounding in time with her heart, her snatched cries rasping her throat.

It seemed like hours later when she slithered to a halt outside the stables. 'Mudd! Mudd!' Her legs turned to jelly and went from under her, and she collapsed in a heap, her chin resting in a pile of dung.

Hands reached under her arms and hauled her upright. 'Come along, Mudd's gone out to look for the captain. He'll find him, don't fuss yourself.' Leah wiped her hand across her cheeks and pushed her hair back from her face.

Mary licked her lips 'How do you know?' A rising wave of hysteria tinged her voice.

'Captain's horse came back. Mudd knew something weren't right. Let's get you inside and cleaned up.'

'It's my fault. I shouldn't have ...'

'Hush! Nothing's your fault. We all know what the captain's like after a night in town. Mudd'll fetch him home.' Leah wrapped her plump arm around her shoulders and guided her towards the house, while the image of James's staring eyes filled Mary's vision and guilt curled like a snake in her belly.

Mrs Rudge bundled her upstairs, telling Leah in no uncertain terms to bring warm milk and bread. Slumped like a rag doll, Mary let Mrs Rudge wipe her filthy hands and face, brush her hair and help her into her nightgown. Not asking any questions, not speaking, lulling her into a semi-conscious state.

Mary's eyelids drooped and she turned her face to the pillow, the blessed oblivion hovering—until the door flew open.

Leah teetered on the threshold, a bowl of bread and milk in her hands, her face a matching pasty blur. 'Mrs Rudge.' She cocked her head to one side and together they stepped outside the room. The door pulled closed.

Mary sat up and swung her legs over the side of the bed, knowing full well the message Leah brought.

'His neck was broke. Naught anyone can do.'

The room twisted and twirled, and her stomach churned and more by luck than design she heaved foul-tasting bile into the chamber-pot.

Leah's cool hands cradled her forehead and eased her back into bed. 'Rest now.'

She lurched upright. 'Tell me, Leah. Did Mudd find him?'

She perched on the side of the bed and clasped her hand. 'Mrs Rudge says you're to rest.'

Mary wrenched her hand free. 'I know. He's dead.' Racking sobs shook her body. 'It's my fault.'

'Your fault?' Leah's voice wavered.

'He's dead.' She inclined her head, flicking her hair back from her face.

'How can it be your fault?'

Mary inhaled, then let the breath trickle from between her lips. She batted down the sense of relief that James could never hurt George, never strike her or force her to submit to his demands. But no matter how badly James treated her, she hadn't intended to kill him. 'I screamed and darted across the path, the horse reared, and James fell.' She covered her face with her hands, pressing her fingers into her eye sockets, trying to erase the picture of the snorting, sweating stallion and James's blind accusing stare.

'No, it can't be your fault. Mudd said he's not surprised. The new stallion's a hellish handful and the master was drunk, very drunk.'

'How can he know that?'

'The stench of brandy on him.'

Mary inhaled again, the smell of blood and sweat filling her nostrils. Her stomach heaved and she clapped her hand over her mouth. Leah thrust the chamber-pot under her chin but this time she swallowed down the bile.

Six

James was buried in the church in Bristol where they'd married, and Mr Caldicott, Papa's man of business, commissioned the Greenway Brothers to erect a headstone. Guilt rankled, but Mary couldn't bring herself to tell anyone that the Greenways would be the last people James would have wanted to create the monument to commemorate his life.

The household closed ranks. Curtains were drawn and doors covered in black wreaths, the clocks stopped at the very hour of James's death. Although Mrs Rudge, Leah and Mudd refused to acknowledge that her foolish actions had caused the stallion to rear—that she was in any way responsible for James's death—it did little to lighten the darkness engulfing her.

Days merged into nights and nights into horrifying dreams peppered with accusations and guilt. Not only guilt for her role in James's accident but also, in the darkest moments of the night, the knowledge that James's death had brought her relief.

The sun continued to rise every morning, bringing with it the warmest summer for years, but she remained in her bedchamber, convinced Mrs Rudge or Leah would somehow read in her face her innermost thoughts, and know that she had wished James gone.

And all the while her belly grew, larger and larger, as if defying her despondency.

Leah and Mrs Rudge tried to convince her that it was her responsibility to ensure the best for the new baby and constantly brought George to visit her, recounting his newly acquired skills, his ability to sit and pull himself onto his feet, pointing out his chubby legs and radiant smile, his curiosity and awareness and his fascination with water, inherited no doubt from his father. But she couldn't find the energy or the courage to bear the burden of her guilt. Had she deliberately leapt from the path, startled the horse? The thoughts whirled round and round in her head.

In the end it was Leah who rescued her from the doldrums—after she lost her temper. 'You're thankless and ungrateful,' Leah harrumphed, arms akimbo, staring down at Mary's huddled form.

Mary turned her face into the pillow and closed her eyes, but Leah simply moved to the other side of bed, scraped Mary's hair back from her face and peered deep into her eyes.

'What's the matter with you? You've got more than most women ever have, a beautiful bonny baby boy and another child on the way, to look after you in your old age, a wonderful home, more money than I'll ever see in my lifetime.' She paused, pinched her lips together, then exhaled. 'It's time this grieving stopped. It's not as though you loved the man.'

Mary pushed into a sitting position, her mouth yawning wide. 'He was my husband.' The man Papa had chosen for her, had trusted with his most treasured possessions.

'He was a tyrant, a drunken sot, and you were nothing more to him than a brood mare.' Leah's words filled the room like gathering storm clouds, swallowing every breath of air. She snatched up the untouched breakfast tray. 'And if you don't eat something soon that baby ain't going to thrive and you'll have more misery on your plate.'

Dumbstruck, Mary sat staring at the slammed door. Her face heated, and she dropped her head into her hands, diminished, embarrassed, weak—as though James's conduct was her fault, that she shouldn't have behaved in such a way to cause him to treat her so badly. Lifting her head, she ran her fingers through her hair and scraped it back from her face. Her skin felt taut, and a band of metal tightened around her head.

She should never have married James, never have blindly accepted Papa's carefully orchestrated matchmaking. He'd been so convinced he had covered every eventuality in the marriage settlement, it hadn't crossed his mind to consider Captain Fripp, a man he'd known and respected for many years, would care any less for his daughter than he did. The shock of Papa's death, his unexpected departure from her life, had rendered her incapable of a single independent thought and she had fallen into the role James had carved for her. In truth Papa had handed her, and his hard-earned paradise, over on a platter to a man who had blindsided him. She might as well have been sold into slavery. It was not what Papa intended for her and she had no one to blame but herself.

She had blithely accepted the role James forced upon her, allowed him to dominate and isolate her. He had manipulated and humiliated her, chipped away at her sense of safety and independence.

She, like every other woman, had the right to pursue her own interests. James might have been her husband, but fate had decreed he was no longer her keeper. It was enough.

Liberated by the truth, she felt the clouds lift, and her self-confidence stirred, slowly flexing its long unused muscles. After a few moments she swung her legs over the edge of the bed; the room tilted but she sucked in a fortifying breath and persevered.

With each step her legs gained strength and, tottering over to the window, she drew back the curtains. The summer sun streamed in.

In another four months the baby would arrive; nothing would change that. In the meantime, she had no one to answer to, and the house was her own, as she had always dreamt. Finally, she had no need to dance to any man's tune.

The mirror told an ugly story. Her hair hung in lank strands, accentuating her pale, greasy face, and deep, dark smudges shadowed her eyes. She picked at her chapped lips and pinched her cheeks—to no avail.

Leah's words played over and over an unyielding refrain— *tyrant, drunken sot, brood mare*—and try as she might, she couldn't summon any argument. She drew in a deep breath, and with it the sour odour of her body, and she shuddered. A sluggish movement coursed through her, and as she cradled her stomach the baby twisted beneath her fingers, reminding her of its existence—she wouldn't live with another death on her conscience.

She poured a drink from the carafe beside the bed and sipped the cool water, staring out past the garden to the woodland beyond. She shuddered. She'd never walk there again—Mrs Rudge's tales of the bluebell fairies had more to them than she'd allowed. She shook the thought away before the great black clouds descended again and instead inhaled the warm, sweet-smelling air drifting in the window from the lilacs outside, bringing with it the promise of the future. She picked up the little bell Mrs Rudge had placed on the table, and rang it, then she opened her clothes press. All her gowns had disappeared from the hanging space, apart from the heavy silk she'd worn to the funeral, and another lightweight, pitch-black crepe gown.

By the time Leah's face appeared around the door she'd arranged the conveniently placed crepe on the bed. 'I'd like to take a bath, Leah, and could you perhaps bring me a cup of tea and a biscuit or two. I missed my breakfast.' She offered a frail, sheepish grin—more of a grimace, truth be told.

Leah beamed. 'I'll be back in the twitch of a lamb's tail. Mrs Rudge's made some fruit cake, I'll bring some of that with the tea.' Without waiting for a reply, she clattered back downstairs.

Seven

It was a slow and tedious crawl back into the light but each day Mary's spirits lifted, and her strength increased. She made the most of her improving health although she didn't set foot in the woods, nor did she ask Mudd to take her driving. She confined herself to the gardens, concentrated on her exploration of the architectural books in the library, re-read Elizabeth Wilbraham's journal, paying particular attention to the passages referring to her relationship with Wren, and revisited her father's books from India. She became her own companion and tutor as she filled her sketchpad with copies of Lady Wilbraham's drawings and, later, more creations of her own. Every afternoon she and baby George enjoyed a walk. He had celebrated his first birthday and gambolled around with increasing dexterity. Given the slightest opportunity he headed directly to the river, leading Leah a merry dance.

One morning as she sat in the library enjoying the warm breeze through the open sash a flash of movement caught her attention, followed by the low rumble of conversation. As befitted her continued state of mourning, visitors were few and far between, and even Mr Caldicott continued to write, rather than call. He'd informed her he'd dealt with Francis's bill for the headstone and was still working on James's papers and, bearing in mind her situation, would continue to manage the finances, a fact that appealed to her no end.

She stepped through the lower sash onto the flagstones and shaded her eyes. Some sort of commotion echoed from the stables. Mudd's bulky frame blocked her view but from his belligerent stance it was obvious he was attempting to discourage the visitor from coming up to the house.

When Mudd stepped to one side he revealed Francis, sporting, as always, his moss-green coat and brilliant white cravat, looking just as she remembered. A fluttering sensation spread through her insides; the baby stirring because of her sudden movement, no doubt. With a widening smile she swept the strands of loose hair back from her face and hurried towards the stables.

Francis spotted her almost immediately and doffed his hat in greeting.

Mudd, unfortunately, wasn't so enthusiastic. He held up his hand, stalling Francis, and rushed to her side. 'He wants a word.'

'That's perfectly fine, Mudd. Tell him I'm in the library and send him in, perhaps through the front door, not the sash, and then ask Mrs Rudge if she can bring us some refreshments.'

'But you're not receiving, not in your situation.' He emphasised his words with a wave of his hand towards her midriff.

James's accusations about Francis flitted through her mind. The thought that her dealings with Francis might have fuelled James's rage crossed her mind but she pushed it away. He'd made no mention of Francis after his initial outburst. 'I will receive who I like, when I like.'

Totally aghast, Mudd clenched his fists. 'The man should know better.'

'I'll make that decision, thank you.' It was more than three months since James had passed, and as for her situation, there was no reason why she shouldn't receive visitors at home.

Without waiting for Mudd to reply, she slipped back into the library and sat down at the table, quickly arranging her books. There was so much she wanted to discuss with Francis, including her final drawings for Manali and particularly the portico, which she had enlarged to include six stone steps, plinths, pilasters and columns. Once Mr Caldicott gave her his final reckoning, she intended to engage Francis to draw up the plans and organise the building.

'Come in,' she called at the first sound of a knock, unable to control the hint of excitement lacing her voice.

The door swung open. 'Mrs Fripp.' A lopsided smile lifted the corner of his mouth and he bowed. 'Mary. Please forgive my intrusion but I have come to offer my condolences.' He inclined his head.

'Mr Greenway, it's a pleasure.' She sketched a quick curtsy. 'Won't you come and sit down.' Indicating the chair at the head of the table, she resumed her seat. 'I've asked for some refreshments to be brought. You must be parched after your walk.'

'Not much of a walk. I had Olive and John drop me off at the end of the carriageway. I saw Mudd outside the stables and wasn't sure if you would be receiving.'

'I'm delighted to see you. I believe Mr Caldicott settled your account.'

A hint of colour tinged his cheeks. 'Mr Caldicott did settle the account.' For the first time she noticed a vulnerability in him, hesitation in his long slim fingers as he drummed them on the table and muttered under his breath then turned to face her. He appeared haggard, the spark in his hazel eyes dimmed.

Without thinking she reached out and touched his sleeve. 'Are you well?' Rather a personal question, but he had insisted they were to be friends and friends enquired about each other's wellbeing.

He stared off into the distance for a moment or two, ignoring her familiarity. 'Physically, yes. Thank you.'

'But?'

'Business is never easy. All the talent in the world doesn't free one of the monotony of daily life.'

'Are you still working on the Clifton Assembly Rooms? The building must almost be complete.'

A scowl darkened his face, and he gave a disgruntled huff and shrugged. 'Externally it is, but until we receive payment, we can't progress any further.'

So that was the problem. What Francis needed was a sponsor, a patron, someone like Elizabeth Wilbraham with funds to tide him over. 'Is there no one who could sponsor you? I've been reading Lady Wilbraham's diaries. I found them in Papa's collection. Did you know she had a great influence on Sir Christopher Wren's designs?'

He shot her a look of pure disbelief. 'You can't believe everything you read.'

'But this is her own journal. I found it—oh, I can't remember when, so much has happened in the last months.' And most of it had disappeared into the cloud of misery and guilt that had shrouded her after James's accident. 'It's fascinating reading. Some of her designs are most interesting.'

'I'm sure they are and I'm certain Wren benefited from her patronage.'

'I have no doubt you're correct.' She bit her lip, not game to even hint at the possibility a woman might have had a hand in the design of some of London's most famous buildings. 'Which brings us back to my suggestion that you find a sponsor. Is there no one else you could approach? You made mention of the Duke of Norfolk.' How she wished she might be able to help him, but until she'd spoken to Mr Caldicott and understood her financial position, she could make no commitment.

He gave no response but eyed her through the spikes of his lashes as if he was trying to read her thoughts, then with a shake of his head he pinned her with his gaze.

Annoyingly she blushed as if she had something to hide.

'It is an interesting thought, but I doubt very strongly the duke would be in a position to assist me.'

'Unfortunately, neither am I, as much as I would like to. James's assets will pass to George and then …' Unwittingly her hands reached for her belly. 'Perhaps a small loan to tide you over? I shall speak to Mr Caldicott when he calls.'

'I would be most grateful.' He interlaced his fingers and sat for a moment, his gaze fixed on the open books on the table, most particularly her sketchpad. 'I see you have been keeping busy.' He pulled Mary's drawings closer. 'Unless I'm very much mistaken this is a copy of Wotton House.' He turned the page. 'And this … How delightful. It has overtones of the gatehouse at Thornbury Castle. Did you visit?' The warmth in his hazel eyes tickled her skin.

'I did. Your design and plans so impressed me …' Her words tapered off and a flush heated her cheeks. 'Mudd took me for a drive. We only viewed the outside; we didn't leave the carriage. We stopped at the gatehouse, but the place appeared deserted.' A strange tension swirled in the air. Should she not have gone? 'Is there any reason I should not have been there?'

'Not anymore, no.'

'Why do you say that?'

He cleared his throat, pushed to his feet and stared out of the window, his broad shoulders straining the velvet of his coat. 'It's of no consequence.'

Leah's knock heralded the arrival of their refreshments and Mary cleared a space on the table. 'Thank you. Just leave it here.'

'Would you like me to stay, ma'am?'

'No, no thank you. I can pour.' She arranged the cups and plate of biscuits then lifted the teapot and paused. 'Would you like tea, Mr Greenway? I'm afraid I am quite addicted to the drink, or would you prefer something else? Ale, brandy, a glass of wine?'

'Tea suits.'

'Thank you, Leah. You may go. I'm certain George would enjoy your company.'

'Mrs Rudge said …'

'Never mind Mrs Rudge.'

Leah pouted, dropped an uncharacteristic, exaggerated curtsy and huffed out of the room, Mrs Rudge's message conveyed and ignored.

Once the tea was poured Francis resumed his seat, and, determined to ease the unspoken tension, Mary searched for another subject. Everything seemed so very different. During their previous meetings conversation had flowed seamlessly but there was an undeniable atmosphere in the air, a sense of unease.

'Have you any new commissions?'

'There is a great deal of building going on in Clifton—the Prince of Wales Crescent, Royal York and Lower Crescent. I'm working on a set of plans for a man named Doolan, retired Colonel Richard Doolan, no less. I'm hopeful that we can weather the storm.'

Weather the storm. That sounded a little dire. 'I do hope the loss of the work on Manali isn't to blame.'

'Unfortunately, my financial woes extend far beyond your late husband's unfulfilled contract.' He passed a weary hand over his eyes. 'To be honest we have lost the commission for the internal fit-out of the Clifton Assembly Rooms. It's hit hard. However …'

his face brightened, '... we have been asked to undertake the repairs to St James, Mangotsfield. We are seeking work wherever we can: paving stones, statuary for the aristocracy ...'

Which, even she understood, was no substitute.

'We hope to have the assembly rooms completed externally by the end of the year and stave off bankruptcy. But enough of this.' He reached across the table for her hand. 'Tell me about your designs, Mary. I may continue to call you Mary, may I not?'

She inclined her head. 'And I shall call you Francis. We have, after all, been friends for several years now.' Bankruptcy. She hadn't imagined the situation was so grim. A change of subject was needed while she digested this latest piece of information.

'Let me show you this. It was one of Papa's favourite buildings.' She opened the extravagantly bound folio containing the large-format plans and elevations of the monuments from Delhi, Agra and Faizabad. Francis's eyes lit up as she turned to the first illustration, her fingers caressing the heavy paper.

'This is the Taj Mahal. It's a mausoleum, built by Shah Jahan.' She ran her fingers over the breathtaking white marble monument. 'It's on the banks of the Yamuna River, south of Delhi. It's amazing to think it was built two hundred and fifty years ago. It took twenty-two years to complete.' Tears filled her eyes and she searched fruitlessly for her handkerchief.

Francis pressed his own into her hand and moved his chair closer.

'Please excuse me.' She mopped her cheeks. 'It's such a poignant story. Papa used to tell it to me as a child. I always believed he would have built such a monument to my mother had he not been forced to bury her at sea. I'm sure it is where his interest in architecture stemmed from.' She forced a smile. 'I'm sorry, I seem to be a little emotional. It's ...' She bit her lip; it would be totally unseemly to mention her condition.

'It's understandable. Your life has been turned upside down. Tell me the story.'

It wasn't one a practical man like Francis would relish. 'It's pure romance. A tale that appeals to women.'

'It appealed to your father, and it holds memories of both of your parents. It's important to you, and therefore to me.' His touch strengthened. 'A man named Shah Jahan, you said.'

'Yes, the grandson of Akbar the Great, the fifth emperor of the Mughal Empire. When he was sixteen, he met the fifteen-year-old daughter of the soon-to-be prime minister. It was love at first sight, but he had to first marry another—an arranged marriage. Five years later she became his second wife—she was beautiful, clever and tender-hearted. He gave her the name Mumtaz Mahal—jewel of the palace. They went on to have fourteen children. Only seven survived infancy. It was the birth of the fourteenth child that stole her life.'

Mary's hand cradled her stomach and her mind darted to the possibility of losing George, or this new child she carried within her—making the story take on a deeper significance.

'Despite being with child Mumtaz Mahal insisted on accompanying Shah Jahan on a four-hundred-mile journey to repel a usurper. Her child was born in a tent in the middle of the camp. Shah Jahan rushed to her side, and at first all was well but just one day later she died in his arms. According to tradition she had to be buried immediately. In his anguish Shah Jahan mourned for eight days, and when he emerged from his tent his hair had turned white, and he had aged immeasurably.'

Francis leant closer, his fingers running over the huge, shelled dome and the four thin white minarets of the perfectly symmetrical building. 'And?'

'When the feud was over, he had his wife's body brought back to Agra accompanied by thousands of soldiers and mourners. She was buried on the site where the Taj Mahal now stands—the first mausoleum to be dedicated to a woman.

'It's inlaid with delicate flowers and vines using precious gem-stones, lapis lazuli from Ceylon, jade from China, turquoise from Tibet. There are pictures further on in the book of the work and inscribed with passages from the holy book. It is exquisite ...'

He lifted her hand and for a wild and magical moment she believed he intended to press a kiss upon her skin. 'I never thought to meet another person who would understand.' His warm breath brushed the back of her hand. 'It is not the design and creation of the buildings themselves; it is what they represent, the echoes of our lives, our traditions, our very being. Take your Taj Mahal. Its beauty and creativity tells a permanent story that will never be forgotten, which is what Shah Jahan intended—thank you. I thought I knew everything there was to know about architecture. You have proved me wrong.' His gaze roamed her face, soft and warm as his hand.

Her heart quickened embarrassingly, and her lips curved in a smile. 'I've enjoyed our talk; please feel free to call again if you have the time.'

But despite her invitation, Francis once again stayed away.

As the leaves on the oak trees started to turn Mary knew her time was close. She had little recollection of George's birth, and it was with some trepidation, and the reawakened memory of Mumtaz Mahal's story, that she approached the impending event.

On a warm autumn day, her pains began. By the following morning little William Moore lay in her arms, named for Papa, and from the very first moments he displayed the placid nature of his namesake. Ironically it seemed that her body was well equipped to deal with the rigours of childbirth, and according to the midwife her preference for long walks and fresh air had played to her advantage. A wet nurse was employed again, but this time, as mistress of her own fortunes with no one to answer to, she refused the weeks of confinement and within five days ventured outside to make the most of the last days of autumn.

It was as though she had been granted a new life, handed her freedom on a plate. She had every intention of pursuing her passion for architecture, arranging with Mr Caldicott sponsorship for Francis to ease his financial woes, and learning all she could. And ... her heart fluttered annoyingly at the thought of him, his handsome rugged face and lively hazel eyes, the way he tipped his head to one side as he listened to her, as though her words, her thoughts were of great significance. She felt as if she was standing on a precipice peering down into the unknown—her heart telling her one thing, her head another, and in the odd quiet moments, she wondered what James would think.

'Mr Caldicott is insisting on seeing you.' Mrs Rudge's glowering face appeared around Mary's bedroom door. 'He won't take no for an answer.'

'That's perfectly fine, Mrs Rudge. I asked him to call.'

'It ain't proper. You not out of your child bed but a matter of days.'

'I'll see him in the library. Please bring refreshments, some tea and cake perhaps.'

'I don't know. I just don't know.'

'Now please, Mrs Rudge.' Mary pulled her Indian shawl over her grey dress, revelling in the splash of colour after so long. She peered into the mirror, straightened her hair and with a nod of self-approval followed Mrs Rudge downstairs and into the library.

Hands behind his back, Caldicott seemed engrossed, peering out into the garden.

'It's a pleasure to see you.'

The wizened little man turned with a jump, almost as though he hadn't expected her.

'Mrs Fripp …' His lugubrious face quivered. 'I do hope I'm not disturbing you. Your note sounded most urgent.'

'Would you like to sit down?' She took a seat at the table and gestured to the chair opposite. 'I am keen to speak with you. I have a business proposition I wish to discuss.'

His eyes bulged. 'A business proposition?'

'Indeed.' The coil of excitement in her stomach tightened. 'I intend to sponsor the architect Francis Greenway and I would like your advice.'

'Sponsor?' The word spluttered across his lips, leaving a blob of spittle on his cheek.

'Yes. The Greenway brothers have suffered a setback; their commission on the internal fit-out of Clifton Assembly Rooms has been withdrawn and they are facing some financial difficulties.' She had no intention of mentioning bankruptcy, and besides, she didn't know whether it had eventuated. 'Sponsorship would give the Greenway brothers the opportunity to trade out of their difficulties. They have been busy seeking work wherever they can, providing paving stones, statuary for the aristocracy, and their repairs to St James church at Mangotsfield are progressing apace, and Francis … Mr Greenway is working on a set of plans for a house in Lower Crescent for a man named Doolan. He has such a talent. It should be fostered. Architecture is an art which, as you know, my father held in high esteem, and I feel he would approve such a move.' The words poured out of her mouth, and it wasn't until Mr Caldicott cleared his throat that she noticed the look of total horror on his wrinkled face. His raised, open hand shook and his mouth hung slack, but she couldn't halt her torrent of words.

'I understand that James will have left the property in trust for George, his eldest son, but I would like to make use of my dower. I would like you to draw up papers. It is an arrangement that would not only benefit us all, but allow me to pursue my own interests.' Mary beamed across the table at Caldicott, but he wouldn't make eye contact with her. How could he possibly object? Couldn't he see her enthusiasm? Apart from anything else it was not his position. He could offer advice, but he had no control over her activities.

Caldicott rummaged in the pocket of his greatcoat and produced a sheaf of papers. The action seemed to buoy him. He thumped them on the table and rose. 'Mrs Fripp, I hope you agree it is my duty as your late father's man of business to offer you the best advice and ensure the wellbeing of yourself and your sons at this difficult time. It is necessary that you are in possession of all the facts.' His Adam's apple bobbed most alarmingly, and he cleared his throat, yet again, then drew in a lungful of air. 'As you rightly surmise your late husband left the property, Manali, in trust for your eldest son, and there is a …' he cleared his throat again, '… a dower which passes directly to you for your use.'

Mary couldn't contain herself a moment longer. 'Then I fail to see what the problem is, Mr Caldicott.' She was entitled to spend her dower any way she saw fit and until George, and William, came of age she would remain at Manali and ensure their inheritance.

Caldicott's response dried on his lips as a knock sounded on the door.

'Will you take some tea, Mr Caldicott?' Mary crossed the room, pleased to have the opportunity to gather her thoughts.

Why was the man being so obtuse? Papa had amassed a large fortune through private business dealings and prize money before he and Mama left India and he prided himself on the investments he had made, particularly in the tea trade. 'Thank you, Leah. Put the tray on the table, and that will be all. I shall pour.'

Once the door closed, Mary turned back to Caldicott. 'As I said, I fail to see the problem. Perhaps you can explain.' She fiddled with the teapot and arranged the cups; until the man gave her a satisfactory answer, she had no intention of serving him. Her days of subserviency were behind her—well behind her. She cast her gaze to the painting of Mama and Papa hanging over the fireplace, convinced they approved of her stance.

'Very well.' Caldicott dusted his hands, a look of determination on his face. 'I had hoped to explain the situation more fully at a later date but if you insist.'

'I do insist.' She sat and folded her hands in her lap, head tilted to one side, a look of what she hoped was businesslike attention on her face.

'Your father's dying wish was to see your future secure and to that end he arranged your marriage to Captain Fripp. As your husband, he controlled the property and all your father's investments.' He annoyingly cleared his throat yet again. 'I have to inform you that the lavish lifestyle and ensuing outstanding debts incurred by Captain Fripp have eaten into the capital and I can see no other recourse but the sale of Manali and its contents.'

Lavish lifestyle? 'What lavish lifestyle?' And debts incurred by James? 'What debts?'

Caldicott took a large slurp of his tea before he continued, 'Captain Fripp made some unfortunate investments … the maintenance of the houses in Bath and Ascot and his stables at the racetrack.'

Mary shot to her feet. 'What houses in Bath and Ascot? What activities on the racetrack? What unfortunate investments?'

'It is not my position to explain Captain Fripp's activities but suffice to say the houses, and this estate, will have to be sold.'

'But the estate belongs to George.'

'We are obliged to settle Captain Fripp's debts. I doubt there will be many assets left.'

'Everything?'

'Due to Captain Fripp's liabilities the estate, the houses and contents are all encumbered. You will be able to keep a few personal possessions—your clothes, some books, possibly a painting or two as mementos.' His eyes strayed to the picture above the chimney, and he shook his head. 'I am so sorry, my dear.'

'Mr Caldicott, I require a complete reckoning. I feel certain there must be some mistake.'

'I'll leave these papers with you for your perusal.' He placed his hands flat on the tabletop and eased to his feet. 'If you have a question or two, please don't hesitate to contact me. As soon as you are ready, we will put matters in progress.'

A question or two? She had a thousand. But more importantly, never again would she be placed in this position. She would take control of her own life and that of her boys.

Eight

Mary sat staring blindly out of the window as the winter sun sank behind the trees, the shadows lengthened and the flurry of confusion in her mind settled. She had no doubt that Caldicott's reckoning would be accurate. It had never crossed her mind to wonder about James's activities. The business he conducted while he was away, the meetings he spoke of, his attendance at Ascot, the string of horses in the stable. A house in Bath and another in Ascot. And it was her own fault. She had never questioned her role—a brood mare, a well-heeled brood mare to boot. A dry laugh caught in her throat. It had taken Leah to have the courage to make that clear.

And what of Francis? What of her offer to advance him a loan, her thoughts of sponsorship? She'd painted such a rosy picture, imagined a life further from all possibility than those stars she'd reached for as a child, peering through Papa's telescope. She had never questioned James's authority, his business dealings, his plans for the future. She'd blindly accepted her role as a daughter, and then as a wife.

She picked up the bell on the small table and rang it ferociously. Leah appeared in less than a second. Obviously she'd shown

Caldicott out and had been hovering since, most probably at Mrs Rudge's insistence. Oh, Mrs Rudge! She'd have to tell her, and Leah, and Mudd.

'Leah, could you ask Mudd to come and see me? I have a note that needs delivering to Mangotsfield, and perhaps you'd like to go with him if Mrs Rudge agrees—you can call in and see your sister.' And probably start spreading the gossip of the downfall of the Manali household. She had to speak to Francis before that happened. He couldn't hear it from anyone else.

By the time Mudd appeared she had a note written asking Francis to call at his earliest convenience, as it was most urgent.

'Would you take this to Mr Greenway immediately, please, and wait for a response.'

Mary spent the remainder of the day working her way through the tangled maze of Caldicott's accounting, hoping against hope she'd find an oversight, a misunderstanding, a blunder, but she didn't. Hot tears stung the back of her eyes. It wasn't as though she had no understanding of matters of business. Before Papa passed, they'd often talked about his long and distinguished career, as Commodore William Moore of the East India Company, the company that had monopolised the tea trade and the enormous wealth of the Indian subcontinent. Commanding a 44-gun warship and two smaller ships, he accrued sufficient wealth through investments and prize money to allow him to retire to England and build Manali.

She and Papa had spent many a winter evening in front of the fire discussing his investments and the security they afforded—he seemed to recognise her interest, and thrill at her ability to comprehend the finer points of his financial dealings. But her marriage, that Papa had so promoted, had rendered her invisible and hamstrung. James had insisted on taking full responsibility for financial matters, and what a mess he had made. Caldicott hadn't misread the situation—if anything he'd underplayed the full extent of James's tomfoolery. George's inheritance was no more, Manali was mortgaged to the hilt and she and the boys were destined for a life of destitution.

A rap on the window brought her from her reverie. Francis stood, silhouetted against the darkening sky. Despite her despondency and disappointment her spirits lifted at the sight of his cheerful coat.

She threw up the sash, and he stepped through into the library. 'Mary.' He reached for her shaking hands. 'I came as quickly as I could. Mudd gave me a lift. I hope it is not too late.'

'Not at all.' She withdrew her hands and folded her arms. 'I'm afraid I have some bad news. Shall we sit down?'

She led the way to the table, gathered the spread of Caldicott's papers into a pile and tapped the sheaf on the tabletop to align them. Her mouth had dried and suddenly she couldn't frame the words. Just a day ago she'd believed her future secure and her dreams of pursuing her passion for architecture coming to fruition and now this ... She licked her lips. 'The conversation we had prior to William's birth was, I'm afraid, a little premature.'

She lifted her eyes to his face. He'd stilled, not a flicker of emotion in his face and a cat-like stealth to his limbs. What had she expected? That he'd toss her remarks aside and claim it was of no consequence? No matter how he might respond, she knew what it would mean to him. Years ahead of working to overcome the stigma of the loss of contracts, working with his hands, shifting rocks, recreating another's artistic dreams. No longer an architect—a builder, a stonemason at best.

She sucked in a deep breath. 'Mr Caldicott called this morning. It seems that James has left me in a difficult financial situation and I will have to sell Manali.' No need for him to know how difficult. She wanted no one's pity. She had only herself to blame. Legalities aside, she could have made more of an effort to secure Papa's hard-earned wealth, to question James about his largely absent, expansive lifestyle. 'I will have to renege on my offer to advance you a loan. Please accept my apologies.' She propped her elbows onto the table and dropped her head into her hands, unable to face the disappointment she knew she would see reflected in his face.

Very, very slowly she lifted her head and turned to him. Tears pooled in her eyes. 'I am so sorry.' They were so close she could feel the heat of his skin. Her own tingled in response as her blood warmed. She reached out for his hand, then snatched her fingers back. It was so wrong, so very wrong, this attraction, with James barely cold in his grave, and his sons needing all the protection and love she could offer.

'Mary, Mrs Fripp, forgive my bluntness but I am in love with you. I will never hamper your desire to express your ideas, in fact I would welcome your thoughts. Our love would not impede our lives but enrich them. Together we can make our mark on the world. I have no doubt of my ability to attract commissions, and I am in no need of a loan or sponsorship, with you beside me as my wife.'

She met his gaze, chin tilted to enable her to look into his hazel eyes. His statement seemed as revolutionary as her dreams. 'But what of my boys?'

'Why they will live with us. We will put the past behind us. My offer stands—my hand ...' he lifted his palm to his chest, '... my heart willingly given; we will be a family.'

Mary's mind stilled as she gazed into his eager eyes. Marriage. In spite of her secret feelings, it was the last thing she had imagined—a business relationship, but not a marriage. As the

possibilities blossomed, she found her voice. 'Mr Greenway ...
Francis. I thank you for your kind words, but I must bid you
farewell.'

'But you will consider my proposal?'

'I will.' They both stood and she went to step past him but the
space between them contracted. How was it that from one terrible, tragic accident so much happiness could eventuate? Their
eyes locked, a great trembling overtook her, and, in that moment,
she knew she would accept him.

Nevertheless, his kiss came as a raw shock. Kiss after kiss,
until he'd stopped her breath. She pulled away, her heart thundering and her mind swirling—her first kisses, after all those
years of marriage to James, and nothing as she imagined. Clamping her hand over her buzzing lips, she stumbled through the
open sash. His voice echoed, calling her name, but she didn't
stop, not until she reached the protection of the hedgerow, then
she bent double, catching her breath, resting her hands on her
knees, the taste of him still on her lips, the birdsong wild and
ecstatic.

Sometime later she made her way back into the silent library,
where his scent still lingered. Why had she run from him? Hand
shaking, she clasped the banister and climbed the stairs, a different woman to the one who had greeted Francis less than an hour
earlier, and the thrill of his kisses mingled with a spike of fear.
What now?

To love someone, to be loved in return, scared her, made her
skin feel raw. She wanted this, but she also wanted to pursue her
dreams. She couldn't imagine her life without him now—there'd
be no colour, no spirit, no brilliance, no radiance. Yet the thought
of loving someone so much—and being loved back—made her
exposed and vulnerable and scared.

She couldn't refuse him but she determined that this time it would be different. There would be love but also a meeting of minds, as they shared the same passion. They would explore the world together and strive for a better future—fine thoughts, fine words. She gave a wry smile. No matter what the future brought, she would never again be a woman defined by her relationship with a man.

Nine

1811
Bristol, England

Francis's bellow brought Mary running.

'What is it?' She skidded to a halt in the doorway.

'The effrontery of the man.' Francis whipped around, eyes blazing. 'Joseph Kay requests the pleasure of our company to celebrate the opening of his—*his*—great achievement. An important era in the annals of fashion, if you please, in one of the most elegant and complete … did you hear that … *complete*, establishments for public entertainment.'

Mary sank into the nearest chair. For months no one had talked of anything else, and she'd expected an outburst from Francis at some stage. He still hadn't got over the indignity of losing the commission for the internal fit-out of the Clifton Assembly Rooms, and the animosity between Francis and Kay had become legendary. An invitation was simply rubbing salt in the gaping wound of his pride.

'Will we go?' she asked. Truth be told she'd very much like to. 'It was your design, no one can deny that, and Kay could hardly

82

complete the interior without your inspiration and external construction. It's a magnificent building. You should hold your head high and be justly proud. The interior will change over time, but the facade will stand for hundreds of years—testament to your vision.' And she wasn't biased. People stood in awe to admire the nineteen bays of dressed limestone, the central block flanked by recessed wings and six Ionic columns that rose two storeys from the basement, crowned with the largest triangular pediment Bristol had ever seen.

Francis turned from the window and brushed back his hair with an impatience that always made her smile. No matter how erratic his temper, given time she could talk him around. Besides, he should attend and be acknowledged. Not only that, she should also stand proudly by his side. Sour grapes were poor medicine. She bent down and retrieved the screwed-up ball of paper from the floor and smoothed it out. 'It's a few days after George and William's christening.' When, finally, they would be a real family, the boys taking Francis's name, the past truly behind them.

It had been over two years since she and Francis had married, two years that had seen a complete change in their circumstances. In a gesture of defiance they had married on the very day the Greenway brothers' bankruptcy was declared. Francis's sister Mary and his brother John witnessed their marriage but no one else attended the ceremony.

When the vicar inscribed her maiden name, Moore, and wrote *spinster of the parish* on the register, she had leant forward to correct him, but Francis stilled her hand. 'We want no memories of the past, your previous life. George and William have never been baptised. Let us arrange that and they, like you, will carry the Greenway name forever.'

And so Mary Fripp vanished into oblivion and Mary Moore, spinster of the parish, left the church as Mrs Francis Howard

Greenway. Manali was sold, James's debts were cleared, and Mary, George and William moved to Francis's rented house at Ashton, just outside Bristol. Leah and Mudd went with them, and Mrs Rudge declared her working life over and retired to live with her daughter, much to Mary's relief.

All Mary had to remind her of her past were a few of Papa's books, her painting and drawing materials, and Mama's small rose cameo dangling from a silver bail. However, since the settlement of the Greenway brothers' bankruptcy charges and the subsequent sale of the business materials, Francis and his brothers were slowly trading out of their difficulties. Now she turned her face up to him and offered a loving smile. 'The opening would be the perfect way to celebrate, to show the world that despite all we have endured the Greenways are here to stay.'

Mary surveyed the elegant rooms with the faux marble columns, mahogany couches, and green and orange velvet drapery. They were soon to be used as tearooms, for cards and dancing and, with the large folding doors thrown open, for ticketed assemblies. It was an extravagant and luxurious public venue for those who took their leisure in fashionable Clifton, and all who set foot in the place would admire the building Francis had created.

'Mrs Greenway?'

Mary smiled down at the diminutive woman in a simple blue gown.

'Is your husband present?'

'Indeed he is.' Her gaze roamed the crowd; she'd lost sight of Francis while admiring the soaring ceilings. She searched in vain for his green coat amongst the flourishing crowd.

'Miss Bingle wondered if you could spare her a moment.' She extended her hand to indicate two wingback chairs placed in front of one of the windows overlooking the Mall. The woman's face was hidden but the top of her head, sporting a ruby red, feathered turban made her impossible to miss.

The name Bingle didn't conjure any specific person, which was unusual; she had a good memory for both names and faces and in the last two years had made a point of cultivating the ladies of the town. 'I'll fetch Mr Greenway.'

'Miss Bingle would prefer to speak to you alone.'

How very unexpected. With a final glance around for Francis she inclined her head and crossed the room, coming to a halt in front of the window.

The woman's inquisitive gaze melted into a friendly smile. 'Ah, Mrs Greenway. How delightful. Thank you for your time. Please take a seat.' Her sharply featured face was handsome rather than pretty, with an aristocratic nose and piercing grey eyes. They were of a similar age, neither young nor old. Mary did not recognise her.

'Thank you.' Mary perched on the edge of the chair, hands in her lap, and raised her eyebrows. 'How may I help you?'

'I wondered if you would like to call on me, tomorrow afternoon.'

Oh dear. Another interminable round of chatter, ladies with their embroidery who were more concerned with the actions of others than their own—although she should accept for Francis's sake. He liked her to cultivate people whose acquaintance might be beneficial and possibly lead to a commission. And, in all honesty, her curiosity was aroused.

Miss Bingle leant forward in her chair, eyes narrowing. 'I have a message for you.'

An invitation was one thing, a message completely different. Mary squeezed her interlaced fingers tight; another commission would benefit Francis immeasurably.

'We are in Bath at the moment—a break to take the waters and catch up with friends before we return home to Taunton.'

Mind made up, Mary drew in a sharp breath. Taunton was becoming quite the spot for country retreats. A fact she should mention to Francis. 'That would be most kind. Where will I find you?'

'Bennett Street, number nineteen, a short walk from the Royal Crescent. Four o'clock?'

'I look forward to seeing you.'

The moment Miss Bingle rose from her chair, the woman in the blue gown reappeared. Together they left, making no attempt to bid farewell to any of the other guests.

It wasn't until she and Francis returned home, and they sat with a nightcap, that Mary broached the subject of her strange encounter. 'I received an invitation today.'

Francis lifted his head from his pile of papers. 'Indeed.' His tone made it obvious that he had no interest in her statement. 'I am of the opinion symmetry is essential both inside and outside a building. Kay seems to have managed to ignore that principle.'

She peered over his shoulder at the piece of paper in front of him. He had redesigned the interior of the assembly rooms, adding additional columns and removing many of the couches and paintings.

'Frippery simply detracts from the intrinsic design. If I ...'

'I have been asked to visit Bath tomorrow,' she interrupted, knowing full well Francis's musings would lead to a storm of recriminations and a sleepless night. 'A Miss Bingle. Do you know the name? They have a house in Taunton and are visiting Bath for a short break.'

His head came up and his eyes narrowed. 'Did she wish to speak to me?'

'She said she had a message.'

He let out a derogatory snort. 'But didn't deliver it.'

'I thought that a little strange too, and she left immediately after we spoke. You were nowhere to be seen.'

'I was offered the singular pleasure of a tour of the remainder of the building.' His lip curled; the disappointment of the lost opportunity still rankled. 'The south wing and the apartments in the centre of the building will provide accommodation. The north will be a private house for our esteemed proprietor, and needless to say the hotel will be named for him. The Auriol, no less.' He lounged back in the chair and tossed back the remnants of his glass of port in one gulp. 'Will you go and see this Miss Bingle?'

'Yes, I think I will. I cannot imagine what message she might have but you never know, it could be beneficial. Word of mouth is without doubt the best way to foster business.'

Mary arrived at Bennett Street on the dot of four. After a sleepless night she still hadn't managed to come up with a reason why Miss Bingle had asked her to call, nothing that made sense. Quite why she hadn't demanded more information before she agreed to the visit, she had no idea. Why couldn't Miss Bingle have passed said message directly to her at the assembly rooms?

The carriage drew to a halt and Mudd jumped down to assist her. 'I'm not expecting to be very long. Please wait here.'

A neatly dressed young girl opened the door almost the moment she knocked and, before she had the chance to give her name, she was ushered inside and led into a small parlour at the front of the house. 'Mrs Greenway is here, ma'am.'

Miss Bingle had obviously watched her arrival from the window. She smiled and gestured to two chairs and a small table in front of a cheery fire.

'Come and sit down. Can I offer you any refreshments? A cup of tea perhaps?'

Mary resisted the urge to decline and demand she get straight to the point. 'Thank you. It's quite chilly this afternoon despite the sun.'

While Miss Bingle poured, Mary gazed around the cosy room. A large oil painting of a ship under full sail, battling a rough grey sea, hung above a small desk that stood against one wall. There was not a piece of paper or letter on the desk, just the pristine leather insert and a pair of silver inkpots. Other smaller paintings hung around the room, largely of a maritime theme, a strange choice for a woman. Tucked in one corner was a wheeled chair with a wicker seat and a blanket neatly folded over the backrest.

'Milk, lemon?'

Mary dragged her attention back to her hostess. 'No, thank you.' She took the fine porcelain cup and saucer and balanced them on her lap. 'I have to admit I am quite intrigued by your invitation. A message, you said?' A little rude but the thought of small talk simply made her more impatient.

Miss Bingle held the handle of her teacup between her finger and thumb and took a sip, her gaze never leaving Mary's face. She swallowed and gave a small sigh of pleasure. 'My friends believe the message may be of some interest to you.'

Shifting forward on the chair, Mary placed her tea on the table, ready to receive a piece of paper containing the message. None was forthcoming. 'You have a letter for me?'

'Oh no, a verbal message, and I must ask for your discretion.' · Her eyes hardened over the rim of her cup.

Stranger and stranger. Mary made a vain attempt to mask the frown of confusion creasing her forehead and nodded. 'Of course.'

'I have it on very good authority that there is a position available for an experienced architect. We wondered if Mr Greenway might be interested.'

Her heart gave a little jump. How perfectly wonderful, but why not approach Francis directly? 'I'm sure Mr Greenway would be delighted to discuss the matter.'

'We thought it might be better to seek your advice first.'

Whatever was she talking about? Francis would make his own decision. He frequently asked her opinion on a design, even requested she sketch her ideas on occasion, but he was very particular about meeting clients and discussing their requirements himself. She shook her head. The whole trip was a total waste of time. Why hadn't Miss Bingle asked to speak to Francis when they'd met yesterday? He would take it as an affront if she relayed the message. 'I'm not sure I quite understand. Mr Greenway always makes his own decision about commissions.'

'Ah, yes. Men make all the decisions, do they not, but in this case, as it would affect you and your two young boys, we thought it better to approach you first.' She pressed her fingertips together and brought them to her lips, her curious grey gaze making Mary's skin prickle. 'Once the front door is closed on the world a woman often has the final say, don't you think?'

Miss Bingle might well be correct, but it wasn't anything Mary would admit to. In the two years of their marriage, she had learnt Francis's erratic disposition demanded careful managing, but she wouldn't change her situation for the world. Not only did she love her husband, she adored the partnership they had formed, the opportunity to hone her skills and the hours they spent discussing architectural designs.

'More tea, my dear?' Miss Bingle didn't wait for a response but simply filled Mary's cup with the pale liquid.

Already the visit had lasted longer than she expected, and how did Miss Bingle know about George and William? Had she mentioned them when they'd first met? She didn't think so. 'What exactly is the message you would like me to convey to Mr Greenway?'

'We don't want you to convey any message until you have had time to mull on the offer.'

Mary pressed the back of her hand to her damp forehead to ease the ache. The wretched woman was being so obtuse. 'Perhaps if you told me a little more.' She tried and failed to keep the impatience out of her voice.

Miss Bingle leant towards her and murmured, 'Macquarie is urgently in need of a government architect.'

A government position. A tickle of anticipation traced Mary's skin. Would that mean a move to London? All government matters were dealt with in the capital. Francis would be thrilled, particularly if he found himself working alongside his mentor, Nash. Who was this man? What position did he hold? 'I'm not sure I know of Mr Macquarie.'

'Lachlan Macquarie. The governor of the Colony of New South Wales.'

'The penal colony?' The delicate cup rattled in the saucer. 'Why would a penal colony be in need of an architect?' She knew nothing of New South Wales except that it was the dumping ground for the worst type of prisoners, the home of pickpockets and cut-throats. A picture of ragged, starving men shackled in leg irons danced before her eyes.

'Times are changing, and the colony is outgrowing its doleful function. Many of the convicts choose to remain once they have served their sentence and received their pardon, and free settlers are taking up the challenge of a new life. With land grants and convict labour they establish themselves with the greatest of ease.'

Miss Bingle must have heard tell of Francis's financial woes. It was a commonly held belief that a charge of bankruptcy resulted in debtors' prison but that wasn't always the case—not if alternative arrangements could be made with the creditors. Francis and his brothers had fortunately escaped the horrors of a stint in Newgate, the foul medieval gaol in the centre of Bristol. 'Mr Greenway has committed no crime. He has been granted a certificate of bankruptcy and released from his debts. He and his brothers are seeking work and repaying their creditors.'

Miss Bingle didn't respond for a moment, then she nodded. 'Governor Macquarie has requested a government architect be sent to the colony to plan and superintend the erection of public buildings. He has high hopes that one day Sydney Town may become an elegant and well-appointed city. We believe Mr Greenway might be interested in the position, as a free settler.' She emphasised the words *free settler*. 'Many well-to-do families are making the move. They say opportunities abound and, interestingly, that the sun always shines.'

Mary's mind spiralled. A thousand questions batted like moths seeking the light. So many, many questions, but also possibilities if Francis was prepared to accept such a position. A curl of excitement stabbed at her breast—a chance, a new start, away from the clouds of mistrust and disappointment Francis's bankruptcy and her own financial straits had caused, a chance of regaining everything the past had stolen from them. 'Who should I tell Mr Greenway to contact?'

Miss Bingle cleared her throat. 'If you would be so kind as to convey Mr Greenway's answer to me, I will relay it to the relevant parties.' She rose. 'I give you good day, Mrs Greenway. I would appreciate it if you only discussed this matter with Mr Greenway.

The position has not as yet been made public. Thank you for your time. I look forward to our next meeting.'

Moments later Mary found herself standing on the doorstep, the door firmly shut behind her. Mudd spotted her and drew the carriage alongside. By the time she had settled, Miss Bingle was hurrying from the house, down the street in the direction of the large semi-circle of townhouses aptly named the Circus.

It wasn't until they left behind the crowded streets and reached the open road that her mind returned to Miss Bingle's exact words—her use of the word *we*. Who was she representing? Surely not the governor of the Colony of New South Wales.

Ten

1812

'Not now, Mary, I am busy.' Deep in thought, his face etched with a frown of concentration, Francis raked his fingers through his hair and gave a derogatory snort. 'Doolan has reneged on our arrangement for the house in Lower Crescent and destroyed his copy of the contract. I cannot believe this is happening a second time.'

'A second time?'

'Indeed. It reminds me very much of when that scoundrel Fripp tried to pull out after my initial plans for the improvements to Manali. Doolan is threatening to employ that swindler, Kay.'

'I thought the matter was resolved.'

'It is not. As a result of the bankruptcy, he is within his rights to withdraw from the contract, but he still owes me two hundred and fifty pounds for the preliminary inspections and plans and is refusing to pay. Even if the contract cannot be found, a gentleman's handshake is legally binding.' He flapped a sheet of paper at her. 'You should go and see the boys; Leah is at her wit's end.'

Two hundred and fifty pounds outstanding! How could that be? What she couldn't do with that—even half the amount would be a godsend. George had outgrown his clothes and poor William had never worn anything but his older brother's cast-offs, not to mention the frayed cuffs of Francis's threadbare coat and the soles of her own shoes worn through and then there were the outstanding wages she owed Leah, never mind Mudd. There was hardly anything left of the money she'd received after Manali had sold and James's debts settled. Ever since the bailiffs had demanded the sale of Francis's goods and furniture, they'd barely made ends meet, which didn't seem to bother Francis one iota. The security of a position as a government architect would remedy the situation in a flash.

She tucked George and William into their beds, kissed them goodnight and dimmed the lamp then made her way down the stairs. A sliver of light still shone beneath the door to the dining room. She pushed it open.

Francis sat, hair standing on end and a jumbled array of papers spread out on the table in front of him. She tiptoed across the room and rested her hands on the back of his chair. 'Francis?'

'I'm busy.'

'Francis, I have something very important to tell you.'

'Not now. Have you any idea where my copy of Doolan's contract is? Half my papers are missing. Did you clear the desk drawers before the bailiffs took the furniture?'

Mary eased around the table and reached for his hand. 'Francis, please, this is far more important. Governor Macquarie is in search of a government architect.' There, she'd said it.

'The papers from my desk drawers—where are they?'

'You told me not to touch them. I thought you would have dealt with the desk. Is the contract in your portfolio?'

The chair scraped across the floor, and he leapt to his feet. He snatched open his portfolio and scattered the contents over the table. 'No, it is not.' He flapped his long fingers at the profusion of plans, designs and drawings that lay in wild abandon. 'I must find the Doolan contract. Solicitor Cooke said he'd see to the matter of the two hundred and fifty pounds. That he would annotate the front page. If it is in writing on my copy, then Doolan won't have a leg to stand on.'

'Let me help you tidy these, and perhaps we will find it here underneath some of the other papers. Is it possible Mr Cooke has it?'

'Why would he have it? I believe it was at his instigation that Doolan destroyed his copy—the ridiculous clause allowed him to do so because of the bankruptcy. So much for a solicitor working in one's best interests. Doolan may as well employ Cooke. The jumped-up, high-handed, officious little man. Who does he think he is, parading around in his uniform? The man's retired. Have you ever seen Admiral Phillip strutting in his uniform other than on official occasions?'

'It's said the admiral is much recovered.' Mary tried for a change of subject. 'He and Mrs Phillip spent the summer in Clifton. I believe they've left now. His wife is such a delightful woman. I met them one afternoon, when they were promenading with Miss Chapman and Mrs Powell.' Mary stacked a pile of papers and drummed her fingers on the table. 'There's nothing resembling a contract in this lot.'

Sucking air through his teeth, Francis pushed the pile away and pinned her with a quizzical gaze. 'What were you saying about government architects?'

'The governor of the Colony of New South Wales, Lachlan Macquarie, has requested an architect be sent out to superintend the erection of public buildings and they wondered if you would be interested in the position. It would be such a marvellous opportunity, a fresh start. We could travel as free settlers and ...' The words poured out of her mouth, filling the room with such a sense of promise her skin prickled.

'And who exactly are "they"?' He threaded his fingers together and perched his chin on his hands. 'And how have you come by this scuttlebutt?'

'I told you, Miss Bingle, the woman I met at the opening of the assembly rooms, invited me to call on her. She passed on the information. I intended to tell you as soon as I came home but you appeared busy, and I had to attend to the children. I am to let her know whether you would be interested in learning more about the position.'

A loud, explosive and derogatory guffaw filled the room. 'Why would we be interested in a position fifteen thousand miles away from all that is civilised? The place is nothing more than a penitentiary!'

'Miss Bingle said there were hundreds of people ...' a slight exaggeration but the idea filled her with such enthusiasm, '... travelling to New South Wales as free settlers, and opportunities abound.'

'And if, just if, the position appealed, how do you imagine we could fund it? We would need money for the passage, money for accommodation.' He shook his head. 'Go to bed, Mary. I have more important matters to attend to.'

The bankruptcy had stripped Francis both mentally and physically. Gone was the inspirational genius who had so moved her when they had first met—it seemed almost a lifetime ago. There had to be some way she could overcome Francis's negative thoughts.

When Mary awoke Francis's side of the bed remained undisturbed, but she was hardly surprised; he frequently snatched an hour or two in the chair by the fire if he was working. She found Leah already in the kitchen, deep in porridge and sticky little fingers.

'Boys!' She dropped a kiss on each of their heads. 'Leah, do you know where Mr Greenway is?'

'He left about an hour ago, ma'am. Said he had business to attend to.'

Still chasing Doolan and the missing contract, no doubt. Perhaps he'd gone to see Olive and John. They'd remained at Limekiln Street, although the premises had been cleared in the same way the house had, and the contents of the workshop sold to help pay their outstanding debts.

Nibbling on a piece of dry toasted bread, Mary wandered into the dining room where the usual mess of papers littered the table along with an empty bottle of port, several sticky rings on the table and a dirty glass. She threw back the curtains, revelling in a pale, watery, winter sun, and shivered. There must be something she could do.

Mary spread the portfolio out on the table and searched through the papers for Francis's plans and elevations, drawings she'd become as familiar with as her own: the planned restoration to Thornbury Castle, the extensions to Manali, Prince of Wales Crescent and Royal York Terrace ... so much talent and vision, all of which sadly had come to nothing. Much to her amazement her own suggestions were noted and pinned to Francis's original plans.

If nothing else the glorious facade of the Clifton Hotel and Assembly Rooms, the market hall at Carmarthen and the repairs to St James at Mangotsfield were solid testimony to Francis's ability. She smoothed the creases and laid the plans, one at a time, inside his worn leather portfolio.

A somewhat screwed-up, flimsy piece of paper caught her eye. Not the usual cartridge paper Francis preferred, it looked as though it had been torn from a notebook or journal, and was covered in Francis's looping scrawl, a random and largely illegible scrawl interspersed with tiny drawings, a sweaty thumb print blurring the letters in places. She turned it over—34 LOWER CRESCENT, CLIFTON was written across the top in capital letters and underneath was the facade of one of the terraces, and below that a floor plan. Without a doubt it was a set of preliminary working drawings for Doolan's house. Francis often sought her opinion while he sat after supper sketching—his way of thinking, he always said—but she'd never seen these before.

Stretching her shoulders, she placed it in the portfolio and pushed to her feet. The day had turned gloomy and from the look of the darkening clouds, rain threatened. She pulled her robe tighter against the chill. Leah hadn't lit the fire, which was hardly surprising when she had the demands of two small children to deal with, demands Mary assisted with most mornings and here she was still in her nightclothes. With a shake of her head, she bent and collected the papers littering the floor then dropped to her hands and knees to retrieve a couple of pieces from under the table ...

Contract between Colonel Richard Doolan and Francis Howard Greenway for the ...

Pain blossomed as her head crashed against the underside of the table. Raising her hand, she gingerly threaded her fingers beneath her hair. No blood but an incessant thump. She crawled out from under the table, the contract clutched tightly in one hand. How had Francis missed it last night—how had she?

Easing into the chair, she spread the paper before her. It was without a doubt a copy of the contract between Francis and Doolan. Nothing looked unusual. The first page carried only the title and a date—January 1809. Six months after James died and just two months before the *Bristol Gazette* had announced the first notice of bankruptcy. She flicked the page over; again, nothing unusual but for a clause that work should be commenced within three months of signature. Francis's and Doolan's signatures and the sum of thirteen hundred guineas being full and final payment to be received within three months of completion. But there was no mention of the two hundred and fifty pounds for preliminary drawings. Why hadn't Mr Cooke annotated the contract as Francis had asked?

She rubbed at the lump on the back of her head. Had it been just a gentlemen's agreement, a handshake? What a load of poppycock! A clause about payment should have been included in the contract, as Francis had requested, and the payment should be made. After all, Francis had worked on the preliminary drawings—the proof was tucked in his portfolio—but obviously he hadn't presented them because he was tied up with the bankruptcy proceedings and prevented from commencing new work until the certificate was granted.

A surge of rage swept through her. The money would make all the difference to their hand-to-mouth existence. Then the pounding in her ears stopped and the world went still. The money might well pay their way to New South Wales—to a new life, the position and recognition Francis deserved. The prospect made her giddy.

Her pulse quickened and her palms grew clammy. Picking up her nib pen, she studied the front of the contract, chewing her lip. A plan began to form in her mind; there was something she could do. After all, if Doolan had destroyed his copy of the contract, who was to say an addendum *hadn't* been added by Mr Cooke to Francis's copy?

Francis didn't deserve to be treated in this high-handed fashion.

Sweat broke out on her forehead and a breath whistled between her lips, breaking the heavy silence. Doolan did in fact owe Francis the money; the preliminary plans proved it. Dipping the nib into the inkwell, she wrote in the perfect copperplate Papa had insisted upon:

Colonel Doolan to pay Mr Greenway £250 in addition to the 1300 guineas for finishing the house.

She leant back in the chair and studied her addition. Her penmanship matched the rest of the contract. There. It was done. Francis could take it to Doolan and demand payment. Then she would explain her plan for their new life to him—he wouldn't refuse if they had the funds to cover the trip, and they could always come home if the position wasn't to his liking. She would return to Miss Bingle and tell her they had discussed the offer, as suggested, that she'd spoken to Francis, and they would be travelling to New South Wales as free settlers where Francis would present his portfolio to Governor Macquarie. Who could knock back the proof of such genius? He would be offered the position of government architect in a heartbeat. Government Architect to the Colony of New South Wales. It had a certain ring.

'Ma'am, ma'am. Come quick, little George ...' Leah's panicked voice broke through her reverie. She snatched up the pen; a final signature was needed.

M

Her hand stilled and her blood turned to ice. What was she doing? A small squeak slipped between her lips. She'd almost written *Mary Greenway*. Swallowing the lump in her throat, she attached the letter 'r' and then wrote *Cooke*.

Mr Cooke

Perfect, just perfect. Mr Cooke was bound to support the claim rather than admit he hadn't followed Francis's instructions. The matter would be resolved, and the outstanding debt paid. 'Coming, Leah.' She scooped up the contract, tucked it in her waistband

and raced into the kitchen where chaos reigned. William sat beneath the table howling like a banshee, a trickle of blood running from the top of his forehead down the side of his face, and Leah was on her hands and knees trying to reach George, who was brandishing a wooden rolling pin.

'Stop it this moment!' She scooped up William. 'George! Put that down. Leah, take the rolling pin away from him.'

George darted across the room and hid himself in the corner behind the door while Mary turned her attention to poor little William. A cloth and some warm water revealed the extent of his injury and as his sobs diminished, she turned her attention to George who had curled up into a small ball and lay quaking as Leah loomed over him, hands on hips. 'Now, what happened?'

'I'm sorry, it's all my fault. I gave William some dough to play with and when I turned my back ...' She threw her hands up. 'They're becoming quite a handful.'

Leah was right. With only fifteen months between them, the two boys were in constant competition. 'Come over here, George, and apologise to your brother.' She dabbed at the small cut on William's head, which had already stopped bleeding, and although he had a large round bruise blossoming on his temple, she doubted George had inflicted any serious damage.

'Sorry.' George lisped his apology and patted his brother on the head, causing another scream from William.

'Look, William,' she said, lifting his hand to her head. 'Mama has a bump, too.'

Two sets of sticky fingers poked and prodded at her head and then George wiped the wet cloth across her head, sending a trickle of water down her cheek.

'All fixed now.' She settled William on the floor with his dough and broke off a piece for George. 'You play here quietly.'

She scooped up the rolling pin and handed it to Leah. 'I think we both deserve a cup of tea.'

'I'm so sorry. Look at your poor head.'

Ignoring the pounding, Mary smiled. 'Nothing a cup of tea won't fix.'

By the time Francis returned with a huge grin on his face peace was once more restored and the identical eggs sported by Mary and William were rapidly turning a delicious shade of bluish-purple.

Francis gathered William into his arms, turned him upside down and spun around. Much squealing ensued, and some concern about William's injury, but no harm was done and when Francis finally tired of the game Mary could hardly contain herself. It was the perfect time to tell him of her plan. She hadn't seen him so buoyant in a long time.

'Francis, I must speak with you. Leah, can you manage the children?'

'Their dinner is all prepared.' She jiggled William on her ample hip.

Francis threw an arm around Mary's shoulder and pulled her close. 'And I have news for you. Wonderful news! Come, I think it deserves a small sherry. Leave William here.'

Eleven

Francis led Mary into the dining room and closed the door. 'You've been busy.' He surveyed the tidy table and his neatly filled portfolio before pouring two glasses of sherry and handing one to her. 'Come and sit down and let me tell you my news.'

'I have news for you too, Francis.'

'Mine first.' He beamed at her.

Determined to make the most of his good humour, Mary sat back in the chair and took a small sip of the sherry and tried to stop her nose from wrinkling. The oversweet, sticky drink had never appealed to her and seemed only to intensify the pounding in her head.

'I have today placed an advertisement in the *Bristol Mercury* offering a reward of ten guineas.'

'For what?' she squeaked. Or more importantly, where would he get ten guineas? It would take every penny of the two hundred and fifty pounds from Doolan to pay their outstanding debts and passage to New South Wales.

'For the return of the missing contract. Doolan may or may not have destroyed his copy, but I am firmly convinced my copy was in the desk drawer. Whoever bought the desk when the furniture was auctioned is bound to have stumbled upon it. Apart from anything else the return of the contract will expose Doolan as the conniving swindler he is, his ungentlemanly behaviour will be publicly revealed, and he will be shamed. He won't be able to hold his head up in polite society if he doesn't pay up.'

Mary swallowed the lump in her throat and took another sip of the sherry. She coughed. 'What will you do if no one hands the contract in?'

'Hush, hush. I am convinced it will resurface. I shall take it directly to the assignees and state my case. I have plans to prove I had completed preliminary work on the project.' He tipped back the rest of his sherry. 'I'll finalise my drawings. I haven't shown them to you. I would appreciate your thoughts. When Doolan sees them, he may well change his mind and ask me to complete the project. The assignees will back me because a percentage of any money paid will go to my creditors and reduce the debt. No one stands to lose.' He beamed again, his hazel eyes glittering in the sudden shaft of sunlight illuminating the room. 'I shall sort through the rest of the paperwork. I intend to make a good copy of my plans for Doolan to support my claim. I don't want to hear any more about it. My mind is made up.' He turned to the table.

Mary's heart hammered in her chest; her breath came in short sharp puffs. Thank heavens she hadn't left the contract on the table. A cold shiver traced her shoulders. She hadn't thought this through.

'When will the advertisement appear in the paper?'

Francis lifted his head and sighed. 'Tomorrow morning. I have no time to waste with these plans. Not another word on the matter.'

Mary couldn't get the advertisement out of her mind, and she filled the remainder of the day with mindless chores. A trip to the butchers, sorting out George's old clothes for William—the poor child might never have anything he could call his own—and snapping at Leah and the children and still Francis wouldn't listen. Once the boys were tucked up safely for the night, she retired to her bedchamber and buried the contract under her chemises, trying to wish away her foolish scrawl, and finally sat flicking through the pages of Lady Wilbraham's diary, unable to concentrate on any of the words that had once provided her with such solace.

The morning dawned grey and dismal and once again Francis's side of the bed remained undisturbed. She found him sitting at the dining-room table with the morning copy of the *Mercury* spread out in front of him. 'It's here.' He stabbed the centre of the page and with his pencil drew a large circle around the double-column advertisement. 'Now we wait and see what transpires. I have finished the good copy of the plans. What do you think?'

Mary bent to the table. The facade of the five-storey terrace was little changed, but the internal floor plan presented a quite unusual layout. The front door opened onto a large hallway with a wide curved staircase. The next floor consisted of a dining room and three sitting rooms and a further staircase leading to the bedrooms. Above them in the attic were servants' quarters and the basement contained the kitchen, scullery and storage rooms. 'It seems very sumptuous.'

Francis tilted his head to one side and threw her a puzzled frown. 'Nothing else? What do you think of the enlarged windows? The view from upstairs will extend to the gorge and river. What about the staircase?'

'I think it is perfect.' She couldn't concentrate on the plans. 'What will happen if your copy of the contract is not handed in?'

'It will be. I am convinced it was in the desk drawer.' He sat back and stretched out his legs. 'Doolan's ruse will be revealed. I have left a promissory note for the ten guineas reward. I shall go and collect the contract, inform the assignees, and leave the matter in their hands. Now let me get on.'

Mary stilled and then her stomach sank. Francis's copy of the contract couldn't be handed in because it was sitting upstairs buried under her motley assortment of undergarments. If only Francis had told her he intended to place the advertisement.

A knock on the door brought her out of her reverie. 'Yes, Leah?'

'Mudd wants a word, ma'am.'

'I'll be right there.'

Leaving Francis to his plans, she followed Leah to the kitchen. She found Mudd on his hands and knees galloping George around the kitchen table. He gave her a sheepish grin. 'Off you get, young master, this old horse needs a rest.'

George slithered off his back and Mudd struggled upright and brushed down the knees of his trousers. 'I've got a note. Young boy delivered it.'

She held out her hand, her mind still consumed by her dilemma. 'Thank you.' She tucked it into her sleeve.

'The boy said it was urgent; he's waiting for a reply.'

She glanced at the folded sheet of paper; the handwriting was unfamiliar.

'It's from Bennett Street,' Mudd murmured.

She scanned the note. Miss Bingle wanting to know whether she could spare the time to call tomorrow morning. 'Come with me, Mudd. I'll write a reply right now.'

Mudd followed her into the sitting room and shuffled his feet while she sat at the small table and wrote a quick reply saying she'd call in at eleven. She folded the paper and held it out to Mudd. 'Give that to the boy.' And then she made a snap decision.

'Do you know the offices of the *Bristol Mercury*? I have something that needs to be delivered. Perhaps you could do it while I'm at Bennett Street tomorrow.'

'It's a good twelve miles to the offices—they're in Bristol, Broad Street. I'd be late picking you up. You weren't at Bennett Street much longer than half an hour last time.'

No, she didn't want that. Miss Bingle seemed to be very precise, and it would hardly reflect well if she was seen standing around in the street waiting for Mudd.

'Haven't got anything on this afternoon.'

Her head came up. This afternoon. Now. Then it would be done and there'd be no going back. It would secure the money from Doolan and when she saw Miss Bingle, she could accept the offer on Francis's behalf knowing the funds for the passage to New South Wales would be forthcoming.

'Why don't you come for a drive? Sun's out now and you look a bit peaky. You could do with some fresh air.'

'Very well.' She couldn't remember the last time she'd taken a drive. That was very much a luxury of the past. It wasn't until she'd worked her way through the documents after that fateful meeting with Mr Caldicott that she'd discovered Papa had bequeathed the coupé carriage and pair to Mudd as a token of thanks for his years of service, and it had never belonged to James—how it must have infuriated him. These days Mudd hired it out and was making a tidy sum—thankfully he didn't charge her. 'How soon should we leave?'

'As soon as possible.'

She glanced down at her dress and shook her head. She'd have to change. 'Very well, give the boy the note and I'll be ready in a few minutes.'

She bolted upstairs. It was the only solution. The prospect of handing over the contract filled her with such a great sense of relief. Her forgery wouldn't be questioned if the contract had been handed into the newspaper office anonymously and besides, she'd hate to spoil Francis's perceived one-upmanship with Doolan … and since he believed the amendment was already there, what harm would be done?

She rummaged beneath her undergarments and pulled out the contract, wrote a quick note saying no reward for the return of the contract was required, and tucked them both in her reticule. She then washed her face and hands, fastened her hair up under her bonnet and pulled on a matching pelisse. She'd be quite warm enough in the carriage and she'd have time, and a bit of peace and quiet, to decide what she should say to Francis this evening to convince him they should explore the opportunity afforded by the position in New South Wales. No more acting on impulse.

Francis barely lifted his head when she told him she was going out and before long she was tucked in the carriage with, at Mudd's insistence, a blanket over her knees, and they were bowling along the main thoroughfare.

When they arrived Mary sat well back in the shadows as Mudd took the small package containing the contract and note and disappeared into the newspaper offices.

Two minutes later he returned, touched his hand to the brim of his hat and, without speaking, clambered up, and the carriage once more rolled off down the road.

Beneath her hand Mary's heart thundered. Right or wrong, it was done. And she was pleased.

Once they were out of the city confines, she rapped on the box and Mudd stopped. 'Did they mention the reward?'

'I told them, like you said, there was a note inside the package and no reward would be collected.'

She threw Mudd a wry look. 'What would I do without you?'

'Not something you need to worry your pretty head about. I made a promise to your father that I'd look out for you.'

'Mary, Mary! Where are you?' Francis's voice boomed through the small cottage. 'I was right. They've just delivered the contract.'

Mary tucked William on her hip and clattered down the stairs, heart in her mouth. He'd simply refused to settle since he'd bumped his head but there seemed to be little else wrong with him.

Francis stood at the front door waving a handful of papers in the air, his excitement palpable. 'I knew it. Knew it had to be in the desk drawer.'

She licked her lips. 'Who handed it in?' It hadn't occurred to her to wonder whether anyone had recognised Mudd. Unlikely. He'd had his hat pulled well down and hadn't been in the office more than a moment or two.

'No idea. One of the print-room boys dropped it around just now. He didn't know. Said there was an anonymous note declining the reward. Must be our lucky day; that's saved ten guineas. Now to take it to the assignees and insist they commence action. I'll get the plans; there's not a moment to lose.'

Now. She had to do it now. She couldn't live with her duplicity a moment longer. 'Francis, I …'

'Look at this.' He stabbed his finger on the front of the contract. 'I wasn't mistaken—Mr Cooke had added the promissory memorandum. What a good fellow. See right here.' He traced the words she'd written. '*Colonel Doolan to pay Mr Greenway £250 in addition to the 1300 guineas for finishing the house.* He's even signed it. We've got him.'

Mary clutched William tight to her chest. He let out a monstrous wail and burst into tears. She jiggled him up and down, tears blurring her vision. 'Francis! Stop, listen to me. It's important.'

'Here, give William to me. I can't hear a word you're saying.' He took the boy from her arms.

'I wrote it. I found the contract amongst your papers and added the clause. I didn't know you were going to place an advertisement. I found your preliminary drawings. It made me so angry. You deserve payment for the work you have done. We could take up Miss Bingle's offer, travel to New South Wales. A new life, the position and recognition you deserve. I tried to tell you but there never seemed to be a moment.'

Francis stared at her, his mouth hanging open. William's cries settled to a whimper, and he stuck his fingers in his mouth and turned his big blue eyes on her. Francis's low, rich laugh took them both by surprise. 'Oh, my darling Mrs Greenway. What a stroke of genius.'

'Genius?' The word spluttered out of her mouth.

'I told you; when the contract was drawn up Cooke and I discussed the matter and he agreed the memorandum should be added. He's not going to dispute it.'

'But it's not his signature.'

Francis held the paper up high, out of reach of William's grasping fingers, and squinted at the signature. 'Not a bad facsimile, but now you mention it I can see the "M" at the beginning has the little curlicue you favour when you sign your name. No matter. Leave it to me. Here, take William.' He pushed the child back into her arms. 'I'll get the plans and go directly to see the assignees. I won't even mention it to them. I'll explain to Cooke afterwards; he won't question it. He was there when Doolan and I discussed it and shook on the deal. A gentleman's handshake is legally binding.' He rubbed his hands together in glee. 'I can't wait to see Doolan's face when he is forced to pay up.' With that Francis bounded out of the room, his feet barely touching the floorboards.

Mary sank down onto the bottom step and blew out a shaky breath of relief. Nothing, nothing had gone as she expected.

When Francis returned he was, if anything, even more exuberant. The assignees had taken the contract and the plans, listened to his explanation, and agreed to discuss the matter with both Cooke and Doolan.

'There was absolutely no problem at all.'

'And you told them I had amended the contract?'

He shook his head. 'Cooke will do the right thing. Once he sees the plans he won't dispute the matter.' He loosened his cravat. 'Doolan might well try and wheedle out of it, but he hasn't got a leg to stand on. Even if there was nothing on the contract Doolan knows full well a handshake between gentlemen is legally binding.'

Mary relaxed back in the chair. The angst of the last couple of days was finally seeping out of her body, leaving her boneless, enveloped in a sense of calm. 'I'm to call on Miss Bingle tomorrow. She will want to know whether you are interested in the position in New South Wales. I'm certain the two hundred and fifty pounds would cover our passage and you would no doubt receive a salary once we arrived. If it wasn't to our liking, we could always return.'

'There's talk of Nash being appointed the government's surveyor general in London. I rather prefer the title Government Architect. It has a nice ring to it, and they do say opportunities abound for free settlers in New South Wales.'

Mary bit back her smile as Francis parroted the very words she'd spoken earlier.

'The voyage might be arduous, however thousands of people have lived to tell the tale and I'm certain a government position would come with a free passage. Which will leave us with two hundred and fifty pounds to ease our settlement costs. I would insist you and the children accompany me and that we receive a land grant in the town.' He wrapped his arm around her shoulder and pulled her head against him. 'Imagine the house we could design and build, the perfect advertisement for my services. We might even receive agricultural land. I have made some enquiries and it appears there are many opportunities.'

Opportunities she had only dreamt of. In the warmth of the small sitting room, with the fire blazing and the possibility of their financial woes behind them, the horizon seemed bright and full of promise. Mary closed her eyes, imagining a life in a country where the sun always shone. A life where Francis's genius would be rewarded, and the stigma of his bankruptcy forgotten.

'Perhaps I should come with you and meet this Miss Bingle. I'd very much like to know who she is representing. Get rid of this cloak and dagger nonsense.'

A knock on the door startled Mary and she lurched upright.

'Now who can that be this late at night?' Francis grumbled. 'I've told Mudd he is to confine his visits to Leah to respectable hours.'

'His visits to Leah?'

'Oh, come now, Mary, you can't be that blind. He's been court-ing her for years.'

The knock sounded again, more insistent.

'And keeping her from her duties by the sound of it.' He pushed the stack of papers away from him and pocketed his pencil. 'I'll go and see who that is—and give them a piece of my mind. It's past eleven.'

Mary stretched out her legs, eased off her shoes and wiggled her toes in front of the fire. The rumble of voices from the hallway grew in volume but she couldn't catch a word. Then the door slammed, and everything went quiet. She sat basking in the promise of the future, waiting for Francis to reappear.

A draft whipped around the back of her neck, and she spun around. Mudd towered in the doorway, an expression of undisguised shock on his usually placid face.

'What is it?' She scrambled to her feet.

He cleared his throat, scratched at his head. 'It's Mr Greenway. They've taken him away.'

'What do you mean, taken him away?' She brushed past Mudd and threw the front door open, scanning the empty street.

'Constables have taken him to Newgate. They've refused bail.'

'On what grounds?'

'A sworn deposition—something to do with a forgery.'

Twelve

The gaol, Newgate Bristol, lurched drunkenly against the walls of the Cat and Wheel on the low-lying, damp ground between the old castle moat and the River Frome. Noxious, insanitary and appalling, the prison tainted the air with the stench of misery.

Mudd drew the carriage to a halt, jumped down and opened the door.

Mary choked back a sob and covered her nose and mouth with her handkerchief and stared up at the tall, once whitewashed building. She was thankful Mudd had refused to bring her the night before, insisting it would be better in daylight. 'How do we get in?'

'You stay here. I doubt we'll get inside but we can at least make sure he's here.' He turned up the collar of his greatcoat and tugged his sleeves down over his hands before crossing the stinking excuse for a street, where he ambled up to a narrow, barred door and raised his fist.

After an excruciating wait the Judas window squealed open. Mudd stuck his face close, gesticulated madly, the fingers of his big hands splayed, then stamped his foot.

Unable to stand the agony, Mary lifted her skirts and jumped out of the carriage, narrowly missing the open sewer. Mudd's fingers closed on her sleeve before she managed to right herself. 'Get back inside the carriage. It's no place for a lady.'

'Is he here? I must see him.' And ask him why he had let them take him away, why he hadn't told the truth.

'He's here. I got that much out of the turnkey, but we're not getting in there without someone in authority or a purse full of coin. Never mind what you might catch. The stink's worse than a whore's ... beg pardon.'

Mary's mind spiralled. 'There must be someone ... take me to Mr Cooke's offices.' Francis's solicitor would know what to do. Maybe the assignees. They'd managed to save the Greenway brothers from a stint behind bars—but that was for debts, not forgery.

'Trouble is forgery's a hanging offence.'

The world wavered and spots danced in front of her eyes. 'A hanging offence?' How had she not known?

Mudd reached out and steadied her. 'Thought you'd know that.'

She hadn't given it a thought, certainly not when she'd blindly written Cooke's name on the contract—and then handed it to the newspaper office for all to see. A squeal of horror slipped between her lips. 'I must speak to Mr Cooke.'

'Cooke's not going to be much help. Nor the assignees. They must have informed the authorities. Like I said, this is no place for a lady.' Mudd's hairy eyebrows pulled together in a frown, and he pursed his lips. 'Best leave matters as they stand right now.'

Mary drew in a deep breath and regretted it instantly as the stink of the open sewer stuck in her craw. 'I don't know what to do.'

'No point hanging around here. Besides, you've got an appointment with Miss Bingle.'

Thoughts of Francis incarcerated in that terrible place sat like rocks in her stomach. 'I haven't got time for that. I must see Francis.'

'Might be Miss Bingle can help you. Heard tell she's got powerful friends.'

'How would you ...?' Mary pressed her lips together. She tended to forget that Mudd spent a lot of his time driving people around Bath and Bristol and was privy to all sorts of scuttlebutt. Besides, he was correct. How else would Miss Bingle have known about a government job in the colonies if she hadn't got friends in high places? Although when she heard of Francis's latest dilemma any offer of a position as government architect would take flight.

As soon as they left the narrow confines of the old streets Mary forced down the window, took off her hat and unpinned her hair. The stench of the prison clung to her like a second skin, turning her stomach every time she inhaled. Poor Francis. Whatever must it be like to be locked up inside that foul cesspit of a place? She had to get him out. Mr Cooke would understand if she went to him and admitted what she had done—apologised and explained how much she regretted her foolish, spur-of-the-moment action which Francis knew nothing about. Once she admitted the truth, told him she was responsible, he would have to see to Francis's release. He was a gentleman, he'd understand, and no gentleman would see a lady incarcerated in a prison with a reputation like that of Newgate.

They arrived at Bennett Street with barely a moment to spare and the young girl opened the door before Mary had the opportunity to knock. Once again, she was led into the small parlour on the ground floor and offered a cup of tea. She accepted, hoping to wash away the taste of the gaol that still coated her mouth.

'So, my dear.' Miss Bingle sat down and handed her the cup of tea. 'Have you reached a decision?' She leant forward in anticipation. 'How did Mr Greenway respond to our offer?'

The air wavered before Mary's eyes again as the gaol's walls loomed in her imagination and all hope of a new start, a new life, disappeared into an interminable pit of misery.

'Mrs Greenway.' The teacup vanished and Miss Bingle pressed a handkerchief into her hand. 'Mop your eyes now. Nothing can be that bad.'

Mary lifted her hand to her face and found her cheeks wet. She was crying! She never cried. Not even in her darkest moments, and there had been plenty of those. She dabbed at her eyes then studied the sodden handkerchief and shook her head.

'Take a minute. Sit quietly and let your breath settle. Do you require smelling salts?'

'No, thank you. I'm sorry. I don't know what came over me.'

'You don't strike me as someone who resorts to tears. How can I help?'

'I'm not sure you can.' She swallowed the lump in her throat threatening to choke her, remembering Mudd's comment about powerful friends. What had she to lose? 'Mr Greenway was very interested in the position but unfortunately he has been taken to Newgate on charges of forgery.' Her lower lip trembled. 'It's a hanging offence.'

Miss Bingle's gaze hardened, and she raised a pointed finger. 'Don't you dare cry again. I forbid it. You must be strong.'

Mary shuddered and choked back a wail.

'If he has been falsely accused, he must have representation. Now what exactly happened?' Her narrowed eyes held a look Mary couldn't quite read.

She lifted her shoulders, steadied herself to tell of her involvement, then stopped. Francis must not have said anything about the part she'd played, otherwise she would have been arrested. If Miss Bingle and her friends could help, better not confuse the issue. 'The constables came to the door and took him away. I went to the gaol, but they wouldn't let me see him.'

'I see.' Miss Bingle smoothed down her skirt, walked a few steps, paused, then turned back. 'Drink your tea and try to settle. I shall be back in a few minutes.'

Mary sipped at her tea. The sound of footsteps on the stairs echoed. She heard a gentle knock, a murmured response, a woman's voice pitched so low she couldn't decipher the words, then the click of the door closing. It hadn't occurred to her to wonder if anyone else might be in the house. The carriage clock on the mantle ticked away the minutes. She put down the empty cup and paced the floor. How much longer would Miss Bingle be? The few minutes she'd promised had well and truly passed. Through the window she could see Mudd's stocky frame lolling against the side of the carriage, the smoke from his pipe drifting into the air. She clenched her fist, raised it to knock on the glass …

'Very well.'

Mary spun around. Miss Bingle stood framed in the doorway. 'I'm afraid there is nothing more you can do for the time being. Go home and see to your boys. Evidence will have to be gathered; an indictment prepared. In the meantime, this should ease Mr Greenway's plight.' She held out a small pouch. 'Get that man of yours to grease the turnkey's palm, arrange a basket of provisions and stay away. Newgate is no place for a lady, and there is nothing else you can do. I'll contact you the moment we know more.'

We. Again, the use of the word *we.* 'I can't take the money.' She clutched her hands behind her back.

'My dear, please. Now is not the time for pride. Have you the funds to ease Mr Greenway's situation?'

Mary's cheeks flamed. Now her measly inheritance had dwindled away, they relied entirely on the money allocated to Francis by the assignees when he completed a job and there wouldn't be any more if he was incarcerated and unable to work. Maybe Olive or John? No, they had their own responsibilities, not least their mother. Her stomach turned over. How was she going to explain the situation to Francis's family? 'I can't take the money without knowing who it is from.'

'My dear, you're simply going to have to trust us.' Miss Bingle pushed the pouch into her hand. 'Off you go. I shall be in contact the moment I know the next step. Not a word to anyone.'

Unlike her previous visit, Miss Bingle showed her to the door. Mudd snapped to attention, helped Mary into the carriage and climbed up onto the box seat. She lifted her hand to wave farewell, but the door had already closed. A curtain twitched at the window on the second floor, a bedroom window, no doubt. The shadow of a face—a woman's face, of that she was certain—hovered. She blinked and it was gone. When Mudd had said Miss Bingle had powerful friends, she'd imagined a man, several even, not another woman.

Mary rested her aching head as the carriage bumped and bounced along the three-mile stretch of road back to Ashton, the pouch of money clasped tightly in her fist. Snippets of the conversation with Miss Bingle danced around in her mind, hotly followed by thoughts of her own duplicity. She couldn't continue to allow Francis to take responsibility for her actions, to let him wallow in the filth of Newgate. Then Mudd's words echoed, backed up by Miss Bingle: *It's no place for a lady* … She'd blithely presumed Mudd was simply referring to the gaol, but it was almost as though they both knew what she'd done. Then she remembered Mudd's suggestion that Miss Bingle had powerful friends, which brought her right back to Miss Bingle's statement that she would have to trust—she hadn't said *her*, she'd said *us*.

Mary lurched upright and rapped on the window. Mudd slowed the horses and pulled to one side of the road. She opened the carriage door and jumped out.

Mudd slipped off the box seat and came to her side.

'Who are Miss Bingle's powerful friends and how do you know about them? Is it fact or scuttlebutt?'

He shifted from one foot to the other, groped in his pocket for his pipe, and made a great play of prodding the bowl and sucking.

'Mudd?'

'Not sure. But I'm more than certain Miss Bingle doesn't live at the house in Bennett Street.'

A picture of her slipping furtively down the road after their first meeting, and then the woman at the upstairs window, flashed before her eyes. 'Then why would she see me there?'

'She's what might be best described as a go-between.'

Whatever was he talking about? 'A go-between?'

'Someone who speaks for another, passes on messages and directions for another.'

'Well, who is Miss Bingle go-betweening for? Who is the person who doesn't want to make themselves known? It all sounds very ... what was the expression Francis used ... cloak and dagger. And why?'

Mudd shrugged his shoulders. 'Don't rightly know but I could hazard a guess.'

'Go on then.'

The tops of his ears turned brick red. 'I might be wrong, and I wouldn't want you going around quoting me.'

'Why would I do that? Are you going to help me or not? Miss Bingle says I need to get a basket of provisions to Francis before he starves.' She jangled the pouch under his nose. 'I want to know who's paying.'

'Last I heard Admiral and Mrs Phillip purchased the house in Bennett Street, good five years or so back. He hasn't been a well man, but they say he's on the road to recovery after taking the waters at Clifton.'

'Yes, I met him and Mrs Phillip some summers ago, but I didn't know they lived in Bath.'

'Come on. You've missed the point. Admiral Phillip, Arthur Phillip, founding governor of the Colony of New South Wales. Retired now.'

'Ohhh!' Mary covered her mouth with her shaking hand. Government architect, Governor Macquarie, Governor Phillip. The blocks stacked neatly in place. 'And you think Miss Bingle is the go-between.'

'Stands to reason, don't it?'

Thirteen

'Any hope of Francis getting the position is long gone.' Mary dropped her head into her hands. 'If he's a convicted forger he'll …' The word *hang* danced on her lips. She spat it aside.

'Come on, it's not that bad. He's still got to be sentenced.' Leah took the two bottles of ale from Mudd's hands. 'That's right, isn't it?'

Mudd lifted his shoulders and turned down the corners of his mouth. 'Like I said, I might be wrong, but it seems to me there's more to all this than meets the eye.' He cocked his head to one side. 'Might just be matters are falling into place quite nicely for some.'

It was highly unlikely that Francis would see it like that. Neither would she if Francis chose to tell the truth. She reached for one of the bottles of beer. 'I thought you were getting provisions for Francis, not ale. I must see him.'

Mudd plonked himself down at the kitchen table and threw Leah an exaggerated wink. 'Have you told her the plan?'

Leah shook her head. 'Thought I'd leave that for you.'

'Plan, what plan?' Ever since they'd carted Francis away control had slipped through Mary's fingers. She blamed Mudd, but looking at the flush on Leah's face she wasn't too sure. Everyone seemed to be conspiring to keep her in the dark— Miss Bingle included. 'Wouldn't it have been better to spend the money on food?' she snapped.

'I've sorted out a basket of provisions.' Leah hefted a large wicker hamper onto the table. 'The ale's for the turnkey. Might make him look the other way if we need him to.'

'Why would you need him to look the other way?' She took a sideways glance at Mudd, who'd thrown Leah another wink. 'What are you two up to?'

'Leah's coming with me. Need someone to keep an eye on your back in a place like that.'

'You told me it was no place for a woman.'

'Nah. I told you it was no place for a lady. Leah knows how to handle herself in a pinch.'

Mary shot to her feet, hands on her hips. The audacity of the man. He'd become far too familiar. He still saw her as the young girl he'd kept an eye on when Papa was at his books. 'And I don't?'

'Your father'd have me hide for leather.'

'Papa's not here. I need Leah to mind the children.' As if on cue a wail drifted down the stairs. 'See to William, please, Leah.' Mary chewed on her lip, waiting for Leah to leave the room. If Mudd was happy to take Leah, the woman he had more than a soft spot for, then their dire predictions about the gaol had to be exaggerated. Besides, if she went it would give her the perfect opportunity to find out why Francis had taken responsibility for her forgery. He couldn't stand trial for her foolishness. Miss Bingle had said an indictment had to be drawn up. How was that supposed to happen if no one knew the full story? 'I'm coming with you. Not Leah. I must speak to Francis.'

Mudd narrowed his eyes and folded his arms, his muscles flexing, in a stance she had become familiar with over the years. 'There's no point in looking at me like that. I've made up my mind.'

'You'll spend the whole time retching into your handkerchief.' He raised his hand to his mouth and made a particularly disgusting noise.

'Don't be ridiculous. I know what to expect now.'

An exasperated huff issued from behind Mudd's hand. 'You'll have to do something about those shoes, and your clothes come to that.'

'What's wrong with my clothes?' Mary looked down at her slippers, the memory of her near miss with the open sewer springing to mind. She'd told Leah to give away all her gardening clothes when they'd left Manali. These were the last decent pair of shoes she had, and the fine lawn of her dress snagged at the slightest opportunity. 'I'll borrow Leah's boots and …' A snort stopped her in her tracks as Leah appeared with an armful of clothing.

'If you're determined to go you better wear these.' She threw the pile of clothing down on the table. 'It's the things you told me to get rid of when we left Manali. I thought they might come in useful one day.'

It wasn't until Mary had dressed in her oldest boots, squeezed into one of the heavy cotton gowns she'd favoured in the garden before the two boys were born and covered her head and shoulders with a ratty old shawl, that Mudd, and Leah, finally gave their nod of approval.

Mudd left the carriage outside the old town walls, and they made their way on foot through the darkened streets, dodging the sewers, potholes and steaming piles of freshly deposited horseshit.

Raucous shouts, laughter and the occasional groan and thump of a well-placed punch signalled their arrival outside the Cat and Wheel. With an apologetic grin, Mudd slipped an arm around her shoulders and chose the safest path to the gate. 'Let me do the talking. You just keep your eyes downcast and your mouth tightly closed.' He rapped on the wicket and the Judas window opened, bringing with it a wave of fetid breath and a wizened, weather-beaten face.

'You again. Told you. No visitors.'

'Thought this might oil the hinges.' Mudd held up two of the bottles of ale. 'We've got a basket of provisions for the prisoner.'

The Judas window slammed closed.

'What's the matter with the old fool …' The words knotted on her tongue when Mudd brought his finger to his lips. The clang of rusty bolts being drawn and the rattle of keys filled the silence. The wicket groaned open, revealing a dank, dark passageway.

Mudd stepped inside first. Mary followed and the door slammed behind them, cutting off any light. She reached for the back of Mudd's coat. He grunted in approval and took a step. As her eyes adjusted to the darkness the ancient, seeping walls seemed to close in, but Mudd never hesitated, leading her past a series of closed, barred doors and up a flight of worn stone steps. 'How do you know where to go?'

'Might have had a brush inside these walls in me misspent youth. Nothing's changed since King Charlie got the chop.'

'That was in London, a hundred and fifty years ago.' Maybe more.

'Still Newgate. Come on. We're heading for the day rooms—there's two of 'em, there's a sleeping room off it. He won't be in "the pit" because he ain't being transported. It's a nasty suffocating hole. Wouldn't wish it on me worst enemy.'

A shudder worked its way down her body, and she stumbled. If that's what they did to prisoners awaiting transportation, what about those with a death sentence hanging over their heads? Mudd snatched at her arm and caught her as her foot slipped in a fetid puddle. 'Not much further now.' His words heralded the hum of voices and as they rounded the corner a dim light wavered and grew brighter. 'Tennis court.'

'What?'

'Tennis court. It's the exercise room. We'll see if he's in there.' Mudd stepped into the large room. A sudden, oppressive silence descended, and all eyes turned to them. 'Gentlemen, we're after a Mr Greenway.'

A hoot of laughter greeted Mudd's words and a tall, skinny fellow with a pockmarked face framed by wisps of greasy hair bowed low, held out his arm and gestured to the back corner of the room.

Mary's heart missed a beat, then picked up a furious pace as she flew across the flagged floor. Francis sat on a stool, lolling against the wall. He lifted his head, gave a shake, and drew himself up to his full height, his chin thrust out. He locked eyes with her, and a cry slipped between her lips. Dark sunken circles marred the pale skin beneath his eyes. In the two days since she'd seen him, all colour had leached from his face. 'Francis!' She sank to her knees at his feet, eliciting a licentious roar and a series of catcalls from the audience of pickpockets, prostitutes, shoplifters and worse.

Francis tossed his head and inhaled loudly. 'What are you doing here?' He shot to his feet, reached for her hands and hauled her up.

'We've brought you some provisions.' She snatched a glance over her shoulder and lowered her voice. 'I have to speak to you. You shouldn't be here. You've done nothing wrong.' If she could only erase her foolish, foolish action, Francis wouldn't be here rubbing shoulders with Bristol's worst.

'Hush your mouth. You are my wife. I am responsible for your wellbeing.' He pushed past her and fronted Mudd. 'What have you done? Did you not give a single thought to your actions? Get her out of here.'

No. She wouldn't leave. She had to speak to Francis, tell him what Miss Bingle had said. Tell him she would confess. Squaring her shoulders, she stepped up next to him. 'Come, have something to eat, you must be starving. Mudd, is there somewhere we can go to be more private?'

'Not unless you've got another one of those pouches.'

Francis's head jerked up. 'Pouches. What pouches?' He dragged her into the corner of the room and sat her on the stool. Mudd followed, his broad back shielding them from the rampant curiosity of the other inmates.

'Well?'

'I went to see Miss Bingle.'

'Lower your voice,' he snapped.

'I told her what had happened, that you'd been brought here on charges of forgery.' She lowered her voice, trying to keep her tone even, trying to control the scream bubbling in her throat.

'She gave me money, said she and her friends would discuss the matter and decide what should be done. She said an indictment would have to be drawn up and that you would need representation. I'm going to see Mr Cooke and tell him ...'

'You will do no such thing.' Francis's raised voice bounced back from the solid stone walls and the other prisoners raised their heads.

'Forgery is a hanging offence. A forgery I ...'

He slammed his hand over her mouth, shutting off her words, and then the tension left his body and he knelt in front of her, drawing her down, taking her cold hands in his. 'If I had claimed innocence the finger of blame could have come to rest on your shoulders. I am your husband. When we married I vowed to cherish you, love and protect you, and I will do that until my last breath. Let matters take their own course.' He pressed his fingers against her lips. 'What's in the basket? I'm starving.'

Pleased for the moment's respite to gather her thoughts, she pulled the basket towards her, brought out a pork pie and handed it to him. It disappeared in three bites.

'If you hadn't done it, I would have. That's the end of the matter.' He chewed slowly as though thinking, then the corner of his mouth lifted in the beginning of a smile. 'Once I have an opportunity to state my case the matter will be resolved. Cooke knows Doolan's in the wrong.' He wiped away the pastry crumbs with the back of his hand.

'How long will they keep you here?'

The darkest scowl crossed his face, and he tightened his grip on her arm. 'Until the charges are laid, and then I will have the opportunity to put the record straight. In the meantime, Mudd, I am happy to receive sustenance, but Mary will not set foot in here again.' He wrapped his arms around her, gave her a quick embrace and whispered, 'I love you.'

'Come along.' Mudd prised her fingers from Francis's lapels and led her away. 'You look as though you've been to hell and back.'

They retraced their steps, Mudd's arm around her shoulders guiding her. When the wicket slammed behind them, they both blinked owlishly in the light.

'Are you all right?'

Mary nodded, tried for a smile, and failed. The stench of the gaol clung to her clothes, invaded every inch of her skin. She swayed against him.

'You don't look it. Your face is whiter than Leah's washing. Let's get you home.'

No matter how hard Mary scrubbed her body she couldn't remove the taint of the gaol. In accordance with Francis's wishes she stayed away while Mudd worked his way through the contents of the money pouch and delivered daily provisions. She still hadn't heard from Miss Bingle.

The note arrived when she least expected it, on a Saturday afternoon, asking her to attend the morning service at the church of St Nicholas the following day. She had no idea where the church was nor why she hadn't been summoned to Bennett Street.

She found Mudd and Leah in the garden sharing a bottle of ale—hopefully not part of Francis's rations—and George and William bowling a hoop up and down the path to the privy. 'Mudd, do you know where St Nicholas church is?'

He struggled to his feet and scratched his head. 'Not right sure I do. Leah, have you any idea?'

'Which one? Bristol or Bathampton?'

Mary's heart sank and she pulled out the note from her sleeve. She hadn't read any further than the initial sentence. She scanned Miss Bingle's neat hand and at the bottom of the page found a line that read *Church of St Nicholas, Bathampton*. 'Bathampton. How far is that?'

'Be about fifteen miles or so.'

'It's down near the river,' Leah said. 'Me granny's buried there. I can show you the way.'

That was the last thing Mary wanted. 'It's business, Leah. I need you to stay here and take care of George and William.' She shot a glance at Mudd.

'They'd like a ride. It's been weeks since they've been any-where. There's plenty of room.'

Mudd raised his eyebrows, Mary shook her head. 'You'll stay here, Leah. It's not something for women and children.'

'Better make sure you're dressed like a lady then.' With a grunt of annoyance, Leah marched across to the privy, snatched the hoop from George and with one child dangling from each hand flounced back into the house.

'I'm sorry, I should have spoken to you alone.'

'She'll do as bid. I don't want her involved any more than you do. Her nose has been out of joint since we went to the gaol—likes a bit of adventure does our Leah.' Mudd gave a rueful smile. 'We'll have to leave before nine if we want to be there by eleven. Why not Bennett Street?'

Sometimes it seemed she was stumbling around in the dark, controlled by some mighty puppeteer who declined to offer any explanation for the moves she was forced to perform. 'I've no idea.' She grimaced and lifted her shoulders.

'No point in wondering. You'll find out what's what tomorrow. There's not much left in that pouch, enough for one more hamper. I'll take it Monday. See what you can do about getting some more.'

By the time Mary came downstairs on Sunday morning Leah had recovered her good humour and the boys were shovelling in their morning porridge.

'Do I look the part?' Mary gave a small spin then smoothed down her blue pelisse and adjusted her hat.

'That you do. I'll expect you back by dinnertime. I've got a nice chicken and the last of the carrots and potatoes. Wouldn't want to miss that.'

Mary placed a hand on her arm. 'Thank you, Leah. I don't know what I'd do without you.'

'Can't see anything like that happening, especially now this nonsense about going to the colonies has passed.' She gave a bright smile. 'Mudd's got the carriage ready. No time to waste. Say goodbye to your mam, boys.'

George and William chorused a farewell through their porridge as she smoothed their soft hair. 'I'll be back soon. Be good for Leah.' She closed the door behind her, not wanting to leave. Leah's words echoed in her mind with a prophetic toll. She'd lain awake most of the night drenched in despondency. If only she hadn't endorsed the contract, she might well be meeting Miss Bingle to finalise their departure to New South Wales, the future full of promise and Francis's position secured. Instead, all her dreams and hopes lay buried beneath Francis's honour and her own stupidity. A fine sponsor she'd turned out to be.

The miles to Bathampton ticked over in a flood of self-recrimination until Mary had convinced herself that Miss Bingle would wash her hands of them. When Mudd drew the carriage to a halt she sat for a moment willing her stomach to settle. The church bell tolled, and a stream of people, none of whom looked remotely like Miss Bingle, traipsed into the ancient church.

Mudd's face appeared at the window. 'You ready?'

'She's not here. I've been watching the people go in. There's no one who looks anything like her.'

'Maybe she's sent someone to pass on a message.'

Which was exactly what Mary feared. That would be the easiest way to step back and avoid any recriminations. Pretend it had never happened—that she had never suggested Francis should take up the position of government architect.

'Here we go.' Mudd cocked his head. A carriage meandered across the bridge, the two immaculate horses stepping in perfect time.

'How do you know?'

'Trust me. I know decent horseflesh when I see it and that carriage is worth a quid or four.'

The carriage drew alongside, and a gloved hand pulled the curtain aside revealing, for a fleeting moment, Miss Bingle's face beneath a wide-brimmed hat. The door opened.

Mudd handed Mary down and she slipped into the carriage and settled on the plush seat.

'I thought perhaps we'd take a turn around the village.'

Mary could do no more than nod. Her heart was pumping nineteen to the dozen and her chest felt as though it would explode.

It wasn't until they had left the church behind them and were crossing the bridge that Miss Bingle lifted her head and folded her hands in her lap. 'Matters are resolved.'

Licking her dry lips, Mary waited for the axe to fall.

'We will attempt to make Mr Greenway's stay in Newgate bearable through regular payments to the gaolers; perhaps your man would be good enough to organise that. We expect it to be a month, maybe two, while the indictment is prepared and evidence gathered, and then the matter will come before the court.'

Mary glanced back across to the graveyard to where Mudd leant against the carriage, unsure why Miss Bingle would continue with the foolish charade. A month, maybe two, seemed an eternity.

'Food, bedding and clothing will be provided, and we will ensure he has his own cell. I suggest you restrict your visits to one a week and that you arrange some books to help him pass the time.'

'Miss Bingle, please, stop. I'm very grateful for your offer of assistance but why?' Mary held out her hands, palms up in defeat. All possibility of a job in New South Wales would be gone. 'Francis has been accused of forgery. It is a hanging offence.' Her voice caught on a sob.

'And is Mr Greenway no longer interested in the position in New South Wales?'

'He is still very much interested but …'

'As I said, we will organise representation for him. Someone will call at the gaol to discuss the matter and instruct him.' She held out another pouch. 'Take this and once the trial is over, we can meet again. In the meantime, I must ask you to tell Mr Greenway that despite any recommendations he receives from elsewhere he should plead innocent otherwise there will be no option but the death penalty. As you correctly point out, forgery is a hanging offence.'

Fourteen

'I will ask you once more, how do you plead?'

'Guilty.' Francis's voice rang out with not the slightest hesitation, his chin tilted with that all too familiar jut of defiance. His hollow and unwise laugh sent a shiver down Mary's spine.

A communal sigh rose, filling the crowded courtroom, then faded. 'He'll hang.' A lone voice echoed in the chamber. 'They'll string him up from the gallows. He'll swing, mark my words.'

Mary lurched to her feet and spun around to face the row of women, smug smiles on their rosy-cheeked faces. 'You miserable bunch of trollops. He's done nothing.'

'Order!' The clerk brought the hammer down on the bench.

Olive and John dragged her back down. Only the scratching of the clerk's nib broke the silence as he recorded Francis's belligerent plea, and her bones chilled to their marrow. This wasn't the way it was meant to go. Miss Bingle had assured her that if Francis pleaded innocent, the full sentence of the law would not be passed—that he would not hang.

Beneath the royal coat of arms, Sir Vicary Gibbs sat motionless, his face beneath his judicial wig furrowed with confusion, as he studied Francis for a long moment. The sound of the clerk clearing his throat echoed in the high-ceilinged room and, disturbed from his contemplation, Gibbs raised his head and placed the black cap over his wig.

A bead of sweat tracked a path from her temple down her cheek. Guilty. Why had he pleaded guilty? Miss Bingle had been emphatic that his plea should be innocent.

Gibbs threw a melancholy stare at Francis. 'You shall be taken from this place to the place from whence you came and thence to the place of execution.' Shaking his head, he removed the cap and pushed to his feet.

'All stand,' the clerk's voice echoed in the chamber. Feet scraped and a wave of confused murmuring swelled. The turnkey led Francis, docile as a lamb, from the dock until he stood below her. Leaning over the gallery railing, she stretched out her hand, a foolish, futile gesture, for even if their fingers met, she wouldn't be able to convey her confusion nor the depth of her sorrow.

Francis halted, turned his head, his hazel gaze locked with hers as he too stretched out his hand, then clasped his fingers tight, trapping the silent communication that passed between them. He brought his fist to his chest, covering his heart with a thump that resonated in her breast, speaking to her more eloquently than the tenderest kiss or the sweetest words, intricately entwining them forevermore.

The turnkey tugged at Francis's chains and led him from the chamber, the iridescent glow of her husband's moss-green velvet tailcoat her last sight of him.

All strength left her, and Mary sank onto the wooden bench, tears stinging her eyes, her shoulders shaking, but she didn't utter a sound. Why? Why had Francis pleaded guilty? What had possessed him? No one had expected that. Not his legal advisors, nor Sir Vicary Gibbs. In fact, with a stunned expression on his face, Gibbs had only yesterday adjourned the hearing, asking Francis if he was aware of the awful step he was taking and offering him time for further reflection.

She'd visited Newgate that evening, hoping to find out what had prompted Francis's refusal to follow advice, but the turnkey had denied her admittance. Instead, she'd spent a sleepless night pacing the floor, praying Francis would alter his plea as directed. However, a night of introspection had made no difference and once again Francis had, with not a shred of hesitation, pleaded guilty. Why?

How long she sat in contemplation she couldn't fathom, but when she raised her head, the chamber had emptied save for Francis's stalwart brothers flanking her, their expressions stony, their faces paler than whey.

Lips tightly sealed to hold back the howl of misery fighting to escape, she allowed Olive and John to lead her through the mayhem, their strong hands steadying her, shielding her from the demands of the broadsheet writers—the answers they sought were a mystery, and not hers to give.

Mudd had the carriage waiting outside the court. He tipped his hat in recognition and held open the door. Olive and John moved aside. She clambered aboard, every muscle taut with the strain, and cleared her throat, her paltry, prepared excuse snatching at her throat. 'Please forgive me, I would rather be alone.'

The brothers exchanged concerned looks, but neither of them questioned her. She lowered her lids, raised her handkerchief to her eyes and sank back against the plump upholstery.

Once the carriage turned out of Small Street, Mary rapped on the box. Mudd's face appeared at the window. 'Bath, ma'am?'

She nodded. Mudd knew her better than anyone.

An hour later, the carriage drew to a halt in Bennett Street and Mudd jumped from the seat and offered his broad, callused hand. 'I'll wait right here.'

The front door of the terrace opened, and she ran up the steps.

'Mary? Come in, my dear. Good heavens, you're as pale as a ghost. Is it as we hoped? Thank you, Mudd, that will be all. Call back later this afternoon.' Miss Bingle led her into the front parlour.

Away from prying eyes, Mary's composure evaporated. Her muscles cramped and she swayed. 'Come and sit down.' Miss Bingle steadied her, slipping an arm around her shoulders.

'Sir Vicary Gibbs passed the death sentence.' The words exploded from her mouth and panicked screams ricocheted around inside her head, bouncing from one side of her skull to the other. Her mouth yawned open as if something had disconnected from her mind and she could no longer control her actions. She covered her ears with her hands, but the screaming continued unabated.

'Hush, Mary.'

Diabolical images blurred her vision, the noose tightening, the convulsive shudder as Francis's neck snapped, the roar of the crowds as his body swung in the misty morning air, hands splayed—hands that had held her, loved her, comforted her.

Her body shuddered. Someone clutched her shoulders, struggled to still her writhing.

'Drink this.' A glass, cold against her lips. Liquid, thick and sickly sweet, trickled down her throat. Her limbs loosened, and darkness descended.

When Mary awoke a fragile light flickered through the muslin curtains and Miss Bingle's face drifted into focus, her fingers soothing as she brushed the hair back from her damp brow. 'What time is it?'

'Late evening. Mudd's waiting outside.'

A rush of panic blurred her vision. 'The children ...' She struggled upright, failed as a wave of dizziness threw her back against the cushions. Leah would be with George and William, but she always kissed their sweet-smelling faces and tucked them up for the night.

'They will come to no harm.'

But they wouldn't settle, hadn't since they'd been uprooted. 'I must go to them.'

'You need to rest and let the laudanum wear off.'

Laudanum ... she had no recollection. It would account for her unusual weakness and disorientation. She ran her swollen tongue around her dry mouth. 'May I have something to drink?'

Miss Bingle raised a glass to her lips and she sipped the cool water. 'You were very upset when you arrived. I thought you were aware of the possible consequences.'

'But not that Francis would plead guilty, that they would pass the death sentence, that he would hang.'

'No. It came as a shock to all of us, but I have it on very good authority that due to the recommendations of several gentlemen of high standing ...' she gave a sympathetic smile, '... the full sentence of the law may not be executed.'

'It's all my fault.' Mary's pitiful wail filled the room.

'Come, come. No matter how responsible you might feel you cannot dictate another's actions. What Mr Greenway did was of his own volition.'

'You don't understand. Francis did not forge the amendment on the contract. I did.'

Miss Bingle's usually composed face paled then flushed an alarming red, and her mouth opened and shut like the Judas window. She took several steps back and reached for the chair and lowered herself into it, all the while waving her hand around as if to stir her tangled thoughts. 'I think you had better explain,' she spluttered, her lips thin with tension.

An icy shudder crawled over Mary's skin. 'Francis insists on taking responsibility for my actions. He says it's his duty as my husband, because he vowed to cherish and protect me.'

'Unfortunately, since he has chosen to ignore our advice and plead guilty there is little more we can do. The matter remains in the hands of the recorder, Mr Vicary Gibbs.'

'When will Mr Gibbs make his decision?'

'Hopefully soon. I have it on good authority that he is leaving Bristol on the overnight coach. If he rescinds the death sentence ...'

A shiver traced Mary's skin ... could Francis be kept under lock and key in that horrible dungeon for the rest of his life? A yelp of pure horror slipped between her lips. 'Is there nothing that can be done?'

'Representations have been made on Mr Greenway's behalf by people in far more powerful positions than I can aspire to.' She glanced up at the clock on the mantel. 'I am hopeful that we will receive intelligence within the hour.'

Mary closed her eyes and inhaled slowly through her nose. An hour. It would no doubt be the longest one of her life.

'No matter what the outcome Mr Greenway will not walk free. If he is spared the death sentence there will be a further penalty to pay—imprisonment, transportation ...' Miss Bingle shrugged her thin shoulders. 'Best not dwell on conjecture. Suffice to say we will make every effort to ease his incarceration. As I told you, money will be provided for the remainder of his stay in Newgate, for a cell of his own, books, writing materials, anything he requires to pass the time, and you will be free to visit him.'

It was on the tip of Mary's tongue to explain to Miss Bingle that Francis refused to allow her to visit when a sudden knock sounded—not on the door but from above. She craned her neck and whipped around in time to see Miss Bingle racing to the door. 'One moment. I believe we may have received news.'

Mary leapt to her feet, heart pounding.

'Stay here.'

The door banged shut and Mary slumped back onto the sofa. It was impossible to bear, this lack of control. This inability to deal directly with anyone but Miss Bingle. She wanted to charge up the stairs and confront whoever was in those rooms—the pale face she had seen at the window, the owner of the wheeled chair.

Clutching her interlaced fingers, she resorted to pacing the small room. Twelve paces one way, a quick turn and another twelve to the window. Backwards and forwards and still the hands on the clock refused to move. Leah always insisted there was no point in mourning spilt milk but what she wouldn't give to wind back time. She should have simply handed Doolan's contract to Francis when she'd found it—or better still exercised some small degree of patience and waited for Francis's return before she'd chased off to the *Mercury* offices. Another wail built in her throat and the door opened to reveal Miss Bingle, her face beaming. 'It seems our overtures were accepted.'

A bubble of joy replaced Mary's threatened wail. 'And ...'

'Mr Greenway's sentence has been commuted.'

'He's free to go!' She threw herself at Miss Bingle. 'I can't thank you enough.' Tears of triumph and delight coursed down her cheeks. Francis would be freed—they could put the whole devastating experience behind them, perhaps even take up the position in New South Wales, use the funds Miss Bingle promised for Francis's prison stay, and travel as free settlers to the colony.

Miss Bingle untangled Mary's arms from around her shoulders and eased her down into a chair. 'Not quite. Do you understand the expression "commuted"?'

Of course she did. It meant the sentence wouldn't stand. It would be reduced to something smaller, a fine, an apology—though she couldn't imagine that would please Francis.

'In judicial terms, it means his sentence has been reduced to a lesser one. Mr Greenway will not suffer the death penalty.' She let the words dangle and an awkward hush descended.

Miss Bingle's right eyebrow arched. 'He will be transported to the Colony of New South Wales. Unfortunately, because of Mr Greenway's plea, the best Mr Gibbs could do was to *commute* ...' she emphasised the word like a frustrated schoolteacher and colour rose to Mary's cheeks as she took the reprimand, '... the sentence to fourteen years transportation.'

Fourteen years! Tears welled in Mary's eyes and a wave of nausea swept her body, dizziness washed over her, and pinpricks of light sparked behind her eyes. Banished to the Colony of New South Wales, not as a free settler but as a convict destined to work in chains, his aspirations and ambitions shackled. He could die of some dreadful disease, be beaten to death, and he wasn't guilty. 'Fourteen years!'

'It is a lenient sentence. A commuted death penalty usually incurs a life sentence.'

Hardly lenient. Francis would be fifty, an old man, by the time they were reunited, if he survived the voyage, the hard labour, the dreadful diseases, and the savages Mudd said roamed the colony. She slumped down, head in hands. No! There had to be an alternative. She had to be strong. No matter what Francis said she would hand herself over to the authorities. A woman wouldn't be treated as harshly.

'Come, my dear. You are overwrought. It is not as bad as it sounds. Let me explain. For the time being Mr Greenway will remain in Newgate, and we will see to it that he is made as comfortable as possible. Then he will be taken to one of the hulks off Portsmouth to await transportation. We will attempt to facilitate his departure so that his time on the hulks is not a burden, not drawn out.'

The word itself was enough. *Hulks* conjured all kinds of horrors. 'But what about the children, and me?' A pathetic griping churned her stomach as a picture of the workhouse loomed.

Fifteen

Two weeks later, with Mudd's assistance, Mary once more entered Newgate. This time they didn't have to bribe the turnkey with bottles of ale; someone had already taken care of that. Instead, they were greeted with a toothless grin as a door at the back of the turnkey's cubbyhole opened. Armed with Francis's portfolio, paints, two new canvases and a commission Miss Bingle had organised—a title page and the replacement of some damaged sheets in a copy of *The Chronicles of Fabyan* for Mr Harford, the barrister and book collector—they were led up a steep flight of steps.

Mary teetered on the irregular stones. Mudd's guiding hands were as full as her own, with a large hamper of provisions, an easel, more books and sketchpads, and a change of clothes.

Once they reached the top of the steps the turnkey turned to the right and stopped at the fourth door. He held up the lantern, shot the three rusty bolts and shouldered the warped door open, releasing an indescribable stink.

A barred window let in a frail shaft of light but there was a bed and a chair and a rickety table bearing the marks and names of untold prisoners. The underlying stench of urine and sweat snatched at her throat.

Unshaven and grey, Francis lay on the trundle bed alongside one wall, his arm thrown over his eyes to block the beam of sunlight slanting through the barred window high up, close to the raked ceiling. She dumped the canvases and paints and rushed to his side.

He rose from the bed, lurched to his feet, and drew her into a warm embrace. 'I hate it here. I think I'd rather be out with everyone else.'

'Just be patient. I'm sure you'll be allowed to exercise. We've brought you supplies and your paints and easel, some drawing materials, and clean clothes and a commission; it is explained in the letter.'

'One visitor only. You've got an hour, no more, no less.' The turnkey tipped his head to the door and hoicked a thumb at Mudd. 'You. Out.'

'I'm not leaving Mrs Greenway.' Mudd deposited the hamper with a thump, folded his arms across his chest and glared down at the wizened turnkey.

'Fair enough. Both of you out. Now.'

'No. Mudd, I will be perfectly fine.' The reek of misery, mixed with the dreadful stench of sweat, and other odours she didn't want to consider, cloaked Francis. She needed time alone with him, to tell him what had happened and prepare him for what was to follow. 'Perhaps you could organise some water so Francis can wash before he changes his clothes. Come back and fetch me please when our time is up.'

Mudd sniffed his disapproval but stepped out of the cell and with a rattle of keys the turnkey locked the door.

'Why, Francis? Why did you plead guilty? It wasn't what we arranged, what you were advised.'

Unfathomable thoughts raced behind his gold-flecked eyes. For a moment she wanted to make him suffer, suffer for the anguish he had caused by his plea, yet the blame was hers.

He sank down onto the bed and linked his fingers behind his head. 'How many times must I tell you? You are my responsibility, my wife. The obligation is mine. It is better I am imprisoned. You wouldn't last a moment in here. There are hundreds jammed between these walls, the women's quarters are worse, and at night time ...' he shook his head, '... the women ... we will not speak of it again.' He struggled into a sitting position and studied her face through unfocussed eyes. 'How have you arranged all this?'

'It seems we have some very powerful friends.'

'Someone must have greased the turnkey's palm. I should be grateful for that.'

'We have Miss Bingle and her friends to thank. The death sentence has been lifted.'

His eyes widened. 'At what price? What has Miss Bingle and her far-reaching influence arranged for me? I need to be assured that I am not being manipulated.'

That she couldn't do but she could give him some hope for the future. 'You will remain here at Newgate, for a few weeks, maybe a month or two. Miss Bingle has gone to great lengths to ensure your stay will be as comfortable as possible. Mudd will continue to bring hampers, and there are clean clothes for you, which will be replaced with every hamper. If there is anything you need leave a note in the hamper. I will come as often as I can.' Mary sat down beside him on the bed and took his hand in hers, swallowing the rank odour of his body.

'And after that?' He smoothed his palm over her hand.

Her throat dried. 'The death sentence has been commuted to fourteen years. You will be moved to the hulks at Portsmouth to await transportation to New South Wales.'

He let out a bark of harsh laughter. 'Along with hundreds of other felons, left to rot in the stinking estuary. So much for the position of government architect, a free settler in a land full of promise and opportunity.'

Mary swallowed down her frustration. She could do no more and if he refused to allow her to admit the truth, there was nothing else, unless she went against his wishes and took matters into her own hands. But then what would happen to the boys? 'Miss Bingle has …'

'I am tired of Miss Bingle.' He dropped her hand. 'I must accept my fate.'

She stilled. There was one more alternative. Why hadn't she thought of it before? Her heart pounded. 'The children and I will come with you to the colony. Most of the convict ships carry free settlers.' She squeezed his hand, her heart lifting. Perhaps as a free settler she could ask to have Francis work for her. What was it Miss Bingle had said? *Many are taking up new lives as free settlers, with land grants and convict labour they establish themselves with the greatest of ease.* It would mean half a year alone on a ship, then heaven knew what, but he was her husband in more ways than James had ever been, and her saviour. She would follow him to the very ends of the earth.

The rattle of keys sounded. Mudd, hopefully with bath water, and the turnkey no doubt.

'Francis, I must go now. A bath, a change of clothes and some food will make everything seem better. I will come back and see you again in a few days. Is there anything else you require?'

Francis lay back down on the pallet and turned his face to the wall.

Closing her eyes and taking a deep breath, Mary leant down and dropped another kiss on his unshaven cheek. At least when she returned next time, she would perhaps be able to offer a solution, then take him in her arms and prove to him how much she appreciated his determination to protect her.

Once the carriage left the narrow streets of the old town Mary opened the window and inhaled the fresh air. As before the stench of the gaol clung to her and she couldn't rid her mind of the sight of Francis sprawled on the bed, cloaked in misery. Misery she had caused by her foolish action—but at least she now had a plan. She had to see Miss Bingle again. She rapped on the window. 'Mudd. Stop, please.'

The moment the carriage came to a halt she leapt out. 'I need to see Miss Bingle as soon as possible. Do you think we could leave a note at Bennett Street?'

'We can, don't know it'll do you much good though.'

'We can try. Go there directly. I'll write the note on the way.' She threw herself back into the carriage and rummaged in her reticule for her pocketbook. She tore out a page. Hopefully Miss Bingle wouldn't be offended by the scrap. The more she thought about it the more her idea grew. It was the perfect solution. If she could convince Miss Bingle and her friends to advance her the money for the passage she and the boys could travel on the same ship as Francis. But first she had to ask Miss Bingle's opinion, find out if, as a free settler, her husband could be assigned to her, if she could be granted land, preferably in the town, and then she and Francis could design a house, prove his capabilities. Her mind sang with the possibilities.

With the note written, requesting a meeting at Miss Bingle's earliest convenience, Mary leant back and allowed her mind to roam. There had to be building materials available in New South Wales. She was certain Admiral Phillip wouldn't have spent his entire time under canvas and there had been several governors since then. If only she could speak to him, or even his wife, glean some understanding of the man and his time in the colony. Tall sash windows would be essential, to allow the light in, and a second storey ... Her mind raced. A staircase winding its way to the second, maybe even third floor. A view—what the view would be she had no idea. There would have to be some sort of harbour ... The rocking of the carriage lulled her.

'Wake up.' Mudd's grasp on her arm shook her from her reverie. 'We're there. Got that note written? Want me to take it?'

'No. I'll do it.' She had no doubt one of the staff would recognise her. Maybe even the woman she'd seen at the window would be at home, or better still Miss Bingle might be there.

Mary stepped out of the carriage and before she had the chance to mount the steps the door opened. Miss Bingle, dressed in a smart pelisse, stepped out.

Her breath caught. Their luck had changed, she just knew it had. She licked her dry lips. 'I wondered if I might have a word. I've just been to the gaol.'

Miss Bingle pursed her lips, glanced over her shoulder, and, unexpectedly, closed the door behind her. 'Mrs Greenway. Perhaps you'd like to walk with me.'

Much to Mary's surprise Miss Bingle slipped her arm through hers and led the way down the steps. She nodded to Mudd and walked off in the direction of the Circus.

'I wanted ....'

'Not yet, my dear, not yet. Let us walk a little.'

Mudd's eyes bored into Mary's back, and she glanced over her shoulder. He raised his eyebrows and indicated that he would follow. She nodded and concentrated on keeping pace with Miss Bingle.

Once they rounded the corner Miss Bingle slowed, and it became obvious she hadn't wanted their meeting to be witnessed.

A flash of irritation heated Mary's cheeks. More clandestine nonsense. She lifted her hand and waved Mudd alongside. 'May we give you a lift somewhere?'

'Thank you. That would be most kind.'

In a flash Mudd had the door open and he handed Miss Bingle into the carriage, his face a picture of subservience.

'Drive on, Mudd. I shall give you instructions later.' Mary sat opposite Miss Bingle. She had every intention of studying the woman's face as she spoke. The time to take some form of control was long over. It wasn't that she didn't appreciate all Miss Bingle and her friends had done. But now she had decided the path to follow. She had every intention of making sure she got what she wanted; besides, it was the perfect solution.

'I wanted to thank you for the efforts on Francis's behalf. I've just visited him and taken his paints and canvases. He is in a private cell and is in much better spirits. He asked me to convey his thanks.' Mary couldn't bring herself to look into Miss Bingle's eyes. She licked her lips and prepared to continue. 'I do, however, have another request. This is not from Francis, although I believe it will benefit him greatly.' She lifted her gaze, able to stare into Miss Bingle's face now she was telling the truth. 'I would like to accompany Francis to New South Wales.'

Miss Bingle's brow creased into a frown. 'You would leave your boys?'

'Oh no. Not at all. I believe the convict ships carry fare-paying passengers. I would like to travel aboard the same ship as Francis with the boys and settle in the colony.'

'Have you any idea what you are asking? Fare-paying passengers do not mingle with the prisoners, there would be no opportunity to ...' she cleared her throat, '... have any contact with your husband, and what about your children? Would you subject them to a six-month voyage aboard a convict ship, fraught with danger and disease?'

Mary had never felt more determined about anything in her life. When she had first conceived the idea, she had been twisted with anxiety. Children died on voyages. How would William and George manage being confined to a vessel for months with appalling food and fouled water? Was there a doctor aboard ship to tend them? But she'd pushed the thoughts away. She had no option. She owed it to Francis and, besides, she had always intended that the boys would travel with them; they'd never had a day's sickness in their life. 'My mind is made up. I will take my maid, Leah, with me to help with the children.' Although quite how she would pay their passage without Miss Bingle's assistance she had no idea.

'You said that free settlers could establish themselves with the greatest of ease and are offered grants of land.' Her mind skipped, imagining the possibilities once more. 'You also said that Governor Macquarie requested an architect. Mr Greenway's credentials are obvious. His actions were nothing more than a foolish mistake, and being accused of forgery in no way impedes his ability as an architect.' Mary snatched a quick breath and caught a twitch lifting the corner of Miss Bingle's lips.

'It is an interesting proposal.' She rapped on the carriage roof and Mudd drew to a halt. 'This is my destination. Thank you for the ride.' And without another word Miss Bingle allowed Mudd to hand her down from the carriage.

Mary sat, heart pounding, as Miss Bingle's figure disappeared around the corner.

'Now what?' Mudd asked with a raise of his eyebrows. 'You've got that look on your face, as though you're up to no good.'

'I have the perfect solution to all our problems.'

Sixteen

1813

It wasn't until the new year that Mary finally plucked up the courage to tell Mudd and Leah her plan. They sat stunned, their mouths gaping. Sensing the strange atmosphere, William let out a whimper and clambered onto Leah's knee. She buried her face in his mop of curly hair.

'You're out of your mind.' Mudd folded his arms and rocked back in the chair. 'I won't allow it. Your father would never forgive me.'

Mary cupped her chin in her hands and rested her elbows on the table. 'Francis and I intended to travel to New South Wales when he was first offered the position, and Papa's not here. I think he would understand and approve.'

'I made him a promise to look out for you,' Mudd said. 'I've got more work than I can handle, my business is going well, I'll take over the lease on the house. You and the boys can live here, at least until Mr Greenway gets himself to New South Wales and finds out what's what.' He walked around the table and rested his hands on Leah's shoulders.

Leah lifted her face, her eyes bright. 'Mudd's asked me to marry him. I've said yes. I'll be here to help you look after the children.'

Mary forced a smile and smoothed down her skirt, her thoughts of Leah accompanying her to New South Wales taking flight. 'That's wonderful. I'm so happy for you both.' She walked to the window and gazed out. Life in Ashton with Mudd and Leah for the next fourteen years didn't bear thinking about. She was responsible for Francis's incarceration—the least she could do was stand by his side. 'I've asked Miss Bingle to arrange passage for me and the boys. My mind is made up.' Without another word she climbed the stairs and threw herself down on the bed. Nothing, just nothing was going the way she'd hoped.

The days passed at a snail's pace. Every morning Mary sat waiting for a note from Miss Bingle, but none was forthcoming. The purse to cover Francis's expenses arrived regularly and Mudd dealt with the food hampers and additional payment for Francis's cell, but she received no reply from him to her letters pleading to visit him. On one occasion she'd attempted to grease the turnkey's palm herself only to be refused—the prisoner's instructions were that he should not receive visitors. Despite Miss Bingle's earlier assurances, it seemed as though Francis would remain in Newgate forever.

And then one morning when she'd all but given up, Mudd flew through the back door with a grin from ear to ear, sporting a familiar folded piece of paper. 'Thought this might cheer you up.' He handed her a letter. Heart in mouth, she tore it open with shaking hands, then raised her gaze to Mudd. 'Do you know what it says?'

'How would I? I didn't open it.'

Her pulse thundered in her ears. What if something had happened to Francis? What if they had decided to rescind his reprieve? What if ...

'For goodness sake! Read it.'

Mary damped her lips, swallowed and peered down at the cramped handwriting. Not the usual summons to Bennett Street. She scanned the page, let out a moan and clenched her fist, screwing up the paper into a small ball. 'He's to be taken to the *Captivity*, one of the Portsmouth hulks, to await transportation.'

Mudd snatched the ball of paper from her hand and smoothed it out. He let out a dismissive grunt. 'Did you read the rest of it?'

Mary shook her head. What was the point? In the back of her mind, she had come to the conclusion that the delay meant Francis would not be taken to one of the hulks, the notorious decommissioned naval vessels that littered the estuaries housing prisoners awaiting transportation. She couldn't dwell on the stinking rat-infested abominations—not that she had ever seen them, but she'd overheard Mudd and Leah debating the likelihood of Francis surviving his time there. No amount of money would ease any convict's lot—floating dungeons, Mudd called them. He reckoned that if a prisoner was lucky enough to survive the cramped, damp and dismal conditions below decks, the clanking chains and manacles and the daily manual labour, they invariably died of typhoid or some other foul disease.

'She says he will then be transported on the *General Hewett*, leaving in August, and passage has been booked for you and the boys as free settlers. She apologises for the fact that your maid can't travel with you ...' Mudd raised a quizzical eyebrow and shot a look at Leah.

'It was simply a suggestion, before I knew you and Leah were to be married.' Suddenly the weight she'd carried for so many months lifted. 'I must see Francis and tell him myself. Will you take him a note?' What was the point of that; he had ignored all her previous pleas. 'No, better still I'll go myself. Disguise myself so the turnkey doesn't recognise me.'

'You're not going alone.'

'Mudd, I am, and that is an end to it.'

Two evenings later Mudd drew to a halt outside the walls of the old town. Mary slipped from the carriage, hoping to disappear into the darkness before he had the opportunity to upbraid her yet again. When she'd told Leah of her plan to get past the turnkey she'd broken into fits of giggles, clapped her hands together and shot off up the stairs, but Mudd was less impressed—much less impressed—and stormed off.

A few moments later Leah had reappeared with an armful of crimson silk and handfuls of other bits and pieces. 'I've got just the thing for you to wear. Where's Mudd gone?'

Leah scooped everything from the kitchen table.

'He had a job to do. Won't be back for a couple of hours.'

A pungent odour of dust, sour perfume and something far more unsavoury filled the kitchen as Leah shook out the material and laid it carefully on the table.

Mary's breath escaped in a puff of amazement as she arranged the skirt and the miniscule bodice before tightened the lacing to create a cinched waist. 'Where on earth did you get it? I'll look like a harlot.'

'That's the general idea. Guaranteed to get you past the turn-key in exchange for …'

'For what?' Mary snapped.

'Something better than ale.' She caressed the dirty silk and rearranged the bodice, which would undoubtably reveal a vast amount of bosom.

'Francis will think I've taken to the streets.'

'He might like it.' Leah threw her an exaggerated pout. 'I'll give you a few pointers.'

Still smiling at the memory of Leah's pantomimed instructions, Mary sashayed across the filthy street leading to the Cat and Wheel.

Her first mistake. A series of whistles and catcalls greeted her approach.

With a quick glance over her shoulder, she slipped into the shadows of the gaol walls and eased her way to the wicket, bunched her fist and rapped with as much force as she could muster. The Judas window opened, and the crumpled face of the turnkey peered out at her.

'Visitor for Mr Greenway,' she trilled, hoping he couldn't hear her pounding heart.

'And who might you be?' A cloud of fetid breath wafted between the bars.

'Kitty, Kitty Fisher.' Where did that come from? She adjusted her decolletage and thrust forward—Leah would be impressed—then batted her eyelashes and pouted. 'He requested my services.'

The wicket creaked open and two gnarled hands reached for her shoulders and dragged her over the threshold.

Mary wrenched aside. Not a chance. Not a hope in hell. ''ands orf.' She slid a flask of brandy out from under her cloak. 'Like a quick tipple to warm the cockles of your heart?' The cork popped, the turnkey's eyes lit up and he licked his flaccid lips.

His hand rose to snatch the flask, then dropped. 'You first.'

Mary lifted it to her lips, heart thumping. Leah had carefully wiped the top after she'd added the laudanum but warned that she shouldn't let the spiked liquid touch her lips. She raised the bottle, tipped back her head and twirled around. Her cloak flew open, and the dress billowed out. The turnkey groaned and reached for her again. She thrust the flask towards him, and he knocked back the contents in one slug.

Now what? Leah had said the mixture should work in a matter of minutes.

With a lecherous leer he tossed the flask aside, grasped her breasts and lunged forward. Teeth gritted, she stayed put, trying to master her uncontrollable shudders as his clammy hands roamed her skin.

Suddenly his body went limp, his knees buckled and his splayed fingers worked their way down her skirt until his knees hit the flagstones with a resounding crunch and he came to rest in a puddle at her feet.

Sucking in a deep breath, she thrust out her foot and nudged him aside. He groaned and rolled over, his mouth gaping. God! Was he dead? It hadn't occurred to her to question the amount of laudanum Leah had added to the brandy, trusting that she knew the dosage. Her eyes darted around the small, fetid space. She had to get out; there'd be no commuted sentence for her if she was caught standing over a corpse.

The flicker of light from the oil lamp glanced off the flask lying on the flagstones where the turnkey had fallen. She scooped it up. Take the evidence. Leave nothing. Leah's instructions again.

A shuddering snore broke the silence. The turnkey's chest rose and fell, and another snore filled the small space. Her breath whooshed out between her lips, and she smiled.

Moments later, with a swish of her dirty skirts, she slipped through the door and up the winding stone steps and along the passageway. The fourth door on the right. She counted each one then bent down and wriggled the first bolt free.

Not a sound came from the cell as Mary struggled with the second and third bolt and eased the door open. With his back to her, Francis slouched, paintbrush in one hand, studying an unfinished painting. It showed a disparate group of prisoners in the day room, some well-dressed, others barefooted, playing cards, smoking, eating and drinking. There were children in rags, even a cat. It was nothing like the scene that had greeted her the first time she'd visited.

'Francis.' His name caught in her throat, and all she wanted to do was throw herself into the security of his arms. How she longed for his comforting embrace.

He turned slowly, eyes vacant and staring, then frowned. 'Mary?'

'Oh, Francis!' She threw herself at him, wrapping her arms around him, resting her head on his shoulder. 'I have missed you so much.'

He pulled away, held her at arm's length. Her cloak fell open and his eyes widened. 'What is all this? Why are you dressed that way?' He sketched a wave over her bosom, his shaking hand stalling a mere inch above her skin.

'It was the only way I could get in to see you. The turnkey refused me admittance, said you didn't want visitors. I have news, so much news. I have seen Miss Bingle and …' The words poured out of her mouth in a torrent. 'You will be taken to the *Captivity*, a hulk at Portsmouth, to await transportation on the *General Hewett*, leaving in August.' She paused, gathering strength. He had to agree. 'And passage has been booked on the same ship for me and the boys, as free settlers. We will be coming with you.'

Mary reached out, took his hands, and squeezed them. 'I will follow you to the ends of the earth, my love.'

He threaded his fingers through her hair and drew her lips to his then rocked back on his heels. His gaze fixed somewhere between her chin and her cinched waist. After a moment or two he stepped closer, backing her against the wall. She lifted her hand and caressed his cheek. Their eyes caught. The passion that had always been between them sparked. He didn't break her gaze as his hands encircled her waist, drawing her close against him. She closed her eyes, her hair swished against the back of her neck and the curl of excitement peaked as his lips dropped to her bosom.

Francis propped his head on his elbow and traced the curve of her cheek. 'Although I have reservations about subjecting you and the boys to the rigours of a voyage, I have to say I am thrilled to know that you will be accompanying me. The new start we promised ourselves, and if luck is on our side and Macquarie is prepared to accept a somewhat tarnished government architect, I might still make good.'

Mary snuggled closer, letting his words wash over her as her mind darted back to Mudd's observation before they'd first visited the gaol with provisions for Francis. She'd been convinced there was no possibility of Francis getting the position as government architect once he was sentenced. Mudd hadn't agreed. What had he said? That matters might be falling into place—for some. 'Oh my!'

Francis dropped a kiss onto her forehead. 'What is it, my love?'

'I think you may be right. All is not lost. You will make good. I'm certain of it.'

'The other prisoners reckon if I can earn a ticket-of-leave, and start to make my own way, it shouldn't be too bad. I will have to take my portfolio; if I let Macquarie see what I have to offer he can hardly refuse.' He ran his finger down her neck. 'I rather like this outfit. Where did you find it?'

'Leah,' Mary murmured. 'Something she found in the markets and couldn't resist.'

'I wonder what Mudd thinks of it.'

'He may well have seen it; he has asked Leah to marry him. They intend to take over the house at Ashton. He is making a good living with Papa's carriage.' And she had left him sitting outside the gaol twiddling his thumbs waiting for her. He'd be frantic. 'Francis, I have to go. The turnkey ...' She paused. No need for Francis to know about the laudanum. She struggled to her feet, righted her dress, and wrapped her cloak around her shoulders. 'I will come and see you again before you are sent to the hulks. Not long now, my love.'

Seventeen

Two days later, Mary's words came back to haunt her as she stood, heart pounding, a note from Miss Bingle screwed tightly in her sweaty hands. 'Mudd, where are you?' She raced outside and scanned the street for any sight of the carriage, then swung around and bolted back into the house. 'Leah! Leah! Where is Mudd?'

'Got a job. Said he'd be back around midday. You look dreadful. What is it?'

'This.' She waved the crumpled piece of paper under Leah's nose. 'It's from Miss Bingle. She's got word Francis is to be taken to the hulks in the next day or so. I must see him before he goes. They won't let me near him once he's there.' A great sob rose in her chest.

Leah's comforting arm wrapped around her shoulder. 'Mudd'll be back before long. Take yourself off and get changed. Boots and skirt, not the Kitty Fisher garb.'

Dear Leah. Such a rock, so steadfast. How she wished she could go with her to the colony. 'You're right, as always. I'll go and get dressed. If Mudd comes back …'

'Yes, yes, I'll call you the minute he comes in. I'll make a sandwich or two. Keep your spirits up.'

Mary trailed off, a strange mixture of trepidation and excitement swirling. Although she wouldn't wish Francis any more time in the hulks than necessary, it was the beginning of their journey. She needed to find out what he wanted to take with him and what she should take for him. He'd need his portfolio, his folding rule and measuring compass, pens and paper, Chambers's book … what else? She twirled around in the small room searching for inspiration then pulled out the clothes she'd worn on her first visit to the gaol—sturdy boots and skirt, as Leah had said, and a shawl to cover her head. Nothing that would draw attention.

Leah's call came sooner than she expected. She wrangled her hair into a tight knot at the nape of her neck, tucked her shawl into her waistband and rushed to the kitchen to find Mudd with his mouth wrapped around two large chunks of bread and cheese. Never had she been so pleased to see him. 'Oh, Mudd! We must go to the gaol. Francis is due to be sent to the hulks. Miss Bingle said in the next day or so.'

He nodded, swallowed his mouthful and grinned. 'Good job I've got nothing on for the afternoon. Are you ready?'

'I am.' She straightened her skirt and tossed a look at Leah, hoping for approval.

'You'll do.' Leah thrust a sandwich at her.

'I can't eat that in the carriage.'

'Dressed like that you can. Now get a move on. The boys will wake from their nap in a minute and then you'll never get away.'

While the carriage swayed and bumped its way through the streets of Bristol, Mary sat biting her nails, the sandwich uneaten in her lap. It hadn't occurred to her to bring anything to pay off the turnkey. Maybe Mudd had remembered—if not, perhaps a cheese sandwich would do the trick. The wizened old fellow looked as though he could do with a decent meal. She shuddered, the memory of his creeping, crawling hands and rancid breath making her skin stipple.

As before, Mudd drew the carriage to a halt against the old walls of the town and she slipped down, avoiding the stinking puddles with a skill she didn't know she'd mastered. Mudd rapped on the Judas window and the gnarled face appeared. 'What?'

Mudd stepped in front of her. 'Here to see prisoner Greenway.' He pulled a bottle of ale from under his cloak.

With a creak and a groan, the wicket swung open. A hand reached out and grabbed the bottle, then the wicket slammed shut again.

'What the bloody hell ...' Mudd pressed his face against the Judas window. 'What's the matter with you, you stinking rat?'

Two bloodshot eyes peered back at them. 'Wasting your time. He ain't here. Taken to the hulks before dawn. If you get a move on you might make Portsmouth before he goes aboard.' He pulled the cork from the bottle with his teeth, and spat it aside. 'He's gone to the *Captivity*. There, that's payment for your ale.'

All the air whistled from Mary's body, and she slumped against the wall. What now? She couldn't go to Portsmouth. It had to be over a hundred miles away and then they wouldn't let her see him. Miss Bingle had made that clear enough.

'You all right there?' Mudd hauled her to her feet. 'Not the best place to take a breather, stinks worse than a cesspit.'

'What am I going to do?'

'Not much you can do, 'cept bide your time until you sail.' He pushed his hat back and wiped his brow. 'Hang on a tick.' He spun on his heel and rapped on the Judas window again.

A lot of arm-waving ensued, then head-shaking and fist-thumping, but she hadn't the strength to find out the reason. Then Mudd stormed back, his face like thunder. 'The putrid little shit.'

'What?'

'The turnkey, the bastard ... beggin' your pardon ... but he's got all Mr Greenway's belongings bundled up and wants five quid for them. Otherwise, they go to the highest bidder.'

Mary slammed her hand over her mouth. How could she have forgotten? Francis's portfolio, his paints, easel and canvases. 'I haven't got the money.'

Her shoulders slumped; with one ghastly problem a stepping stone to the next, she didn't know if she had the stamina. Miss Bingle. Maybe she could help. But she couldn't go cap in hand again. Not after her friends had paid the cost of the voyage.

'But I have.' Mudd's cheery face filled her vision.

'I can't take your money.' Not even as a loan. She had no means of paying it back.

'It's earmarked for you anyway. Leah and I have been saving a bit here and there. Thought we'd pay you for what's left of the furniture when you leave.' He thumped his chest with the flat of his hand. 'I've got it hidden, safe and sound, on me person.'

The man was a godsend.

But the turnkey wasn't to be trusted. What if he'd already sold Francis's possessions? 'No, that won't work. Get me inside, into the turnkey's room, and I'll check he's telling the truth.'

'Not a chance.'

'What do you mean? I thought you said you'd lend me the money.'

'Didn't do that. I'll *give* you the money. He's still got the stuff; he wouldn't have offered it if he'd already sold it. Would have denied all knowledge, sworn Mr Greenway'd taken it with him. I'll go and sort it out. You stay here. We don't want anyone recognising Kitty Fisher.' Without giving Mary a chance to reply Mudd turned on his heel, raised his fist and hammered on the wicket again.

Moments later the Judas window creaked open, and Mudd stuck his hand inside his coat, pulled out a wodge of notes and waved them under the turnkey's nose. The wicket cracked open and Mudd disappeared inside.

Mary couldn't remember ever feeling so useless. She kicked her boots in the dirt, took several steps towards the gaol, remembered Mudd's warning about Kitty Fisher, turned on her heel, marched back to the carriage and stood with her forehead resting against the paintwork, counting the thumps of her heart. It had been bad enough when Francis was locked up but at least she'd known where he was—that, thanks to Miss Bingle's money pouches, he wasn't starving or beaten—but this, this was different. She had no idea where he was and what was happening to him. And now to add insult to injury she owed Mudd and Leah money. She let out a long, sorrowful groan.

Perhaps she could sell the painting she had seen Francis working on, if and only if, it was with Francis's belongings. Maybe his brothers would lend her the money, surely Francis was owed some wages ... and then the street noise and the raucous shouts from the Cat and Wheel faded and she remembered the commission Francis had been working on for Mr Harford. If he had completed it, he would be entitled to payment. She had no idea how much the work was worth, but Miss Bingle would know. Where was Mudd? Surely he hadn't come to any harm; he was twice the size of the turnkey. She paced up and down, the wait becoming intolerable as the minutes passed.

Then suddenly Mudd appeared, a large hessian bundle thrown over his shoulder. She bolted across the street. 'I thought something terrible had happened to you.'

'I'm all right. Come on, let's get out of here.'

Once they'd stashed Francis's possessions beneath the seat and firmly fastened the doors of the carriage Mary climbed up on the box next to Mudd. 'Did you go through Francis's belongings?'

'That I did. Didn't really know what I was looking for but thought I remembered a few bits and pieces. I reckon it's all there. His portfolio, instruments and drawings and a couple of paintings, and that book he was working on. The Chronicles of somebody or other.'

It was there. What a relief. She would be able to take it to Miss Bingle, and hopefully repay Mudd. She reached out and placed a hand on his arm. 'I can't thank you enough for this, for every-thing.' Tears sprang unbidden and she scuffed them away. Leah and Mudd had become so much more than servants—they were the closest thing she had to family.

The next day, Mary wrote a note to Miss Bingle and a reply came in a matter of hours. She duly presented herself at Bennett Street and was shown in.

'I was sorry to hear that you had missed Mr Greenway. The information we received said he would remain at Newgate for another three or four days.'

'It can't be helped. Thank you for the advice. I collected his possessions yesterday and …' She ran her hand over the package on her lap, trying to decide whether to explain about Mudd's money, but she'd discovered in the last months that sometimes it was bet-ter to wait and see what people would say before she laid her cards on the table. 'Mr Greenway completed the work on Mr Harford's book.' She unwrapped the calico and passed it to Miss Bingle.

'Why this is remarkable. Such an excellent facsimile.' The hint of a smile tweaked the corners of Miss Bingle's mouth—with-out a doubt she was about to make some remark about Francis's ability to copy, forge even, documents. After all, who better than an accused forger to make a replacement copy of a missing page? 'I will pass this on to Mr Harford and ensure you receive the monies owing before you leave.'

Mary's spirits rose. She would so very much like to be able to repay Mudd and Leah. She had every intention of leaving all the furniture with them, and hadn't dreamt of asking for payment.

'Which brings me to another matter.'

Mary snapped back to the moment.

'We would like to give you this to help ease your ...' she cleared her throat, '... resettlement costs.' She held out a folded piece of paper. 'A promissory note for ten guineas drawn on the High Street Bank, Bath. I have it on good authority it will be accepted in the colony along with foreign coins, rum and barter. All are an acceptable substitute for coin.'

Mary choked back a sob, or was it a laugh. Payment from Mr Harford *and* ten guineas. More than she'd dreamt of, but still she didn't know who was responsible for this largesse. 'I can't thank you enough for your assistance. I would very much like the opportunity to personally express my gratitude to those people who have assisted us.' She couldn't leave without knowing who was behind the strange series of events.

With a strangled cough, Miss Bingle turned her gaze to the door as though waiting for someone to appear and give her instructions. After an exaggerated silence she cleared her throat again and leant forward. Much to Mary's surprise she took both of her hands. 'My dear, I understand and applaud your sentiments, however I am not at liberty to divulge ...'

It was ridiculous. 'I believe Admiral Phillip and his wife Isabella own this house.' There, she'd said it. Was Mudd correct? She'd find out soon enough.

Miss Bingle stilled, her eyes wide as her damp fingers clenched Mary's hands. 'I am not at liberty ...' she repeated, her voice cracking.

But there was nothing stopping Mary from offering an opinion. 'Allow me to paint a scenario.' And if she was correct Miss Bingle would not need to divulge anything. It was a gamble, but what had she to lose? Francis was on his way to the hulks and her passage was secured. Miss Bingle would hardly repeat her words. 'When we first met, after you'd approached me at Clifton, you said Governor Macquarie was looking for an architect. I believe you were aware of Greenway Brothers' financial position and thought Mr Greenway's services would be easily secured, possibly at a favourable rate. Am I correct?'

When she received no response Mary continued. 'Then unwittingly, Francis and I played into your hands. An accused felon, a convict, was obliged to work for the government without recompense—a much cheaper option.'

Miss Bingle's face paled and she pursed her lips. 'I may have underestimated you, my dear. I must ask you to keep your assumptions to yourself. Promise me you will never reveal the extent of our involvement in your husband's trial. It would not do for *him* to be seen to be involved in judicial or colonial matters now he is retired.'

Confirmation of her suspicions. As Mary had intended, Miss Bingle hadn't needed to betray any confidences. 'I have no intention of making my assumptions public, but I need to know my family will be looked after when we arrive in New South Wales.'

'I can assure you that will be the case. The slate will eventually be wiped clean.'

Time telescoped as Leah and Mary worked to ready the trunk and sea chest with all the things Mary would take to New South

Wales: clothes for the boys, for herself and Francis, precious treasures, reminders of her life at Manali, not of James but of the halcyon days before her marriage—Lady Wilbraham's journal, Francis's copy of Chambers's treatise, a collection of her drawings neatly filed in Papa's old leather folio and Francis's plans and elevations in his own portfolio, his measuring compass and folding rule, a range of pens, black and blue ink, cartridge and blotting paper. How she wished she could contact him and tell him that his possessions were safe and sound.

The trunk and Papa's sea chest were packed, repacked and emptied again until finally Mary began to believe it was not all a dream. She secured the clasps of the chest, promising herself she would not open them again.

'Mary!' Leah's voice echoed up the stairwell.

'I'm coming.' She was halfway down the stairs when a wave of dizziness swept her, her feet slid on the worn timber runners, and she landed with a thud at the bottom. Carefully, she eased upright and waited for the world to right itself.

'Oh dear!' Leah reached out her hand. 'Let me help you up. What happened?'

Mary blinked away the clouds of confusion. 'I have no idea. One minute I was at the top of the stairs then the world turned upside down and I found myself at the bottom.' She grasped Leah's hand and eased upright. 'There. Nothing wrong. Just a misstep. Tiredness I expect. I've finally locked the trunk and chest. I have no intention of reorganising anything.'

'There's a note from Miss Bingle. At least, I think it is. A boy delivered it.' She held out the familiar sheet of paper. 'Come and sit down. I'll make a pot of tea. I've got some meat pies for lunch.'

With paper in hand Mary settled at the table and opened the letter and her heart jumped. 'We have a sailing date! Thursday, twenty-fourth August.'

'I'll bet Mr Greenway will be pleased when he finds out. Can't be much fun in those hulks. Here—eat this, you missed breakfast.' Leah pushed a plate with a slice of pie under her nose.

Mary's mouth filled with saliva, her stomach roiled, she slapped her hand across her mouth and bolted into the garden, retching again and again until her legs shook and her eyes watered.

'Here. Wipe your face with this.' Leah handed her a damp cloth. 'I was in two minds about that meat, but the boys ate it last night and it didn't do them no harm.'

Clutching the cloth, Mary sank down, dropped her head between her knees and inhaled several slow and steadying breaths. She hadn't even had a chance to smell the pie. The wave of sickness had come from nowhere, and she hadn't eaten since the night before.

'Drink this.' Leah handed her some water. 'Wash your mouth out. It'll make you feel better. You haven't been at the brandy, have you?'

Bile rose in her throat again. No brandy, no meat pie. 'Oh God.' She dropped her head again and waited for the world to come to rights, and as it did reality dawned. She counted back, tried to remember the last time ... 'Leah, I think I'm carrying.'

'Oh! Ah! Yes, well that'd make sense, you were real sick with William.'

'And George.' But that was before Leah had come to work at Manali.

'But when? Who?' Leah clapped her hand over her mouth. 'Beg pardon.'

And so she should. 'I hold you responsible.'

'Me?' Leah squawked.

'Yes, you and the wretched red dress of yours.'

Leah let go a great belly laugh. 'Told you he'd like it. So that means you'd be due ...' she counted off on her fingers, '... around about December. A Christmas baby.'

A Christmas she would spend aboard the *General Hewett* … An ice-cold shudder rippled across her shoulders and worked its way down her body. She cradled her belly. 'What am I going to do?'

'Ain't much you can do about it. They have doctors on board them ships, don't they?'

She lifted her chin. There was no alternative. She'd promised Francis. George and William were already planning their life aboard ship. Miss Bingle had organised their passage. She retched again.

'Why don't you go upstairs and have a lie-down. I'll take the boys for a walk. Give you some peace and quiet. Here.' Leah hauled her to her feet. 'Can you manage those stairs?'

Mary nodded, made her way to the kitchen door, steadied herself, sucked in a deep breath, squared her shoulders and carefully mounted the stairs.

Once she'd reached the bedroom, she closed the curtains and lay down. The sound of the boys in the yard filtered up through the open window and the curtains billowed gently in the breeze. She let her mind slip back.

On the eve of Mary's marriage to James, when she'd finally reached a suitable age, she'd plucked up the courage and asked Papa about the story of her birth. His harrowed face and the tears pouring unchecked down his cheeks made her regret her decision, but he'd insisted. He'd laid no blame on the surgeon who'd treated more broken bones than he'd had hot dinners but knew nothing of midwifery. No pain relief but rum, prolonged labour, excessive bleeding, followed by an infection that had taken Mama's life.

'No!' She bolted upright. Her long, drawn-out cry echoed, pain racking her body. The small room swayed and came into focus, and she reached for Francis. Gone! Not there. Incarcerated in some filthy wreck of a ship. She'd promised. She couldn't break her promise. She had to. Francis's first child. She cradled her belly again, searched for a sense of movement. Nothing. She rolled onto her feet, studied the bedding, lifted her skirts searching for the telltale stain of blood. Nothing.

Footsteps thundered on the stairs and the door flew open. Leah's frightened face gaped at her. 'What is it? I heard you cry out.' She led her back to the bed. 'Rest. I'll bring you tea, black tea.'

'The boys?'

'Downstairs playing. We've had our walk and came back. Mudd's home. Don't fuss yourself.'

Mary drew in a shuddering breath. 'I can't go. I can't risk the baby.'

'Oh! Your mother.' Leah clapped her hand across her mouth. 'I'm sorry. Mrs Rudge told me … You stay right there.'

'No. I'll come down. I need to write to Miss Bingle and explain.'

Mudd delivered her letter, and two days later at eleven o'clock Mary descended from the carriage and knocked on the door at Bennett Street. As usual she was shown into the front parlour and found Miss Bingle gazing out of the window.

'I hadn't expected to see you again before you embarked.' She turned and faced Mary, her face stern. 'This is an unexpected event. It would be foolhardy to make the journey given the situation. Your passage has been cancelled.'

Mary cradled her head in her hands. What would happen to Francis? He would board the *General Hewett*, expect her to be there. Think she had deserted him. 'I have to see Francis.'

'That's not possible. A message perhaps can be arranged but not until he has left the hulks. When he embarks.'

Mary's shoulders dropped but now she had to ask the next question. Would it be too much? Could she expect Miss Bingle and her friends to organise another passage? 'Do you think it would be possible … after I …' she sketched a wave over the barely visible bump beneath her skirt, '… to organise another passage?'

'That I do not know.' Miss Bingle held the door open.

Eighteen

Francis John Greenway, named for his father and uncle, but known to one and all as Frankie, entered the world on a cold windy evening, with as little difficulty as his older brothers. He was baptised on the twelfth of February and ten days later Mudd and Leah, still protesting Mary's decision, accompanied her and the children on the one-hundred-mile trip to Portsmouth to join the *Broxbournebury*, bound for the Colony of New South Wales.

Mary gazed up at the sullen sky shrouding the Isle of Wight, Miss Bingle's voice echoing, repeating the words she'd uttered so long ago telling her the sun always shone in New South Wales. She prayed it was shining down on Francis, that they would be reunited, and their life could begin again, free from the trials and tribulations of the last years. There would be new opportunities—there were always opportunities. She simply had to keep her mind open and ensure she and Francis made the most of every single one.

Clutching baby Frankie tight, she shepherded William and George aboard the lighter that would row them out to the ship swinging in the strengthening breeze. Not that George needed much encouragement—aided by one of the other passengers, he bounded aboard. An affinity with the sea, inherited from his father and grandfather, apparently ran deep in his veins.

The hull of the *Broxbournebury* towered above them. With a crash and a splash, the watermen shipped their oars as the bosun's chair was lowered. Mary had been warned about this strange device—a swathe of canvas slung between a cat's cradle of ropes which would haul the passengers aboard.

Obviously familiar with the contraption, the gentleman who had assisted George slipped the ropes over his head and he lowered himself onto the sling without a moment's hesitation. 'It's no more than a garden swing,' he called as one of the crew members hoisted him high. The chair swirled and swung like a dervish until it reached the ship's deck. A boat hook snatched at the ropes and pulled the sling aboard, and the gentleman was deposited safely on the deck before the whole rigmarole began again and the next passenger, windswept and dumbstruck, reached the deck.

They made it aboard, Mary nursing Frankie on her lap and a burly sailor clasping William in his arms, but George would have nothing to do with them, insisting on riding alone on the sling packed with cloaks and blankets, and a grin of pure pleasure lighting his face. She'd never seen him so at home.

'Follow me, ma'am, and I'll show you to your cabin.' A broad-chested, pockmarked sailor led them down a series of ladders into a darkened passageway and threw open a small door. Flabbergasted, Mary surveyed the tiny cabin: one bunk, a single porthole, a hinged table and a small chair—and this for fare-paying passengers. Whatever had Francis endured, manacled below deck, unable to see the sun rise and set for months on end? She didn't even know if he'd survived the voyage. For all she knew he could be resting beneath the sea with Mama.

George and William suffered none of her despondency. With a whoop of excitement, they launched onto the narrow bunk. The burly sailor edged towards the cabin door.

'Is it possible to bring another mattress in here for the boys? We won't all fit in the bunk.'

He dived under the bunk and brought out two rolls of canvas. 'No mattress, but these should do the trick.'

The boys would never sleep on that, not on the damp wooden floor, especially when the weather chilled. Perhaps if they topped and tailed … she studied the bunk, a twist of despair churning her stomach. Whatever had possessed her to imagine she could do this? Not a few minutes of discomfort or terror but six long months. If she spread her arms, she could almost touch both walls of the cabin.

'This should do it. Want to give them a try, boys?' The sailor's hoarse voice broke her despair, and she whipped around in time to see George and William scrambling into two hammocks swinging from the beams of the cabin roof. 'Then you take them down during the day and it'll give you a bit more room. Now where do you want these trunks? Sure you wouldn't like them below decks? They'll take up a fair bit of space.'

'No. They can't go in the hold. I must have clothes for the children, the baby especially.' She hitched Frankie up onto her hip. He was a good baby, more settled than William and George had ever been, but he still needed clouts, and she'd only recently weaned him onto a bottle. Captain Pitcher had assured her there would be cow or goat milk available on board. She'd sleep in the hold herself rather than leave Francis's instruments, books and portfolio unattended in the bowels of the ship.

'Right you are, ma'am.' He tipped his finger to his forehead. 'Hot meal around four. Give you a chance to meet the other fare-paying passengers.'

No, she didn't want that at all. 'The children and I will eat in our cabin. Can that be arranged? I'll need some fresh milk for the baby.' If only Leah was with her. She'd taken her for granted, relied on her far too much. She sank down on the bunk and let her shoulders drop. She couldn't, wouldn't, dwell on the rightness or wrongness of her decision to follow Francis. She drew in several long slow breaths—she'd do this, and once they joined Francis, they'd face the new world together.

By the time dinner arrived, potatoes and some sort of boiled meat, she'd organised the small table, and with the boys sitting on the bunk and she and Frankie sharing the single chair they made short work of the offering. Even the baby took a taste of squashed potatoes mixed with the watery gravy.

Sounds wafted through the open porthole: the creak of the hull, the cries of the men hauling ropes, and shouts and thumps that she presumed heralded the hoisting of the sails. The sooner they set sail the sooner the journey would be over. It was an event she and the children should witness, possibly the last sighting of the land of their birth. 'Would you like to go up on deck?'

Once she'd wrangled the boys back into their coats, she wound her shawl around her shoulders, made a sling and tied Frankie tight against her body. 'Come along. William, hold my hand, and George, take William's.'

Sidestepping, they made their way up the steep ladder, past the captain's cabin and onto the crowded deck.

'How do you do, ma'am.' A gentleman with a sharp nose, triangular face and flyaway hair surveyed her. 'Mr Jeffery Bent, at your service.' He gave a sketchy bow. 'Soon to be first judge of the Colony of New South Wales.' He puffed out his scrawny chest and straightened his skinny legs. Mary couldn't think of a better acquaintance—to date, people in high places had stood her in good stead. 'We're to catch the outgoing tide, travel through the calmer waters between the Isle of Wight and the coast then head out into the English Channel. Our last sighting of England will be the southernmost tip of Cornwall—Lizard Point.'

A gasp caught in Mary's throat. She clasped Frankie tight and edged nearer to George and William, who were hanging over the taffrail staring at the churning waters. How would she manage? There was no going back.

'Very brave of you, my dear, with three young children,' said Mr Bent, obviously adept at mind reading. 'Have you no maid to assist you?'

She shook her head. She didn't begrudge Leah's decision, was thrilled that she and Mudd had found happiness, but what she wouldn't give to see her unflappable, smiling face. The boys had accepted her explanation with barely a glimmer of regret; in their young minds Mudd and Leah belonged together.

'Let me have a word with Mr McLachlan, he's the surgeon, responsible for the welfare of all one hundred and twenty female convicts. There must be one amongst them with some experience with children. I'm sure he could arrange a suitable girl to give you a helping hand.'

A convict maid? She couldn't trust a convict girl to care for her boys. She opened her mouth to refuse his offer, then snapped it shut. What was the matter with her? The children's father was a convict. The surgeon would have records of all the prisoners, and surely wouldn't recommend anyone unsuitable—and how she'd love some help. 'That would be most kind.' As the Lizard retreated into the smudged horizon the *Broxbournebury* turned its bow to the future and Mary tucked her loose hair behind her ear, braced herself against the roll of the ship and led her small family down below decks.

After a sleepless night—fraught with waking dreams of drifting down, down to the ocean floor where poor Francis and Mama lay in their shrouds with stitches through their noses—Mary staggered to her feet, jostled baby Frankie into a clean nightgown, shouted over her shoulder at George and William, who were more interested in swinging in their hammocks, and mumbled a string of words she'd learnt in the stables. A knock on the cabin door stilled her tirade. 'Come in and shut the door behind you.'

The door opened and closed before she'd had the opportunity to fasten Frankie's clothing and look up. 'Just put it down on the table.' Perhaps breakfast would get the boys out of their hammocks. Not that the prospect of the gruel and hard biscuits Leah had warned her of was inviting.

When the expected clatter didn't eventuate, she clasped Frankie to her shoulder and whipped around.

Abundant, unconstrained, nut-brown hair framed a freckled face with red-rimmed eyes and spidery lashes.

'I'm Hannah, ma'am. Surgeon McLachlan sent me. Said you needed help.' She wiped her grubby hands down the front of her stained calico blouse.

Not exactly what she had in mind but nothing a good wash wouldn't rectify. 'Oh yes. Yes, I do. The baby is Frankie, and those two tearaways are George and William. Get down, boys, and come here.'

With a groan the boys untangled themselves from their hammocks and thumped to the deck.

'Shall we get those hammocks away and then go and find some breakfast?' Hannah offered a gap-toothed smile and within minutes she had the boys straightened out, the hammocks stowed, and Frankie tucked on her hip.

Mary's heart rate settled, her sense of relief palpable until the ship bucked and reared and threw her off balance. She landed with a thud on the edge of the bunk, stomach churning and a foul taste in her mouth. She clamped her hand over her mouth.

'Oh, ma'am, are you feeling poorly? What you need is something in your stomach.'

The mere thought turned her insides upside down again. She'd only heave it back up. If only Hannah would go and leave her alone, amuse the children. She couldn't be with child, and this was worse than any sickness she'd suffered then. Perhaps the stew she'd eaten the night before …

'It's seasickness, ma'am. It will pass. If you can manage, spend time above deck, where you can see the horizon, as it helps settle the stomach. But there's something nasty brewing. The sky's as grey as a goose's wing.'

Mary sat very still, cold and sweaty, shivering. She wiped away the sheen of moisture on her forehead, fingers tightly grasping the edge of the bunk trying to counteract the plunging, rolling ship, unable to believe the boys showed no symptoms. Above them the crew scuttled across the decks, banging and thumping as they did whatever they had to do with the sails and ropes. The hull creaked and squeaked in complaint.

'Come on, boys, let's leave your mam to have some quiet.'

She couldn't do that. She didn't even know what Hannah had been convicted of. 'Not so fast. Why were you convicted?' Oh, that was far too blunt.

A hint of colour tinged Hannah's cheeks. 'I stole a duck.'

'A duck?' Better than she dared hope, not a hanging offence.

'Me mam had a hankering for duck when she was waiting for the littlest to come and I … I know I shouldn't have done it but she wanted it so badly.'

'How many brothers and sisters do you have?'

'There's twelve of us still breathing last I heard. I'm the eldest.'

'Twelve! Good heavens.' Mary took a deep breath, struggling to her feet. She'd have a word with the surgeon and see what he thought but Hannah sounded like she'd manage quite well with her three boys. The ship heeled to one side and threw her against the table.

'You'll find your sea legs soon. The first bout is the worst.' Hannah's practical tone brought a sense of calm, and Mary relaxed.

At that moment the ship gave a violent lurch and Mary catapulted across the room. Her head slammed against the wall, and she surrendered to the darkness.

Frankie's cries brought Mary to her senses. Hannah hovered over her, a damp cloth in hand. Mary's watery gaze darted to the bunk where George and William sat, picnicking on warm rolls, eggs and cold meat, Frankie wedged between them, their eyes bright with excitement.

'Why don't you lie down, ma'am? I'll take the boys up for some fresh air. There's a carafe of water and a bucket for you. Believe me, it will pass. I ain't lived all me life in Portsmouth not to know.'

Too weak to argue, Mary allowed Hannah to help her up, lips clamped tight, while the children were buttoned into their coats and led away. She passed the remainder of the day in a queasy, clammy fug made worse by the increasing intensity of the storm. When Hannah brought the children back down, she reported that six sheep had been washed overboard and drowned and the screaming from the convict women couldn't be borne. 'The silly numbskulls think they're headed for a watery grave.'

The silly numbskulls might well be right. Thank the heavens she'd had the foresight to see Frankie baptised before they left England. She was not deeply religious but she couldn't think of a good reason not to hedge her bets. Mary buried her head under the pillow and prayed the sip of water she'd managed would stay where it belonged.

Once Hannah had tucked Frankie in beside her and jostled George and William into their hammocks, she dropped down beside the bunk. 'Ma'am. It's a bit forward of me but I wondered if you'd mind if I had a word with Mr McLachlan. I thought maybe if I slung another hammock in here with you, I'd be on hand in the night if you needed me.'

Mary rolled over. There was nothing in Hannah's tone or manner to suggest she had any ulterior motive, and the thought of her help should the weather worsen cheered her no end.

'Now we're heading for open waters the storm, like as not, will blow up even more,' Hannah added. 'I'd say we're in for another three or four days of it.'

Hannah's prophecy proved correct and once the ship reached the rougher open seas of the North Atlantic most of the passengers succumbed to seasickness and stayed locked in their cabins, unable to tell day from night.

It was as if there was no one else in the world other than the five of them hunched in the tiny cabin, shaken and torn, buffeted and broken, while the heavens thrashed and roared; perhaps wreaking vengeance on an audacious woman apparently undaunted by the prospect of a fifteen-thousand-mile voyage in the company of two children under the age of seven, and a babe in arms. In the darkest moments of the storm, images mingled in a horrendous medley of events. Mama's death giving life to her, the loss of her boys to the same watery grave, caused by her foolishness, a thoroughly deserved recurrence of events—didn't they say history repeated itself?

Gradually, as the winds eased and took with them Mary's sickness, the *Broxbournebury* limped into the Spanish port of Corunna to make repairs and take on fresh water, vegetables and livestock. Most of the male passengers took the opportunity to stretch their legs and see the sights. The women, convicts or not, remained aboard.

When Mary responded to the knock and opened the cabin door, a delicious warm, sweet scent filled her nostrils and Mr Bent's beaming face appeared around the large basket clasped to his chest. 'My dear Mrs Greenway. I knew you had chosen to stay aboard while we're in port, but I didn't feel you should be deprived of the wonderful treasures we found in the markets.' Without waiting to be asked he stepped into the cabin and put down the basket—on top of all her papers, but she could hardly complain. 'Have you ever tasted fresh oranges? The crew assured me your boys would benefit from them and their health-giving properties; they are particularly good for the children's teeth and gums, I am told, and I couldn't resist adding a few little extras.' Like a magician, he delved into the basket. 'Chocolate! There is nothing quite like a cup of chocolate with oranges, believe me. Also for you alone ... some Dutch cheese and a bottle of Malaga sweet wine.'

She couldn't accept the basket. It must have cost a fortune and she hadn't the money to waste on such luxuries. 'Mr Bent, it's so very kind of you to think of me and my boys but I really couldn't ...'

'I will hear of no such nonsense. Your courage and determination through our dreadful ordeal demands reward. Enjoy! That is an order.' He gave her a broad smile and turned on his heel, closing the door behind him.

Her dreadful ordeal. Truly it had been most unpleasant, and without Hannah's help she wasn't sure they would have managed, but to accept such a gift—more to the point, to present such a gift to a married woman—surely he didn't … She shivered. She could hardly return the basket. The last thing she wanted to do was to land in the colony having snubbed the soon-to-be first judge of the Colony of New South Wales. He was the very sort of person she should be cultivating, for Francis's sake, and for her own for that matter. She had no idea what to expect when she arrived, had deliberately pushed all thoughts along those lines to the back of her mind. She sucked in a deep breath, inhaled the sweet, sweet smell, and couldn't resist.

She sank her teeth into the thick skin, which had an unpleasant bitter flavour that made her grimace. 'Ouf!' She wiped the back of her hand across her mouth then sank her thumbs into the skin and peeled it back. There had to be an easier way and if, as Mr Bent had said, oranges were good for the children, then she had to discover it.

Some time later, covered in sticky juice and having eaten at least one whole orange, she had a pile of segments ready for the boys when they returned from their walk around the deck. None for Frankie, not yet. She wasn't sure if they would be good for him and, since he didn't have many teeth to worry about, the health-giving properties of oranges weren't important. A cup of warm chocolate would make a delightful change to the watery coffee or tea on offer, but it could wait until she could send Hannah to find some extra milk.

With a small beaker of wine beside her she collected up her papers, none the worse for being trapped beneath the basket, and opened her sketchpad. The notes from Miss Bingle lay between the last page and the cover. She wasn't sure why she'd kept them. She moved them aside and folded the back page, this way and that, until she had made a small pocket, then slipped the notes inside. If it hadn't been for Mudd drawing her attention to the link between

Governor Macquarie's request for an architect, Bennett Street and Admiral Phillip, she would never have guessed who was behind their good fortune. She unfolded the letter that had arrived on the day of her departure, took a sip of her wine and for the hundredth time read the words.

> *Bennett Street, Bath, England.*
>
> *To whom it may concern*
>
> *It is my sincere pleasure to strongly recommend Mr Francis Howard Greenway. His skills and scientific knowledge as a civil architect are second to none and his designs and work are amongst the best. Despite the unfortunate situation in which he finds himself, through no fault of his own, I believe he will be of enormous benefit to the Colony of New South Wales.*
>
> *Arthur Phillip*
>
> *Admiral of the fleet*

The moment she set foot in the colony she would have the letter delivered to the governor. If, as Miss Bingle had said, Macquarie had requested an architect be sent to the colony, then he would be thrilled to know his request had been granted. Francis would immediately be released and begin to make his mark on the colony.

How she wished she'd had the opportunity to thank the admiral personally. She closed her eyes and tried to summon an image of the man. She'd only met him that once. A narrow-faced, elderly gentleman, with a big beak of a nose and large ears—but then most elderly gentlemen seemed to have large noses and ears—and that strange gap between two of his front teeth. Her nib flew across the page as she tried to recreate his image.

Mary rocked back in the chair and surveyed her handiwork. The drawing was a little audacious—no, more than a little. Akin to something that might be printed in a broadsheet but nevertheless a recognisable likeness. She blew on the ink, waved the page in the air to dry then slipped it into her folio.

Once the ship reached the Southern Ocean the weather calmed and was nowhere near as vicious as it had been on the first leg of the voyage. Life for Mary changed too … the storm had removed the last vestige of the girl she had once been. She had become a woman, a woman who knew there was no help other than that she could give herself … except perhaps for Hannah, and chocolate and oranges. Responsibility for the wellbeing of her family lay firmly in her hands.

Under Hannah's watchful eyes the boys romped, wondered at breeching whales and soaring albatrosses, fed the goats, pigs and chickens in their cages on the upper deck and learnt a series of expressions Mary refused to sanction but forgave when she discovered Hannah teaching the boys their letters.

She spent much of her time in the cabin going through all of Francis's paperwork, plans and designs, and her own sketchy attempts. She pored over Lady Wilbraham's journal, learning as much as she could while musing on the strange series of events that had led her to this place. All the while Frankie slept and ate and grew; he would be almost eight months old before he met his father.

At four o'clock every afternoon she left Hannah in charge of the boys' meal and dined with the other fare-paying passengers, conscious of the need to make the acquaintance of these people who would form part of Sydney society. The food was surprisingly good: meals of soup, boiled beef, roasted duck and curry served with a variety of vegetables sourced from their ports of call and invariably finished off with plum pudding and a glass of port or sherry. On occasion when the weather was fine the convicts would be allowed on deck. Captain Pitcher would order the drum and fife and the ship would resound to the sounds of singing and laughter, twirling and prancing as the women flashed their ankles and danced the evening away, apparently unconcerned about what lay ahead.

Her heart went out to them. Over dinner at the captain's table she'd heard appalling stories about the allocation of female convicts, no better than slavery. The military had first pick, then the settlers, and the girls had no choice in the matter. The younger, prettier ones were chosen first and then the others, the older women or those with children, were sent to the 'factory above the gaol' in Parramatta, some miles outside Sydney, where they lived in squalor spinning the wool and linen used to make the convicts' clothes or they were sold off for as little as the price of a bottle of rum into a life of prostitution. It was barbaric and she had no intention of seeing it happen to Hannah. She would speak to Mr Bent and ask his advice before they got to Sydney.

The general opinion was that they would be off the coast of New South Wales in four to six weeks, weather willing. Mary couldn't wait to set her feet on dry land, be reunited with Francis and resume their life together as God, and Admiral Phillip, had intended.

Nineteen

Sydney Town

Great slabs of stone fringed the vast expanse of sparkling azure water, ringed with vegetation that ranged from scrubby, mean-looking bushes to soaring stands of bone-coloured trees with peeling bark. Lace-edged coves and bays dotted the craggy shoreline and search as she did, Mary couldn't see a single dwelling or any sign of humanity. It was as though they'd arrived in an uninhabited paradise.

The ship's cannon boomed, signalling their arrival at Port Jackson. According to Mr Bent it would alert the pilot boat who would guide them through the channel to Sydney Cove. Mary leant over the taffrail, the heaving waves turning her stomach, but she forced down a surge of nausea and lifted her gaze in search of the horizon. To no avail. The treelined hills surrounding the shore and the sweeping cliffs were as disorientating as the slapping of the water against the hull.

'Are we in the right place?' Unable to mask the quiver in her voice, Mary turned to Mr Bent. 'It's deserted.' Perhaps in the time they'd been aboard ship the savages had attacked the settlement and burnt all trace of … what ridiculous nonsense. She'd been listening to Hannah's gossip.

'I have it on very good authority that the country is far from deserted.' He pointed to a signal flag fluttering in the breeze atop one of the towering cliffs. 'Fear not, I'm sure we will see signs of life soon. The pilot boat will come out to meet us.'

As the words left his lips the wind changed direction and the crew raced to furl the sails. Moments later the pilot drew along-side and led them past another towering cliff face adorned with six cannons, past a white-crested, treacherous-looking reef and down towards Sydney Cove. Mary's shoulders sagged and her pent-up fears subsided as a bustling harbour appeared, crowded with trading ships, masted schooners, whalers and what looked remarkably like canoes, frail craft made from nothing but bark and held together with twine.

'Matters are moving along apace, I see.' Mr Bent pointed his finger this way and that. 'There we have the new hospital, and that squat little building is the church of St Philip, and there what appears to be the beginning of the new military barracks and another wharf.'

How Mr Bent could speak with such authority about a place he'd never visited she had no idea. She could only presume that he had the intelligence from his brother who, he'd told her over an evening meal, had been in the colony for some time.

'On the right is the two-storey Government House amid the trees, with the governor's wharf jutting into the cove. On the sky-line beyond are the long dormitory blocks of the soldiers' barracks where York Street runs. Further to the right, can you see the pair of lofty windmills crowning the ridge line? So much progress has been made.'

Mary let Mr Bent's words wash over her. She'd find out soon enough. The air brought with it the taint of smoke, something vaguely antiseptic and beneath that the distinct reek of odours less savoury, a reminder of the slaughterhouses behind Bristol's docks. Shelters clung like limpets to the steep hill and below a cluster of buildings ringed the shore where several wharves stuck like fingers into the water.

With much bellowing the great anchor chain rattled its way through the bow. Unsettled and vaguely sick, her heart pounded. Nothing was as she'd imagined. How would she find Francis? The only sounds were the creaking of the ship's timbers, the slap of the waves against the hull and the strange calls of the seabirds. 'Why aren't we going ashore?'

'Because our arrival hasn't been acknowledged.' Mr Bent puffed out his scrawny chest. 'There will be a thirteen-gun salute from Dawes Point.' He waved his hand in a wide arc. 'As befitting a ship carrying such important personages as myself.'

Drawing in a deep breath, and beating back a curl of annoyance, Mary peered out across the water at the windmills on the hills turning lazily in the breeze. But for Mr Bent and his insistence that his arrival should be heralded by a thirteen-gun salute they would have disembarked hours ago, not remained tethered like some recalcitrant animals offshore.

A wherry, much like those that provided services across the Avon, cut through the waves. Two burly men, arm muscles rippling, heaved the oars in remarkable unison. A man dressed in a smart naval uniform sat in the centre of the boat, another at the stern had one arm loosely wrapped around the mast, his bright green coat a beacon … wait—his bright green coat?

Her heart lurched and she wiped the spray from her eyes. 'Francis!' The wind whipped her joyous cry away as she leant further over the taffrail, her feet skimming the deck. Russet hair, longer than she remembered, was swept back from his brow by the wind.

All thoughts of decorum flew away as she cupped her hands to her mouth and screamed his name again, her heart swelling. 'Francis!' Fifteen months since she'd last seen him … Her heart thrummed. The Francis she knew and loved had survived the voyage, and by the erect posture, the determined confident tilt of his head, he'd more than survived—he looked like the man she'd first met.

In the darkest hours of the journey, she'd feared she'd arrive to find Francis manacled, in chains, with ragged clothes, hollowed stomach and jutting ribs. Instead he stood tall and upright, dressed as always and looking, if anything, healthier and more animated than the last time she'd seen him in Newgate. 'Francis! Francis Greenway!'

In a moment of serendipitous fortune, the breeze abated and in the sudden silence her voice carried across the water. He turned his head and their eyes locked. His right fist rose to his chest, covering his heart, while he waved his other hand above his head, a broad smile lighting his handsome face.

Unable to control herself, she leapt up and down, hands waving high above her head.

'It would appear you have located Mr Greenway.' Mr Bent's voice, laced with humour, bought her to her senses.

She dropped her hands and tightened her shawl around her shoulders in a vain attempt to restore some form of dignity.

'Yes, yes, I have.' She might have managed to bring her enthusiasm under control but even to her own ears her sense of excitement was as plain as the nose on her face. 'I had expected to find him in irons.' Mary gave voice to her greatest fears.

'Not at all. Only for the gravest of misdemeanours, or second offenders. Someone skilled, like Mr Greenway, would have had his irons removed the moment he set foot on dry land.'

'But how would he survive?'

'By his wits, and from the look of it he has managed to arrive with those intact. He will have been left to provide himself with lodgings and every morning at dawn when the bell rings, report for work. A weekly ration of meat and flour is provided. But I'll leave it for him to tell you all. They'll bring the wherry around to port. Hopefully they are carrying an answer to my note to Macquarie. Perhaps Mr Greenway is the bearer of good tidings. This lack of respect is deplorable. I have no intention of disembarking until we receive a respectable welcome.'

Mary couldn't give a toss for any thirteen-gun salute, or any other number of guns, for that matter. She wanted to feel Francis's arms around her, hear his soft honeyed laugh, rest her head on his shoulder and know that after all this time she could heal the cruel blow of fate her actions had inflicted upon him.

'Mr Bent, Mrs Greenway.' Captain Pitcher snapped a smart salute in their direction and made for the taffrail where two of the crew were lowering a rope ladder to the cutter.

'A response from Macquarie, no doubt.' Mr Bent rubbed his hands together, a satisfied smirk playing across his sharp features. 'We should be suitably greeted and ashore within a matter of ...'

Before he could finish his sentence, a tousled head appeared, and Francis scrambled aboard. Ignoring Captain Pitcher, he reached for her arm. 'Mary ...'

She buckled into his embrace, inhaled his comforting, if sweaty, presence and spoke over his shoulder. 'Mr Bent, Captain Pitcher, may I introduce my husband, Mr Francis Greenway ...'

'Not now, Mary, show me the way to your cabin.' The grasp on her elbow tightened and he spun her around. 'Which way?'

'Francis, please. Mr Bent has been so very kind to me and the children on the voyage ...'

'Where is your cabin?' A fierce glow lit his eyes, determination or ... a shudder traced her skin ... a hint of mania? Who knew what the voyage and five months in this hellhole could have done to him. 'I feared I'd find you manacled,' she said.

'Only those who reoffend are manacled.'

And since Francis hadn't offended, not even once, he certainly deserved to be at liberty. She relaxed her stance to lead him across the deck. 'Down here.' Regretfully she loosened his grasp. 'The children will be delighted to see you, and you've yet to meet Francis, little Frankie. They have been so very good on the voyage and on Mr Bent's advice I have employed a maid. She's a delightful …'

'Not now. I need my papers, my portfolio. You have brought them, haven't you? I was enraged when they refused to let me take them to the hulks but in retrospect it was for the best—conditions were appalling below decks. I've been on tenterhooks since the pilot posted the passenger manifest and I knew for certain you were aboard. We must hurry. I cannot miss the return trip to shore.'

Mary threw open the door to the cabin. George and William lifted their heads from their game of cards, their mouths agape.

'Papa!' George was the first to recover. 'Papa!' He launched himself at Francis.

He finally took notice of George and William and then his eyes lit on the baby in Hannah's arms. 'And who is this?'

Mary swallowed. 'This is Francis John, your son. He was born in December, after you left.' For a moment her stomach fell. She had no idea how he would react. He scooped baby Frankie from Hannah's arms and held him high above his head. 'What a fine boy. My son. Very good, very good. Come. We've no time to waste. My papers.'

Mary clamped her teeth and shot a look at Hannah, and caught her wide-eyed, halfway to a curtsy. The poor girl, stunned no doubt by Francis's determined manner, snatched Frankie back.

'George, William, go to Hannah. I must find your father's papers.' Find wasn't exactly the right word because she knew exactly where they were and had spent the voyage committing everything to memory.

'My portfolio. That is what I need. Macquarie has no idea of architectural design. He has me copying a plan that has absolutely no claim to classical proportions or character. I must show him my earlier works—Carmarthen, Thornbury Castle and Clifton. Come along, come along. There is no time to waste. I can't have the wherry leaving without me.'

'I have them all here.' Mary tried for a placating tone; she had been quite correct about the glint of mania in his eyes.

'Macquarie's asked for samples of my work. I will have to write a letter to accompany my designs.' A staged sigh slipped between his lips and in that moment she understood. He wouldn't ask for assistance, of that she was certain, but if she offered …

'Perhaps we could do that now.' She reached for her nib pen and unscrewed the inkpot. 'Hannah, would you take the children up onto the deck for some air. If Mr Bent is to be believed the pilot will soon be guiding us to our mooring. He is anticipating an official salute to acknowledge his arrival. The boys will enjoy that.'

As the door of the cabin closed Francis's shoulders drooped, his bumptious demeanour evaporating as a heavy silence enveloped the cabin.

Mary stretched out her arms. 'Come.'

'Oh, my dear, my dearest dear.' He collapsed against her. 'How I have missed you. When I received your letter telling me you wouldn't be aboard the *General Hewett* I thought my world had ended. I've been a ship without a mooring floundering in a towering sea, my shrivelled heart barely able to pump the blood around my body. Now you are here, and we have a fine son.' He clasped her tight, so tight she could feel the beat of his heart echoing against her own.

Her lips curled into a smile. Her Francis. His fierce ambition and impulsiveness honed, not diminished, by his ordeal. He had so very much to offer the world. 'I am here now. We've been given an opportunity, a new beginning. Let's make the most of it. Now tell me what has happened with Governor Macquarie, and we will write this letter.'

Francis sat at the desk, his long legs stretched out and his arms folded, in a familiar pose. 'Macquarie is aware of your arrival. I will write and ask him for permission for you to come ashore at the earliest possible moment, although it will have to be after that wizened little fellow Bent.'

Ah, Mr Bent and his salute. 'That is wonderful, and have you spoken about the governor's plans for the town?'

Francis let out a long sigh. 'He is a procrastinator. He has required verbal reports on minor matters, but no role or official position has been forthcoming.'

Which she wouldn't have expected. Everything Mr Bent had told her led her to believe convicted prisoners were required to work for the government in exchange for rations and clothing. Francis certainly hadn't accepted the clothing. He looked as always, well dressed, although his cravat was a little less than pristine and a bath wouldn't go amiss.

'He hasn't asked to see any of my plans. Simply made some ludicrous request that I should copy a design he has in mind for a courthouse.' He gave a derogatory sniff. 'I couldn't do it. I have already written to him and told him that the building is totally unsuitable. A courthouse for goodness sake—with no claim to classical proportions or character.'

Mary bit her lip. Had Francis no understanding of his position? A convicted prisoner disagreeing with the king's representative—the governor of New South Wales. She swallowed a stern retort and rested her hand on his shoulder. 'I am certain that once he sees your portfolio ...'

'Indeed. I must show him my work immediately.'

Not spend time with his wife and firstborn son after an absence of so many months. She pushed the irksome thought away. 'I also have something else I believe might sway the governor.' She untied her folio and pulled out the letter of recommendation. 'I think you'll be very happy to see this.' She unrolled the letter and handed it to Francis. 'Read it.'

'I require my portfolio, not some letter from England.'

'It is a letter of recommendation from Admiral Phillip.'

Francis snatched the paper from her hand. His eyes scanned the page, the corner of his mouth twisting, then a frown crossed his forehead, and he lifted his gaze to her. 'How did you come by it?' His head snapped up and his hazel eyes locked with hers. 'Not another forgery, I hope.'

'Miss Bingle gave it to me. I believe the governor would be most interested.' She batted down the flush rising to her neck. 'It states you are an architect of some eminence and recommends your services to Governor Macquarie.'

Francis gave a somewhat derogatory sniff and stuffed the letter into his breast pocket before stretching out his hand for his portfolio.

With a grunt of satisfaction, he took out his earlier works. 'I must write a note to Macquarie to accompany my designs. We have no time to waste.'

Her heart lifted. Perhaps with some gentle nudging she could encourage Francis to remedy his arrogant stance on the courthouse. 'Would you like me to act as scribe?' She held up the nib pen.

He pushed aside her hand. 'No, I would not. This must come from me.'

But perhaps a little female intervention would spread oil on the seemingly already troubled waters of Francis's relationship with the governor. As Mr Bent had pointed out, life without the governor's patronage would be impossible. She doubted the promissory note she had received from Miss Bingle and the money for the household furnishings Mudd had pressed on her would cover more than a few months' living expenses. The children had to have a roof over their head; as free settlers they wouldn't even have convict rations to fall back on. Mr Bent had made it only too clear that life in Sydney Town was expensive, a fact she had no doubt was accurate given his brother's experience in the colony. She drew in a deep breath. 'Perhaps this is the perfect opportunity to apologise to the governor for your impetuosity.'

'Impetuosity? What impetuosity?'

'About the courthouse. If you include a copy of the courthouse design along with the other plans in your portfolio, I have no doubt he will understand your initial reaction.' One could only hope. Why hadn't she enquired of Miss Bingle some intelligence as to the governor's character?

'Since you seem to have acquired such an understanding of diplomacy what do you suggest I write?'

Mary cleared her throat. 'Perhaps first tell him you will make copies of the courthouse design as he requested and beg his forgiveness for any offence you may have caused?'

The nib scratched across the paper and after an interminable wait Francis lifted his head and slid the paper towards her. Her gaze scanned his words, and she tamped down the beginning of a smile threatening to lift her lips.

I will according to the request of your Excellency make a copy of the Design of the Court House. And I sincerely lament that I should

have written any thing to give offence. I most solemnly declare that
I had no such intention but quite the contrary. I hope & trust there-
fore that you will not consider it in any way to have been intended
as in so doing you will add another injury which I feel conscious I
do not deserve.

She knew Francis too well, could see his sarcasm shining through, but hopefully, after only one meeting, the governor would give him the benefit of the doubt. 'I think that is perfect. Now perhaps you could request that the children and I go ashore. After all ...' she lifted her hand to her forehead; it was a game she could play as well as Francis, '... we have had a terrible voyage and but for the assistance of Mr Bent I doubt we would have survived.' Quite the perfect time to sing the praises of the first judge of the Supreme Court of New South Wales. If she had learnt only one lesson in the past two years, she knew patronage was important.

Francis let out an exasperated breath and drew the page towards him and began writing. A hardness, a glint of determination she hadn't seen before, flickered in his eyes. Hopefully, she hadn't gone too far. She cranked her neck and read over his shoulder as the words poured from his pen.

I now humbly beg your Excellency will grant an order for my
wife & three children to come on shore. Her health requires it as
she has preserved on a long and dreadful voyage only through
the humanity of Mr Bent, I ask this favour for merit & virtue
in distress which will be sufficient to claim the attention of your
Excellency.

... and if your Excellency will grant me the power as an
architect, to design and conduct any public building or work, I
will exert myself in every way to do your Excellency credit as a
promoter and encourager of the most useful art to society, which

will add to the comforts of the colony, as well as the dignity of
the Mother country …

Francis pushed back the chair and glowered at her. 'Satisfied?'

'Perfect.' Mary clasped her hands together tightly. 'Just a vale-diction. Your Excellency's most obedient and humble servant, perhaps? Macquarie is, after all, the king's representative.'

He didn't bother to sit again but scrawled the words and his signature and, not waiting for the ink to dry, folded the sheet of paper, and tucked it inside the designs he had removed from the portfolio. 'I must go immediately. I will find you the moment you are permitted to disembark.' Without another word he ducked his head and disappeared from the cabin.

Twenty

Finally on Friday 29 July, after a 156-day voyage, Mr Bent's thirteen-gun salute boomed out across the water from Dawes Point. A Captain Piper, the apparently recently appointed naval captain, tall and dark, resplendent in a brilliant uniform, arrived and escorted Mr Bent ashore for a much-anticipated meeting with his brother. Lesser mortals had to wait to be ferried ashore by a succession of wherries, which required another unpleasant ride in the bosun's chair with baby Frankie clasped tight to Mary's chest and Hannah and the boys clamouring behind.

The quay swarmed with people of all shapes and sizes, mostly men in a ragged assortment of clothes. A cacophony of shouts and yells followed orders, responses and unfathomable discussions about moorings as the tide of humanity surged. There were no streets, simply muddy walkways strewn with rubbish and stinking to high heaven. For a fleeting moment Mary's heart twisted— it was a far cry from the gentle peace of Bath and not for the first time she wished James to a fiery hell for squandering her inheritance.

Clasping Frankie tight, Mary clambered onto the wharf while Hannah wrangled the two boys. George and William could barely contain their excitement and bounced around like India-rubber balls. Quite how she would have managed without Hannah she had no idea; she was so grateful that Mr Bent had talked the surgeon into allowing her to accompany them on the condition she reported to the authorities as soon as they were settled and that Hannah would be assigned to her. It was the least she could do to repay the girl for her hard work and kindness during the voyage.

After so many months at sea the ground beneath her seemed anything but solid and she swayed and stumbled, clutching for Hannah's arm, terrified she'd drop Frankie. She was thousands of miles from home with nothing but a leering, jeering crowd, and piles of crates, boxes and barrel-laden barrows. Oh! Where was Francis? She straightened her shoulders and drew in a deep breath of malodorous air.

Keeping the children under control and not losing sight of them in the swarming masses while they waited for her trunk and sea chest to be deposited on the wharf rivalled her worst nightmares. Then an almighty crash rocked the wharf, followed by another and another. The boys clung onto her skirts and the baby set up a mournful yowl. 'What was that?'

'Just the deck hatches, that means the women will be out soon.' Hannah hitched her single bundle onto her shoulder.

'Mrs Greenway, can I assist?' Mr Bent's welcome voice soothed her rising sense of panic. 'The salute from Dawes Point was most rewarding. Perhaps we can arrange a barrow. Mr Greenway has presumably organised accommodation for you.'

She had no idea whether he had or not. No idea where they would be staying; in some convict barracks somewhere? Nothing made sense. All these swarming people couldn't be free settlers, some of them had to be convicts. Where were the men shackled in chains and the irate overseers? 'Francis said he would meet me when we disembarked.' He couldn't have missed their landing. The noise of Mr Bent's salute had rocked the whole settlement and the smell of gunpowder still hung in the air. 'I'll wait here. Thank you for your concern and your assistance during the voyage.' She tried for a smile but suspected it was more of a fearful grimace.

'It was my pleasure, Mrs Greenway. I hope to see you and your lovely boys soon.' He snapped his fingers at the barrow boy, lifted his hand and resumed his conversation with Captain Piper as they disappeared into the crowd.

William yanked on her hand, struggling to free himself, as George slid between a well-dressed pair walking arm in arm.

She transferred the baby to her other hip and William's sweaty hand slipped from hers. She scanned the crowd yet again, almost choking on the rank stench from a cavalcade of convict women from the ship flouncing along the wharf. 'Stay close, boys. I don't want to lose you. Can you see your papa?'

In answer to her question George tugged her hand and pointed.

Francis, head bent, pencil in hand, ambled along, stopping every few steps to jot something down. She could guess what. By tomorrow there would be a drawing, tall warehouses and even a marketplace, something that resembled the market hall he had designed in Carmarthen. A smile played on her lips and she pushed back her bonnet to let the sun onto her face, basking in its benign warmth. There must be a mistake—it couldn't be winter.

'Welcome, welcome!' Francis greeted her. 'Come, I have no time to waste. I have an appointment.'

He couldn't expect her and the children to go to an appointment. 'Francis, you must take me to our accommodation. The children need to be settled and we have the trunk and chest.' She gestured to the barrow boy kicking his heels, and no doubt adding up the moments that would turn into payment. 'You remember Hannah, don't you? She's been a great help to me. Mr Bent says it might be possible for her to be assigned but she must ...'

'One thing at a time, my dear. We have been allocated a small house. Just down here. An excellent spot. Right in the middle of the business district, not a stone's throw from Mr Campbell's warehouses, cheek by jowl with some of the more affluent merchants. Come along!'

The boys paid no attention to their father. They had ground to a halt, faces bright red, and despite Hannah's entreaties they refused to budge.

'I'm too tired!' George wiped his grubby hands over his filthy face.

William pinched his nose and made a particularly disgusting vomiting sound. 'And it stinks.'

Whatever would Francis think? That she'd allowed them to turn into ill-mannered monsters?

Francis gave a bark of laughter and shepherded them along the rutted mud track. 'Wait until the summer. When I disembarked in February, the heat and the humidity was more than I could bear and then the weather broke and a thunderstorm struck, the likes of which you've never seen. Not a month after my arrival we suffered a violent dust storm. It smashed every window in the town including those in Government House. The weather is the most ferocious you will ever see.'

Mary doubted that after their trip to Corunna. Nothing could be worse than those first two weeks when she'd been convinced she and the boys were bound for a watery grave.

'One moment the skies are the brightest blue and then dark as night with the loudest thunderclaps and lightning splitting the sky.' Francis waved his hands around, spreading his arms as though to encompass the entire town.

'I thought the sun always shone.' That's what Miss Bingle had told her.

'Fear not, the climate is generally clement, and we will have a garden plot and I'm sure you will be able to coax some vegetables to grow. It is far easier than in England, although we will have to keep out the scavengers—human and feral.'

Mary bit back a smile. The boys still weren't listening to a word Francis said, more intent on shuffling through the dirt on the side of the track. 'I had visions of you in chains, on a work gang under the lash.'

'As did I but almost as soon as I arrived Macquarie granted me a ticket-of-leave.'

'Ticket-of-leave?'

'It means I can seek my own employment, live and work as a private individual, even though I'm still a convicted felon. My movements are restricted, and I have to report regularly, then if I'm lucky I can apply for a conditional pardon.'

So, Mr Bent was correct and that was why Francis was able to roam around the town with no apparent restrictions. There was so much she had to learn, so much Francis had learnt in the five short months since he'd arrived.

'I am not assigned as others are. I am making use of my connections. I met two gentlemen on the voyage out. Harris has already employed me to design some alterations and additions to his house, Ultimo, on the southwest outskirts of the settlement, and then Captain Piper, another passenger on the *General Hewett* and our recently appointed naval captain, has plans for a house on a point overlooking the ocean. He has asked my advice.'

Mary swallowed the wave of nausea swirling as she inhaled the foul smell of the water and stared in despondency at the mudflats and the rows of dilapidated cottages.

She had to stop thinking of England. This would be their home for the next fourteen years—maybe forever. Would she ever get used to the stench? She covered her mouth with her hand and forced back a retch.

Francis eyed her with a sympathetic smile. 'You'll get used to the odours. The town was largely built on either side of a small watercourse—named the Tank Stream for its storage capacity, but in truth an open sewer. Come along, we have no time to waste.'

Like a band of raggle-taggle gypsies they wound their way along the bustling thoroughfare, skirting potholes and piles of animal droppings until Francis drew to a halt at a corner.

'Here we are. Eighty-four George Street.' He pushed open the gate and led the way up the path. 'It was originally used by the corporal's guard, and over there's the hospital.' He gestured across the track to a long low building, which looked more like a dilapidated row of tents than anything else, and a group of whitewashed buildings perched on a slight slope surrounded by a tumbledown picket fence. 'The other buildings are Wentworth's quarters, he's the surgeon general, then next door is Redfern's accommodation—he's the assistant surgeon. Interesting chap. Bit of a dubious past, apparently a convict mutineer but now sits at the governor's table. Made a name for himself on Norfolk Island, earned a pardon. He's been assistant surgeon for nigh on ten years.'

Mary's stomach plummeted as she surveyed the small, whitewashed cottage with a shingle roof that was to be their home. The open door swung on a single leather hinge revealing a large dirt-floored room that spanned the width of the building, with a fireplace. She swallowed her cry of despair.

Francis placed his hand on her shoulder. 'There are two more rooms at the back of the house. It's only for the time being, Macquarie has promised me Redfern's barrack.' He gestured to a double-storey building across the track from the cottage. 'He'll leave as soon as his quarters at the new hospital are finished, though from the look of the construction I doubt it'll stand more than a year or so. They call it the Rum Hospital.' He gave a bark of laughter. 'Only in the colony. Built in exchange for the licence, a three-year import grant, to sell rum. Still, Wentworth means well enough, though they say Redfern's the better doctor. Come.'

At the back of the cottage the remnants of an overgrown vegetable garden took up most of the space bisected by a narrow winding stone path to what had to be the privy.

'That'll need some work, a new one dug. I'm told it's the place to plant fruit trees. That building behind Redfern's house, that's the hospital laboratory. Redfern apparently had the intention to produce a cowpox vaccination, but I'm not sure if he had many takers. The building will make a decent stable and accommodation for the help once we're settled. Let's take a better look inside.'

Needles of bright sunlight pierced the gloomy space. Rough mortar, sandstone rubble walls, dust mites floating in the air. Rats, spiders and unrecognisable insects scuttled away from the light, and patches of damp blossomed on the walls. Francis threw open the timber shutters, revealing the four huge warehouses that dominated the foreshore and to Mary's right, if she craned her neck, a view of Sydney Cove.

'What do you think?'

Mary ran her tongue around her dry lips. The two smaller rooms at the back of the house could be used as bedrooms and perhaps they could curtain off a corner of the larger room for Hannah. It made the little house in Ashton look like a palace, never mind Manali. She drew in a breath and regretted it. Rodents and … She tilted her head towards the ceiling, hoping the air might be fresher. An ear-splitting scream rent the small space.

George crouched below the lintel pointing his finger to the corner of the room where a plate-sized spider hovered, its banded, hairy legs waving. The scream came again.

Hands clasped her and she flinched away, clutching baby Frankie so tight he bellowed.

'Mary! Stop. Stop screaming.'

She clamped her spare hand over her mouth—the scream had come from her, not the children.

'It's only a spider; I have it on good authority they are harmless.'

They couldn't live here; more importantly, the children couldn't. They had to find somewhere else. Her mind darted to the paltry collection of coins and notes in her purse and she moaned—what hope had she of keeping Miss Bingle's promissory note for emergencies? Life was an emergency.

Sensing her misery, Francis slipped his arm around her shoulders. 'It will be perfectly fine. Macquarie himself told me we will be housed in better conditions as soon as Redfern removes to his new quarters.'

His words floated somewhere above her as her gaze raked the three rooms. Not a skerrick of furniture. No beds, no chairs. Just a rickety table and a straw palliasse and thin blanket thrown into one corner of the larger room. Legs barely supporting her, she stumbled after Francis.

'It really is quite satisfactory. Nothing some furniture and a good clean won't cure.'

'Where have you been living?'

Telltale colour flooded his face, the price he paid for his auburn hair. 'Right here. I told you the governor himself has provided this accommodation for us.'

Mary narrowed her eyes. 'And before the governor provided this house?'

'Wherever I could lay my head. Convict quarters.'

'Prison barracks.'

He gave a snort of laughter. 'No, there are no prison barracks as yet.'

It hadn't been as easy as he'd implied. She reached for his arm and squeezed it, in thanks for sparing her the worst.

'Macquarie's a good man, with honest values and ideals. He intends to show the way and build a town worthy of its inhabitants. He believes the convicts will rise above their current station and flourish. We have a lot of work ahead of us.'

Mary bit back a smile. Francis's experiences hadn't dimmed his ardour and what's more he didn't see himself as a felon. She cast a glance around the larger of the three rooms. A misshapen kettle hung on a tripod over the remains of the fire, next to a sordid array of pannikins and metal plates. More pots would be required, and stools or benches for the table, which was the only piece of furniture.

'I promise, it will clean up well enough and we will secure additional furniture.'

'And how are we going to pay for it?' She couldn't see Miss Bingle's draft lasting very long.

'I told you, Macquarie has provided this accommodation. I have already acquired a commission from Harris, and Captain Piper has approached me about the mansion he intends to build.'

Two clients, well and good, but that was not going to see them establish themselves. 'Have you considered advertising your services?' Mary cocked her head to one side. What had Mr Bent said? That an increasing number of free settlers were looking to make their mark on the new colony. Perhaps she could approach him about a commission; he couldn't live with his brother forever.

'An advertisement, you say.' Francis rubbed his thumb and forefinger across the stubble on his chin, accentuating his grimy cravat and collar. She would have to ensure a woman's touch if he was to make his mark with the upper echelons of society.

The next few weeks passed in a flurry of buckets and brooms and unaccustomed experiences. More than once, Mary blessed Hannah for her common sense and apparent ability to understand or at least find out how to make the most of the situation. She had duly reported to the authorities and been assigned as Mr Bent had said she would be. Thanks to the governor's largess they each received a rug and a palliasse and a weekly allowance of seven pounds of salt pork, six pounds of wheaten flour, four pounds of maize flour and half a pound of sugar, tea and tobacco and soap from the stores so they managed well enough, but it was a far cry from the life they'd known in England.

Francis disappeared every morning before sunrise and rarely reappeared until nightfall. The boys revelled in their newfound freedom and baby Frankie learnt to love the wooden fruit crate Hannah had managed to acquire and repurpose as a cot.

The town's brash nature suited them all and Francis was a different man, keen and enthusiastic. After such a long time apart their marriage was new, and the world full of promise.

At night bright, unfamiliar stars twinkled in the ink black sky, and a warm breeze drifted through the open shutters. Mary rolled onto her back and laced her fingers behind her head. 'Francis.'

'Mmm.' He reached out and stroked her cheek.

'The time has come to place the advertisement we spoke of in the *Sydney Gazette* offering your services. Mr Harris and Captain Piper can't be the only people with money to spend on a new residence. Mr Bent said competition was fierce amongst the free settlers and military to be recognised as committed and entrenched.'

Francis rolled onto his side and propped his head on his hand. 'No doubt you have already thought of the wording for this advertisement.'

She smiled into the darkness. 'I have. *FH Greenway, 84 George Street, from a Practice of many years as an architect in some of the most extensive Concerns in England, public, speculative, and private and having been several years connected with one of the Improvers of Estates flatters himself that he may be of service to those Land Holders who may be aware of the present of as well as future Advantages of such Improvements in this Colony.*'

'What would I do without you? Write it down for me in the morning and I will see it placed, but right now we have other matters to attend to.' He enfolded her in his arms.

Twenty-One

The new year brought with it a flurry of warm humid weather and Francis's promised thunderstorms, but they did little to dampen his enthusiasm. He returned home after a summons to Government House, drenched to the skin and covered in mud but in remarkably good spirits.

'Macquarie is most impressed with my portfolio, and the letter of recommendation from our good friend and patron, Admiral Phillip. He's asked my advice on the Rum Hospital. I am to produce a report on the structure and he is now talking of a lighthouse. I suggested once again he might like to employ me as his public works architect.'

Mary slumped down on one of the upturned crates that served as a stool. Francis still appeared to have no sense of his position in the colony. 'Was that wise?'

'There's no one else in the colony who can do the job, certainly not design the buildings Macquarie envisages. I am rather taken with his vision. He believes emancipated and reformed convicts should fully participate in business and society and the colony can be transformed by a large public works program. I am the man for

210

the job.' He brushed his sopping wet hair back from his beaming face. 'I have no doubt further commissions will be forthcoming. It would appear I have his patronage.'

But as yet no official position. Mary bit her lip to prevent her words escaping. Was she being impatient?

The squawking and flurry of Hannah's panicked chickens interrupted Mary's thoughts and sent her through the door and into the garden. She still had no idea where Hannah had acquired the moth-eaten bunch of half-feathered fowl but after Hannah's admission to her original sentence for duck stealing, she didn't dare ask. No one in the colony questioned another's past; it was one of many unwritten rules she had already learnt.

As she ushered the chickens into their pen she came face to face with a scruffy young boy waving a letter. 'Thank you.' She took the missive without offering a tip and the boy thumped off. The familiar handwriting sent a trickle of apprehension down her spine. Ripping open the seal with shaking fingers, she ran to escape from the pelting rain.

The letter brought the news that Admiral Phillip had, less than a month after she'd left England, succumbed to his illness. It also brought the information that all record of Francis's trial had been destroyed. The slate wiped clean, just as Miss Bingle promised, and with it Mary's own tomfoolery. There was also a reminder that it was still essential Mary didn't divulge to anyone the degree of the admiral's involvement in Francis's trial.

She leant against the door jamb and exhaled a relieved breath.

Francis sat up a little straighter, his piercing hazel gaze riveted on her face. 'Is there something you haven't told me?' The corner of his mouth quirked in a half-smile.

Mary twisted the scrap of paper in her fingers while she debated whether to tell Francis or not. Not the fact that the admiral had died, but the full extent of his role in saving Francis from the gallows. 'I've received a letter. It's not all good news, I'm afraid, and it will be in the *Gazette* by tomorrow, I am sure. Your friend and patron, Arthur Phillip, passed away last August.'

'That's a shame. Though he lived to a reasonable age considering the toll his time here took. I would have liked to thank him for his recommendation. Who is the letter from? I didn't know you were on familiar terms with the family.'

'It's from Miss Bingle.'

'Ahhh!' Francis's long, drawn-out exhalation hovered in the air. 'Have you received regular correspondence from her?'

'No, not at all. I wrote to tell her the boys and I had arrived safely and we were reunited, but nothing since.'

'I should write to her. Thank her. After all, she was responsible for securing Phillip's letter of recommendation which must have held sway with Macquarie, and I'm sure she would like to know Macquarie has promised me an official appointment.'

Colour rushed to Mary's cheeks. Francis could not possibly write and thank Miss Bingle for the letter of recommendation; she might think Mary had revealed Phillip's involvement in Francis's trial and his reduced sentence. She fanned her face with the letter; she simply wanted the whole experience behind them, to get on with their new life. 'This humidity is dreadful. Why don't you give me the admiral's letter and your early plans? I'll keep them safe in my sea chest in case the governor wishes to refer to them again.' Mary clenched her fist, trying to restrain her impulse to snatch up Francis's portfolio.

'Does Miss Bingle have any other news? I haven't received any communication from Olive or John. They would most likely be interested to hear of our situation.' He shuffled through the papers in his portfolio and passed over his earlier plans and the admiral's letter.

Mary's heart rate settled. 'Miss Bingle has no additional news other than the usual Bath gossip which I'm sure wouldn't interest you. I'll write and thank her and tell of your commissions. Would you like me to write to your brothers?'

'Thank you, my dear. I intend to immerse myself in this structural report for Macquarie on the Rum Hospital. It is a shambles. There are no classical proportions to the columns and the shaft is set all wrong in the base. Sarah Howe and her husband, George, want plans for a two-storeyed premises in Charlotte Place and I also must meet with Harris again. I have an idea for a geometrical staircase of stone once we have recast the old house.' He interlaced his fingers and stretched out his arms above his head. 'My first private colonial commissions must catch everyone's eye.'

The first days of March brought relief from the scalding heat. Mary threw her shawl around her shoulders and tucked the ends into the belt she'd taken to wearing around her skirt, blessing Leah once again for her foresight. Slippers and a velvet pelisse were no good in Sydney Town. Sturdy boots and a serviceable skirt were what was needed to navigate the stinking refuse-ridden streets. She may be a free settler, but these clothes marked her as a convict. Whatever her status it was immaterial. She had Miss Bingle's promissory note burning a hole in her pocket and the remains of the money Mudd and Leah had pressed on her. As with all things, Miss Bingle had been proved correct: promissory notes, foreign coins, rum and barter were all an acceptable substitute for coin, despite Macquarie's innovative attempt to establish a local currency. The ingenuity of his plan made her laugh. He'd converted forty thousand Spanish dollars, sent out by the Colonial Office, into local coinage by having the centres stamped out, creating 'holey dollars' and 'dumps' but as with everything in the colony there simply wasn't enough to go around.

She elbowed her way in through the crowded marketplace, holding tightly to baby Frankie while William and George swung like pendulums from Hannah's hands.

'The free market's out the back; that's where they have all the interesting stuff. Do you want to have a look?'

Quite why she hadn't visited before she had no idea but since she'd received Miss Bingle's letter the weight of concern over their future had lifted and now that work had commenced on Harris's house, and Francis was due to receive a sizeable commission, she could at last think beyond their hand-to-mouth existence. 'Yes. Perhaps we can find some cheap pots and pans. Maybe even some beds. I'm sick of sleeping on the floor.'

Hannah led the way towards the back of the cavernous building and there, spilling out into the lanes, they found the free market. The place bulged with goods and chattels, fruit and vegetables from as far afield as Parramatta, Windsor and the rest of the Hawkesbury—not that she had any idea how far afield that might be, because she'd hardly set foot beyond George Street.

A blast of hot air brought her up short: wagons and drays parked in higgledy-piggledy profusion, men standing alongside, some even balancing on the seats throwing their arms around, shouting themselves hoarse, spruiking their wares, to the amusement of a couple of redcoats lounging against the back wall. She definitely needed iron bedsteads; it would be sheer luxury to sleep off the floor away from the rats, snakes and cockroaches that invaded the house despite Hannah's vigorous cleaning. Two for the boys, preferably another for her and Francis, and something for poor Hannah—she never complained but Mary knew she lived in fear of the snakes. They also needed some more seating and a small table for Francis to use as a desk, more pots and pans—it was impossible to cook a decent meal for the six of them with only the old camp oven and the kettle she'd discovered in the privy.

'Hannah, can you manage Frankie and the boys?' She stopped at a crammed dray and sneaked a look from beneath her straw hat at a tall, rangy young man perched above her, arguing with a girl with a large basket dangling from her arm.

'Sixpence'll see you clear.' The young man squatted down and held out his hand for the coins. The girl lowered her eyelashes and gave a pretty smile before handing over the money.

'See you next time.' He straightened up. 'And how can I help you, my lovely?'

'Take the boys over there, Hannah, against the wall.' She handed Frankie over and waited until they'd moved away then faced the hawker. 'I'm looking for some beds, a bench seat or some stools, a small table to use as a desk, buckets, brooms, pots and pans and ...' She threw her hands up in defeat.

'That'll set you back a pretty penny or four. Don't take credit like they do in there.' He tossed his head back towards the Commissariat Store. 'Makes no matter to me whether they're supplying your food and clothing—or not. This is the free market.'

'I can pay ...' Her hand stalled. No point in showing the man her money until she was sure he had what she needed, though from the look of the dray he had just about everything anyone could desire. 'Can you deliver the goods?'

'Can organise a barrow boy. Now show me what you can use, and we'll agree on a price.' He swung down from the dray and landed soft as a cat beside her.

Ten minutes later the pile alongside the dray had grown to enormous proportions. 'How much will that cost?'

'You're looking at around ten shillings I reckon.' He scratched at his chin and eyed her with a look that suggested he'd wasted his time.

'Ten shillings?'

'Got enough to furnish a mansion there.'

'I've got eight shillings. English shillings.' The remainder of the money Mudd had given her. How she wished they hadn't had to pay the wretched turnkey for Francis's belongings.

'Have you indeed.' He rubbed his hands together. 'Well, I reckon if we take this out …' he bent down and pulled out an enamel basin and one of the three buckets she'd chosen, '… I can do it for nine shillings—since it's English coin.' The corner of his mouth hitched as though he was having trouble controlling his smile.

Her face flamed. What a fool she was. She should have asked him the price of each item. The sooner she remembered thieves and swindlers populated the colony the sooner she'd get ahead. Sucking in a deep breath, she thumped her hands on her hips and glared at him. 'I bet you didn't charge the young girl those rates.'

'Susie? Yeah, but I know her. Works for Mr Lord. He's reputable.'

'And I'm not?'

'I don't know you. You look like a convict, emancipist at a push, but speak like an exclusive, and they don't come down here, they send their dogsbody. You want to be careful; there's no love lost between the two. Macquarie does his best but the free settlers reckon they've got a God-given right to rule the roost.'

'My husband …' She clamped her lips closed, didn't give him the opportunity to react. 'I've got sterling, shillings and pence. No holey dollars or dumps. I want all of it and the services of a barrow boy, and you can throw in that rag rug you've got over there. My money's as good as anyone's.'

'Show us the colour then.'

She licked her lips, wrenched the pouch from her waistband and emptied the coins, a scattering of shillings, pennies and farthings into her hand. 'That's all I've got.'

'Nope. That's not going to do it. Forget the rag rug, and those buckets.' He reached down and threw them back onto the dray.

Damn the man. How was she supposed to make a home without the necessities of life? Well, maybe the worn, faded rug wasn't a necessity, but it reminded her of the one in the kitchen at Manali. She eyed him warily. Could she trust him? Had she any choice? She slipped the folded note from the cuff of her blouse. 'It's a promissory note, drawn on the bank in Bath.'

'Is it indeed.' He tried to whisk it from her fingers, but she tightened her fist and snatched her hand back. He made no attempt to ask for the money, just peered at her this way and that. 'From the West Country, then?'

'I beg your pardon?'

'Just got here, from the West Country. Date on that's not twelve months yet.'

She thrust the promissory note back in her sleeve, suddenly concerned it would somehow reflect on Francis. What would happen if his wife was found flashing promissory notes around the free market?

The man pinned her with an intense gaze, and she saw what she hoped was honesty in the depths of his eyes, eyes that reflected the blue waters beyond the harbour. 'Give me the coin you have, and the goods are yours, but not the rug and I'm not touching the promissory note.' He narrowed his eyes and peered at her, making her cheeks flush. God, she felt guilty, as though she'd forged or stolen the wretched thing, and she'd done nothing. 'You want to take that to Mrs Reibey; she'll know if it's worth the paper it's written on.'

Was he implying it might not be? She wouldn't be foolish enough to indulge in another act of forgery. 'Mrs Reibey?'

'Mary Reibey, you'll find her at her new premises, 12 George Street. One of the richest traders in the colony. Runs the business since her husband died. Got a finger in more pies than I can count.'

Mrs Reibey. A woman, a trader! If she cashed the note the extra money would make all the difference to their life. New clothes for the children, a change in their diet, a new shirt and cravat for Francis, even another coat; she'd noticed his frayed cuffs only a day ago.

'Well, what do you want to do?' The hawker studied her, almost as though he could read her mind.

'What about the barrow boy?'

The man stuck two fingers in his mouth and let out a piercing whistle. Seconds later a half-starved urchin with a barrow almost bigger than he was appeared by his side.

'The lady wants this lot delivered.'

'Where to, miss?'

'The girl will show you.' She gestured to Hannah; Frankie was tucked into her shoulder and her other hand grappled with the two boys. 'Load it up.'

'Hannah, will you show the way and take the boys home. I have some business to attend to.'

'Oi! Not so fast, you haven't paid me yet.'

'Off you go.' She gave Hannah's back a push, then turned back to the blue-eyed hawker. If a woman could be a successful trader in this topsy-turvy place, then she would refine the art of bargaining. 'Right, let's get this sorted.'

With a smirk, and a tip of his chin, he grinned at her. 'How do I know to trust you, Miss …?'

Greenway hovered on the tip of her tongue, and she bit it back. Did she really want to admit to who she was? She hadn't done anything wrong, Miss Bingle had given her the note, but who would believe her? Any repercussions would come straight back to Francis. If he was blamed, he'd be accused in a flash, labelled a second offender, and carted off to Norfolk Island or sent to work the mines of Coal River, any one of the dreadful places of punishment Hannah kept going on about.

She tossed a quick look over her shoulder. Hannah and the barrow boy had disappeared through the stores, nowhere in sight. 'Mary ...' She looked across at the dray next to them, stacked high with fleeces, some bundled and marked for London from a Mr Macarthur in Parramatta, or so the stencilled letters said. 'Mary.' What were the sheep called? They'd spoken of them on the voyage out over the captain's table. 'Mary Merino. Thanks for your help. Are you here every week?'

'Not every week. You bought those things as is, there's no returns.' He stuck his hand out and she emptied the coins into his large palm.

That wasn't the reason she'd asked; it was more that she'd rather deal with the same hawker if his goods proved satisfactory. 'I might be needing other items for the house, and I want to plant some fruit trees and a vegetable garden. Where do you get your stock?'

'Here, there and everywhere. From Sydney to the far reaches of the Hawkesbury.' He rammed his hat down and climbed back into the dray. 'Always here in the same spot. I'll see what I can do.'

With a smile Mary patted the promissory note safely back inside her sleeve and fastened her shawl. She could do this. She could deal with these convicts and ticket-of-leave men with no difficulty at all. Now to find Mrs Reibey.

It was only when she got out into the fresh air and her thoughts cleared that she paused. Perhaps it wasn't such a good idea to go and see this Mrs Reibey immediately. She'd been foolish to show the promissory note to the hawker, even to take it with her. It was all she had left and although they wouldn't starve thanks to the government rations and the money Francis would earn from his private commissions, she might well have need of it. She plonked down and rested her back against a pile of sandstone waiting to be carted from the quarry.

By the time Mary returned home the light was fading and there was no sign of the barrow boy. Her purchases balanced precariously against the front wall of the house. She'd rather hoped he would help cart everything inside. 'Hannah! Tell George and William to come out here and give me a hand.' She pushed open the door. 'Oh my God! What is that smell?' Mary clasped her stomach and inhaled deeply. 'It's fish. Fish pie. Where did you get it?'

'Bloke down at the Three Squares gave me a fish on the way home.'

'Gave it to you?' Mary shot a look at the boys sitting at the table, their faces scrunched in concentration as they practised their letters, knowing full well there'd be no leaving the table until they'd completed their page. 'Boys, you can leave your work on the condition you go and bring in some of the things outside.' Not needing to be told twice, they vanished in a flurry of arms, legs and whoops of delight.

'Why would someone give you a fish?' Mary studied Hannah's flushed face, which had nothing to do with the heat from the fire. 'You promised ...' She let the words stall. The last thing she wanted was to have a conversation about Hannah's recreational time within the boys' earshot. George was already spending too much time down at the wharves and becoming far too worldly. 'I'm sorry, Hannah, you're doing your best. I know.'

'I didn't do nothing improper, just gave him a hand when we were passing. Me grandaddy used to have a trawler at Portsea, I know all about gutting fish. The bloke said he'd got some oysters and fish from the natives and I liked the sound of it so I gave him a hand.'

'Oysters too? I've been dreaming of oyster pie and roast pigeon.' Mary rubbed her hand over her belly.

'Oyster pie.' Hannah rolled her eyes, flopped down on the stool then shot back to her feet. 'We could have oyster pie if we were brave enough.'

Mary's stomach rumbled in appreciation. 'And how are we going to manage that?'

'We'll go and buy our own—from the natives.'

'We couldn't. It's too dangerous.'

'We won't be going anywhere near any men. It's the women that do the fishing. They're down at Farm Cove in their canoes, early in the morning. I reckon if we take the boys, talk woman to woman, they ain't going to do nothing to hurt a child.'

Mary inhaled. 'Oysters. What I wouldn't do for an oyster pie.' She sighed. 'I'll go and round up the boys and we'll bring the goods in, if you can settle Frankie. Francis will be home before long.'

The following morning Mary tripped into the kitchen. Hannah stood over the big black pot throwing in the usual mixture of faded root vegetables. 'I dreamt of oyster pie last night.'

Hannah's red face grinned at her through the steam. 'Then we'll go?' Without waiting for an answer, she untied the cloth she'd wrapped around her waist to protect her already splattered skirt. 'Come on, boys, leave your books. We're going for a walk.'

George and William didn't need to be told twice, and neither did Mary. Francis wouldn't be back until two o'clock at the earliest. 'I'll get Frankie and my bonnet.'

An hour later, having carefully skirted the stretch of shoreline where the military took their baths, they reached the edge of the sandy cove, where small waves lapped at their booted feet. Half a dozen bark canoes drifted on the calm waters and a low humming sound filled the air. 'Can you hear that, Hannah?'

'They're singing as they fish. And see the smoke? They have a little fire in the base of the canoe to cook their catch. Look over there.'

Mary followed Hannah's finger to the fringe of the cove where several women crouched, pulling oysters from the rocks, while a group of children leapt into the water, their lithe bodies sparkling in the sun. 'It seems strange to see so many women and children. It makes me realise that there are an awful lot of men in the colony, and very few women.'

'I want to swim.' William thumped down on the sand and stripped off his shoes and stockings. George followed suit.

'No swimming.' Not yet, not until she was convinced they wouldn't cause a problem by encroaching on the women's territory. 'Take your boots off and you can paddle in the shallows.'

The boys streaked off across the sand.

'What should we do, Hannah? Shall we just wait here and see what happens?'

'Won't have to wait long.' Hannah tipped her head in the direction of the rocks where a woman had hefted her open wooden trug onto her hip. With a quick glance over her shoulder at her friends she set out across the sand. 'Let's stay here. We're not doing nothing wrong, just watching the children, same as what they're doing.'

The humming sound increased as the woman drew closer, drifting in across the water. All the other women sat in their canoes or on the rocks, their eyes firmly fixed on the woman walking across the sand. She dropped to her heels and offered the trug, full to the brim with oysters, their shells still wet, glistening in the sun, the pristine scent of the salt and brine strong. She pushed them towards Mary, then with a flick of her wrist she prised one of the oysters open and offered it.

Mouth watering, Mary took the shell and tipped the oyster down her throat. The subtle fish flavour mixed with the fresh taste of the ocean filled her mouth and she swallowed it down with a gasp of pure pleasure. Better than the muddy offerings she'd eaten at home. 'Oh, we have to have some.' She reached out to the trug. 'May I buy some?' She gestured with her hand and felt in her pocket and remembered that she hadn't a single coin with her.

The woman barked out a laugh and shook her head, then offered the trug again.

She couldn't take the oysters, that wasn't what she'd intended.

'Leave it be.' Hannah gestured to the group of women who'd been harvesting the oysters from the rocks and now gathered in a semi-circle around them. 'I don't think this was a good idea.' Hannah shot to her feet and took off towards the water. 'Boys! Come back here.'

Mary struggled to her feet. She didn't sense any danger, just a feeling of goodwill. Women talking, sharing. Two other women stepped forward and dropped more oysters into the trug and pushed it into Mary's hands while another bent and chucked Frankie under the chin before they drifted off across the beach, back to the rocks.

The wonderful fresh smell filled Mary's nostrils.

'Come along, boys.' Hannah wrangled the boys up the beach, their annoyance clear in their grumbles. 'I don't think we should have done that. Now they're going to expect something in return if we come again.'

'I'll bring some coin next time.' She bent and picked Frankie up from his nest in the sand. 'Let's go home. Have we got enough flour to make some pastry? Francis loves oyster pie, he'll be thrilled.'

Mary rinsed out her mouth and spat into the bushes outside the privy. There was no doubt about it. Her body had never lied before so why should it now? She pulled back her hair, fastened it in a loose knot and made her way to the kitchen.

Hannah's smiling face greeted her despite the ruckus. 'Porridge it is, again. I'm sorry, but we haven't …'

Mary covered her mouth and swallowed down the threatening bile.

'Oh, you're not well. Come and sit down.' She pulled out the chair and Mary sank down thankfully. 'Hurry up now, boys. Give me your bowls; you've got a few minutes to play out in the yard and then it's time for your lessons. George, make sure William and Frankie wash their hands.' Hannah shooed the boys outside. 'Now what is it? Can't be the oyster pie because Mr Francis is already out and about no worse the wear and neither are the boys, or me for that matter … Oh.' Her hand came up to her mouth. 'You poor dear.'

Any thoughts Mary had of keeping her secret fled on that one 'oh'. She took the wet cloth Hannah handed her and wiped her face. 'It seems I am in a delicate situation.' A laugh bubbled up. 'It'll pass. It always does.' She'd suspected she was carrying and prayed every night it would be a girl. A confidante, a friend, someone to help her as she aged. 'Do you think you could see to George and William's lessons this morning. They've got a page of their copy book to do and a sheet of numbers. What I need is some fresh air and exercise.'

'No, you need to go and lie down. We don't want you straining yourself.'

'Believe me, Hannah, after three children I know how matters progress.'

Twenty-Two

'I am heartily tired of Macquarie and his philandering.'

Francis's outrageous statement brought a smile to Mary's lips. The esteemed governor was devoted to his beautiful wife. The strength of their commitment to each other was common knowledge. They could barely stand to be apart, and she even accompanied him on his journeys beyond Sydney Town, most recently to the Blue Mountains, and played an active role in all colonial matters. 'I'm sure Macquarie is not a philanderer.'

Francis chuckled. 'Perhaps not in the true sense of the word but it is time he stopped vacillating, gave some thought to my role. I do nothing but give him verbal reports. I'm no more than a surveyor or engineer, no pay, no salary, no remuneration of any kind.'

But a lot more freedom and responsibility than most ticket-of-leave men.

'It is time I approached Macquarie again; I shall write immediately and explain that I should be employed as his architect of public works.

'Perhaps.' Mary bit her lips, silencing the caution she wanted to offer. Francis could sometimes be such a bull in a china shop. 'If you had a plan for the town, showing necessary, anticipated public buildings and the like, he might be more inclined to consider the matter.'

'May I leave it with you? Something to keep you amused while you await the arrival of our bundle of joy.' Mary nodded. She was quite capable of drawing up a town plan, and she'd enjoy walking the streets and imagining the vista. Francis had discussed his thoughts with her on numerous occasions and it might smooth the waters. If he requested an audience with the governor, demanded a position, he could well lose it before it was offered. 'A letter with the suggestion for a town plan?' She injected as much innocence into her tone as she could muster.

'The letter must make it obvious I am the man for the job. Architect of public works is not a position to be taken lightly.'

A shriek echoed from the kitchen and George bolted through the open door into the front yard, hotly pursued by William. 'Boys!' Mary's gaze followed them as they barrelled down the path and came to a grinding halt at the gate and greeted a diminutive man stooping to open the gate.

'Is that Dr Redfern?'

Francis came to Mary's side and peered over her shoulder. 'Indeed, it is. Stay here. I'll deal with him.' He walked down the path to greet the doctor.

Redfern took little notice of Francis but approached Mary with a smile. 'Mrs Greenway.' He doffed his hat, revealing a head of thick grey hair. 'I believe you may be in need of my services.' His gaze settled on her expanding midriff without a moment's hesitation or embarrassment.

'Thank you, Dr Redfern, but I am well.' She interlaced her fingers and rested them on her belly. 'This will be my fourth child. I am prepared.' As she spoke Frankie's sticky hand tugged at her skirt. 'This is my youngest, Francis—Frankie. Those two tearaways you met at the gate are George and William.'

'Please don't hesitate to call on me if you have any concerns. I also came to apologise for my tardiness. It is ridiculous that you and your family are crammed in this tiny cottage. I will have my belongings removed to the hospital immediately and you can put these men of yours to good use and move into my quarters before your impending event. It's a much larger dwelling and there's the old laboratory out at the back which would give you more space if you require it. I'm afraid it'll need a bit of spit and polish.' He beamed at her, replaced his hat and ambled back down the path where he and Francis exchanged pleasantries, and then with a wave he disappeared around the corner into the swarming crowds in George Street.

'Well, that's a turn-up. Nice chap, Redfern. Counts amongst his patients some of Sydney Town's finest, the governor's wife included I'm led to believe, and is a frequent guest at Government House.' He rubbed his hands together as if relishing the fact that they might one day receive an invitation to dine with the governor.

'Redfern said he'll send some men to clear out his belongings and that the place will be ours tomorrow. It will be a delight to have more space. The entire interlude has inspired me. I'll go and put pen to paper and tell Macquarie of my plans for the lighthouse. Matters are looking up.'

Francis's prediction proved accurate and everything proceeded without a problem. Their new quarters on the south-western corner of George and Argyle Streets were a sheer delight after the cramped confines of the cottage. With a shingle roof and thick whitewashed walls, the house was warm in winter and cool in summer. Francis insisted on describing it as a barrack but Mary didn't care. There were sufficient rooms for the children and Hannah to have their own space in the attic, and she and Francis had a bedroom downstairs. There was a room for Francis to use as his office and a separate sitting room with a cosy fire for winter.

A covered walkway led to a kitchen and beyond that was a privy and an expansive, fenced garden. Plenty of room for Hannah's chickens, fruit trees and as many vegetables as they could tend, including wild parsley, celery and spinach, which had formed an important part of the settlers' early diet and still grew in abundance.

The move in March also heralded the arrival of their first daughter, named Caroline—not Mary, as Francis suggested. Mary insisted upon Caroline, meaning 'free woman'; it personified their new life and their hopes for the future. Her daughter would grow up knowing none of the restrictions of the old country. She would flourish in a land where women could own and run their own businesses, marry or not, dictate their own future, and become whoever or whatever they wished regardless of their heritage.

Three weeks later Mary sat in the garden, Caroline at her feet kicking her legs in the afternoon sun, idly turning the pages of the *Sydney Gazette*. 'Hannah, has Mr Greenway returned?'

'Still out and about.' Hannah leant against the door, cloth in hand. 'Is something wrong?'

'No. No, not wrong. Francis's appointment has been gazetted—acting civil architect and assistant engineer. He didn't tell me.'

'I expect he'll be home soon. I'll go and round up the boys. Food's on the kitchen table.'

Francis must have known yet he'd said nothing, except that he had to meet with the governor that afternoon. Mary scooped Caroline into her arms and bent to retrieve the newspaper.

'Ah! You've seen the *Gazette*.' Francis strode down the path towards her, then reached out and took Caroline and jiggled her up and down, blowing raspberries.

'Have you seen the governor?'

'I have. Good news and not so good, as always. Come inside and I'll tell you; it affects Hannah too.'

Francis sat at his place at the head of the table, with the boys and Hannah down either side and Mary perched at the other end. It was such a pleasure to have more room, although they still spent most of their time in the kitchen because Francis had taken over what might have been the dining room as his office.

Francis cleared his throat and folded his arms, chin tilted up in his usual fashion. 'I have just seen the governor and it is now official. I have been appointed to the position of acting civil architect and assistant engineer.'

George, William and Frankie dutifully clapped.

'And the bad news: I will be supervised by Captain Gill.' He gave a derogatory sniff. 'He wears the dubious title of principal engineer. Time will tell.' Then he brightened again. 'Not only that, I am to receive three shillings a day, paid quarterly, the use of a government horse and reimbursement for my travelling expenses while on government business.'

At long last, not only recognition but also some security. Dr Redfern had kindly left them some of his old furniture, but they still needed more, and if she could secure some fruit trees, seeds for the garden and more chickens … Her thoughts drifted for a moment. It was time to cash Miss Bingle's promissory note.

'Not only will our rations continue, the governor has confirmed Hannah's position and our right to reside in this glorious abode.' He swept his hand around the kitchen then wove his fingers together, arched his arms above his head and made a pillow of his hands. 'I venture to suggest that our ship has finally docked. Now I have the opportunity to make a mark on this colony.'

Mary shot to her feet. 'My dear, it is wonderful, all your hard work has paid off. Civil architect and assistant engineer. You are a man of vision, with rare imagination and the ability to transform the mundane into dreams. The governor doesn't know how lucky he is.'

He drew her into his shoulder. 'I'm not sure we will become rich on the proceeds, but the situation is looking up.'

'You are on your way to regaining your rightful position.' One he'd proved time and again he was more than capable of fulfilling.

'I shall also discuss a percentage payment with Macquarie, on completion of the buildings.'

Francis might as well have dumped a bucket of cold water on her head. He couldn't imagine he'd be able to negotiate the position. Could he? She doubted it, considering his status as a convict, something he seemed to constantly forget.

'Now, I have work to do. I need to let Sanderson know about his Masonic aprons.'

'Sanderson?'

'Captain Sanderson of the 46th. A friend of Piper's, I believe. He's asked me to decorate and gild a collection of seven aprons.'

'Aprons?' This was becoming more ludicrous by the moment.

'The foundation stone for Piper's Henrietta Villa is to be laid with full Masonic rites and Sanderson is the Worshipful Master and thus in charge of the ceremony. He's left me very little time and watercolour paint is simply not going to hold in this hot country without varnish. Not only that, I've promised Harris his plans for the footings, and the labourers have close to nothing between their ears. William could make a better job of it. As you said I need a town plan. Macquarie has requested a map of the streets and the intended buildings. How is it coming along?'

'I've made a start.' With the new baby, three young boys to see to, the move and the constant scrimping and scrounging to make the best out of their rations, she and Hannah were run off their feet. 'I'll attend to it tonight after the children are asleep.'

'I think that's all we can do now, Hannah.' Mary pushed back her straw hat, wiped her hands down her skirts and grimaced. The clothing issued by the government stores was far sturdier than anything she'd brought with her. She'd never wear any of the English dresses still folded in the trunk absorbing the fading scent of the English lavender Leah had scattered over them before she'd left. As each day passed, she looked more and more like one of the inhabitants residing in Sydney Town at the government's pleasure. 'George, William, Frankie, brush off your hands and go with Hannah. It's time you had something to eat.' She bent over and dropped a kiss on little Caroline's cheek. She was such a perfect baby. All sunshine and smiles and already sleeping through the night.

'Hannah, if you can see to the boys I'll go and wash up. I've got to go to the stores and pick up our rations, and I'll see what I can find in the way of vegetables.' And while she was out she'd pay a visit to Mrs Reibey and get Miss Bingle's promissory note cashed; Francis still hadn't been paid. 'I saw the Parramatta drays come in this morning. Now we've cleared the new plot I'll see if I can find some fruit trees and vegetables. Give them a good start before the worst of winter is upon us.' Her mouth filled with saliva at the thought of a fresh juicy peach or apricot. Rumour had it they'd grow if she could keep the water up to them, and then they could preserve the fruit to eat during the colder months.

Mary hurried along George Street, basket tucked over her arm, past a ragged group of newly arrived pale-faced convicts, eyes wide and looks of confusion on their faces as the solid ground wavered under their feet after the constant motion of the ship. Bypassing the Commissariat Store, she continued on towards the Tank Stream looking for Mrs Reibey's warehouse. Number twelve, the hawker had said. It couldn't be that difficult to find.

She came to a halt in front of a solid two-storey building, the rear almost hanging out over the water and a verandah fronting the street, the name *Entally House—Reibey's Warehouse* emblazoned above the doors.

She pushed open the panelled door and approached a young man, head buried in a ledger, seated at a desk. 'I'd like to speak to Mrs Reibey.'

He raised his eyebrows. 'And you are?'

'My name's Greenway, Mary Greenway.' No Mary Merino here; his canny gaze would pick her lie in a moment. 'I have an English promissory note which I would like to exchange.'

He scrambled to his feet. 'I'll see if Mrs Reibey is available.'

Mary wandered around the high-ceilinged room, the walls lined with paintings of trading ships, the name of each engraved on a brass plate attached to the frame.

By the time the young man returned she'd made a full circuit of the room and waited at the door, peering out into the bustling activity of George Street. 'Mrs Reibey will see you now. Follow me.' He led the way up a flight of stairs, knocked on the first door he came to and opened it without waiting for a reply. 'Mrs Greenway, ma'am.'

'Come and sit down.' A plump-faced woman, with a pair of pince-nez balanced precariously on the bridge of her nose, gestured to the chair across the desk.

'So, Mrs Greenway. Your husband is the architect, I presume. I've heard a fair bit about him. Governor Macquarie seems to think he's got a lot to offer the colony.'

That was encouraging but how would she know? Perhaps she dined at the governor's table—all well and good if you were a free settler with money behind you.

'The situation has changed a lot since I arrived and now we have to deal with the aspirations of the free settlers and the military, who like to see themselves as a cut above us mere mortals.'

Mary narrowed her eyes; was she saying what she thought? Had this woman, Mary Reibey, come out here as a convict? Surely not. She looked no more than forty, with her thick brown hair, shot with occasional strands of grey, pinned practically in a low chignon. How to ask the question? The hawker had said she was one of the richest traders in the country. Not that she was once a convict. Curiosity bubbled like a cauldron. She couldn't ask. It simply wasn't done. 'You've been in the colony for some time?'

A smile tweaked the corner of Mrs Reibey's lips. 'Indeed I have. I arrived in 1792 at the tender age of thirteen.'

'But how ...' Mary waved her hand around the office, at the sumptuous desk with its leather insert, the comfortable chairs, the bookshelves housing row upon row of bound ledgers, the paintings on the walls, trading ships, and through the window men swarming like ants unpacking the latest cargo.

'My husband died some years ago, leaving me with seven children and even more business interests. It seemed a shame to let all our hard work go to waste. Opportunities abound for a woman of education and talent, away from the uncompromising attitudes of England.' Mrs Reibey rested her elbows on the polished cedar and propped her chin on her interlaced fingers. 'Do you have a talent, Mrs Greenway?'

A flush heated Mary's cheeks. Hardly a talent, nothing that could be mentioned in the same breath as this woman's achievements. 'Not what I would call a talent but an interest in architecture, that I share with my husband.'

'Ah! You and Mrs Macquarie have something in common then.'

Mary couldn't imagine she'd ever be in a position to find out.

'She's a delightful person and very interested in the architectural development of the colony.' Mrs Reibey pushed back her chair, took a key from her pocket and placed it on the desk. 'Shall we conclude our transaction?'

Mary handed over the promissory note.

'Ten guineas, drawn on the High Street Bank, Bath. I can't see that would be a problem.' She held the paper up to the window and squinted at it through her pince-nez, twisting and turning it in the shaft of sunlight.

'Hopefully in the new year you will be able to take such notes directly to the Bank of New South Wales.' She gave a satisfied smile, which might possibly have been a smirk. 'Despite the refusal of the Colonial Office in London to provide funds, we've taken matters into our own hands and raised the money through public subscription. The premises will be in Macquarie Street.'

Having unlocked the top drawer of her desk, Mrs Reibey counted out a variety of coins and notes and slid them across the desk before standing and holding out her hand. 'It's been a pleasure to make your acquaintance, Mrs Greenway. If I can be of any further assistance, please don't hesitate to call on me.'

With a polite smile, Mary slipped the money into the reticule tucked in her basket and made her way out of the office, her mind whirling at the variety of characters who called the colony home.

A constant heckling and buffeting greeted Mary the moment she set foot inside the Commissariat Store, where she found a quiet corner to give herself a moment to recover her senses and plan her route—salted meat, pork and beef. She'd happily give away both in exchange for fresh meat, but it was harder to come by, so it would have to wait until another day.

Rations kept a body alive but there were no luxuries. Enough flour and maize to make a gritty loaf of bread a day and a pound of meat, usually salted, less if it was pork, a paltry amount of sugar and a quarter of a pound of tea.

She waited patiently in the queue, her gaze darting this way and that. Some mangy turnips, onions and cabbage on the stall to her right. A strange assortment of dresses, fit for the theatre or a whorehouse—something Leah would relish—tumbling out of a leather trunk, and leaning against the brick wall next to the doors was a dilapidated pair of leather chairs which with a bit of love and polish would be a delight. The money clinked tantalisingly in her reticule.

She took two steps and stopped as the woman behind her elbowed her aside, then she changed her mind. Food first, luxuries later. 'Excuse me.' Mary nudged her way back into the line, refusing to acknowledge the string of words that would have made a sailor blush.

She whipped around.

'Oi! Mary Merino. It's me, Bill.'

Her pounding heart settled. The blue-eyed Hawkesbury trader. The very man. Her shopping could wait.

'Bill. I was looking for you. I'm in need of seeds for my garden and some fruit trees. Have you still got that rag rug and those basins and bowls? Can you help me?'

'Can you pay?'

'Yes, I can,' she huffed, willing the colour in her cheeks to fade. 'I've just been to see Mrs Reibey.'

'In that case, come with me. My dray's out the back.'

Mary followed Bill through the throng and out behind the building where she'd first found him, her mind darting this way and that. If a thirteen-year-old girl could rise to the position of one of the colony's richest traders then the world was at Francis's feet. She gave a little skip and caught up with Bill. 'Did Mary Reibey come to the colony as a convict?'

He let out a huge belly laugh. 'Indeed she did, not any old convict either. A horse thief no less, dressed as a boy and calling herself James Borrow, to boot. They didn't get wise to it until the doctor examined her after she'd been convicted. Mind you she doesn't usually advertise the fact these days. You must have had quite a chat.'

'We did. She's a fascinating woman. She made me realise the opportunities women have right under our nose, if only we are brave enough to take them.'

'I reckon you're brave enough, Mary Merino. Come on, let's see what I've got for you.'

As before, Bill's laden dray was filled to the brim with anything and everything anyone could want. 'Have you still got that bucket you wouldn't sell me last time?'

He winked. 'Might have something better for the architect's wife.'

She groaned. So much for keeping Francis out of her dealings. 'If you know who I am why did you call out to Mary Merino?'

He lifted his shoulders. 'If that's what you want to call yourself, that's your business.' His shrewd gaze made her skin prickle. 'As you've just discovered there's plenty who reinvent themselves. Besides, it suits you, Mary Merino. Just be careful—there's a strict line between emancipists and exclusives, and God help you if you try to cross it.'

For goodness sake, what did it matter? They were all in this together, trying to do the best they could. In a show of bravado

Mary thumped her hands on her hips. 'Are you going to talk all day or are you going to sell me the goods I'm after?'

'Depends what you want.'

And that was where she needed his help. 'I want vegetables I can plant now, and fruit trees, oranges, lemons, apples, pears, whatever you can get me, and some chickens, point of lay pullets.' Or so Hannah had informed her. 'Not roosters.'

He lifted the lid of an old timber box, rummaged inside and produced a pile of folded pieces of newspaper. 'Cabbage, carrot, onion, parsnip, spinach, turnip, swede.' He thumped each one down on the back of the dray. 'I've got seed potatoes, asparagus crowns, rhubarb too—come spring you'll thank me for those. Get them in quick as you can, give them a start before the weather cools down.'

'I'll take them. What about fruit trees?'

'Ain't got none today. You can put in an order. You want them bare rooted to plant in winter.'

Bare rooted? What in heaven's name did that mean? Did trees grow if their roots were bare? Where was Hannah when she needed her? She'd know, or she'd know who to ask. 'I'd like orange and lemon trees.'

'Leave them till the soil warms up again, in spring.'

'Right, I want two of each.' Especially the orange trees, in memory of Mr Bent who unknowingly had provided her with succour and comfort in the time of her greatest need. 'Next time you're here.'

'Can't guarantee I'll have them next time. You'll just have to call in.'

She balanced her basket on her hip and reached for the seeds.

Bill's warm hand came down on hers. 'Payment first. That'll be two shillings for the seeds and five for the trees.'

'That's daylight robbery.'

'No, it ain't. It's Sydney Town prices. Want them or not?'

'Two now, the other five shillings when I get the trees. Unless you've still got the bucket and the rag rug.' She glared into his eyes, trying to ignore the twinkle of amusement.

'Right you are.' He dropped the seeds into her basket package by package. 'You'll want some good strong fencing, too. Keep the ferals out.'

'What ferals? We don't see many kangaroos in George Street. We've got fencing.' She pulled out two shillings and offered them in the palm of her hand.

'Human kind, not the animal variety. If that lot grows, you'll have enough to feed the neighbourhood. Why don't I call in and drop off the rug. I haven't got it with me today.'

'And the buckets?'

'Them too, and I can check the fencing at the same time. You can show me where you want to put the fruit trees.'

Mary tucked the seeds down into her basket, more to give herself time to think than anything else. There was something about his brash manner that made her trust him, and he certainly seemed to know his way around town. 'Thank you. That would be very helpful. We live on the corner of ...'

'George and Argyle, Redfern's old barrack.' He grinned down at her.

Twenty-Three

Mary pushed aside the town plan and wiped the damp hair from her forehead. She couldn't think straight since summer had arrived in an explosion of hot, humid days. 'Hannah, I'm going to take a walk. I promised Francis I'd have this plan finished but there's something wrong with the coastline. I need to go and have a look. I'll take Frankie with me—a birthday treat, it's not every day a boy turns three. We'll see if there's any fish to be had at the same time. I quite fancy a pie.'

'Are you sure? George and William can keep an eye on Frankie, and Caroline's asleep.'

'No, Hannah, I'm determined. Please go and call Frankie for me while I find my bonnet.' She collected her basket and tucked her sketchpad under the chequered cloth and within a matter of moments was outside with Frankie's sweaty little hand clasped in hers, to prevent him dodging out amongst the carts and barrows and getting trampled. Only a few weeks after she'd arrived in the colony a poor little boy had been run over and hadn't lived to tell the tale. Some said it was the governor's carriage, but there was so much scuttlebutt in the colony a body never knew who to believe.

'Come along, Frankie. We'll walk over to see the ships and then go down and see if we can find the fisher women. You can have a play on the sand and paddle your feet. What do you think?'

He turned his shining face up to hers and nodded furiously. Despite their restricted diet his ruddy cheeks, clear skin and bonny good health put the two older boys to shame. At his age they'd been pale little things but life in the colony had its advantages. The children all seemed to thrive, as long as they didn't come to grief around the bustling port.

Their walk took them past the Commissariat Store and the wharves and then across the Tank Stream, each with their thumb and forefinger clamping their noses. Frankie darted ahead towards the rocks on the point and barrelled straight into two immaculately dressed gentlemen leaving the governor's Domain.

'I'm dreadfully sorry,' she puffed as she pulled up short. 'Mr Bent, good morning.' And, unless she was very much mistaken, the tall, burly man with him was his brother. She smoothed down her skirt and waited for an introduction.

Silence hung as Frankie shuffled his feet and the two Mr Bents studied her as though they'd narrowly missed treading in an offensive pile of animal droppings. 'Are you acquainted, Jeffery?' The other Mr Bent peered down his aquiline nose and sniffed.

'I don't believe we are.' He gave a curt nod and stepped around them.

Mary stood, mouth gaping, as their loud conversation carried on the breeze. 'The convict architect's wife and one of her brats unless I'm mistaken.'

'I trust they're not heading for the Domain. I shall have words with Macquarie. It really isn't suitable, the riff-raff making use of his private gardens.'

Mary gritted her teeth, restraining the impulse to charge after the man and remind him he'd as good as sought her company as a fare-paying passenger aboard ship. So much for planting an orange tree in his honour. Then Bill's words came back, something about strict lines between emancipists and exclusives and God help anyone who tried to cross it. It seemed he was right, and attitudes changed the moment a person hit Sydney Town. 'Come here, Frankie, this minute.' She grabbed at his hand and towed him along the path.

It wasn't until they'd clambered around the rocks and covered the first stretch of sand that she stopped and shaded her eyes. Farm Cove was empty. No sign of the fisher women or their canoes. There'd be no fish pie tonight. Maybe they were around the point. Her stomach gave a rumble of disappointment. 'I'm sorry, Frankie, no fish pie today.' She ruffled his hair. 'You can take your boots off now.'

It was a perfect spot for the children, with no waves to speak of, just the gentle movement of the water in the protected cove. With the place to herself she settled down on the sand, her back against one of the rocks. Frankie dropped down beside her and struggled out of his boots—he was such an independent child, forced by his two older brothers to look after himself or be left behind. 'Push your trousers up above your knees but don't get them wet. That's as far as you can go. No water to touch your clothes. Do you understand?'

He nodded furiously and took off across the sand. She waited until he'd found a spot at the water's edge and dropped down to dig in the sand with a handy stick then delved into her basket and brought out her sketchpad.

She swung around, gazing up at the lie of the land with her eyes half closed, bittersweet memories surfacing as she imagined a grand mansion, in the style of Manali, overlooking the sweeping vista. Pencil in hand, she made the first few tentative lines. It was so long since she'd drawn for pleasure, and then instinct took over and she lost herself in the drawing as before her eyes the house took shape—part Manali, part pure imagination, on the rise above the cove.

When she next lifted her head her breath snagged, and her stomach lurched.

No sign of Frankie. He'd vanished.

A pile of sand and his stick marked the spot where he'd been digging. She leapt to her feet, pulled off her bonnet and scanned the stretch of sand back towards the Tank Stream.

Nothing.

She cupped her mouth. 'Frankie! Frankie!' Dropping her hands, she whirled around in the other direction. And there, almost out of sight, were two small boys running and chasing, arms spread wide like the gulls swooping across the water, droplets of water falling from their hands, glinting in the sunlight.

Unsure whether to be angry or relieved, she tucked her sketch-pad into her basket, picked up Frankie's boots and made her way down to the water's edge.

'Boys. Boys. Come here.' Finally, her voice carried and Frankie stopped in his tracks. He turned to his little friend and then pointed at her and together they ran across the sand, their feet flying, kicking up the sand in their wake. They screeched to a halt in front of her, breathless and laughing.

'You've found a friend.'

The boy scuffed his booted feet and looked down.

'What's your name?'

He looked up at her through pale lashes. Much the same age as Frankie, maybe a little younger, fair hair longish around his narrow face, a shadow of guilt on his sharp features. He most certainly wasn't one of the boys who hung around the wharves making a nuisance of themselves and stealing anything that wasn't tied down. The boy's miniature velvet coat flapped in the breeze and his pristine white shirt spoke of wealth, more in keeping with Captain Piper or the Harrises and their lavish lifestyles.

'Lachlan! Lachlan!' A plaintive cry drifted down the beach. It came again. 'Lachlan! Lachlan!' The rising note of hysteria laced the breeze. One she recognised well enough—a mother's pan-icked tones. She took Frankie's hand in hers and grabbed the other boy before he could run away and marched them towards the woman. 'Did you not tell your mama where you were playing?'

Lachlan hung his head.

'Don't worry, we'll explain. I expect you and Frankie were so busy you didn't notice how far you'd run. Come along.'

As she strode out along the sand the woman's cries ceased. Skirt hitched, untamed copper-coloured curls flying, she ran towards them.

When they met, she snatched the boy into her arms. Tears streaked her pale cheeks. 'My darling boy, I thought I'd lost you. Thank you, thank you so much for finding him.'

'I don't think he was truly lost. My boy, Frankie ...' she ruffled his shiny hair, '... was playing on the sand and their paths crossed. They were having a fine time.'

'This is Lachlan. He knows better than to run from me.' She placed a proprietorial hand on his shoulder. 'Lachlan Macquarie. I am Elizabeth Macquarie, the governor's wife.'

Pale winter-blue eyes pinned Mary with a direct gaze. She smiled and held out her hand. Take that, Mr Bent. 'Mary Greenway, my husband is ...'

'Oh, good heavens! Are you the architect's wife?'

She'd never thought of herself like that. 'Francis Greenway is my husband, yes.'

'And your son, named for his father, as is Lachlan. Are they not a joy and a trial, these boys.'

'Indeed, they are. We call Francis Frankie to differentiate between him and his father.

'And Lachlan is Lachie, for the same reason. Is Frankie your only child?'

Mary laughed, the picture of the hubbub that always filled the rambling house foremost in her mind. She'd imagined once they'd moved into the larger premises life would have become more settled, but they had simply expanded to fill the space. 'He has two older brothers—George and William—so I am familiar with boys' antics.'

A shadow flickered across Mrs Macquarie's face. 'Three boys.'

'And a girl, Caroline, she's nine months old.'

'How very, very lucky you are. I have not been so favoured.' She drew in a deep breath and her face brightened. 'Lachie is very special to me; he is our only child. We lost our daughter, Jane, when she was only two and a half months old.' Her voice hitched. 'Lachie is all we have.' She squeezed Lachlan's hand then proceeded to smother him in kisses, something he didn't appreciate one little bit.

'Perhaps the boys could play a little longer. They were having such fun. It is lovely for Frankie to have the company of someone his own age. His brothers are several years older than he is.'

'Why not. It's early yet. Will you walk with me? There's a spot on the point where I like to sit. The view is very fine.' She let Lachlan's hand drop, and without pausing for breath he and Frankie took off. 'We could talk while the boys amuse themselves under our watchful eyes. Something which would make me much happier.'

Obviously the governor's wife didn't suffer from the same social inhibitions as the gentlemen of the High Court. 'Let me fetch my basket. I was hoping to find the fisher women down here.'

'At first, I thought there was no rhyme or reason to the days they chose but lately I've noticed it depends on the wind. They seem to know when the fish are running. My husband is very keen to encourage the natives. He presented a proper boat to them some time back, hoping to ease their toil, as their own canoes are such frail little things.'

Frail little craft that seemed quite suited for their purpose. Mary buttoned her lips and collected her basket while Mrs Macquarie held tightly onto the two boys. Then they set off along the path until they reached a large sandstone outcrop.

'Here we are.' Mrs Macquarie came to a halt and spread her arms. 'My favourite spot in the colony. Can I offer you some refreshments?'

The shallow cave was a perfect height and shape to sit. There were sumptuous pillows and cushions and a jug of what looked remarkably like a fruit cordial covered with a lace doily, a glass waiting, and an open book—obviously Mrs Macquarie had dropped it in her frantic search for her son. She delved into a hamper and produced a second glass and raised her eyebrows. 'I like to be prepared.'

'That would be lovely, thank you. I am thirsty.'

Once they were settled on the cushions with drinks in their hands Mrs Macquarie let out a long slow breath. 'I believe you arrived on the *Broxbournebury*; you had excellent company. Our Chief Justice, Mr Bent, the Reverend Vale, Sir John Jamison, and Sarah Blades and her three children to name but a few.'

Was there anyone in the colony Mrs Macquarie didn't know? Less said the better perhaps. 'I kept mostly to my cabin though Mr Bent was very kind.' Mr Bent and his wine, chocolate and oranges had done more to bolster her courage than anything else on the terrifying voyage. It was a shame he'd wiped away his good deeds earlier with one sweep of his gloved hand.

'He spoke very highly of you. Sadly, his time here is proving difficult, swayed I believe by his brother's expectations. Rumour had it he believed a knighthood might be in the offing.'

Which might go some way to explaining his toffee-nosed attitude when they'd met.

'And now you are living in George Street in the assistant surgeon's old residence?'

'Yes, Dr Redfern kindly vacated the premises just before Caroline's birth. There are repairs to be done but it is more comfortable and larger than the little cottage we had originally. Much more comfortable than many, I fear.'

'The trials and tribulations of our life here in the colony. Government House is a shambles. When it rains, we have a veritable torrent of water through the back of the house and every surface becomes covered in mildew, in winter the August winds seem to find every gap in the walls. I'm hopeful we might have a new residence soon. I believe my husband intends to speak to Mr Greenway about the possibilities. Before his arrival we managed some repairs and an extra room or two in between the construction of the church of St Philip and the new wharf. There is so much that needs to be done.' Her mouth pulled down at the corners and she let out a long sigh.

Mary couldn't curb her smile. She'd hazard a guess that Mrs Macquarie's life was very different to hers, very different to most women in the colony, surrounded as she must be by servants accommodating her every whim.

'Do you take an interest in your husband's work? I find myself constantly drawn into Lachlan's affairs.'

Mary's hand strayed towards her basket, about to show Mrs Macquarie the drawing she'd been working on earlier, but then she snatched it back. 'I can admit to an interest in architecture, but I rarely do more than offer an opinion.' Possibly better not to admit too much interest in Francis's work—after all, she had no role in Mrs Macquarie's eyes other than that of a convict's wife. 'I do the occasional drawing.' She swallowed the lump in her throat. One day she would.

Mrs Macquarie glanced over her shoulder. 'I frequently find myself acting as secretary, writing letters, particularly those to England.' She raised an eyebrow and peered intently at Mary's sketchpad poking up out of her basket.

'Just some foolish doodling, I find it calms my mind.' Mary tucked her sketchpad deeper into the basket. 'In fact, I was being a little maudlin, remembering the past.' There was no way she was going to get out of the corner she'd backed herself into. 'My father was very involved in the design of the house I lived in as a child.' No need to mention James. Her life with him seemed like a distant dream—a nightmare she wouldn't wish on any woman. 'It's simply a sketch of my home in England. I first met Mr Greenway when he came to suggest some additions.'

'May I see?' Without waiting for an answer Mrs Macquarie helped herself, a tiny frown marring her forehead as she leafed through the pages until she came to Mary's original drawing of Manali with the portico. 'This is delightful. It is exactly what we need at Government House in Parramatta, the building is as flat and bland as cold custard. I have been working on some repairs and renovations for several years. We sought inspiration from a lovely book of designs by Gyfford, and my husband's aide-de-camp Captain Watts has been a great help to me.'

So Mrs Reibey was correct about Mrs Macquarie's interest in architecture.

'Would you ask Mr Greenway if he could draw up some plans for a portico?'

'It would be my pleasure.' However, she doubted he'd have to work overlong on it because she had already drawn up the plans and elevations when Francis had first lent her Chambers's book and they were neatly tucked in her folio in the sea chest.

'You must miss your home. My childhood home in Scotland holds so many memories for me. We used a similar design for the Female Orphan School at Parramatta and laid the foundation stone several years ago but sadly progress has been slow, and we still haven't managed to move the children. Perhaps Mr Greenway could ...' She raised an eyebrow. 'I must speak to Macquarie again. I would very much like to see the poor girls away from the pernicious influence of the town.'

Mary nodded in agreement, although she most definitely was not going to become involved in the orphanage, particularly as the odious Samuel Marsden was said to be supervising the construction. Francis had been on the receiving end of one of his tongue lashings not long ago. As the only Church of England cleric in the colony and magistrate to boot he was very much a champion of the exclusives and had little time for anyone tainted by a convict past. She doubted the children under his care had an easy life.

In an attempt to change the subject, Mary took back her sketchpad and turned to the drawing she'd made while Frankie was playing, of the house on the rise overlooking the cove. 'I transplanted my original home to the rise behind us, with a few additions.'

Mrs Macquarie studied it for many moments, then lifted her face and beamed. 'Why it is glorious, such whimsical splendour. A building like this would be perfectly fitting as the governor's house.' Her finger traced the soaring dome cupola. 'This is most interesting.'

'My father had a fascination for the buildings of the Mughal emperors. He spent many years in India.'

'And this, what is this?' She indicated towards the two drawings Mary had made after her visit to Thornbury Castle.

'Nothing but more scribblings, a place called Thornbury Castle. Mr Greenway was asked to suggest repairs after it fell into disrepair.'

'Mr Greenway is a very lucky man. I have no doubt you are invaluable to him … I hadn't realised …'

How had she allowed this to happen? No one realised, and it was better it stayed that way. 'I was simply taken by the solidity of the building, the sense of permanence, and I particularly liked the gatehouse.' She flipped to the quaint little building she'd drawn and redrawn numerous times.

'Permanence and solidity. That is exactly what we need to create in the colony. These commodious and castellated buildings are perfect.' Mrs Macquarie swept her hand up over her head and around to encompass the vista towards the ocean then, behind her, the treed slope and the somewhat shambolic house where she lived. 'May I show the governor your designs?'

Mary's stomach sank. No! She most definitely could not. Whatever would the governor think? That Francis relied on a woman, albeit his wife, to fulfil his role as civil architect? She shuddered. His reputation would be in tatters. He could lose his position and then where would they be? She swallowed, drew in a breath, and took back the sketchpad. 'I couldn't bear to think of you showing my paltry scribblings to the governor. Perhaps he could speak with Mr Greenway and ask him to produce some designs which would be worthy of your attention. I would hate to intrude on Mr Greenway's position; he is a proud man and I owe him more than I can ever repay.' Whatever had let those words fly free? A change of subject was needed. 'I'd like to draw a picture of Lachlan and Frankie playing on the sand, would you mind?'

'I'd be delighted. I shan't disturb you. I shall take a wander and keep a closer eye on them.'

Relieved she had escaped such a close call, Mary leafed through the pages at the back where she kept her portraits: George and William as little boys, Francis standing, arms crossed, a proud tilt to his head, outside the Clifton Assembly Rooms. Not that he'd posed for the portrait; she'd done it from memory, wanting to mark the occasion of its completion—something he would never agree to after his run-in with Joseph Kay, and on the back the sketch of Arthur Phillip that she'd completed on the voyage out while musing on his role in Francis's trial and incarceration. She smoothed the drawing of George and William and turned it over. Maybe she could ask Bill if he could find her some more paper— Francis would be in need too.

A laugh drifted in on the breeze: the boys, hunkered down in the sandy soil burrowing with all their might, searching for buried treasure or digging to China under Mrs Macquarie's watchful gaze. Mary picked up her pencil.

As always time slipped away and when she next lifted her head the sun had dipped behind the trees and a chill wind blew from the water.

'You're very talented.'

She jumped; she hadn't heard Mrs Macquarie return. 'It's just a sketch.'

'May I have a closer look?'

Mary tipped the page towards Elizabeth. 'I'll find some time one evening to fill out the details.'

'If I may be so bold I would very much like a portrait of Lachie, to send to my family, to my dear niece. You share a name—she is Mary, Mary Mclaine.' Mrs Macquarie's voice hitched, and she ducked her head in a vain attempt to hide the tears pooling in her eyes.

'It would be my pleasure.' Mary reached out and touched her shoulder. It hadn't occurred to her to imagine the governor's wife would be less than happy with her situation. 'Frankie and I must be leaving. I have indulged myself far too long. Caroline will be wanting to be fed and I have no doubt George and William are running riot; they detest their lessons.'

Mrs Macquarie rose from her embroidered cushions and held out her hand. 'I have so enjoyed our chat. Can we not meet again? Perhaps when your drawing of Lachie is complete. I'm sure the boys would love to play. Send me a note when you are ready, and please call me Elizabeth, and I will call you Mary. We shall be friends. We have so much in common.'

Mary inclined her head. 'It would be my pleasure.' Quite when or if she would ever be ready depended very much on Francis's response to her encounter, or perhaps she simply wouldn't tell him. She should take a lesson from Mr Bent's attitude. She didn't need to make a name for herself, or Francis, by breaching the social boundaries of Sydney Town.

Mary held tightly to Frankie's hand as they made their way down George Street. Despite the crippling heat the pubs became busier as Christmas approached, with bodies spewing out onto the street, staggering men, and boisterous banter. It was much later than she intended but she'd been so caught up with her meeting with Elizabeth she hadn't noticed the sun sinking. Poor Hannah had been alone with Caroline, George and William all afternoon. The boys were becoming more and more of a handful and if Francis got home their antics would send him into a flat spin.

She pushed open the gate and ushered Frankie up the path to the open door. The house was unnaturally quiet, never a good sign.

She was greeted by the sight of George and William sitting on the doorstep, both their faces pale and the streak of tears down their dirty cheeks. 'Boys! Whatever has happened?'

William buried his head in his lap.

'George, what have the two of you done?'

'Nothing!' George bounded to his feet. 'Hannah sent us away. Said we shouldn't see it.'

It was like squeezing blood from sandstone. 'See what?'

A howl from William took her attention.

'There, there. It'll be all right.'

William shook his head. 'There's blood, blood everywhere. I don't like that man.'

'What man? Has something happened to Hannah?'

'It's Papa. The man horsewhipped him.'

Her stomach churned. 'Horsewhipped? Don't be ridiculous.' Even the worst convicts weren't horsewhipped—flogged, and horribly so with a cat-o'-nine-tails, but not horsewhipped—and besides, how would William know what it meant to be horse-whipped? 'Stay here and look after your brother.' She dumped Frankie down, closed the door behind her and bolted to the kitchen.

Francis sat on a stool, stripped to the waist, blood dripping from his head and a long snaking welt running from his shoulder, across his back all the way down to his waist. 'Whatever has happened?'

When he lifted his head the look of anguish on his face seared her heart.

'Looks like he's caught the wrong end of a horsewhip to me.'

Mary spun around. 'Bill! What happened?'

'Found him in the narrow lane between the markets, where the old fellow who keeps my spot throws his blanket. Thought Mr Greenway'd had too much and needed a hand home, but he's not drunk. Needs his wife and family around him at a time like this. The military think they're God's gift.'

She snatched the cloth from Hannah and made a hopeless job of dabbing at Francis's battered skin.

'Leave me be.' He pushed her hand aside. 'I'm going to have him charged with assault.'

'Who?' She shot a look at Bill, making himself at home, lounging against the back door. 'Why are you still here?' she hissed.

'Thought I might be able to help but I'll be off now. Let me know if you need anything.' He tugged the brim of his hat and slipped out into the darkness.

Mary crouched down and peered into Francis's ravaged face. 'Who did this?'

'Sanderson.' His lip curled, as though the taste of the man's name on his tongue was more than he could bear.

Captain Sanderson! As dreadful as Francis's injuries were, she had to dissuade him. No one would pay any attention to a ticket-of-leave fellow, civil architect or not, against a member of the military. Not just any member either, he was also the Worshipful Master of Captain Piper's Masonic lodge.

She dabbed at the wound on his shoulder. 'I'm sure it is just a nasty misunderstanding.' She of all people knew how easily Francis could snap, and heavens only knew how he might have retaliated.

'I'd like to believe my own wife would side with me. The man summoned me to the barracks. I dutifully appeared and he ushered me into a small, unfurnished room, slammed the door behind him, all the while ranting about the insulting language I had used when I'd written the letter explaining the matter of the Masonic aprons.' Francis flinched as she reapplied the pressure on his shoulder.

Not one letter but several, one to the judge-advocate no less, and in truth Francis had incurred Sanderson's wrath prior to any letter writing. He'd failed to properly complete the commission he'd accepted to provide the Masonic aprons in time for the all-important ceremony to mark the laying of the foundation for Captain Piper's intended mansion at Eliza's Point. A clashing of two perhaps over-proud men, but not a matter that should have resulted in a horsewhipping.

'He seized me by the throat and cut at me about the legs with his whip. When I caught hold of it he struck me with his fist, a straight left hook to the face.' He reached tentatively for his bleeding and bruised ear. 'Take my word for it.'

Mary nodded her head. There was no doubting Francis's injuries. 'And then?'

'He abused me yet again, called me a damned scoundrel, swindler, scum, and pushed me out of the room striking me all the while. But for my coat I would have been flayed alive.'

Mary shot a glance at Francis's coat, the marks of the whip plain to see in the velvet pile. Why, oh why, had he written the letters without telling her? Perhaps she could have softened his attitude. Could this have anything to do with the reception she'd received from Mr Bent and his brother? 'Oh, Francis. I am so sorry, but really you should think twice about having the Worshipful Master of the Irish Masonic Lodge and Captain of the 46th charged.'

Twenty-Four

The door flew open and Francis appeared, hair dishevelled, coat-tails flying. He threw himself down at the kitchen table and dropped his head into his hands. Ever since his run-in with Sanderson at Christmas his behaviour had become more erratic as he juggled the demands of the governor, the free settlers, the emancipists, the merchants and the military. True to his word he had charged Sanderson and the case was due to come before Judge Wylde in a matter of days—Wylde, and not Mr Bent, as he'd been removed from office after a dispute with Macquarie. What was it about these men and their pride?

Mary bit back an exclamation and jiggled Caroline, trying to distract her from the papers littering the desk. 'What is it, my dear?'

A sheen of sweat glossed his forehead. 'This!' He thrust his hand into his inside pocket and brought out a crumpled piece of paper. 'This is from Macquarie. His intended building plans.'

She peered over his shoulder, trying to hush Caroline's increasing wail and make sense of the list scrawled in the governor's now familiar hand. No doubt at all that it was genuine and not some trumped-up devilry the engineer Captain Gill or one of his minions had created to make Francis appear incompetent. 'A list of essentially necessary public buildings required yet to be erected at Sydney Town et cetera et cetera, exclusive of those now in progress,' she read aloud.

'Ten buildings! Ten in Sydney: a new Government House, handsome, commodious, and castellated if you please, and a court of offices and stables to match, giving a sense of permanence and solidity.'

Heat flew to her cheeks as Francis parroted the very words Elizabeth had used to describe her drawings.

'Mrs Macquarie will supply a list of the number and descriptions of the rooms.'

A cold shiver traced Mary's skin. Elizabeth must have discussed her drawings with the governor.

'So now I have to deal with the first lady of the colony—perhaps she should use her book of designs and employ the services of her husband's aide-de-camp as she did in Parramatta.'

Mary bit down on her lip as her conversation with Elizabeth came back to haunt her. She hadn't expected her designs to come to anything. She couldn't bear the thought of Francis's reputation suffering.

'A new barrack for male convicts. The foundation stone's laid, a small advantage but an advantage nonetheless. A new church, a new courthouse, a neat and handsome fort at Bennelong's point, neat and handsome, if you please, in keeping with the new Government House ...' He ran his fingers through his hair until it resembled the crests on the wretched cockatoos who raided the garden. 'A Gothic gatehouse to mark the beginning of the Parramatta turnpike.'

No doubt based on her drawing of the gatehouse at Thornbury. Mary shivered, then shot to her feet and paced the floor. A sense of warmth spread through her chest, down her arms, making her fingers tingle and long for a pen; she was certain Elizabeth had described her drawings to Macquarie. She must truly have liked them, admired them even, but how could she ever tell Francis what she had done?

'Another government wharf, a stone wall around the dockyard, a new granary, a house and offices for Judge Wylde, though those I will happily approve of, if his verdict is in my favour, and a house and offices for the Provost Marshall.' The paper fluttered from his hand, and he slumped down in the chair and buried his head in his hands.

Mary cleared her throat. All this work had to be a good thing, a mark of respect from the governor and an indication of his faith in Francis. 'I am sure it can be achieved.'

He lifted his ravaged face. 'That's not the half of it. A further six in Parramatta: a hospital, barracks for the troops, a factory and a barrack for the female convicts, another for the males, a new schoolhouse, a spire and steeple for the church and a portico for Government House—whatever has happened to the aide-de-camp? Then much the same for Windsor, except he wants a lumberyard and marketplace as well.

'A portico?' Mary swallowed her high-pitched squeak. Everything Mrs Macquarie had looked at in her sketchpad was mentioned—Government House, matching stables, the toll house and portico, and now a fort. Goosebumps stippled her skin. However was she going to explain it to Francis?

'And finally, three buildings in Liverpool. A church, a wharf and if you please, stables and coach house. All for three shillings a day.' Francis burst into a shriek of maniacal laughter. 'How does he expect me to complete all the drawings? I have no assistance, not even a copy clerk. I am expected to be out and about by dawn no matter what the season, never mind visiting the lumberyards, quarries and numerous other sites to give instructions to the men and visit Parramatta, Liverpool or Windsor to survey and report on the progress in these places. Whatever happened to a day of rest? It makes me long for the opportunity to attend church! The only time I have to draw up plans, write reports and estimate the bills of quantities and valuations is by candlelight.'

Mary poured a beaker of ale and placed it on the table. There must be something she could do to ease his angst. 'How are the other buildings progressing?' She'd really taken very little time of late to assist Francis, tied up as she was with the children, their lessons and the day-to-day running of the household.

Francis knocked back the ale and wiped his mouth on the back of his hand. 'The military barracks.' He raised a thumb. 'The resident chaplain's house, very nearly completed.' His index finger stood to attention. 'The lighthouse and tower at the South Head is about half finished.' A third finger. 'The foundations for the convict barracks were laid yesterday.' His fingers crumpled and he clenched his fist. 'Why do I feel this is a reprimand?'

'It's nothing of the sort.' Unless it was some way of making Francis appear to be shirking. 'Take a positive view.' She couldn't bear the thought of a further outburst—the two spots of heightened colour on his cheeks and the throbbing vein at his temple, a pulsating blue snake, were sure signs. 'It's a compliment. An enormous compliment. The governor is aware of your capabilities, trusts your skill and ability.'

'Yet he has no understanding of the number of hours in a day or the distance, and time, to Windsor, Liverpool and Parramatta to view the sites, never mind those in Sydney. There simply aren't enough hours to accomplish this.'

'I'm sure he doesn't expect the drawings to be completed overnight.' But it wasn't only the drawings, it was the inspiration, the design, that Francis laboured over. 'Is there any way I can help?'

'You? How can you help? I am the government architect.'

'And I am the architect's wife.' She never thought that she would use Elizabeth's words but perhaps this was a solution. 'I will assist you in any way I can.' She ran a hand over Caroline's hair and smiled at her cherubic face and long lashes. Perhaps her fortuitous meeting with Elizabeth was more beneficial than she imagined. What an honour the governor was bestowing, not on Francis alone but on both of them, because without a doubt Elizabeth had her husband's ear. The very words he had used in his note echoed her conversation with Elizabeth.

A bubble of joy exploded in her chest. What an opportunity— the chance to play a part in transforming the penal colony of Sydney into a town of significance. In her mind's eye she could see the formal streets, the grandiose public buildings and town squares to rival Bristol and Bath, maybe even London.

And then a shiver of jealousy traced her skin. Francis would receive the accolades, the recognition for his talent and his ability to transform the barren landscape into a town of importance … unless … 'Let me give Caroline to Hannah to put down, and then she can deal with the boys. I won't be a moment.' Hadn't Francis, on that very first day they'd met, suggested she had a talent that should be fostered?

Once she'd given Hannah her instructions she raced to their bedchamber and delved into the sea chest, which sat at the end of the bed. Her fingers closed over Papa's leather folio tucked right at the very bottom, out of sight and out of mind. She rocked back on her heels and undid the leather thongs, then took her sketch-pad and leafed through her drawings, the familiarity tugging at her heartstrings—Manali and the portico were such a poignant reminder of her first meeting with Francis, her dream house, and the stables for Mudd. How she missed him and Leah. Tomorrow she would write to them. A door banged, bringing her back to the present. She carefully tore the drawings from her sketchpad, slipped them into the folio and scooted down the stairs.

Francis lounged against the open door, gazing up at the darkening sky. He must have heard her footsteps because he turned and tipped his lips in a half-hearted, almost apologetic, smile.

Mary moved the empty beaker off the table and pushed Macquarie's list to one side before laying Papa's folio—her folio, if her hopes became a reality—on the table. 'Come and sit down. I have had an idea.'

'What is that?'

'Drawings I made in England and others while I was aboard ship and a few newer ones.' She cleared her throat as her plan took shape. It was the perfect solution. She brought out the line drawing she'd made of the house overlooking the cove. 'This would make a fine Government House, don't you think?'

He cast a quick glance at her sketch and frowned. 'I am to provide architectural plans, not sketches.'

She wouldn't rise to his taunt. 'It's a starting point.' She pushed the paper closer. 'Stables and offices could be located in a matching building over here, perhaps.'

He stared down at the drawing, raked his fingers through his hair again then sank back into the chair.

'The stables could be castellated to match the house—like this.' She snatched the drawing she'd made after her visit to Thornbury Castle.

From the distance came a shout or two from the wharves, a raucous chorus from one of the pubs further down the street, but inside the house silence hung like a shroud.

Francis brushed at a speck on his sleeve and held out his hand to inspect his nails, a slow smile lifting his lips. 'My very talented wife. What admirable suggestions.'

Perhaps not a shroud. She patted her warm cheeks.

A curl of embarrassment made her face flush further as he began leafing through her other drawings, all the plans and elevations she'd made during the long voyage, quickly at first then gradually slowing and returning to an earlier one or other. The portico, the gatehouse at Thornbury and the original drawing she'd done after her visit with Mudd and Leah. Mary bit her lip, determined not to spoil the moment by saying something foolish. When it became impossible to stay silent any longer, she tiptoed out of the room intending to check, unnecessarily, on the children.

The next time she ventured into the room Francis had covered the table with her drawings and was marking off the list. Curiosity got the better of her. 'Is there anything that might be helpful?'

He rocked back in the chair and smiled at her. 'I think there is. What about this for an idea? As you said, Government House on the rise, then a little further away, perhaps where the bakehouse and windmill currently sit, a crenulated building, similar to your sketch of Thornbury, for offices and stables, which could then be reflected in a fort on Bennelong's point. Castellated and commodious, just as the governor requested.' He gave a bark of laughter. 'A new wharf and stonewall. That requires little design but if it were continued around the bay where the native women fish it would tie everything together and form a pleasing vista for arriving ships. The barrack for the men is already underway.' He ticked off more items on the list. 'A new granary is hardly difficult. We should mark the existing buildings and possible sites for new ones on your town map ...' He reached out and pulled another sheet of paper towards him.

By the time the first fingers of dawn turned the harbour to liquid gold Mary could hardly keep her eyes open. She had given herself a blinding headache in the quest to produce the perfect vision. Her pen dangled loosely in her hand as she surveyed the map she had drawn from the Domain, around the Tank Stream and out as far as the quarries. From memory she sketched in the north shore—so much land so close and yet separated by the stretch of water glimmering as the sun rose. It couldn't be more than fifty yards or so. Her pencil glided across the page, linking the two land masses. She knew nothing of bridge construction …

'An interesting concept …' Francis's breath warmed the back of her neck as he leant over her shoulder. 'The span is large, twice that of the Avon River and Gorge. Remember, they proposed a stone bridge there then decided on wrought iron. I wonder if the construction has gone ahead yet. Wrought iron would be an interesting concept here, with a deck high enough to allow the masted ships to pass beneath.' His eyes took on a faraway gaze. 'It would connect the northern and southern side of the harbour.'

'Allow the town to expand. Entice more free settlers.'

'Who would all require houses to be built.' Francis reached out and took her hands, his eyes sparkling. 'We could achieve so much. Make the Greenway name great. Greater than it ever was at home.

Francis rarely mentioned England, something she quite understood. He may have a ticket-of-leave but until he was granted an absolute pardon or worked out his sentence—another twelve years, dear God—there was little point. She would remain by his side, serving her sentence alongside her husband. Goosebumps stippled her skin. There would have been no assistance from Admiral Phillip for her if Francis had not pleaded guilty, just the end of a hangman's noose and heaven only knew what would have become of the children.

Working with Francis was the perfect solution. Not only would it save so much time, and repay him for his support, it would give her the opportunity to make her mark on the colony. She could draw the plans and elevations while he worked on the estimates of costs, building quantities and surveys, and dealt with the supervision.

And so, as the weeks progressed, Mary worked late into the night by candlelight after the children were in bed while Francis spent much of his time travelling and overseeing the work on the lighthouse rising on South Head. On the occasions he was at home they relished the precious moments alone, taking the time to talk over their ideas for Macquarie's list.

Gradually her ideas blossomed, the drawings in her folio grew and so did her waistline, although this time there was no sickness, instead an abundance of energy and creativity. A Doric colonnade for the southern end of Macquarie Street next to Hyde Park. A courthouse, forty feet high, on six Ionic columns similar to the temple of Minerva with a portico towards the street, and opposite the barracks. A square surrounded by public buildings with a grand church, like the pictures she'd seen of St Paul's in London, a nod to her original mentor, Lady Wilbraham. Perhaps in one hundred years' time she too would be remembered. How she would love to hand over her plans to Elizabeth, admit that they were hers and see the admiration in her eyes. A long pent-up sigh cooled her lips.

She worked diligently on her design for Government House, incorporating the elements Mrs Macquarie had passed on to Francis, and taking her drawing of Thornbury Castle as the inspiration for both the house and the stables and offices, the fort at Bennelong's point and a toll house at the beginning of the turnpike to Parramatta. The governor and Mrs Macquarie would have their handsome, commodious and castellated buildings, and Francis his recognition.

Twenty-Five

Francis straightened his cravat and stood a little taller. 'I've been asked to attend the farewell to Captain Gill and the celebration to mark the completion of the lighthouse brickwork. I can't say I'll be sad to see the back of the man; we've been at loggerheads since the foundation stone was laid. The governor, Mrs Macquarie and a party of friends, and a parcel of children intend to break their fast there.'

Hopefully there would be no mention of the fact that it had taken seventeen instead of nine months since the foundation stone was laid and promises made. Something she felt sorely responsible for since it had been her suggestion to incorporate a domed viewing room where the governor and Mrs Macquarie could entertain guests while overlooking what was undeniably the finest harbour in the world. 'As it should be. The architect should always attend such occasions.'

'Would you like to come? And William, he has been a deal of help running messages, unlike George, who seems to spend his entire time rubbing shoulders with some of the more unsavoury characters at the waterfront.'

Not quite the case. At ten George was angling for a job with the harbourmaster but feared Francis's reaction. 'He has a great love of all things nautical. I'm afraid we might lose him to the sea in the not-too-distant future.' She'd hoped George would tell Francis of his plans, but they had never been close, and she hadn't wanted to stir memories of the past. He was very much like his grandfather, her papa. 'William and I would love to accompany you, but do you think perhaps ...' She interlaced her fingers over her growing stomach.

Francis reached for her shoulders, turned her this way and that, scrutinising her body. 'He's hardly noticeable.'

'He?'

He shrugged. 'I've no idea. Do you?'

'No, none at all.' Though Caroline had proved to be such an easy-going child she rather hoped she might be carrying another girl.

'It's a family day. You're fit and healthy and months off your time. I doubt anyone will remark.'

Two days later, suitably scrubbed and sporting their rarely worn and somewhat outdated best clothes, Francis, William and Mary joined the other guests aboard the government barge. Bill would be fascinated to hear of the interesting mixture of exclusives and emancipists. What a good job Mr Bent had returned to England! He would not willingly rub shoulders with convicted criminals, whether they had served their sentences or not.

'Good morning.' Mary nodded a greeting while Francis helped her into a seat and introduced the other passengers. What a group they were—Captain Gill, Francis's immediate superior, James Erskine, lieutenant governor of New South Wales and commander of the 48th regiment, the Reverend and Mrs Cowper and, thankfully, Dr and Mrs Redfern. It appeared that every faction of society was represented.

Francis seemed quite at home, unfazed by his status as a convict, but Mary couldn't control the churning in her stomach. She still hadn't mentioned her meeting with Elizabeth almost twelve months earlier to anyone, and when Frankie had told his father he had a new friend she'd glossed over the matter. If Elizabeth greeted her, she'd have some explaining to do; worse still, what if Elizabeth had discussed their conversation, her drawings ... Her thoughts took flight as the governor arrived and handed Elizabeth and young Lachlan into the barge. How very fortunate Francis had insisted only William should attend, as she had no doubt young Lachlan would have recognised Frankie, his play-mate. Her wide bonnet and best clothes seemed to act as some form of disguise as far as she was concerned, or else the poor child was totally overcome by the sycophantic attention paid to him.

The moment the ropes were untied the oarsmen flexed their impressive muscles and the barge cut through the water. Francis held court, explaining all manner of architectural devices he had employed in building the lighthouse—Macquarie Tower, as it was to be known—as well as the exquisite sandstone quarried on site, and the plate glass for the light on its way from England, which would create an impressive beam seen for miles out to sea and announce to all the world that Port Jackson and Sydney Town lay ahead. Not only that, it would replace the flagstaff and old beacon fire that had to be lit and manned every night. He was truly in his element.

Once they reached Watson's Bay, named for the harbourmaster George hoped to work for, and disembarked to walk to the carriages waiting to ferry them up Signal Hill, Mary found herself alongside Elizabeth. She nodded a greeting and received a fleeting smile in return, and then Elizabeth's hand rested on her arm and drew her to a halt, allowing the rest of the party to move ahead. 'It's lovely to see you. I would very much like to meet again.

Lachie and I have been spending time in Parramatta but we are in Sydney now. Can it be arranged?'

A meeting could be arranged, but not if it was publicised. Regardless of her position, the wife of a ticket-of-leave man, civil architect or not, did not rub shoulders with the governor's wife. Imagine the rumours Captain Sanderson would put about. In his mind the military sat only one rung below the governor, way above the emancipists and serving convicts, and Mary, although a free settler, was bound by her husband's status. 'I should like it very much, but I don't wish to make your life difficult.'

'How I detest this hidebound society we find ourselves in. I insisted the governor should extend this invitation to you.'

'Why?'

Elizabeth's face broke into a charming smile, and she tapped the side of her nose with a lace-gloved finger. 'Wait and see.' And without another word she strode off, caught up with the governor, slipped her arm through his and held out a hand to Lachlan. Together they climbed into the first of the awaiting carriages.

Most strange.

Soothed by the warm summer breeze, Mary gazed out at the wonderful vista. To the east the tall sandstone cliffs rose out of the jewelled sea—fifteen thousand miles from the spot where she'd thrown chance to the wind and followed Francis. Would she ever see England again? Would Francis want to return? His star was rising, and he would make his mark on this strange new land. Her duty was to be by his side and until he received an absolute pardon the matter didn't merit thought.

Lost in her thoughts, she jumped when William's warm hand took hers. 'Come, quickly. We are going to climb the tower.' He led her back along the track, to the base of the lighthouse where everyone had grouped around the governor, a fawning Captain Gill at his side.

A round of applause greeted her arrival—not for her but for the governor, who began, in his booming voice, to read aloud an inscription cut in the building's facade. Francis raised his chin and moved to her side.

THIS BUILDING INTENDED FOR THE DOUBLE PURPOSE OF
A LIGHTHOUSE AND BARRACK IS NAMED MACQUARIE TOWER IN
HONOUR OF THE FOUNDER. THE WORK WAS COMMENCED IN 1816
AND COMPLETED IN 1817.
L. MACQUARIE ESQUIRE GOVERNOR.
THIS TOWER MEASURING 76 FEET IN HEIGHT WAS DESIGNED
AND EXECUTED UNDER THE SUPERINTENDENCE OF
CAPTAIN JOHN GILL
ACTING ENGINEER.

The governor beamed at the assembled crowd, but Mary couldn't respond. It was outrageous. Why had they omitted Francis's name from the inscription? Francis made an unintelligible growl, ran his fingers through his windswept hair and lurched away from the assembled party. How could the governor have done that? Ignoring his contribution, his design, was the hardest cut, worse than any horsewhipping.

As she reached Francis's side the governor's voice boomed once more. 'This being altogether a very interesting and auspicious day I present Mr Greenway, the government architect, his emancipation dated today, 16 December 1817.' He held out a rolled paper, neatly tied with a red ribbon.

So that was what Elizabeth had referred to. 'Francis, how wonderful.' She nudged him forward. 'Go and collect it. It's a great honour. You are a free man.'

He glared up at the tower, all seventy-six feet of it, vibrating as tight as the string of a fiddle. 'I'd rather he'd remembered my contribution to the building. It was, after all, my design. Besides it's only a conditional pardon, not absolute. I have to stay within government limits. Nothing to celebrate.'

What was the matter with the man? Sometimes he was so temperamental—cantankerous would be a better word. He was ambitious and clever but his provocative and irrational behaviour could destroy all they'd worked for. Goosebumps traced her skin and, terrified all the world would sense her frustration, she hissed, 'Go, Francis. You must.' She could feel everyone's eyes upon them, most of all Elizabeth's, the compassion in her gaze clear. No matter how affronted Francis felt about the plaque, a conditional pardon was a great honour. The first step on the road to freedom.

After an apparent eternity Francis took a step forward and received his certificate. The governor shook his hand, and they exchanged a few words. Francis seemed to brighten as the crowd dispersed to climb the stone staircase to the top of the tower, but he didn't follow.

He stomped back to her, the rolled piece of paper dangling loosely from his hand. 'It seems my name was *inadvertently* …' sarcasm dripped from his lips like spilt wine, '… omitted from the inscription. It will be rectified.'

Mary reached for his arm, felt the tremor tracing his skin.

He shrugged her away. 'I am to meet the governor at Bennelong's point after they have broken their fast and toasted their achievement with cherry brandy. He intends to lay the foundation stone for the new fort … Fort Macquarie, no less, then the stone for the government stables, hopefully not Macquarie Stables. You must come too. After all, it will be a momentous occasion. The laying of the foundation stone for your first designs.'

'Shh! Francis. Enough. What would everyone say?'

'They will say the architect's wife and son have accompanied him. We may not be able to publicly admit your role but it should be acknowledged between ourselves. My talented wife—what would I do without you?' He waved William to their side. 'Come, we will walk down to the bay and take one of the barges before the rest of the party descend.'

'I should like that.' The trip would give her a moment or two to recover her equilibrium.

Mary, Francis and William arrived at Government Wharf ahead of the official party. The moment she took Francis's hand and stepped from the barge the full intensity of the December sun scorched her face.

A group of convicts sat around on the rocks on the point, possibly the best spot, making the most of the breeze blowing across the harbour.

'I'm going to go and have a word, make sure they've got the foundation stone prepared,' Francis said. 'And the governor's silver trowel; he likes to mark the occasion with a spot of ceremony.'

Mary shaded her eyes, searching for some relief from the sun, but unless she walked up into the Domain there was nothing. She adjusted her bonnet. 'I'll wait here.' She turned slowly, looking out into Sydney Cove at the very view the soldiers manning the fort would have of any approaching vessels, and a smile twitched the corners of her lips. What a splendid sight! Spinning on her toes, she gazed up towards Government House. In her mind's eye she could see the stables on the rise, their battlements pristine against the cerulean sky—Thornbury Castle recreated in the far-flung corner of the world. She clapped her hands, a bubble of excitement growing: her name may never be recorded but nothing, nothing could take away this moment, the sense of achievement and pride coursing through her.

'The governor's barge is on its way.' Francis's voice brought her from her reverie. 'This shouldn't take too long and then it's just a quick walk through the Domain to the site earmarked for the stables. They've removed the old bakehouse.' He reached for her hand. 'How are you holding up? The heat's fierce.'

'I wouldn't miss this for the world.'

'There's the governor, and Mrs Macquarie. Come, let me introduce you.'

Before Mary had time to consider his proposition Francis took her arm and led her down towards the wharf where the Macquaries waited for the other guests to assemble.

Elizabeth noticed their approach long before the governor and her face broke into a welcoming smile as she stood grasping little Lachie's hand. Mary tried but failed to respond. How would Francis react if …

'Ah! Greenway.' As the governor approached, Mary sank into a curtsy, more to hide her confusion than anything else. 'A fine day, is it not?'

'Indeed it is, sir. May I introduce my wife, Mary Greenway.'

'Delighted, I'm sure.' He gave a small bow. 'Now, is everything organised? The stone, the engraving has been completed, I believe. And my trowel, I do like to use my trowel. A way of marking the occasion.' He took Lachie's hand and walked with Francis away from the wharf to the cleared area where someone had hoisted a flag at the spot where the foundation stone would be laid.

Mary let out a long slow breath as she found herself standing next to Elizabeth, somewhat lost for words.

'It seems we are destined to spend the day together. A most exciting day. I haven't had the opportunity to tell you how much I approved of the plans and elevations for the fort and the stables. Today marks a great step towards the future. How proud you must feel.'

'I hadn't imagined I would feel such a sense of achievement.'

'Now Mr Greenway has his conditional pardon I hope we can meet more frequently. I was wondering about the portrait of

Lachie … ' Elizabeth lifted her gaze. 'I do believe our presence is required. Come.'

All in all the laying of the foundation stone, the desultory rendering of 'God Save the King' beneath the drooping flag and the long, hot traipse through the Domain to the site of the stables where the entire procedure was repeated left Mary with a confused sense of hope and impatience. If only she could wave a magic wand, but for now she simply didn't dare believe it until the buildings were a reality.

Twenty-Six

1818

Hannah peered through the window, eyes narrowed against the sun. 'I reckon that's the governor's carriage. The one that ran that little boy over.'

'That's scuttlebutt and you know it.'

'Blimey! It's stopping!' Hannah tucked a soggy rogue ringlet behind her ear and flew to the door.

The child in Mary's stomach performed a series of neat summersaults. 'Stop!' Surely Elizabeth hadn't come to visit? The entire town would know within moments. She glanced down at the portrait of young Lachlan. Just a little of the colour needed deepening then she'd intended to get Bill to deliver it to Government House; she hadn't expected Elizabeth to call to collect it herself. 'I'll go.'

When she flung open the door she discovered a liveried servant, arm extended, offering a folded piece of paper. 'Thank you.' She as good as snatched it from his hand and slammed the door in his face. Away from prying eyes, with her back resting against the timber and her heart beating a ridiculous tattoo, she picked at the seal, in no doubt the note was from Elizabeth. Then she stopped. What was the matter with her? Francis now had a conditional pardon. Not only that, he held the position of civil architect, so why wouldn't the governor, or even his wife, who everyone knew had an interest in architecture, send a note to the Greenway house?

As Mary expected, Elizabeth requested a meeting. She and Lachlan would be at their favourite spot, Mrs Macquarie's Chair, as the governor had christened it, at four in the afternoon. Mary curbed a smile. It seemed Francis was correct and every spot in the colony would bear the Macquarie name. She glanced back at the note: Elizabeth wrote that if Mary and Frankie would care to join them, she would be delighted. No need for a response; it would suit, and Mary had the rest of the day to put the finishing touches to Lachlan's portrait. She hadn't had a moment to think of anything other than plans and elevations. She tucked the note into her waistband and returned to the kitchen.

Varying piles of chopped carrots and beans littered the table. Hannah's eyes bulged as William and George fought over random pieces. 'Boys!'

William dropped his head into his hands and pushed back from the table. 'I can't do it.'

Poor William. He found his numbers so very, very hard, and since Mary had introduced the concept of division he'd lost all confidence. 'George, are you helping or hindering?'

'Helping. It can't be that difficult to share something out between three people.'

'But there's not enough. We don't get the same. We must cut one of them up otherwise it's not fair.'

She really had to make more time for their lessons. Once the baby came, her priorities would change. She quite enjoyed teaching them—it brought back memories of her time in the library with Papa—and both boys would need a sound grounding if they were going to secure decent positions. They may be the sons of an almost-free man, but they would be competing with boys unstained by their father's convict status. 'Very well, that's enough for one day.'

Neither George nor William needed to be told twice. Their chairs scraped back, and they were on their feet making for the door in two seconds flat. 'Where are you going?'

'Down to the harbour. Mr Watson's got a job for me.' George tossed the words over his shoulder as he disappeared.

'And William?'

'I'm to go to the quarry and see how much sandstone is ready for carting.'

It was a form of arithmetic William had no difficulty with, and his fine sense of responsibility was a bonus.

'Very well. I expect you home by midday.' Her words fell on deaf ears as the gate clanged shut.

'I want to go.' Frankie's high-pitched wail rent the air.

'You and I are going out later.' Ears ringing, she bent and whispered. 'To see your friend, Lachie. Can you keep the secret?'

His face lit up and he nodded furiously.

'Help Hannah with the vegetables, and collect the eggs then come and find me.' Which should give her sufficient time to put the finishing touches to Lachlan's portrait. She'd drawn him in the blue velvet coat he'd worn when they'd met, his collar framing his pale face and a hint of a smile on his serious face, most probably a smile reserved for his time with Frankie, truth be told. He was a sad little boy, rarely given the opportunity to be a child. She stretched her back then settled at Francis's desk and flicked through her sketchpad until she came to the spot where she kept her portraits.

Wiping away the perspiration from her forehead, she picked up her paintbrush.

Unsurprisingly, William and George did not return at midday, and Mary sat down with Hannah and Frankie to share some bread and cheese. They had taken to eating their main meal in the evening—not only was it cooler, it gave Francis the opportunity to spend time with the boys. He had little interest in Caroline. She was now nearly two but he hardly knew her, and she was asleep long before he returned home.

'Frankie and I are going to take a walk later on.'

'Is that wise?' Hannah cast a long look at her belly.

'I am perfectly fine; I have no intention of spending the next three months with my feet up.' She smoothed her dress. 'This is my fifth child and I know from experience that exercise is the best medicine for me. Ask Dr Redfern when he next calls if you are concerned. I'll not discuss it again.'

Hannah sniffed. 'I suppose you're thinking about fish pie—same as last time.'

'I certainly wouldn't say no to some fish or oysters, but I doubt the women will be down at the cove. They're usually there in the morning. Come on, Frankie, let's go.'

It was a little earlier than she intended but she'd got a bad case of the fidgets. She didn't understand her need to keep her friendship with Elizabeth quiet. The sneaking suspicion that it would reflect on Francis, that she'd be seen to be currying favour on Francis's behalf? It could hardly be called a friendship as she and Elizabeth had only met twice; once when the boys had played and once at the lighthouse and the laying of the foundation stones.

As she and Frankie made their way through the crowd on George Street and past the wharves, her mind began to calm. Why shouldn't she help Francis with his designs? Elizabeth said she helped the governor with his correspondence, and as much as she'd like to she didn't intend to claim any credit for her work. Francis's acknowledgement was reward enough.

The moment they reached the stretch of sand at the cove Frankie plonked himself down, pulled off his boots and rolled up his trousers. She tucked his boots into her basket, and he rushed off to cavort in the water. A stab of jealousy raced through her. The breeze was pleasant and the sparkling water tempting. Throwing caution to the wind she followed suit, hitched up her skirt and chased after him.

As they rounded the last bend before Mrs Macquarie's Chair, Mary drew to a halt. 'Frankie, come here. We're both sopping wet. Let me tidy you up.'

He pulled away from her and raced back to the water's edge. She could hardly blame him—for the first time in weeks she was blissfully cool. She pulled down her skirt and made a half-hearted attempt to wrangle her dishevelled hair into some semblance of order.

'Mary!' Elizabeth's voice drifted on the wind. She waved, then walked to meet her.

'Please excuse my appearance. Frankie and I were playing in the water.' She swiped again at her hair. 'The breeze is delightful.'

'The boys don't appear to need to be reintroduced. Come and have some cordial. You must be parched.' Elizabeth's eyes drifted towards Mary's basket.

'I have Lachlan's portrait. It's finished.'

'I hope it didn't get wet.'

'It'll be quite safe inside my sketchpad. I trust you'll like it.'

'I'm sure I will. I can't wait to see it.' Elizabeth grabbed her hand and led the way to the rock shelf, which as before was laid with cushions and rugs.

Mary took her sketchpad from her basket and handed it to Elizabeth.

'Why, it is just perfect!' Elizabeth held it to her chest. 'I intended to send it home but I'm not sure I can send it to Mary. My dear, dear boy. How can I thank you?'

'It is a gift, from me and Frankie.' She tore the page from the sketchpad and gazed out at the two boys chasing and splashing in the water. She worried at times that George and William already had too much freedom and were learning the seamier side of the bustling town far too quickly, and Frankie wanted only to follow in his brothers' footsteps. Yet she wouldn't for all the world want Lachlan's life for the three of them. Always on show. Expectations heaped on him from the moment he could walk, and worst of all the mollycoddling she suspected he suffered as Elizabeth's only child.

'I am now doubly indebted to you. The portico at Government House in Parramatta is complete. It has changed the entire look of the house. I do wish I could invite you to see it, for without your guidance I would never have thought of such a thing.' Elizabeth reached for Mary's sketchpad. 'Show me the drawing. I'd like to see how close we came.'

Mary didn't need to revisit her drawing. She had redrawn it for Francis, produced the elevations and measurements, and knew he'd followed her design. 'It's here somewhere.' She fanned the pages, knowing full well she wouldn't find it. It was in her folio with the other planes and elevations that Francis had used. She didn't want to admit to the reason she kept them tucked away, the far-fetched idea that she might at some time receive acknowledgement for her work. The sketchpad pages crackled as she turned them faster and faster, pushing her traitorous thoughts aside.

Elizabeth stilled her hand. 'Why I do believe I know who this is.' She tapped the corner of the page. 'Admiral Phillip, is it not? We met many years ago, before we left England. His letter of recommendation impressed Macquarie no end.' Elizabeth gazed down at the portrait she'd drawn during the long voyage on the *Broxbournebury*.

It was as much as Mary could do to keep her fingers still and not snatch the sketchpad back. Her hand began to shake. Dear God, she didn't want a discussion about Francis's relationship with the admiral nor how the letter of recommendation came about. No one must know of the admiral's involvement in Francis's reduced sentence.

'I wonder if I could impose upon you once again.'

The baby in Mary's stomach performed a cartwheel. She turned to Elizabeth with what she hoped was an innocent, nonchalant expression, eyebrows raised.

'We are to host a ball at Government House to celebrate the thirtieth anniversary of the admiral's landing at Sydney Cove. A portrait would be the perfect centrepiece. Could you possibly enlarge it?'

Mary shot to her feet, shaded her eyes, and studied the boys. More to cover the colour in her cheeks than anything else. No, she couldn't, absolutely not. Nor would she part with the sketch. She had made a promise to Miss Bingle and she intended to keep it.

She sucked in a deep breath and tried to calm the irregular thump of her heart, and disturbed, the baby gave a furious kick. 'Oh!' She sank down on the edge of the sandstone shelf, cradling her belly.

'My dear. Are you well?'

'I'm sorry. It is just the baby.'

Elizabeth's eyes widened. 'You are with child, again? I hadn't noticed.'

Mary nodded. 'I'm sorry.'

'Please, don't apologise. How wonderful. May I?' Elizabeth reached out and touched her suddenly obvious bulge, a look of awe and reverence marking her features. 'Oh, but I can feel the movement. You shouldn't have come, walked all this way. I shouldn't have invited you. I had no idea. Let me call the carriage to take you home.'

'I am quite well. I find exercise helps. Dr Redfern is in total agreement. Just give me a moment.' Mary's breathing settled. Her reaction to Elizabeth's request for a portrait of the admiral had caused her distress and she had transferred it to the child. 'I'm afraid I cannot give you the portrait. It was drawn from memory and without the admiral's permission.'

'But Mr Greenway insisted the admiral was his good friend and patron. I well remember him telling us when he brought the letter of recommendation. Were you not introduced?'

Once again they were straying into dangerous waters. 'Perhaps if the governor asked Mr Greenway. He is a very accomplished oil painter.' Mary pressed her lips together. It wouldn't do to tell Elizabeth of the two paintings Francis had completed while in gaol, but they proved he had the skill without a doubt.

'How foolish of me. How unthinking. To ask such a thing in your condition. Forgive me.'

Mary offered a wan smile. This was not the recognition she hoped for.

'Are you sure I can't call the carriage to take you home?'

The last thing she wanted. The governor's carriage stopping outside their humble barrack again and drawing attention to her personal relationship with Elizabeth. 'No, I assure you I will be perfectly fine. Hannah will have supper prepared and I expect Francis home this evening.'

'Hannah?'

'My maidservant. Although she's become more of a friend. She's been with me since the voyage out. Mr Bent organised it for me.'

'It's good to know Mr Bent had his uses.' Elizabeth gave a wry twist of her lips. 'Do you not have a cook?'

'Hannah and I share the cooking and the care of the children, though George and William need little assistance, except with their lessons. George is hoping to work with Mr Watson, the harbourmaster, and William is of great assistance to his father.'

'My dear.' Elizabeth reached for her hand. 'I have nothing but admiration for your courage. Five children. You are so blessed.'

'It is time Frankie and I made our way home.' Mary straightened her dress, thankfully now dry due to the warm breeze. 'Please ask the governor to speak to Francis about a portrait. When is the ball?'

'January 26. I would very much like to invite you but …' Two pink spots stained Elizabeth's cheeks.

'I understand.' The convict taint. Until Francis had an absolute pardon, they would not be classed as emancipists or be invited to any social function at Government House, no matter how firm her friendship with Elizabeth became; just one more reason why it should remain private.

Francis didn't arrive home until well after dark. The children were all tucked up in their beds and Mary and Hannah were sitting outside the kitchen trying to catch the breeze blowing in from the cove.

'You're later than I expected. Is everything all right?' Mary scanned his face, trying to read his mood. 'Hannah, would you go and prepare a plate for Mr Greenway, please.'

Francis perched on the edge of the chair, back straight, chin slightly tilted to the stars. 'I've been with Macquarie. I have a commission. It seems my skill as an artist has filtered through the colony despite Sanderson's complaints about the aprons.'

Mary dipped her head demurely to hide her smile. 'Indeed,' she murmured.

'I have been asked to paint a portrait of Admiral Phillip for the official ball at Government House to commemorate the thirtieth anniversary of the landing at Sydney Cove, no doubt because of his letter of recommendation. The only problem is I have never met the man.'

'But I have. I met him and his wife in Clifton; they were promenading with some friends. I made a sketch of him; I still have it. Could you work from that? It would be such a great privilege for you to provide the painting.'

Francis ran his hand over the stubble on his chin. 'And the perfect way to celebrate the memory of my patron. Go and fetch your sketch while I see Hannah; my stomach thinks my throat's been cut.'

Mary heaved herself out of the chair. As much as she was loath to admit it, the heat, her walk and Elizabeth's questions, although meant in the nicest way, had sapped her strength. Just ten more weeks until the baby's arrival. She couldn't wait.

Paper in hand, she made her way back to the kitchen and sat down with Francis. 'Here's the admiral.' She slid her pen-and-ink sketch across the table.

'It's rough but I am certain I can make something of it. I'll need a canvas and oils. I'll have to work on it at night but you're right, I would take much pleasure in celebrating his memory.'

And having his name on everyone's lips. 'I have both in the sea chest.' Hopefully the unused canvas and paints had survived the journey. It would save her asking Bill or, worse, traipsing up and down George Street, never mind their dwindling finances—Francis still hadn't received the monies owing to him.

Having perhaps learnt from the matter of the Masonic aprons, Francis completed the portrait and delivered it to Government House in ample time for the celebrations and took great pleasure in knowing that it would be suspended in the ballroom in a wreath for all the guests to see. There was even a piece in the *Sydney Gazette* lauding his masterpiece.

Mary, however, had other matters to occupy her. The heat of summer proved far more trying than two years earlier when she'd given birth to Caroline. Dr Redfern had the temerity to suggest that her age might well be contributing to the difficulties she suffered but finally, on the thirteenth day of March, she proved him wrong, and Charles Capel Greenway entered the world with as little fuss as his older brothers and sister.

A large hamper arrived from Elizabeth, including a tin of China tea, two bottles of wine, cake, figs, grapes and four smooth, plump orange-yellowish heart-shaped fruits, with an attached note saying they had recently arrived on a transport from India. They were called mangoes and Elizabeth recommended them not only for their delicious flesh but also their health-giving properties. Mary inhaled the heady fragrance. 'Hannah, bring me a knife.' Papa had spoken of mangoes; said they were manna from heaven. Her heart twisted. How he would have loved to meet his grandchildren. She took the knife from Hannah, sliced into the plump cheek, and sank her teeth onto the flesh. Juice trickled down her chin. 'It's delicious.'

'You be careful, you don't know what that is. Just 'cause it smells sweet don't mean it won't harm you.'

She licked her lips and swallowed. 'I'm sure it'll do me no harm; the basket is from Eliz … Mrs Macquarie to celebrate Charles's safe arrival.'

'How would she know?' Hannah thumped her hands on her hips and cocked her head to one side.

Mary took another bite of the luscious morsel, more to give herself time to think than anything else. 'I expect Dr Redfern told her, or perhaps Mr Greenway has spoken to the governor.' Although that was highly unlikely because Francis had been out

Parramatta way for the last week putting the final touches to the ground plan for the Female Factory, which would lodge some three hundred convicts enclosed behind a nine-feet-high stone wall. The mere thought of those poor incarcerated women made her shudder. 'Would you like to try some?'

Hannah wrinkled her nose then shook her head and plucked another piece of paper from the bottom of the basket. 'There's another note here.'

Mary tucked it into her sleeve and finished the mango, licking her fingers then wiping her sticky hands on her apron. 'I can hear Charles. I'll go and check on him. Can you find somewhere cool for the hamper, and perhaps make a cup of tea? We haven't had real tea for so very long.'

The moment she left the room she unfolded the note. It contained congratulations on Charles Capel's birth and the hope that Mary would soon bring him to meet her. Proof, without a doubt, Dr Redfern had reported to Elizabeth.

Twenty-Seven

Another three weeks passed before Mary managed to extricate herself from the house. Dr Redfern made a final call and pronounced her fit and healthy, so she wrote a quick note to Elizabeth suggesting a meeting the next day. She hadn't written to thank Elizabeth for the basket after Charles's arrival because she'd always intended seeing her, but time had conspired against her. Under the pretext of picking up their rations, she took off down to the Commissariat Store.

It took very little time to collect their entitlement and with a full basket over her arm she slipped out to the free market, hoping to find Bill and ask him to arrange for her note to be delivered to Government House.

A low whistle caught her attention as she stepped out into the autumn sunshine. Her head came up with a jerk and she stopped in her tracks.

'Mary Merino!'

'Why do you persist with that tomfoolery? You know I am Mrs Greenway.'

'Suits you. There's always two sides to every character. What can I do for you?'

His intense blue-eyed gaze brought heat to her cheeks. It seemed as though Bill was the only person in the colony who truly saw her. 'How do you know I'm looking for you?'

He rolled his eyes. 'Wishful thinking more than like. Haven't seen you about for a while now.'

'I've been busy.'

'And the babe is well?'

Was there anything the man didn't know? 'Yes, thank you. I need someone to deliver a note.'

'There's plenty can do that, unless you want it done on the quiet. Who's it for?'

Mary glanced over her shoulder and took a step closer to him. 'Mrs Macquarie.'

He pushed back his hat, his eyebrows shooting up his forehead. 'Right, and you don't want it to become public knowledge.'

She gave a quick, curt nod.

'She and the governor are back from Parramatta so it shouldn't be too difficult. Give it over.'

She scrunched the paper in her fist, unwilling to part with it. In the past she'd always waited for Elizabeth to contact her; the last thing she wanted to do was cause a problem. She trusted Elizabeth to keep her secrets and for some reason she trusted Bill. 'I don't want just anyone to deliver it.'

'I can sort that out. I've got an errand to run.' He squatted down, reached under the wheel of his dray and hauled out a young girl, hair as pale as moonlight, eyes round and huge in her tear-stained face. 'Me and Aggie have to go for a bit of a walk, haven't we, love?'

Mary's stomach sank. The girl looked terrified, and a large blue bruise marred her high cheekbones. She'd heard more terrible stories than she could count of young girls forced into dreadful positions, sold for an hour or two to any man who wanted them. Bill wouldn't ...

'Who is she?' She couldn't control the snarl in her voice as she reached towards Aggie, intent on dragging her out of Bill's clutches. A sharp stab of pain ricocheted up her shin.

'Leave me alone, you miserable witch.' Aggie cowered behind Bill, eyeing her through thick eyelashes.

Bill reached for her and wrapped an arm around her shoulders. 'You apologise for kicking the lady.'

Aggie wrinkled her nose and uttered a few mumbled words.

'She's me sister's girl. After Annie died, they put her in the orphanage down near the public works depot, but she's got other ideas and keeps shooting through. I've tried time and time again to get them to give her to me, but the Reverend Marsden won't have a bar of it. I think he reckons I've got plans for her.' He raised his eyebrows, his meaning clear. She wasn't the only one who'd jumped to conclusions. 'Too pretty for her own good, she is. I'm going to take her back so I can deliver your note at the same time. Would you be wanting a reply?'

'Just a yes or no.'

'Right. Give me that bag of flour.' He reached into her basket.

Whatever was he talking about?

'I'll send someone around with it if the answer's yes. Fair enough?'

Good heavens, the man was a genius. She handed over the flour, the note tucked underneath. 'Thank you.'

'It's my pleasure, Mary Merino, just be careful you don't get yourself in too deep. I've told you before there's plenty in the colony who don't take too kindly to convicts, even if they have got their conditional pardon, or their wives, hobnobbing with the exclusives.' Bill reached out for Aggie's hand. 'Come on, love, we've got an errand to run and then I'll take you back.'

Not two hours later Hannah came to Mary with a frown. 'Some lad just dumped this on the doorstep. Said you forgot it down at the stores.' She jiggled the small calico bag of flour from one hand to the other.

'Oh, silly me.' Mary pushed her hair back from her face. 'I'm still suffering from too many sleepless nights.'

'Young Charles'll settle given a few more weeks. The problem's the other tearaways.'

'What have they been up to now?'

Hannah lifted her shoulders and groaned. 'George mostly. Running riot down at the wharf. Sooner he gets himself a berth the happier we'll all be. What's more, Frankie's heading the same way.'

There was no one she could blame but herself. Their lessons had fallen woefully by the wayside in the last few months. 'I have errands to run tomorrow and then we'll get back into their lessons.'

When Mary took Charles into the kitchen the following morning, she found Hannah sitting at the table, hands wrapped around a cup of tea, and Caroline playing quietly on the rag rug with a mound of wooden offcuts. 'Where are the boys? I was going to take Frankie for a walk.'

'Long gone, and Frankie with them. Got wind of you talking about lessons.'

'And who would have told them that?' Mary raised her eyebrows. For all her complaining, Hannah's loyalty lay with George and William, had done since they'd bonded on the *Broxbournebury*. Poor little Frankie tagged along, trying to keep up. 'I'll make sure I'm up bright and early tomorrow morning before they escape.'

'Don't like your chances. Still and all, it gives me and Caroline some time to get into the garden. She likes to feed the chickens. Want some tea?' She pushed a cup across the table. 'Can't beat that China tea. Hope you wrote a thank-you note to Mrs Macquarie.'

Mary swallowed down the tea. 'I'll be back in a couple of hours.' She tied her shawl around her neck and tucked Charles against her body. She'd no intention of taking her sketchpad with her. After several sleepless nights trying to settle Charles, who unlike all the other children refused to sleep through, she'd had plenty of time to think and she'd decided the fewer people knew about her contributions to Francis's work the better, and that included Elizabeth Macquarie. Life was becoming far too complicated.

Mary spotted Elizabeth walking towards her not long after she rounded the bend into the cove. Her heart leapt at the sight of her. It had been weeks since she'd seen her, and she'd missed their easy conversations. There was no sign of Lachlan; the poor boy was probably at his lessons as her boys should be.

Elizabeth ran the last few yards and came to an abrupt halt. 'Mary! I am so happy to see you. It's been too long. Show me baby Charles.' Without waiting she tweaked the shawl. Charles opened his big blue eyes and stared at Elizabeth.

'Oh, he is adorable. Let me take him, please.'

'Shall we wait until we settle? I've got him tied up tight to keep him safe.'

'How foolish of me; that's a far more sensible idea. Come. I have wine and cake to celebrate. We shall behave as society ladies. I want to hear all your news.'

'First, I must thank you for the hamper—the tea and the mangoes, such luxuries. I've never tasted mango before; my papa used to talk of them.'

'The governor has some idea we might be able to grow mangoes in the colony. It would be a wonderful addition.'

'Indeed, it would. I believe you've been in Parramatta.'

'We have. I am coming to the conclusion I'd prefer to live there than in town. I've been working with Reverend Marsden on the final stages of the orphanage. The girls are to be taken to their new accommodation in a matter of weeks. I can't wait to get them away from the temptations of Sydney to a place where they can be educated as wives and servants.'

Mary bit down on her lip. It hadn't occurred to her that this was the intention of the orphanage; she'd thought the girls would receive an education that would enable them to make their own decisions, run their own businesses, marry or not, follow their interests. Aggie's battered, tear-stained face filled her vision.

'They are apprenticed as servants when they reach the age of thirteen to families of good character and when they marry, they are entitled to a gift of a cow from the government herd as a form of dowry. Is it not ideal? Now, enough of that. Let me hold your darling child.'

While Elizabeth and Charles cooed and gurgled at each other Mary's mind drifted back to Aggie. Would she become one of the girls given a cow to compensate for her loss of freedom? Snapped into an arranged, loveless marriage because of her pretty face or because she came with a cow? She wouldn't wish a marriage like her first on anyone. She must be able to help Aggie and in so doing repay Bill. He'd rescued Francis after his run-in with Sanderson; she owed him.

'Now tell me how Mr Greenway's plans for Government House are coming along.' Elizabeth's words brought her back to the moment. 'We simply must do something. It is getting worse by the day. I'm dreading winter; the wind whistles through like a banshee and the white ants have invaded the timbers. It is in a ruinous state. Now the foundation stones for the stables and the fort are laid it is time to make a decision. It too should be castellated, built of stone, and suited to the rank and dignity of the governor.'

'Francis has given some thought to it. He has sketches prepared.' The words caught in her throat as she remembered the plan she had drawn in the weeks after Macquarie's list had arrived, but neither she nor Francis had taken the matter further. Was it so very wrong to want acknowledgement for something other than her ability to produce children? She swallowed the thought. 'Shall I suggest Francis submit the plans?'

'I should like that very much. I do hope he has considered that lovely sketch you showed me the first time we met. Now I shall give you back your little man and offer you the wine and cake I promised.' Elizabeth busied herself with plates and glasses, almost childlike in her delight, while Mary attempted to tuck Charles back into her shawl. He, however, had other ideas and started to wail and kick his legs. 'Oh dear, I believe he's hungry. Will you excuse me for a moment. I must feed him.'

'Please, stay here. Come and sit back on the cushions, no one will disturb us.'

Surprised by Elizabeth's understanding, Mary made herself comfortable and tucked Charles beneath her shawl, and in moments his wailing ceased and the familiar rhythmic suck, swallow and breathe sounds merged with the bird calls and the gentle whisper of the waves. 'Thank you, we've had a few sleepless nights but he's a good baby.'

'A good mother I suspect. Your daughter must be growing.'

'She's just turned two and has a passion for chickens.' Mary twitched the shawl and ran a finger over Charles's cheek.

'Five children. However do you manage without a nursemaid?'

'Hannah is a godsend, and the boys are growing fast, becoming very self-sufficient. George is eleven and William turning ten soon.'

'And Frankie is soon to be six, like my darling Lachie.' Elizabeth nibbled one of the small cakes, then took a sip of her wine. 'We should arrange more help for you. One of the girls from the orphanage perhaps, and a cow from the government farm. With all those children you must have a cow. Fresh milk is essential for growing children.'

'Really, we manage very well with Francis's salary, travelling expenses and government rations.' If and when it was paid, but she couldn't expect Elizabeth to chase up Francis's dues. 'Although some extra help never goes amiss.'

'Let me. I will arrange everything. I'd like to. There are some deserving young girls at the orphanage.'

Charles stirred as Mary moved him to the other arm. 'The orphanage, you said?' Now, how to manage this. If she could make it work, she would be able to repay Bill for his kindness, save Aggie from an arranged marriage, bring Hannah some respite and possibly devote some more time to the boys' education, and she'd still have the evenings to work with Francis. 'You are too kind. It would make life a little easier, and if it also helped a young girl, I would feel less demanding. I will have to speak to my husband about it.' More importantly she'd speak to Bill, and find out if he thought Aggie would benefit.

'Then consider the offer open and let me know the moment you have decided. I shall speak to the matron, Mrs Hoskings, and arrange for a girl of your choice to be apprenticed to you. It would be easier if we could organise everything before the girls leave for Parramatta. I think the little man has had his fill.'

Mary glanced down at Charles, his eyelashes half-moons against his peach-like cheeks. Taking great care not to disturb him, she straightened her clothing and tucked him more securely into the shawl.

'Now it is your turn. Wine and cake. The perfect way to seal a deal.'

On her way home Mary called into the free market. The spot where Bill usually set up his dray was occupied by a wizened old man who reeked of rum and soiled clothing. 'I'm looking for Bill.'

'Gone for another load. Won't be back until the day after termorrow.'

'When you see him, please tell him Mary Merino wants a word.'

He winked, tipped back his head and poured a stream of rum down his gullet then leant back against the wall and closed his eyes.

If she wasn't careful Mary Merino would be getting herself a reputation. With a smile, she hitched the sling holding baby Charles over her shoulder and weaved her way through the crowds on George Street towards home.

A blissful calm enveloped her when she walked into the house. Hannah sat dozing at the kitchen table, Caroline asleep on the rag rug at her feet. She pushed open the door to what might one day become the dining room to find Francis in his shirtsleeves, bent over a set of plans. He lifted his head and smiled.

'I wondered where you'd got to. I finished earlier than I expected. The barracks at Hyde Park are coming along nicely. I'd say we'll have the men in there before winter.'

'That's good news. I've been out for a walk with Charles, and I've been thinking.'

'Have you got some ideas for me?' He shuffled the mess of papers and drawings littering the table. 'It seems I am to take over the design for the public fountain in Macquarie Place.'

'I thought it was underway.'

'Some complaint that there should be a niche in the wall and the fellow Mrs Macquarie commissioned, Cureton, his work is not satisfactory. What have you been thinking about?'

The perfect opportunity. 'The girls from the orphanage are being moved to Parramatta in a few weeks and I thought perhaps before they go, we could find someone to give Hannah and me some help with the children.' Francis's face creased in a frown but before he had time to open his mouth she continued. 'It would leave me with a few spare hours in the day to assist you and attend to the children's lessons, as they are falling behind. Frankie hasn't the remotest idea of his letters, and if George is hoping to secure this job with Mr Watson …' She let the remainder of the sentence dangle.

'I don't see why not. Would they be on rations?'

'I don't know. I will have to go down and talk to Mrs Hoskings, the matron, and ask to have a girl apprenticed to us. I believe they are found positions once they turn thirteen. With your salary and travelling expenses owed I'm sure we could manage even if she wasn't on rations. Hannah has done such a wonderful job with the vegetable garden and the chickens.'

'I'll leave it with you. Now come and sit down and give me your opinion.'

'First of all, I need to settle Charles and then we can eat as soon as the boys are home.'

Once Hannah took the children to their beds Mary lit the candles and together, she and Francis spent the evening designing and estimating, drawing and measuring until the pile of plans grew and the remaining items on Macquarie's list dwindled. She made no mention of her meeting with Elizabeth; she'd simply bide her time and hope that when the governor summoned Francis the plans she'd drawn for Government House would be accepted with approval and not questioned. It made Mary smile to think that behind these two proud men stood two women who could, if they so desired, fashion the country in any way they saw fit.

Twenty-Eight

It took a great deal of bribery, threats and promises to keep the three boys at their lessons but Mary was determined they would have a decent education. She handed George and William pens and a page of arithmetic, then settled the inkpot between them.

Out of the corner of her eye she glimpsed Frankie sidling to the door. 'You come right back here.' She settled a slate and tubes of chalk in front of the vacant chair. 'Come on, sit down.' He curled up his nose and pushed the slate aside.

'Don't even start. You don't get pen and ink until you've proved you can form your letters.' Before too long she would have to include Caroline in the lessons—just because she was a girl didn't mean her education should be ignored. Reading, writing, arithmetic, history, geography and drawing and measuring, all the topics Papa had deemed essential, had held her in good stead.

The next hour passed, a sense of resigned tolerance pervading the air until George and William pushed away their pages in unison and chorused, 'Finished.' Their chairs scraped back.

'For today but tomorrow we'll try a little geography. George, I want you and William to go down to the harbour.'

The boys' eyes rounded, and Mary curbed a smile. 'I want a list of all the countries you can discover that the ships in the harbour have visited. Take Frankie with you. Now off you go.'

They were out of the door, feet flying as they headed for the wharf. She wasn't sure where the idea had come from but it was essential they should have an understanding of the world. If they had a globe, they could have studied that. Maybe she should consider sending them to one of the church schools. She tidied up the table, peered out of the window at Hannah and Caroline, who were busy in the garden, and made a decision. She could do a better job herself and they wouldn't be subjected to the rigours of a religious education and the beatings that came with it. She wanted Caroline to receive an education that would encourage rational thought and inspire independence and a desire to contribute to society. She'd go and see if Bill was back in town, ask him how he'd feel if she applied for Aggie, and ... what a wonderful idea. Aggie, who'd had an education at the orphanage, would be able to help with the younger children's lessons.

Mary cupped her hands around her mouth. 'Oi! Bill!'

His head came up with a snap and he swung around. 'Oi! Mary Merino.' His chiselled face broke into an engaging grin.

'I've had an idea, but I wanted to ask you about it first.'

'You don't look much like Mary Merino today. More wine and cake with the governor's wife?'

'Shh!' How on earth ... 'I'm going to employ another maid. I wondered if Aggie might like the job?'

'Aggie? She's nothing but trouble, and six months more to go before she's old enough. They keep them until they're thirteen, you know.'

'I think I can arrange it, but I want to talk to her first, make sure it's what she wants.'

His blue-eyed gaze pinned her. 'Why would you do that?'

'You've helped me out, and Francis, the Sanderson business. The girls at the orphanage have had an education. I need some help with the younger children, and it would get Aggie out of the place.' Away from the prospect of an arranged marriage, but she wasn't about to bring that up with Bill. 'I thought maybe if you came with me, we could speak to her together.'

'I'd have to find someone to keep an eye on me goods. We'll be a while and they won't be letting Aggie go if they think she's coming to live with me.'

'We can get around that problem.'

His eyes narrowed. 'It slipped me mind for a moment, friends in high places.'

'I'm doing this for Aggie, for you, and myself. As I said, I need some help around the house and with the children. Wouldn't you rather know she was in a family home than …' She bit her lips. She hadn't intended to mention the marriage question.

'Than fobbed off to some dirty old farmer with a hankering for a young wife and a cow,' he finished for her. 'Give me a minute to sort this lot and I'll meet you out the front.'

A few minutes later Bill appeared around the corner, hat on, woollen coat a tad too small for his broad chest buttoned, and no sign of his usual confident self. He offered a half-hearted smile.

Convinced there was more to Aggie's story than he'd told her, she rested a hand on his arm. 'Are you sure you want to do this? I thought it would be a help.'

'Yeah, it's just …' He shrugged his shoulders. 'I can't stand that man at the orphanage.'

'Which man?'

'Marsden, better known as the Flogging Parson.' His shoulders rose and fell then he shuddered. 'Was on the receiving end of the lash more times than I'd like to count.'

Which would mean that Bill too had been under the care of the church. No doubt he had a story to tell in his own good time. 'I don't believe we have to see the Reverend Marsden. I've been told we need to speak to a Mrs Hoskings, and request that Aggie is apprenticed out to me.'

By the time they arrived at the orphanage Bill looked ready for the gallows. Mary stopped on the corner. 'Are you sure this is what you want?'

'Yeah, it's what I want and I'm pretty sure it'll be what Aggie wants—she's been at me for months to get her out of the place. She wants to be with me, but that can't happen.'

'I'm sure she'll understand, and you're always welcome to visit. Let me do the talking.' Mary raised her hand and rang the bell attached to the side of a heavy door with a Judas window, and the memory of her visits with Mudd to Newgate made the hairs on the back of her neck prickle until an apple-cheeked, smiling face appeared at the window. 'I'd like to speak to the matron, Mrs Hoskings.'

'Got an appointment?'

'No. No, I haven't but I have been assured Mrs Hoskings would be happy to see me.'

'Name?'

'Mrs Greenway, Mrs Francis Greenway, and ...' She paused. She had no idea of Bill's full name. Bill's shoulders straightened and he lifted his head. 'Mr Edwards,' he said in a firm voice. Two sides to every character, indeed.

The window closed and after some rattling and banging the door swung open and they were led into a small courtyard. 'Wait here and I'll see if she's available.' The girl, dressed in a blue gown with a white apron and cape, scuttled off.

Bill stood shuffling his feet, mumbling to himself. His face was the colour of whey.

'Everything will be fine. Trust me.' It was so strange to see the usually confident young man twisting his hands, a mass of nerves. She couldn't even imagine what he and Aggie must have been through as children, and she didn't dare ask. No one enquired into anyone's past in the colony.

A few minutes later the girl reappeared. 'Follow me.' She led them into the main building, down a corridor, and knocked on a door. 'They're here, Mrs Hoskings.'

The door closed behind them and a tall thin woman with a beak of a nose rose from her desk. 'Mrs Greenway, Mr Edwards ...' her face creased in a frown, '... have we met before?'

Before Bill could answer Mary stepped in front of him. 'Mrs Hoskings, how very good of you to see me. I am looking for a new servant girl, someone young, to help with my five children.'

'I'm sure we can find someone suitable. Our girls are well trained, can read and write, know their numbers, and have excellent needlework skills. We are always keen to house them in good *family* homes.' Her eyes darted once again to Bill.

'My husband is the civil architect, and we have ample room to accommodate another maid.'

'If you'd like to sit down, I will arrange for you to meet some of our more presentable girls.'

Mary sucked in a deep breath. It was now or never. 'I have one particular girl in mind who has been in your care for over five years and is approaching thirteen. Mr Edwards's niece, Aggie.'

'Ahhh!' Mrs Hoskings plopped back down in her chair. 'I thought I recognised the young man. We have several girls who would be better suited.'

'No, I have quite made up my mind and I have discussed the matter with Mrs Macquarie,' she said, throwing down her trump card.

Mrs Hoskings jumped to her feet. 'Mrs Macquarie? She pays a keen interest in our girls and visited only the other day. She mentioned someone who was in need of assistance ... I shall go and arrange for Aggie to come down.' She bundled out of the room.

Bill let out a long slow wheezing breath and then grinned. 'Nicely done, Mary Merino. Though I'm not sure Mrs Macquarie will appreciate her name being bandied about.'

'She herself told me to come and see Mrs Hoskings about a new maid.'

'So that note I delivered ...'

'As I said, let me do the talking. We'll see what Aggie has to say.'

'Mary Merino ...' Bill shook his head. 'Always knew there was more to you than meets the eye.'

Before she could reply, the door swung open and Mrs Hoskings ushered a sour stench and a red-faced Aggie into the room. She took one look at Bill, flew to his side and burst into tears.

'Silly girl. Stop that nonsense at once. This nice lady, Mrs Greenway, she's come to offer you a place.'

Aggie peered at Mrs Hoskings through a curtain of dishevelled hair, then tipped her head up and stared at Bill.

'That's right, love. Mrs Greenway's looking for someone to help her with her children. You'd like that, wouldn't you?'

'I want to go with you.'

'You can't do that, Aggie, love, but if you're a good girl and do what you're told Mrs Greenway will let me come and visit.'

Mary swallowed the words she wanted to utter, taking in the girl's filthy apron, torn dress and scratched face. 'Bill can come and visit but only if you work hard and do what you're told.'

'There'll be paperwork to sign,' Mrs Hoskings interrupted. 'We can't have our charges just leaving with anyone who ...'

'I'd be happy to sign any paperwork and I'm sure Mrs Macquarie will vouch for me. I would like Aggie to start today.'

'I'm not sure that can be arranged ...'

Mary drew herself up to her full height. She hadn't intended to take Aggie immediately, but the poor child was obviously deeply distressed and badly in need of a bath. 'If you'd like to give me a pen and paper, I shall write a note to Mrs Macquarie. I'm certain she'll agree when I explain Aggie's ...' she cleared her throat, '... distress.'

Mrs Hoskings's cheeks filled with air, and she let out a series of huffs punctuated by a few dry coughs. 'No note will be necessary. Go and collect your belongings, Aggie.'

Aggie gripped Bill's hand as though her life depended on it, which it possibly did, and shook her head.

'Please have Aggie's belongings, along with the necessary paperwork, delivered to my home. The corner of George and Argyle Streets—anyone can direct you to Mr Greenway's residence. Come along, Aggie.' Without waiting for a response, Mary turned on her heel and led the way out of the room. She could do this.

When Francis returned home Hannah had taken charge of Aggie and she sat scrubbed and glowing on the kitchen floor building a castle with Caroline from her wooden offcuts. Bill had left, virtually speechless with gratitude, promising to return in the morning.

'Francis, this is Aggie, our new help. I chose her from the orphanage today. Aggie, this is Mr Greenway.'

Aggie bounded to her feet and made a clumsy curtsy. Francis did little more than nod before heading for the would-be dining room and his paperwork. 'Mary, I need to speak with you.' He tossed the words over his shoulder.

Her stomach sank. He couldn't complain about Aggie, he'd agreed only the day before. 'Hannah, we'll all eat together. Can you round up the boys, they're outside in the garden. I'll go and see what Mr Greenway wants.'

Much to her amazement Francis had poured two glasses of wine and stood waiting for her. 'I have news and we should celebrate.'

She took the glass and studied his face, searching for some indication as to his mood. It was always so difficult to gauge— sometimes sarcasm got the better of him.

He proved her wrong and beamed. 'There is to be an official opening of the Hyde Park barracks on June fourth to celebrate the king's birthday. It is a triumph! The opportunity to prove that function and design can exist in harmony. And we, my dear ...' he wrapped his arm around her shoulder and pulled her close, '... will attend with the official party. At long last I feel my efforts are appreciated.'

Not sarcasm, simply genuine pride in his achievements. Before her stood the man she'd first met—enthusiastic, optimistic and confident. Matters were definitely looking up.

Twenty-Nine

Francis's exuberant optimism reached into every corner of the household. George achieved his heart's desire when Francis spoke with Mr Watson and secured him a part-time job in the harbour-master's office and traded his lessons at home for those of Sydney Cove. William spent more time travelling with Francis—learning the trade, he told Mary with a gleeful glint in his eye—and Aggie settled in after a few hiccups, taking responsibility for Frankie, Caroline and Charles as though born to the role, leaving Mary very much the lady of the house.

'Aggie, would you do me a small favour?' She folded a paper and dropped a blob of heated wax to seal it. 'Could you go down to the stores?' She handed over the small purse she kept for house-hold expenses.

Aggie's pretty blue eyes lit up. It was over two weeks since she'd last seen Bill.

'While you're there give this to Bill. He has some seeds for me. Don't forget your bonnet and perhaps Frankie would enjoy a walk. I'll see to the babes.'

The girl was out of the door, Frankie's hand clasped in hers, before Mary could issue any more instructions. It warmed her

heart to be able to make Aggie happy, and a visit to Bill kept
her from straying. She'd no need to give instructions about the
note. Bill would peel off the sealed outer page and see Elizabeth's
name. She wanted to thank Elizabeth for her assistance with Mrs
Hoskings and the tiresome paperwork involved in securing Aggie's
release from the orphanage, and despite the harmony in the house
with time on her hands she missed the opportunity to talk of matters other than the daily routine. She scratched at the back of her
neck; truth be told she wanted to ask Elizabeth another favour.
The idea had come to her only the night before as she'd lain in
Francis's arms, revelling in their rediscovered closeness.

Mary's luck held and not two hours later Aggie returned with a
small box containing a complete range of seeds for winter planting, obviously intended as a gift because she handed back the
purse still containing every one of the coins, and tucked beneath
the seeds, a note from Elizabeth. Mary had no idea how Bill had
managed such a swift response. Elizabeth would be at her favourite spot that afternoon.

'Hannah, can you see to the children's meal? I have business to
attend to.'

'What about you? Have you given up eating? You're not ...'
She waggled her eyebrows.

'I'll take something to munch on the way.' She snatched a piece
of cheese and an apple from the table. 'And no, I'm not. Charles
is barely more than a year old.' Without waiting for a response,
she picked up her folio and made for the door. 'I'll be back before
dark.'

She as good as flew along George Street, cut across in front of
the men beavering away on the rising walls of Fort Macquarie and

headed down to the cove. She found Elizabeth sitting staring out at the ocean, an unnatural slump in her shoulders. 'My dear.'

Elizabeth lifted her tear-stained face. Mary flew to her side. 'Oh, how can I help?'

Elizabeth shook her head and wiped her hand over her face in a strangely childish gesture. 'A little homesickness, nothing more.'

'Has something happened?'

'Nothing unexpected. I shouldn't speak of it …'

Mary took her hand, 'Anything you say will be in confidence. Besides, whom would I tell?' The truth of her words hit with a blow. She wouldn't, couldn't talk to Francis of anything Elizabeth said. Certainly not Hannah or Aggie, and she had no other close friends in the colony, except perhaps Bill.

Elizabeth shuffled back on her cushion and arranged another next to her. 'Come sit. I'm being foolish.'

'If whatever it is has made you unhappy then you are not foolish.'

Elizabeth drew in a deep breath and offered a wan smile. 'We have been waiting for a response to several letters Macquarie has sent to England tendering his resignation and he still hasn't received a reply. It seems we are to remain here forever—no reprieve for the king's representative.' The words flew from her lips and she clamped her hand across her mouth.

The governor had tendered his resignation? Mary's eyes widened. 'Why would he do that? All his hard work, the wonderful progress he has made in the colony, the buildings, the roads, the …'

'It is politics and the tittle-tattle of the exclusives who think he favours the emancipists. It is taking such a toll on his health and his wellbeing. Lord Bathurst is sending out some commissioner, to examine the effectiveness of the colony and investigate every aspect: financials, the church, the judiciary and the convict system. There have been complaints about his extravagant building program, his compassion towards the convicts and his support of the emancipists.' Two red spots highlighted Elizabeth's cheek-bones. 'The implication is that Macquarie is in some way personally benefitting from the system. Bathurst couldn't be further from the truth. Macquarie wants everyone, settler or felon, to thrive.'

The free settlers and the military had been up to no good. It was strange to think that but for her action the Greenways too might have numbered with the exclusives, something she no longer regretted. She applauded Macquarie's sympathy for the convicts and his belief that once they had served their sentence they should be admitted into their previous rank in society. Dr Redfern, Mr Lord and Mrs Reibey were but three fine examples.

'I fear our halcyon days may be over. But enough of such maudlin matters.' Elizabeth shook back her hair and her face brightened. 'I believe you have received an invitation to attend the official opening of the Hyde Park barracks.'

'We have. Mr Greenway is very much looking forward to the occasion. It has cheered him no end. He's once more the man I married, the architect intent on making dreams a reality. He believes the barracks to be one of his greatest achievements.'

'And so it is. It is a man's building intended for men. Clean simple lines, a sense of permanence and stability ...'

'Nothing like the glorious, whimsical splendour of the government stables, Fort Macquarie or the gatehouse?'

'Not a sign of a woman's touch.' Elizabeth winked. 'I do hope we have time to finalise the plans for Government House and get it underway before the odious commissioner arrives.'

Mary laughed. Her secret was safe with Elizabeth, governor's wife or not.

'You have been such a friend to me. I look forward to inviting you to old Government House before it is demolished.'

'Government House?' After all the discussion of Macquarie's difficulties with the exclusives, why would Elizabeth make their acquaintanceship public?

'Why not? The barracks are complete.'

Why would the completion of the barracks bring about such a change?

Elizabeth smiled. 'Wear your best bonnet and brightest smile, Mrs Greenway. You are, after all, the architect's wife.'

The vast clock above the central door of the convict barracks struck one as Mary and Francis walked through the gates into the courtyard of Hyde Park barracks. It had been a mere eighteen months since the governor laid the foundation stone.

Francis straightened his cravat and tugged at his new coat. 'Proof indeed that elegant simplicity and faultless proportions will always out.'

The towering grandeur of the three-storey building overshadowed the impressive group of dignitaries, headed by the Governor, Elizabeth, and young Lachlan, making their way through to the dining room where hundreds of convicts sat down at long trestle tables feasting on beef and bread, plum pudding and punch.

''Tis as good as Christmas in June,' a grizzled man remarked as Mary passed by. Her eyes strayed to Elizabeth, who having reached the podium sat, hands folded neatly in her lap, listening first to her husband's short plain speech and then the more rambling offering from Judge Advocate Wylde. Once Wylde said his piece the governor rose again and, glasses raised, they drank a toast to the health and prosperity of the inmates.

A resounding three cheers from the six hundred men echoed in the cavernous room. Just when Mary thought it was all over, she caught Elizabeth's eye. Her friend lifted one finger and gave a discreet nod.

Macquarie held up his hand, cleared his throat and waited for silence. 'Mr Greenway, if you and your wife would be so kind as to join us.'

Francis's chin tilted and a smile curled his full lips. He gave a slight bow, encouraging Mary to proceed him to the podium.

Elizabeth's comments two days earlier suddenly made sense. Macquarie intended to make Francis's conditional pardon absolute. She didn't know whether to laugh or cry. Heads held high, they would now be able to take their place in Sydney society, accept Elizabeth's invitation to dine at the governor's table and, if Francis chose, return to England, the slate wiped clean. With one stroke of his pen Governor Macquarie had put the past to rest. It was strange to think she and Francis were no longer tied to New South Wales, while the Macquaries were subject to the whims of a government fifteen thousand miles across the sea.

Nine years since that fateful day when Francis had taken his life in his hands by pleading guilty, he was free. Free to take his proper place in society. But best of all, this building was Francis's crowning achievement. She'd offered no suggestions. Hyde Park barracks stood testament to his skill and creative genius, and it had produced the pardon he so richly deserved.

Thirty

When a thirteen-gun salute Jeffery Bent would have envied thundered from Dawes Point, the very air quivered and both Charles and Caroline burst into a torrent of tears. A shiver worked its way across Mary's shoulders. With the arrival of Mr John Thomas Bigge, life in the colony was about to take a turn for the worse. She could feel it in her bones.

Only five days earlier she'd met with Elizabeth, a very different Elizabeth, her hair awry and her eyes flashing. 'Matters have reached such a peak that we are to expect the arrival of a Mr Bigge, Lord Bathurst's under-secretary no less, appointed to enquire into the affairs of the colony. Macquarie is convinced it is for the best and that the progress made turning the wilderness into a haven of civilisation will be applauded. I don't share his optimism. I have it on good authority letters have been flying fast and furiously between certain members of the exclusives and the Colonial Office in London claiming over-spending, corruption and mismanagement.'

'I am sure once Mr Bigge is shown around, he will appreciate all the work you both have done.'

311

'You should prepare Mr Greenway. He will no doubt be asked
to provide financial statements and dragged into the melee.'

The mere thought sent Mary into a flat spin. In his present mood
Francis would not tolerate any questions about his work. It appeared
the official opening of the barracks had done more than establish
Francis's reputation. Full of glee and self-congratulations, his confidence bloomed as his name began to appear on lists of honoured
guests at functions ranging from the laying of foundation stones to
hobnobbing with the gentry, and increasing his private commissions.

Francis now believed he had some kind of divine mission to
fulfill, and his self-importance had reached new heights. Mary
couldn't relay Elizabeth's warning.

She did, however, accompany Francis to Government House,
along with everyone who was anyone, to hear Judge Wylde read
Bigge's commission, administer the oaths of office and partake of
wine and cake.

Her first sight of Mr Bigge did little to allay her fears. He was
red-headed, freckled-faced, with a nose as large as his self-regard
and, if the tittle-tattle was to be believed, a well-matched salary, some one thousand pounds larger than the governor's. Mr
Bigge's arrival didn't bode well. Pleading a headache, caused by
her earlier sense of foreboding, she managed to convince Francis
they should leave rather than interrupt the group of wealthy free
settlers courting Bigge. There would be plenty of time for Francis
to make the commissioner's acquaintance.

The first inkling of trouble arrived with Bill early one evening.
It had become his habit to call in as the sun was setting, bringing little gifts or delicacies from the market, and sit playing
with the children and Aggie. On this particular evening he was

preoccupied, shuffling his feet, scratching at his chin, peering out into the twilight.

'What is it, Bill? Come and sit down, I'll make some tea,' Mary prattled on, her words sounding hollow and forced.

Once Bill had a mug of tea cradled in his large hands, he lifted his head and fixed Francis with a steely gaze. 'I heard from the quarry workers that the newly arrived convicts are to be sent out of town, to work for some of the wealthier landowners to develop their estates.'

Francis's knife stalled halfway to his mouth, and he dropped the apple he was peeling. 'They are going to do what?'

'Send the new convicts to work for the exclusives on their land grants.'

All the plates on the table jumped as Francis slammed his hands onto the table as if he meant to vault over it. 'What a load of bunkum. The governor won't hear of it. He's promised me additional labour for the fort and in return I promised it would be finished in ten weeks.' He flounced out of the room and a few moments later the front door slammed, making the shutters rattle.

Hopefully Elizabeth and the governor were entertaining or, better still, out of town.

Bill dropped his head into his hands. 'I didn't mean to …'

'I know you didn't. Francis has a lot to deal with at the moment. He'll be back to his happier self before long.' The hollow ring to her words rattled her ears as she fought back the sense of doom.

Hannah huffed and puffed and mumbled about wasted food as she scraped the plates and sent Aggie out into the scullery to deal with the washing up. George and William drifted outside with the bag of marbles Bill had acquired, Frankie on their heels, and Mary scooped up Charles and Caroline, one on each hip. An early night, maybe even a peaceful one, would be a fine thing.

Several hours later the slam of the door roused her. She pulled her old pelisse over her nightgown, checked on the children and followed the sound of thumping into the dining room. The slight fishy smell of the oil lamp greeted her as she pushed open the door to find Francis foraging through the piles of paper littering the table. They looked remarkably like his costings, not anything she was permitted to touch. 'Did you see the governor?'

He didn't lift his head, simply grunted.

'Is everything all right?'

She might well have lit an explosive. His head snapped up, eyes blazing. 'No! It is not. And to add insult to injury I am to provide the Bigge man with an estimate of expenses for the government stables—the palace for horses, he called it.'

'You spoke with him?'

'He was dining at Government House.'

Mary clamped her lips, trying to prevent the groan escaping her lips. She didn't dare imagine the scene that must have ensued.

Despite the upheavals and constant demands that Mr Bigge's arrival caused poor Francis, running and jumping from one project to the next, they laid the foundation stone for St Andrew's church and not a month later for the new courthouse. The guard house on Dawes Point was already underway and even Mary's Gothic folly, the turnpike lodge at the intersection of George and Pitt Streets where the road to Parramatta began, took shape. Francis's private practice continued to flourish: a house at Charlotte Place for Sir John Jamison, a cottage in Parramatta and work for merchant Loane.

He was run off his feet, as though, in a most un-Francis-like way, he was trying to prove himself.

Nothing more happened as the months rolled by except Mary's realisation that she was once again with child, and by the time she was back to her usual self Bigge's assault took a more personal tone. He summoned Francis and informed him that instructions would no longer be forthcoming from the governor. He, Commissioner Bigge, would be relieving the governor of the task of overseeing Francis's work and deciding what would be built and when. Mary couldn't imagine Francis's response but something had gone very wrong because when she sent a note to Elizabeth in the hope that they could smooth things over she received a very curt reply stating it wasn't convenient.

Francis's rage exploded one afternoon before he'd even made it through the door, his body angled with tension as if forcing his way through a crowd. 'Now the bastard is slandering me, querying various works, their progress, and demanding full costings.'

He slumped down at the table, shuffling through papers, then turned to her with a sheaf of them in his hand. 'The man has no understanding of building principles, nor any sympathy for design. He is an uneducated heathen.'

Possibly not the case. Bill had told Mary that *the man* had a string of qualifications, had attended Oxford, and been called to the bar before being sent to Trinidad as Chief Justice.

'His list of complaints this week range from delays in construction of the Female Factory at Parramatta, to deciding the schoolhouse is to be converted into a courthouse and a new charity school built nearby.

'To add insult to injury Macquarie has turned his back on me and is suggesting that I have overstepped his original instructions. I have every intention of ignoring his remarks. I will ensure the building program continues as planned. I hear Bigge is intending to visit Van Diemen's Land early in the new year, and we shall make a

big push to finish construction in his absence.' His determined tone
sent a chill down her spine.

'It would be prudent to attempt to keep both the governor and
Bigge on side.' Her patience shrivelled and she didn't care who
heard. 'It's not wise to make enemies of people who wield so
much power.'

'To be honest I cannot be concerned with this petty bickering.
All I care about is the purity of my art. It is the architecture that
is important.' The movement of his shoulder, almost a dismissal,
made her nerves jangle.

Perhaps she should try once more to speak to Elizabeth. She'd
received no word from her for several months, since her curt note
saying they would not be able to meet, though to be fair both she
and the governor had spent time in Parramatta and then embarked
on a tour northward. Not that she would have been in a fit state to
be seen out and about; since Francis had received his absolute pardon, the decorum required was beginning to play on her nerves.
Thankfully Dr Redfern still attended to her despite the trouncing
he'd received from Bigge.

It was all so terribly unfair. D'Arcy Wentworth had retired as
chief surgeon, and the governor had offered Dr Redfern the position, but Bigge overruled the governor and claimed that the naval
surgeon, James Bowman, had already been appointed. Without a
doubt the governor had had enough of Bigge's high-handed ways
because he immediately appointed Dr Redfern magistrate—or so he
thought. Bigge overruled that too, saying that an emancipist couldn't
hold a position of such responsibility. It flew in the face of every phi-
losophy Elizabeth and the governor espoused. What hope had any
convict of regaining their previous position in society if the governor's appointments were to be overruled by a man who appeared, to
all intents and purposes, to be firmly tucked into the pockets of free
settlers and military who had all received large land grants?

More to the point, what would happen to Francis? He had earned his pardon; they were free to apply to return to England, but she knew him well enough to understand that he would not leave his buildings unfinished. She had to speak to Elizabeth, and explain how dire the situation had become. Elizabeth counted both Piper and Redfern, exclusive and emancipist, as her friends, and they frequently dined at her table. Whatever had happened to all the governor's brave words? Was Francis destined to be treated as a convict forever?

In a fit of despondency Mary went to see Bill. He kept his ear to the ground and heard both sides of every story from his contacts in Sydney, Parramatta and Windsor. She couldn't wait until he called in to see Aggie and the children; she had to speak to him alone, preferably when Francis was safely out of earshot too.

Her pelisse refused to button. There was no way to mask her condition—two more months to go if Dr Redfern was to be believed, and he'd been right every other time. Instead, she dug out a set of government-issue slops. She dirtied her face and blended in with the crowd surging down George Street to the free market. Or so she thought.

'Oi! Mary Merino.'

Mary ducked into the shadows behind Bill's dray to catch her breath.

'What're you doing hiding here?'

'I need a word, and some advice maybe.'

'Advice. Since when did an exclusive come to a currency lad for advice, huh?'

'Currency lad? Are you trying to tell me you're a banker now?' Perspiration dripped from her forehead into her eyes.

'You're going to have to learn the local jargon. Currency lad, or lass, is what the exclusives call us, those born in the colony. Sterling if you weren't. Just like the coins you paid me with the first time—sterling. Those holey dollars and dumps are currency, but not sterling. It's a title we wear with pride.' He made a sweeping bow, his nose as good as touching her boots. 'At your service, Mary Merino.'

'Stop your shenanigans.' It was as hot as Hades in the cramped space behind the dray; her chemise had stuck to her back and a river of sweat pooled beneath her arms. 'This is important.'

'Here, come and sit down. You look all done in. You shouldn't be out and about in your condition. Certainly not in this heat.'

Mary blew out a puff of air. Perhaps he was right, though the heat didn't usually get to her until well into the new year. January, February. Not yet. It was the wretched humidity after the incessant rain. She squatted down on an upturned crate propped against the wheel of the dray and wiped her face with the corner of her apron.

'Drink this.'

Mary took the open bottle wrapped in damp sacking, and sniffed at it.

'It's fine, good clean Hawkesbury water, not that Tank Stream rubbish.'

The water revived her, and her mind drifted back to the reason for her visit. 'Do you know if Mrs Macquarie has returned to town?'

Bill shrugged. 'I can find out. I know they're back from their traipsing around up country, but she's been in Parramatta mostly. Tittle-tattle says the new colonial secretary, one Major Goulburn, landed a few days ago. Macquarie's resignation has finally been accepted. Then you've got that Kitchen bloke slandering Mr Greenway all over town. Telling anyone who'll listen that he's receiving an extra five per cent on all the government buildings from the public purse. Rumour has it he's cosying up to Bigge and has got his eye on Mr Greenway's government appointment.'

'Oh, that's just ridiculous. Francis hasn't been paid any extra on anything. He's still receiving the same salary and rations we've always had, apart from a dollop of coal now and again. Not exactly what's needed in this heat.'

'I reckon Mr Greenway should know what he's up against.'

Mary slumped against the wheel of the dray and her temper snapped. 'In that case why don't you come and tell him yourself.' She simply hadn't got the energy. 'Aggie would love to see you and I'll write a note to Elizabeth if you can deliver it. They usually come back from Parramatta when the weather heats up.' She struggled to stand upright, gave up and held out her hands.

Bill heaved her to her feet. 'Are you all right to walk home? I can't leave right now but I can get someone to go with you.' He tipped his head towards the old fellow who minded his spot when he was out of town.

'I'll be perfectly fine and there's a breeze coming off the water.'

Thirty-One

Bill's news went down like a foundering ship off the Sow and Pigs reef, and Mary thoroughly regretted her delay in warning Francis about Kitchen. Standing in the middle of the room, his face purple with rage and spluttering, he gave vent to his feelings in no uncertain terms. 'I've been cheated out of cartloads of money owed to me. As architect I should have been paid a percentage on all the buildings once they were completed, not a paltry three shillings a day, and I've had to fork out my own travelling expenses for the last three years, sixty pounds at least, even though they were promised. I shall have words with Macquarie.' He pulled on his coat and straightened his cravat.

'Francis, there's something else you should know.'

His head came up with a snap, and his eyes narrowed. 'Well?'

Mary sucked in a breath. 'Macquarie's resignation has finally been accepted. The colonial secretary, Goulburn, arrived with the dispatches.'

'In that case I better get a move on.' He reefed off his coat and rolled up his sleeves. 'I shall present Macquarie with a list of monies owed before it is too late. I'm out of pocket for some of the earlier buildings as well. I will not be cheated.' He stomped off into the dining room, ranting. Mary trailed along after him, the cloying heat making every step a nightmare, and any hope of smoothing the troubled waters between the governor and Francis disappearing rapidly.

Francis snatched up a sheaf of papers and read the title. 'An estimate of Work done by the Government under the Immediate superintendence of FH Greenway. Twenty-one buildings completed or in progress, fees due to Mr Greenway as a professional man ...'

He spun around, eyes blazing. 'It's as well I have been working on these costings. Perhaps the odious Mr Bigge has done me a favour. I have earned a measly six hundred and forty-five pounds in the last six years in addition to the generous allocation of rations for my family.' His voice dripped with sarcasm. 'Coal, an old horse and a tumbledown government barrack better suited as a piggery.'

Papers flew this way and that as Francis continued to rummage through the piles of plans, costings, elevations and bills. 'I need to make some final adjustments, but I expect my account to come to well over ten thousand pounds. I shall present Bigge with my reckonings and if they refuse then I shall demand compensation. Macquarie always said that I could build my own house on this site and use the materials from the demolition.'

A wave of nausea swept Mary and the world tilted as a gripping pain razed her body. She clutched the back of the chair to restore her balance and blinked the world into focus. 'Francis, I need Dr Redfern. The baby is coming.'

As before, within three days of the baby's arrival a large hamper arrived containing an array of delicacies and a note from

Elizabeth. Aggie sat on the bedroom floor exclaiming in wonder at the contents—large juicy oranges, a tin of chocolate, wine and cake. Sadly no mangoes, but grapes, purple and green, plump and sweet, better than any she or Aggie had ever tasted.

'There's a note here.' Aggie wiped her hand down her skirt and held up a folded letter with Elizabeth's now familiar handwriting across the front. 'Pardon me, it's got the governor's seal on it.'

Mary took the small, folded square and slid her nail under the wax. Aggie's knowledge of the colony was as well honed as her uncle's. She tilted the page towards the candle to better read Elizabeth's note.

> *My dearest Mary,*
>
> *Dr Redfern informed me of the joyful arrival of your son, Henry John, on the 14th inst. It struck me as an auspicious day, and I wondered if I could take the liberty of suggesting he also bears the name Valentine. It comes from the Latin,* valens, *meaning, as I am sure you know,* strong and healthy *which is everything I would wish for him …*

Mary lowered the letter and smiled. Francis had decided on Henry, after the English architect Henry Holland, she suspected. She had agreed wholeheartedly but it would be nice to have a reminder of Elizabeth once she left the colony.

'What do you think of the name Valentine, Aggie?'

'For the baby?' She ran the back of her hand down his cheek and his eyes flashed open. 'I think he likes it, but I thought Mr Greenway wanted Henry John.'

'He does but it would make a lovely addition. It means strong and healthy.' She smoothed his downy hair. 'Henry John Valentine Greenway, what do you think?'

'He's certainly strong and healthy.' Aggie hefted the swaddled bundle into her arms. 'I think he's already putting on weight.' She reached for the tin of chocolate, eyes sparkling, and dipped her finger in. 'For me, not for baby Henry Valentine.' Her index finger disappeared into her mouth, and she groaned with pleasure.

Mary returned to her letter.

When you are up and about, please let me know. I have missed our meetings and would love to be introduced to Henry Valentine. I thought we might take a closer look at the stables and the fort as they are both finished and discuss plans for Government House.

Plans for Government House. Francis had mentioned nothing— she'd spent hours working on her preliminary ideas but had shown no one. She'd made some changes to the original drawing that she'd first shown Elizabeth, and the floor plans had become a secret delight which had kept her amused while Francis attended to Macquarie's more mundane, necessary public buildings— courthouses, wharves, gaols, military barracks and churches—and now he'd even roped Aggie into his wretched accounting. 'Aggie, tuck the baby into his cot. I think it's time we settled down for the evening. Take the hamper down to the scullery where it is cool and then off to bed, but before you go could you find me my folio. It's in the chest, right at the very top.' She pointed to the end of the bed.

Aggie fussed around and settled Henry in the fruit crate that had served the last three children so well then lifted the lid of the chest and took out Mary's folio. She smoothed her palm across the well-worn leather. 'It's so soft. It must be very old.'

'It belonged to my papa; he used to keep his correspondence in it when he was at sea.'

'How nice to have something that belonged to your father.' Aggie's voice held a wistful note. 'I don't even know my father's name. Now Mam's gone there's no one to ask.'

It was on the tip of Mary's tongue to suggest Aggie should talk to Bill, but he would have told her long ago if he knew. 'You have Bill, and he's the best uncle in the world.'

'Yes, he is, isn't he?' Her face brightened. 'Living here is so much better than the horrid orphanage. Thank you for rescuing me.'

Mary stretched out her arms. 'Come here.'

Aggie hovered for a moment as though unsure how to respond, then with a strangled sob threw herself into Mary's embrace.

The poor, poor child. What a blessing that Mary had, with Elizabeth's help, managed to make Aggie's life a little better. No one deserved to live in the comfortless, cold orphanage under the guardianship of the Reverend Marsden.

After a while Aggie sniffed and disentangled herself. 'I'm sorry.'

'Don't be; everyone needs to be loved.' Mary brushed Aggie's bright hair back from her face and knuckled a tear from her cheek.

'I'll take the hamper down. Little Henry Valentine is sleeping.' She tucked the blanket tighter around him. 'I'll see you in the morning.'

As soon as the door closed Mary lifted her folio to her cheek. How lucky she'd been. She had never known Mama, but she'd had the love of Papa and he had kept Mama's memory alive with his stories of their life together. He would never have condoned her devious behaviour, or accepted that his daughter would have stooped to forgery. Goosebumps peppered her skin as she took out Miss Bingle's notes and letter. They had to go. Nothing could jeopardise Francis's position, most especially if Bigge was scrutinising his accounts. She held them up to the candle one by one. A great sense of relief filled her as the paper curled, crackled and turned to ash. No more. She turned to her designs for Government House. There were better ways to use her talents.

Dr Redfern released Mary from her confinement. The sting had gone out of the heat, and the humidity had eased. She pulled on one of her old muslin dresses and ambled down to the kitchen in search of an orange, and possibly some chocolate. She found Bill sitting at the kitchen table, rolling one of the oranges around in his large hands.

'Oi! Mary Merino. How are you?'

'I'm well, thank you. What are you doing with my orange?'

'Young Aggie was telling me all about the hamper of goodness you received from Government House.'

Really, she was going to have to have words with the girl. She couldn't have news of her relationship with Elizabeth getting out, not after Bigge's complaints of favouritism and extravagant building programs. 'It's not to be discussed,' she snapped.

'I guessed as much, and I told Aggie the same. I've got some news I thought you ought to hear. Hoped to catch you on your own. Didn't want to be upsetting Mr Greenway like last time.'

Mary lowered herself into the chair. 'Where's Hannah?'

'Out fetching some fish for your dinner, though I suspect she's more interested in the bloke down at the Three Squares than his wares.' He winked.

'If that's your news I don't want to hear it. She's a grown woman who has worked out her sentence and is entitled to her own friends.'

Bill nodded. 'You're right. It's not what I'm here to say. Just wanted to catch you on your own. Bigge has refused Dr Redfern's appointment as chief surgeon or magistrate. His emancipist status counted against him despite all the good work he has done in the colony.'

'Yes, I already know, he told me that himself.' Mary folded her arms, inordinately pleased that she was already aware of Bill's news.

'Seems the governor's health isn't the best, a return of the dysentery that has so plagued him, but he's insisting on calling Redfern, not the Bowman chap.'

'Poor man, Elizabeth will be concerned.'

'She's got more than that to concern her. Captain Piper seems convinced Bigge is out to replace Macquarie himself.'

'He can't do that. Goulburn wouldn't have it, and hasn't Bigge returned to England to present his report?' Whatever was Bill on about? He was dishing up nothing but scuttlebutt. 'I'm not surprised you waited until Francis was out; none of your chatter is important.'

Bill propped his chin in his hands and pinned her with his blue, blue eyes. 'But this is, and you need to know. Bigge apparently took a specific stance against what he calls the Gothic follies. Apparently because Macquarie didn't inform Bathurst of the intricate details and expense of the fort, stables and turnpike lodge, all ornamental features on buildings will henceforth be banned.'

Mary folded her hands tightly in her lap, fingernails scoring her damp palms. The stables, the fort, the lodge—her whimsical Gothic designs, the ones Elizabeth had so heartily championed.

Bill raised his eyebrows. 'I thought you might be particularly interested. No doubt they'll feature in his report.'

Heat flew to Mary's cheeks; she licked her lips and cleared her throat. 'I'm interested in all of Mr Greenway's buildings,' she spluttered. 'He's my husband.' She shot to her feet, grasping the edge of the table to steady herself. She was jumping to conclusions. Bill couldn't possibly know they were her designs. Only Elizabeth and

Francis knew … and neither of them would say anything. Francis regarded the designs as his own. She had to speak to Elizabeth and make sure she hadn't said anything. Inhaling a steadying breath, she lowered herself back onto the chair and pushed the orange across the table to Bill. 'Why don't you have it?'

He shook his head. 'Nope. I don't want to eat your orange. I just wanted you to know what's going on. Give it to Aggie. There's plenty coming from out Hawkesbury way. I better be making a move. Nothing you need doing? Notes you'd like delivered? I expect Mrs Macquarie is looking forward to meeting young Henry Valentine.'

'I would like a note delivered to Government House, now you mention it. Can you wait a moment or two while I write it?'

'That I can. I'll take a stroll round the garden. Talk to young Caroline's chickens and see how those vegetables are coming along. Got green fingers, has Hannah.'

Mary and Elizabeth met, as she'd suggested in her note, in the cool of the afternoon at the newly completed arched stone bridge that led to Fort Macquarie. They were in no danger of offending anyone's sensibilities because the governor had long since decreed that the stretch of shoreline that had once been the preferred bathing place of the military was now off limits, and part of the Domain.

A ripple of pride traced Mary's skin and she squeezed Elizabeth's hand as they stood together admiring the perfect symmetry of the octagonal building, the picturesque towers, turrets and bastions and, further up the incline, the matching stables and offices.

'All that is needed now is a new Government House and our vision is complete. Have you had any further thoughts?'

Elizabeth's eyes strayed towards Mary's basket where her folio rested.

'I have.' Mary smiled. 'Shall we go and sit down?'

'Please ... I can't wait a moment longer. Follow me. I know somewhere we can be undisturbed.' Elizabeth darted off the path, sat in the shade of a grove of small trees and slipped the worn leather folio from Mary's basket. 'Show me.'

'In keeping with the stables and fort, I took Thornbury Castle as a model.' Mary took the folio from Elizabeth's hands, pulled out her plan and laid it flat on her lap. 'It's designed around a quadrangle partly open on the southern side. The north side will form the principal entrance and there will be a staircase here, a vestibule, hall and morning rooms.'

Elizabeth's mouth formed a circle of surprise. 'It is beyond my wildest dreams.' She ran a finger over the drawing. 'And this?'

'The domestic apartments and bedrooms. They will look to the east and have a view of the harbour, with a wing attached for all the domestic offices for servants.'

'Yes, I see. The west side will mirror the east.'

'And contain all the state apartments for public occasions with a museum, library and domestic chapel, and apartments for the civil and military staff. Handsome and commodious, in the castellated style, as requested.' Mary grinned, a great bubble of happiness swelling in her chest as she revelled in Elizabeth's rapturous cries.

Until Elizabeth's face fell, and she breathed a long painful sigh. 'It is such a shame we will never live in this wonderful palace.'

'Nor see it built if Mr Bigge and Lord Bathurst have their way. They're opposed to the "Gothic follies".'

'Obnoxious men!' Elizabeth jumped to her feet and paced then stretched her arms wide. 'However, I will at least quit these shores secure in the knowledge two women have created a lasting legacy.'

'And a feeling of guilt on my part.' Mary failed to control the quaver in her voice. 'The three buildings which have incurred Mr Bigge's wrath and caused Governor Macquarie, and Francis, the most grief were based upon my dreams and fantasies.'

'Dreams and fantasies I wholeheartedly supported and encouraged, as did Lachlan. I am only sorry that you have been caught up in this ludicrous political dogfight.'

'Neither of us had any choice in the matter. Nor did the governor and Francis. The blame lays fairly and squarely with the hidebound free settlers who believe they are entitled to preferential treatment.'

'It upsets me so very much to know that Lachlan's vision for the colony has been tarnished. He has strived only to make everyone's dreams a reality. His health is failing; it is time we returned to Scotland. Thomas Brisbane has been appointed governor; it's a position he has wanted for many years. He will take over at the end of the year—and implement many of Bigge's recommendations, no doubt.'

Mary wiped her damp palms down her skirt. 'Elizabeth, it is most important that no one knows of my contributions to these designs.' She patted her folio. 'Francis would be seen as a fool. His genius questioned. His position ridiculed. His reputation destroyed. Please, I beg of you, keep my secret.'

Thirty-Two

When Macquarie rejected Francis's claim for payment, he determined to present his case to Sir Thomas Brisbane. To Mary's horror his itemised accounting concluded that he was owed £11,877/15/6—and sixpence, for heaven's sake! A mere three hundred pounds less than the governor's own annual salary.

Mary was at her wit's end. The Macquaries had left town again, travelling from one end of the colony to the other in some kind of a farewell tour, and all the while she imagined them sleeping under the stars discussing the strange quirk of fate that had seen her designs adopted. Thank goodness they didn't know the rest of her story. In the darkest moments of the night, she pondered the possibility of Francis being accused of poaching her designs but as the sun rose, she'd concluded he was quite within his rights— not only had she freely given him her drawings but she was, as Elizabeth insisted, the architect's wife and as such he had every right to her work.

Meanwhile Francis continued to draw up his own plans for various private commissions and trained Aggie to calculate the costings. It seemed news of Macquarie's displeasure hadn't filtered through to the exclusives, or perhaps it had, and by being out of favour with Macquarie he had unwittingly become sought after. However, Francis, being Francis, refused to let the matter of payment drop.

'My letters have finally born fruit. Macquarie has deigned to see me. I am to present myself at Government House. No doubt to be formally introduced to Brisbane and discuss ongoing projects.'

A cold shudder crossed Mary's shoulders. 'They have returned from their travels?'

'Obviously, and I am expecting every satisfaction.'

She didn't share his optimism. 'When are you seeing the governor?'

Francis gave a casual wave of his hand and pushed back his hair from his red-rimmed eyes. 'As yet a date has not been set. In the meantime, I have work to do. My building program will no doubt continue under Brisbane's watch.'

A breath whistled out between Mary's lips. If she could manage to arrange a meeting with Elizabeth, perhaps she could ease Francis's path, prevent him from doing anything foolish. 'I'll leave you to your papers.' She shot up the stairs and wrote a note to Elizabeth. Francis aside, she would like the opportunity to bid her farewell as it was only a matter of weeks before the Macquaries would be leaving.

Two days later Mary met Elizabeth in their usual spot with Henry strapped firmly to her chest. Once she'd untangled him, she held him out to Elizabeth.

'He's such a bonny lad.' Elizabeth's voice carried a Scottish lilt Mary hadn't recognised before; no doubt she was preparing herself for their homeward journey. 'He must be close to walking.' She held him against her and laughed as he bounced on his chubby little legs. 'If there's one thing I regret about my life it is my apparent inability to carry children to term. It makes Lachie even more special. You are so very lucky, my dear.'

Mary opened her mouth to explain that once, in the now distant past, she too had suffered the same affliction but instead bit her tongue as Mrs Rudge's long-ago whispered reference to the French Disease, common amongst sailors, echoed. How dreadful for poor Elizabeth to blame herself when the fault might not rest with her. After all, despite her own earlier difficulties, she had successfully borne four children with Francis. She shook the thought away and grasped Elizabeth's hand. 'You have Lachie, and he is a credit to you both.'

'He is, as I'm sure this little bundle will be to you and Mr Greenway.' Elizabeth dropped a kiss onto Henry's cheek and put him down on the ground. 'Now, you must promise me that you will write and tell me all the news. I'm sure Mr Greenway's business will continue to thrive. There are so many new settlers who will require houses, in the city and Newcastle and the surrounding area when the Hunter Valley is proclaimed a free settlement.'

Mary let Elizabeth prattle on, waiting for a chance to bring up Francis's demands on the governor. She was in no doubt his claims for payment would be refused. As a ticket-of-leave man he had been obliged to work for the government in exchange for rations. Once he had been appointed civil architect he had received a salary from the government purse. No matter how much he might have wished for a percentage payment on completion of the buildings it had never been agreed.

'Land in the Hunter Valley will be greatly in demand once the convicts are moved to Port Macquarie.' Elizabeth raised her finger to her lips. 'But that is not yet public knowledge.'

Mary's head came up with a snap. Francis had talked of Macquarie's offer of a land grant, and had always presumed it would be the plot between George and Argyle Street, but pastoral acres in the Hunter Valley could be worth a lot to the colonialists in the future. It would cost the government nothing to grant him land, and thus both parties would be appeased. Francis would have the payment he so richly deserved, and Macquarie would not lose face or, more importantly, incur the wrath of the authorities in London. 'Elizabeth, may I speak frankly?'

'Haven't we always been open with each other?'

Mary nodded her head in agreement, although their conversations had always steered away from matters political. 'I'm not sure whether you are aware, but Mr Greenway has presented an account for payment to the governor. He is very bitter, and determined to pursue what he sees as his just remuneration. If only I had known, I could have tempered his letter to the governor.'

'Lachlan is no longer able to authorise any payment. Thomas Brisbane will take over the reins of office tomorrow.' The tremble in Elizabeth's voice tugged at her heartstrings. Bigge hadn't only destroyed her own hopes and dreams of recognition, he'd trampled upon both Elizabeth and Macquarie's aspirations too.

'I wondered if perhaps the governor would see fit to grant Mr Greenway land in settlement of his claim, then both parties would be satisfied ...' The pounding of her heart echoed in her ears. How had she the audacity?

'... and honour would be served. I see your point. Let me talk to Macquarie later today. He will spend the remainder of the year travelling, introducing Brisbane to the country. Now enough of these men. Tell me what you have planned for the future. I want to be able to imagine you and your lovely family on the long voyage home. Perhaps you might return to England now Mr Greenway has an absolute pardon.'

'I doubt that very much. Mr Greenway has his private business here; he hopes to continue as government architect, but

I will not involve myself in his practice any longer. It would be the final straw if any mention was made. His reputation would be destroyed.'

'Mary, let me assure you, your secret is safe, all will be credited to Mr Greenway. Bigge's arrival unleashed a series of disasters, and we are all balanced on the brink of an abyss, surveying the wreckage of our hopes and dreams.'

Mary reached for Elizabeth's hand and squeezed her fingers tight, a wave of relief swelling in her chest, partly because her audacious suggestions had been so well received and partly because she wanted to give voice to a thought that had been keeping her awake at night. A plan, a way to ensure their security no matter how Francis's business progressed, and it would not include any forays into architectural design. 'I must provide for the children. The children, the safety of my family, are my priority.

'I am considering opening a small school. There is a shortage, only those run by the churches. Mine would be a private venture with a dozen or so pupils, girls. At the moment all the tutors are men. I don't want that for Caroline.'

'And you'd employ a teacher?'

'I would teach the children. Aggie has a natural gift for arithmetic and is already running our household budget and assisting Francis with his costings. She would help me. I want the girls to learn more than the feminine arts—to understand they are worthy and capable of more than embroidery and pianoforte, that their lives need not be dictated by a husband or a father. I believe that there are several families who would appreciate such an education for their daughters, which would recognise their skills and abilities.' Her voice rose as the words she'd never dared utter tumbled out. 'If the old laboratory was cleaned and whitewashed it would make a perfect classroom and the money from fees certainly wouldn't go amiss. My pupils would be both exclusives and emancipists—perhaps I can break down some of the preconceived notions that prevail in the colony and continue the work you and the governor have done. It would be a shame for all your efforts to be wasted. I hope we can look towards a time when the convict taint will be washed away. Even if it can't happen for their parents then their children should be free of their inherited stigma. I thought I could balance the pupils by also selecting girls from the orphanage who show an interest in something other than needlework and household duties.'

Elizabeth raised an eyebrow. 'A class of architects perhaps.'

'Not only architects but doctors, lawyers—who knows, one day we might see a woman magistrate.'

'You'd have a way to go since we couldn't get Dr Redfern onto the bench!'

'Nothing is impossible. An educated woman is a force to be reckoned with. After that it's simply a case of self-confidence, a voice of reason and breaking the stronghold the exclusives have.'

'I'm sure the good wives of the colony and their daughters would be fighting a path to your door. A schoolmistress. Whatever next? You are a woman of many talents, Mrs Greenway.' Elizabeth reached into the basket, amongst the untouched wine and cakes, and brought out a rectangular package wrapped in muslin. 'I have something for you. Perhaps you'd allow me to contribute your first textbooks.'

Mary took the package, untied the pale blue ribbon, and unfolded the fine muslin. Two books. A smile tugged the corners of her mouth as she read the titles: Gyfford's pattern books that Elizabeth had brought with her from England.

'There is an inscription.' Elizabeth leant towards her and turned the page: *You have no need of these as I am well aware but please accept them in memory of the delightful hours we spent and remember your secret will remain safe. Your friend, Elizabeth Macquarie.*

Tears sprang to Mary's eyes as, incapable of speech, she enveloped Elizabeth in a long and heartfelt embrace. The pain in her chest was a nagging reminder of all that might be if women had the freedom to express their ideas and follow their dreams.

Thirty-Three

1822

Mary leant against the fence staring beyond the hustle of George Street to the anchored ships in the cove. Two weeks ago Thomas Brisbane had been sworn into office—the end of Macquarie's rule. A strange word to use, but it felt right. He may have been subject to the demands of the Colonial Office, but in many ways he had ruled the Colony of New South Wales for nigh on twelve years. How she'd miss both the governor and Elizabeth.

The rumble of wheels snagged her attention, and her heart skipped a beat when the Macquaries' yellow curricle drew to a halt at the gate. The liveried coachman swung down and approached. For a moment she wanted to turn and flee, keep prying eyes and wagging tongues at bay, but then with a shrug she opened the gate and walked to meet him. Hobnobbing with the governor's wife was one thing but now that Elizabeth was no more than wife and mother, and Francis a free man, no one could complain. 'Good morning. How can I help you?'

'Letter for Mr Greenway.' The coachman held out a square of paper, nodded his head and once she'd taken it bounded back into his seat and pulled off.

Mary turned the letter over and found the governor's seal on the back. A smile twitched her lips. Possibly one of his last missives while still in office. He really was leaving everything to the final hour.

She found Francis at the kitchen table, mug of tea in hand, instructing William in his errands for the day—a check at the quarry next door for available dressed sandstone, instructions for the workers at the Howe residence, some minor issue with the gatehouse at the turnpike ... the list seemed endless, but the set of William's shoulders proved he relished the responsibility.

'There's a letter for you, Francis.'

He reached out and turned it over, raising his eyebrows at the seal. 'Off you go then, William. I'll meet you back here at dinner time. I must see Campbell about his Wharf House.'

'Aren't you going to open it?' Mary pushed the letter closer to Francis's hand, more to resist the temptation of tearing it open herself. Had her request to Elizabeth for land in lieu of wages born fruit? Land in the Hunter, a move from town, new opportunities and possibilities. Mary's mind spiralled and a curl of excitement twisted in her breast as Francis ripped the seal and stilled.

Mary sat biting her lips, her fingers drumming an impatient tattoo on the tabletop. The letter couldn't be long, she could see through the back of the paper. A matter of a few lines. How many times did he have to read it?

Francis's hand clawed the paper, crumpling it into a ball. 'A mockery, a mere mockery.' He tossed the letter aside. 'The measure of my reward, my compensation for hours of labour and toil is ...' he paused as if anticipating a drum roll, '... I am to be granted eight hundred acres of land by way of remuneration ...'

Mary's shoulders dropped. Elizabeth had done as promised, now all she had to do was convince Francis that this was a positive step, an opportunity.

'... and six cows from the government herd. What am I? A virgin bride? The value doesn't even cover my travelling expenses. Fetch me pen and paper.'

'Francis, please. Let us consider this ...'

'The time for consideration is long gone. In fact, I shall present myself to Macquarie and we can discuss the matter. I was promised town land, not in some godforsaken hole on the Coal River. I will not rest until I receive my due.'

'May I look at the letter?' Not waiting for a reply, Mary reached out for the crumpled ball of paper now lying on the tabletop and smoothed it out. Much as she had expected, the date on the top of the letter was November 30. The last day of November, the last day Macquarie held office. Mary dropped her head into her hands. There was little point in Francis presenting himself to Government House, as there was nothing Macquarie could do. He was no longer governor.

A pall hung over the house. Mary, Hannah and Aggie tried their best to keep spirits up while Francis wrote more letters and drew up more accounts. Macquarie had conveniently spent time on a farewell tour of Bathurst, returning briefly after Christmas before setting off on another trip to Cow Pastures and the Illawarra at the beginning of February.

And suddenly the day of the Macquaries' departure dawned.

Ears ringing from the band's somewhat off-key rendition of 'God Save the King', Mary elbowed her way to the front of the jam-packed crowd in time to see Elizabeth, escorted by Sir

Thomas Brisbane, leaving Government House with her husband and young Lachlan. Followed by just about anyone who was anyone, they made their way down through the Domain to the private landing place below young Lachlan's garden. From the melancholy expressions on everyone's face she wasn't alone in her sense of despair—sincere and undisguised regret etched the faces of all but the regiment, who formed the guard of honour.

Onlookers draped the foreshore around Fort Macquarie and the rocks on Bennelong's point and it seemed every craft in the colony had taken to the water: launches, wherries, small sailing boats, even native canoes. Every spot was crowded with those determined to catch a parting glimpse of their beloved governor. Mary searched the crowd around the fort for Francis, the children, Aggie and Hannah, and unless she was very much mistaken, she'd spotted Bill's bright hair, head and shoulders above everyone else. She'd had every intention of staying with them until a ripple of foreboding had stippled her skin and she'd forced her way forward.

Although she and Elizabeth had made their private farewell, she wanted her friend to know she was close.

The government barge was waiting at the steps and, accompanied by Sir Thomas Brisbane and their closest friends, the former governor, his wife and his son embarked. A nineteen-gun salute boomed from Dawes Battery, marking the end of the twelve years of Macquarie's rule.

Within moments the barge rowed out across the cove through the anchored ships, colours displayed and myriad crews at attention marking their passage towards the *Surry*, the ship that would take the Macquaries on the first leg of their journey back to their beloved Scotland.

Mary gave a final wave of her hand, turned her back on what might have been and made her way home alone.

The remainder of the day wore on. Aggie returned with Caroline, Charles and Henry, and news that Francis had business to attend to and Hannah a hankering for fish pie—a hankering for a meeting with her beau more than like, but Mary couldn't summon the energy to respond. A strange numbness had invaded her body, words jumbled in her mind, and she couldn't concentrate on Aggie's gossip or even the children's needs. She sat still and silent as the house quietened and night fell.

Perhaps she dozed, perhaps she dreamt, but when she woke she couldn't snatch a breath. Heat swamped her. She ran to the window and flung it open, gulping in the cooler air. Her head pounded. For a moment she couldn't remember where she was or what she'd been trying to do.

The sun had set, leaving behind a trail of purple clouds. Soon the day would lose its colour, much as she had.

Taking her folio from the sea chest, she flipped through the designs until she found her favourites—the stables, the fort, the toll house, her plan for Government House.

Happy times which she'd known couldn't last. She'd sensed the approach of something—someone, it had turned out to be—large and overwhelmingly dark. It wasn't a premonition, she could see a shadow, the shape of a man—his round florid face, red hair and self-important smirk. She gazed sadly at another drawing, the one that meant more to her than any of the others. The pen-and-ink sketch she had made on that first day when she'd met Elizabeth, the domed house, so like Manali, the one they'd shared beneath the sandstone outcrop. Tears stained the page. In another time, in another life, she could perhaps achieve her ambitions. She folded it and tucked it into her waistband. It would be her only reminder of the past.

The time had come to let her dreams of recognition go. To erase them from the memory of the world. From her memory.

Clutching the drawings tightly in her clawed hand, she made her way to the kitchen.

The fire had burned away, but the embers still glowed. Without pausing, without giving herself the opportunity to waver, she thrust the drawings face down into the coals. Then without a backward glance she shut the door firmly behind her and turned to the future, determined not to weaken and attempt to retrieve her precious dreams.

Epilogue

Two years later

Mary stood at the window, five-month-old baby Agnes pressed to her shoulder as the setting sun painted the sky a fiery red. Fate had decreed that Agnes would be their last child. Seven children, all fit and healthy, and every one a delight—such a far cry from the heir and the spare she'd once felt so obligated to produce.

From the second floor of the old laboratory she had a bird's-eye view, illuminated by the pin-prick lights on the masts of the anchored ships. George Street, now so different from the stinking, refuse-ridden haunt of cutthroats and footpads that had greeted her when she first stepped ashore almost ten years earlier. Paved and guttered, fronted by two- and three-storey warehouses, glass-fronted shops and homes, where strings of carriages and gigs barrelled along at remarkable speed. Hundreds of new public and private buildings flanked a harbour that bustled day and night with the ever-increasing trade.

Not only Sydney Town thrived. The colony now boasted dozens of roads and bridges, not least Cox's route over the Blue Mountains, and new townships along the Hawkesbury and

Nepean rivers prospered. The Greenways could hold their heads high, no matter what the odious Mr Bigge had written in his report about palaces for horses, extravagant ornamental features and Gothic follies; there were churches, courthouses, hospitals, granaries and stores that would stand testimony to their efforts for years to come.

Macquarie had taken the fledgling colony, kicking and scream-ing more often than not, from a rum-infested den of iniquity to a vital and vibrant country. Mary's lips curved in a smile. There had been no official statement but Macquarie's new name for the colony had caught the attention of all the emancipists who missed him so, and the word Australia was on everyone's lips.

Thomas Brisbane had seen fit to dispense with Francis's ser-vices just two weeks after the Macquaries left which, in hindsight, wasn't a bad thing. Francis had plenty of private work and they were permitted to remain in the house on the corner of Argyle and George Streets—the perfect spot to run a business, right in the middle of the commercial district, as Francis had pointed out when Mary and the boys had first arrived. The only downside was that they no longer received rations from government stores. They managed well enough from Francis's private work and Bill had fingers in more pies than she'd ever dreamt. Hannah, who had finally married her beau, still came every day, frequently armed with offerings of fish. The garden flourished, producing an array of vegetables, and the orchard blossomed. Even Mr Bent's orange trees delivered a healthy crop but, as always, a little more money wouldn't go astray.

It was a coincidental meeting that opened the door to the future.

Mary had taken a walk, not along the foreshore as she had on so many previous occasions when she met Elizabeth but along the path from Fort Macquarie, through the Domain. The thrill of seeing the buildings that had once lived only in her imagination never waned but her footsteps led her to her favourite—the government stables.

Sixteen battlemented towers punctuated the quadrangular stable block, square mullioned windows set in the main walls and between the towers large Gothic windows—all perfectly symmetrical, the brilliant white walls piercing against the azure sky. A quiver traced her skin; no matter what the future held, this building would stand testament to her vision.

She'd turned back into George Street and come to a halt outside the Bank of New South Wales. Initially established in Macquarie Street, it had moved to new premises two years earlier.

As she assessed the central recessed arcade, so similar to the facade of Liverpool Hospital that Francis had completed earlier in the year, a voice called her name. 'Mrs Greenway, isn't it?'

'Mrs Reibey.' Mary smiled down at the diminutive one-time horse thief, now pillar of Sydney society. 'How lovely to see you.'

'Are you admiring your husband's handiwork? He's done a remarkable job. Only in Sydney Town could a public house belonging to a member of the Rum Corps become the home of the country's first bank.'

'I'm taking a tour, following my town map ...' Mary bit her lip and swallowed the remainder of her sentence. She hadn't spoken to anyone, not even Francis, of the folio of drawings she'd burnt the day the Macquaries left. 'There have been so many changes. You must notice them more than anyone; you've been here since the beginning.'

'I think we should all be proud of what Sydney has become. Your children must be growing. Are you sending the boys back to England for their schooling?'

'George has a position with the harbourmaster, and William continues to work with his father. I taught them both at home and I've recently enrolled Charles in the Cape School here in Sydney.'

And that was the moment everything had changed.

She'd licked her lips, taken a deep breath and shared her dream. 'I intend to start my own school. Most of the schools in town are run by the churches and the tutors are all men. I want something different for my own daughters and all the other young girls in the colony. A real education, not one that revolves around the feminine arts—embroidery, painting, music and flower arranging. They should learn mathematics, geography and science ...'

'... and architecture perhaps?' Mrs Reibey echoed Elizabeth's words and raised a quizzical eyebrow. 'Fine sentiments but you must attract students whose families can pay fees or, like all businesses, you will fail.'

'I don't intend a school for only the wealthy free settlers. I intend a mix of emancipist and exclusives.'

'Do you indeed. What an admirable notion. Then you will need financial backing, start-up funds. Perhaps you'd like to come inside?' She held open the door to the bank and led Mary into a large office on the right-hand side.

Two hours later Mary flew out onto the street, her feet barely touching the ground. When Mrs Reibey had taken her into the office she had demanded a full rundown of all her plans, the premises, the tutors she would employ and, most importantly, how she would attract students. Mary's answers, thoroughly unprepared, but which she thought showed merit, had not brought the response she'd hoped for and Mary discovered to her horror that, even though Mrs Reibey was one of the bank's shareholders, she was not permitted a bank account, nor could she, as a mere woman, borrow money. What poppycock! However, Mrs Reibey had a solution. All Mary needed was someone to provide private backing, and Mrs Reibey offered to be that someone.

'Mary, Mary.' Francis's voice drifted up the stairs. 'Are you up there?'

'I am. I'll be down in a moment.' In the fading light she cast one more look around the room. The walls were whitewashed and bright, thanks to some hard work on the part of George and William, supervised by Bill, who had somehow managed to source two long trestle tables and benches that ran the length of the old laboratory; not a hint of cowpox vaccine or any medical paraphernalia remained, and at the front of the room was a large cedar table with an etched plaque that read *Mrs Greenway*. Mary hefted Agnes higher up her shoulder, closed the door behind her and made her way carefully down the steep flight of stairs. Francis sat in a leather carver, his booted feet propped on another large table. He peered over the top of the newspaper and grinned. 'All ready for tomorrow?'

'I am.' She walked slowly around the room trailing her fingers along the bookshelves, not all full yet but holding a vast number of donated books that Mrs Reibey had somehow managed to acquire—covering every subject from anatomy to astronomy— and in pride of place the pattern books Elizabeth had given her, alongside Chambers's treatise, Lady Wilbraham's diaries and Papa's set of the plans of the Mughal palaces of Delhi, Agra and Faizabad. 'Bill says he'll drop the slates, nibs and ink in tomorrow along with the copybooks. He must have scoured the countryside. I have no idea how much I owe him.'

'Ask Aggie. I'm sure she'll have a handle on the finances. I noticed she had a ledger entitled "Mrs Greenway's Academy for Young Ladies" and you will be charging seven guineas a term.'

'Aggie is a godsend, as is her uncle. I bless the day I first came across Bill in the markets.'

'Well, tomorrow is the day. How many students are you expecting?'

Mary swallowed the flutter of trepidation. She had advertised, but she suspected the majority had contacted her through word of mouth—Mrs Reibey's mouth, unless she was mistaken. 'Eleven, twelve if I count Caroline.' But most pleasing of all were the three girls from the orphanage recommended by Mrs Hoskings. The remainder could best be described as a delightful mix of emancipists and exclusives. 'I have to admit that I am a tad nervous.'

Francis tucked the newspaper under his arm and picked up the lamp. 'I cannot imagine why. Your accomplishments more than qualify you for the task.'

THE SYDNEY MONITOR

Saturday, 28 April 1832

DIED—On Wednesday night, at her Residence in George-street, after a lingering illness, Mrs. GREENWAY, deeply regretted by her friends. Mrs. Greenway, having educated a great number of the ladies of the Colony, now at the head of families, was generally known, and as universally beloved. Her accomplishments were considerable; but they were equalled, if not excelled, by her fine sentiment and excellent principles, which rendered her society an acquisition to all who had the opportunity of enjoying it.

Historical Notes

As with most of my books, *The Talented Mrs Greenway* is a mixture of fact and fiction. It all began when I learnt that the architect Francis Greenway was buried in an unmarked grave near East Maitland, in the Hunter. It seemed a very ignominious end for the man responsible for the design of many of Australia's finest colonial buildings.

Although Francis Greenway's life is fascinating, and well documented, it was his wife who truly captured my attention— because of the lack of references to her. The first record of Mary Greenway (née Moore) is her marriage to Francis Greenway on 27 April 1809. There is no record of her birth or baptism. A Mary Moore married a James Tripp, who died in 1808, but I have been unable to ascertain if it was 'our Mary', which is why I decided to change the name of her fictional first husband to Fripp. To all intents and purposes, Mary didn't exist until she met the man in the green coat ...

Her first two sons, George (born July 1807) and William (born October 1808) were not baptised as 'Greenway' until 2 November 1811, two and a half years after Mary and Francis married. There is no earlier record to indicate that Francis Greenway was their father. Her third son, Francis John Greenway, was born in December 1813. I have assumed he was Mary and Francis's first son, because of his name, and have used the diminutive Frankie to differentiate him from his father.

Other mentions of Mary are few and far between but I have incorporated them into the story:

Mary's name, and those of William, George and Frankie, appear on the *Broxbournebury*'s manifest and Jeffery Hart Bent, the first judge of the Colony of New South Wales, refers to Mary as 'a favourite' amongst the passengers aboard the *Broxbournebury* in the journal of his voyage to Australia.

The birth of Francis and Mary's daughter, Caroline Ann, in March 1816 is recorded as are Mary's later children: Charles Capel, in March 1818, Henry Valentine, in February 1821, and Agnes in June 1824.

Governor Macquarie described Mary in his papers as 'a pleasant respectable woman' whose 'earnest entreaty' encouraged him to grant Francis Greenway an absolute pardon.

Mary's school is shown in the *Returns of the Colony* as having nine pupils.

And finally there is her obituary in the *Sydney Monitor* and Francis Greenway's tribute to Mary in the *Sydney Gazette*—'the mild, unobtrusive but talented Mrs Greenway'.

There are no other recorded facts that I have found. Given this almost blank canvas I have fictionalised Mary's story; however, it is woven around the well-recorded events of her husband's life.

There is a large amount of scuttlebutt around Admiral Phillip's involvement. Macquarie did write to Lord Castlereagh in March 1810 requesting that a government architect should be sent out to the colony to plan and superintend the construction of public buildings but how that request was managed is unknown. Phillip and his wife Isabella had settled in Bath in

1805. The records of Greenway's trial do not exist; there are only newspaper accounts.

At the age of sixteen, after Mary died, her daughter Caroline took over responsibility for her younger siblings—Charles, Henry and Agnes. George fulfilled his dreams and went to sea, where sadly he died in Timor. Francis (Frankie) became articled to the trader TG Pittman and travelled to the Sandwich Islands. Charles entered the church and in 1882 was appointed the first archdeacon of Grafton. William managed the unproductive land grant Greenway finally accepted on the banks of the Hunter River where he and his sisters spent many years, after Greenway's death, in genteel poverty, making their own clothes and breeding chickens and turkeys until Agnes married and Caroline moved to England with Agnes and her husband.

The original pen-and-ink drawing of Government House and the stables is held in the State Library. It is unsigned, marked 'attributed to F H Greenway'. The elevation and plans for the government stables are also unsigned and the plans for the turnpike toll gate, to the best of my knowledge, have never come to light, nor have the plans for a new Government House.

Lady Wilbraham is not a figment of my imagination and is only recently being recognised for her contribution to architecture. The role she played in the designs for Sir Christopher Wren's buildings continues to be disputed. Her journal, however, exists, and she is sometimes credited with the design of her home, Wootton House, which is now a Country Estate Hotel. Thornbury Castle has also become a hotel and restaurant.

There are references to the book owned by Mary's father, showing the designs of the Mughal palaces, but I have been unable to track down a copy. William Moore, however, is a fictional character. Obviously the Taj Mahal and the story behind that magnificent building is well known.

My use of the expression *cloak and dagger* is incorrect. It was first used by Charles Dickens in 1841. Prior to that *cloak and sword* was popular but somehow it just didn't seem right. The name *Mary Merino* however did exist, at least in print, in contributions to the *Sydney Gazette*, discussing the standards of colonial girlhood. I like to believe Mary Greenway was responsible.

The events in Francis Greenway's life are, I believe, as accurate as they can be although the exact monthly dates may have become a little bent in the writing of what has become a fictional account of Mary Greenway's life.

Acknowledgements

I acknowledge the Gadigal people of the Eora Nation as the traditional Custodians of the land upon which this story is set and pay respect to Elders past, present and emerging, and I acknowledge the Darkinjung, Awabakal and Wonnarua people as the traditional Custodians of the land on which I live and work, and pay my respects to the Elders of those nations also.

I am indebted to the work of MH Ellis, *Francis Greenway, His Life and Times*, Broadbent and Hughes' book *Francis Greenway, Architect* and *A Forger's Progress, the Life of Francis Greenway* by Alisdair McGregor.

As always Trove has proved invaluable, and Mary's obituary is taken directly from the newspaper of the day. *In Her Own Words, The Writings of Elizabeth Macquarie* by Robin Walsh proved a wonderful resource as did the Lachlan & Elizabeth Macquarie Archive (LEMA), an online research initiative by Macquarie University library, and the *Australian Dictionary of Biography*.

My thanks to all the people who have put up with my obsession to write Mary Greenway into history—as always Chief Researcher and plot wrangler, Charles Smith, dedicated genealogist, Lynda Marsh, and my critique partners Sarah Barrie and Paula Beavan have provided immense support. I also wish to acknowledge Kevin Short and Heather Berry from Maitland Historical Society who were with me at the very beginning of this journey and made many, many research suggestions. Also my thanks to Jim Groom for his family's history of Mary Reibey. All errors are my own.

My thanks to the wonderful team at HQ/HarperCollins: my longsuffering publisher and editor, Jo Mackay, Annabel Blay, managing editor, editor Kate James who all helped make sense of my ramblings and checked my historical references, and proofreader Annabel Adair. Thanks to Darren Holt of HarperCollins Design Studio who once again has produced the most perfect cover, to Giacomo Pantalone for the amazing map, and to Josephine Bryant, my campaign manager, Jo Munroe and the HarperCollins sales team for getting this book out into the world.

And finally, to my readers. I hope you enjoy this reimagined life of Mary Greenway.

Book Club Discussion Questions

- What did you know of Francis Greenway before you read the book? Were you aware that he was married?
- Mary Greenway's life is fictionalised. Did her early story seem feasible?
- It is Mary's actions that cause the dramatic change in the Greenways' life. Do you think she should have accepted Francis's decision to take responsibility for her actions or should she have stood trial?
- Arthur Phillip's involvement in Greenway's trial and life is not documented, and Miss Bingle is a fictional character. Do you think it is possible that someone acted as a 'go-between' and arranged Francis's commuted sentence?
- Should Mary have travelled on the *General Hewett* with Francis and risked her unborn child's life or was she right in waiting until Frankie was born?
- When Mary meets Elizabeth Macquarie she is reluctant to reveal their friendship. Should she have gone against the

society's 'rules' and made use of their friendship to foster her husband's position?

- History doesn't tell us whether Mary had any influence on Francis Greenway's designs and plans. Do you think it is within the realms of possibility that she did?

- The story is effectively divided into three parts—Mary's life in an arranged marriage after her father's death; as the wife of a struggling bankrupt architect; and finally life with her husband's status as a 'convict'. Which Mary did you connect with the most?

- Did the story end as you expected it to?

- What was your favourite, and least favourite, part of the book?

- If you could ask the author anything, what would it be?

- How did the story impact you? Do you think you'll remember it in a few months or years?

- Are there lingering questions from the book you're still thinking about?

- Did the book strike you as original?

- Have you read any other books by this author? Which is your favourite?

talk about it

Let's talk about books.

Join the conversation:

 facebook.com/harlequinaustralia

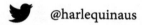 @harlequinaus

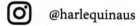 @harlequinaus

harpercollins.com.au/hq

If you love reading and want to know about our
authors and titles, then let's talk about it.